Penguin Crime Fiction
Editor: Julian Symons
The Fifth Simenon Omnibus

Georges Simenon was born at Liège in Belgium in 1903.
At sixteen he began work as a journalist on the
Gazette de Liège. He has published over 180 novels
in his own name, sixty-seven of which belong to
the Inspector Maigret series, and his work has
been published in thirty-two languages. He has
had a great influence upon French cinema and
more than forty of his novels have been filmed.

Simenon's novels are largely psychological. He
describes hidden fears, tensions and alliances beneath
the surface of life's ordinary routine which suddenly
explode into violence and crime. André Gide wrote
to him: 'You are living on a false reputation – just
like Baudelaire or Chopin. But nothing is more
difficult than making the public go back on a too
hasty first impression. You are still the slave of your
first successes and the reader's idleness would
like to put a stop to your triumphs there . . . You
are much more important than is commonly
supposed', and François Mauriac wrote, 'I am
afraid I may not have the courage to descend right
to the depths of this nightmare which Simenon
describes with such unendurable art.'

Simenon has travelled a great deal and once lived
on a cutter, making long journeys of exploration
round the coasts of Northern Europe. He is married
and has four children, and lives near Lausanne
in Switzerland. He enjoys riding, fishing and golf.

D1600829

Georges Simenon

The Fifth
Simenon Omnibus

Penguin Books

Penguin Books Ltd, Harmondsworth,
Middlesex, England
Penguin Books Australia Ltd, Ringwood,
Victoria, Australia
Penguin Books (N.Z.) Ltd, 182–190 Wairau Road,
Auckland 10, New Zealand

L'Ami d'enfance de Maigret first published 1968
Copyright © Georges Simenon, 1968
Translation published in Great Britain by Hamish Hamilton Ltd 1970
Translation copyright © Hamish Hamilton Ltd and Harcourt
Brace and World Inc., 1970
Le Grand Bob first published 1954
Copyright © Georges Simenon, 1954
Translation published in Great Britain by Hamish Hamilton Ltd 1969
Translation copyright © Hamish Hamilton Ltd, 1969
Novembre first published 1969
Copyright © Georges Simenon, 1969
Translation published in Great Britain by Hamish Hamilton Ltd 1970
Translation copyright © Hamish Hamilton Ltd, 1970

Published in Penguin Books 1972
Reprinted 1975

Made and printed in Great Britain by
Cox & Wyman Ltd, London, Reading and Fakenham
Set in Intertype Times

Contents

Maigret's Boyhood Friend

**Translated from the French by
Eileen Ellenbogen**

Chapter One

The fly circled three times round his head before alighting on the top left-hand corner of the report that he was annotating.

With pencil poised, Maigret eyed it with amused curiosity. The fly had repeated this manoeuvre over and over again in the past half-hour. At any rate, Maigret presumed that it was the same fly. It seemed to be the only one in the office.

Each time, it circled once or twice in a patch of sunlight, then buzzed round the Chief Superintendent's head, and finally came to rest on the papers on his desk. And there it stayed for a while, lazily rubbing its legs together, and looking at him with an air of defiance.

Was it really looking at him? And if so, what did it take this huge hill of flesh to be, for that was how he must appear to it.

He was at pains not to frighten it away. He sat motionless, with pencil still poised above his papers, until, quite suddenly, the fly took off and vanished through the open window.

It was the middle of June. From time to time, a gentle breeze stirred the air in the office, where Maigret, in shirt-sleeves, sat contentedly smoking his pipe. He had set aside this afternoon to read through his inspectors' reports, and was doing so with exemplary patience.

Nine or ten times, the fly had returned to alight on his papers, always on the same spot. It was almost as though it had established a kind of relationship with him.

It was an odd coincidence. The sunshine, the little gusts of cooler air blowing through the window, the intriguing antics of the fly, all served to remind him of his school days, when a fly on his desk had often engaged a larger share of his interest than the master who was taking the class.

There was a discreet knock at the door. It was old Joseph,

the messenger, bearing an engraved visiting card, which read: *Léon Florentin, Antique Dealer.*

'How old would you say he was?'

'About your age.'

'Tall and thin?'

'That's right. Very tall and thin, with a regular mop of grey hair.'

Yes, that was the man all right. Florentin, who had been at school with him, at the Lycée Banville in Moulins, the clown of the form.

'Send him in.'

He had forgotten the fly, which, feeling slighted perhaps, seemed to have gone for good. There was a brief, embarrassed silence as the two men looked at one another. This was only their second meeting since their school days in Moulins. The first had been a chance encounter in the street about twenty years ago. Florentin, very well groomed, had been accompanied by an attractive and elegant Parisian woman.

'This is my old school friend, Maigret. He's a police officer.'

Then, to Maigret:

'Allow me to introduce my wife, Monique.'

Then, as now, the sun was shining. They had really had nothing to say to one another.

'How are things? Still happy in your work?'

'Yes. And you?'

'Mustn't grumble.'

'Are you living in Paris?'

'Yes. Sixty-two Boulevard Haussmann. But I travel a good deal on business. I'm only just back from Istanbul. We must get together some time, the two of us, and you and Madame Maigret . . . I take it you're married?'

The encounter had been something of an embarrassment to both of them. The couple's pale green, open sports car had been parked near by, and they had got into it and driven off, leaving Maigret to continue on his way.

The Florentin now facing Maigret across his desk was more seedy than the dashing figure he had seemed to be in the Place de la Madeleine. He was wearing a rather shabby grey suit, and his manner was a good deal less self-assured.

10

'It was good of you to see me without an appointment. How are you?'

After the first formal greeting, Florentin, a little uneasily, reverted to the 'tu' of their boyhood. Maigret, somewhat grudgingly, did so too.

'And you? . . . Do sit down. How's your wife?'

For a moment Florentin's pale grey eyes were blank, as though he could not remember.

'Do you mean Monique? The little redhead? It's true we lived together for a time. She was a good sort, but we were never married.'

'You're not married, then?'

'What would be the point?'

Florentin made a face. His sharp, well-defined features were so flexible that they might have been made of india-rubber. His knack of twisting them into an infinite variety of comical grimaces had been a source of endless amusement to his schoolmates and exasperation to his teachers.

Maigret could not muster the courage to ask what he had come for. He was watching him covertly, finding it hard to believe that it had all been so long ago.

'I say, I like your office. I must admit I never expected to see good furniture in Police Headquarters!'

'So you're an antique dealer now?'

'In a manner of speaking . . . I buy old furniture and do it up. I rent a small workshop in the Boulevard Rochechouart. You know how it is, almost everyone is an antique dealer, nowadays.'

'Doing all right, are you?'

'I can't grumble. Everything is fine, at least it was until the sky fell about my ears this afternoon.'

He was so used to playing the clown that, almost mechanically, his features took on an expression of comical dismay. All the same, his face was grey, and his eyes troubled.

'That's what I came to see you about. I said to myself: he's the only one who'll understand.'

He took a packet of cigarettes from his pocket, and lit one. His long, bony fingers were trembling slightly. Maigret thought he caught a faint whiff of spirits.

'To tell you the truth, I'm a good deal bothered . . .'

'Go on.'

'That's just the trouble. It's hard to explain. I have a friend, a woman. For four years now . . .'

'You and she have been living together?'

'Yes and no . . . No . . . Not exactly . . . She lives in the Rue Notre-Dame-de-Lorette, near the Place Saint-Georges . . .'

His stammering hesitancy and shifting glances astonished Maigret. Florentin had been noted for his easy self-assurance. Maigret had always envied him a little on this account, and also because his father had owned the smartest confectioner's shop in the town, facing the cathedral, and Florentin had had a walnut cake named after him. In time, it had become something of a regional speciality.

Florentin had never been short of money. However much he played up in class, he was never punished. It was as though he enjoyed a special immunity. And, when school was over, he used to go out with girls.

'Go on.'

'Her name is Josée . . . Well, actually her real name is Joséphine Papet, but she prefers to be called Josée . . . I prefer it myself. She's thirty-four, but you'd never think it . . .'

As he talked, Florentin's mobile face never ceased to change and crease and twitch. It was almost as though he had a nervous tic.

'It's so hard to explain, my dear fellow . . .'

He got up and went over to the window, a tall, sharply etched figure against the sunlight.

'It's hot in here,' he sighed, mopping his forehead.

The fly had not returned to its place on the corner of the report on the Chief Superintendent's desk. Cars and buses could be heard rumbling across the Pont Saint-Michel, and, from time to time, a tug, sounding its siren before lowering its funnel to pass under the bridge.

In Maigret's room, as in every office in Police Headquarters, not to mention all the other government departments, there was a black marble clock. The hands stood at twenty past five.

'I'm not the only one . . .' stammered Florentin at last.

'The only what?'

'I'm not Josée's only friend. That's what makes it so hard to explain. She's a marvellous girl ... the very best ... I was everything to her, lover, friend and confidant ...'

Maigret, struggling to contain his impatience, relit his pipe. His old friend returned from the window, and resumed his seat opposite him.

After a silence that threatened to become unbearable, the Chief Superintendent ventured a little gentle prompting.

'And she had a good many other friends?'

'Let me think ... There was Paré ... one. And Courcel ... two. Then there was Victor ... three. And a youngster known as *Le Rouquin* – I never saw him ... that's four.'

'Four lovers who visited her regularly?'

'Some once a week, the others twice.'

'Did any of them know about the others?'

'Of course not!'

'In other words, each of them was under the delusion that he was keeping her?'

Florentin, nervously tapping the ash of his cigarette on to the carpet, seemed to find this way of putting it embarrassing.

'I told you it was difficult to explain.'

'And where, in all this, do you come in?'

'I'm her friend ... I go there when she's alone.'

'Do you sleep at the Rue Notre-Dame-de-Lorette?'

'Every night except Thursdays.'

Maigret, trying not to sound sardonic, asked:

'Because that's someone else's night?'

'Yes, Courcel's ... she's known him ten years. He lives in Rouen, but he has business premises in the Boulevard Voltaire. It would take too long to explain. I daresay you despise me for it.'

'I've never despised anyone in my life.'

'I realize it's a delicate situation, and that most people would frown on it ... But you have my solemn word for it, Josée and I love each other.' Abruptly, he added: 'Or rather, I should say, loved each other.'

Though careful to avoid showing it, Maigret was shaken by this use of the past tense.

'Are you saying that you've broken with her?'

'No.'

'Is she dead?'

'Yes.'

'When did she die?'

'This afternoon . . .'

And Florentin, looking him straight in the face, said, in a tragic manner which Maigret could not help feeling was somewhat theatrical:

'I swear it wasn't me . . . You know me . . . It's because you know me, and I know you, that I've come to you.'

True, they had known each other at twelve, at fifteen, at seventeen, but they had long since parted and gone their separate ways.

'How did she die?'

'She was shot.'

'By whom?'

'I don't know.'

'Where did it happen?'

'In her flat . . . her bedroom . . .'

'Where were you at the time?'

Maigret was finding it more and more awkward to use the informal 'tu'.

'In the cupboard.'

'In her flat, you mean?'

'Yes . . . It wasn't the first time . . . Whenever I was there, and the bell rang, I . . . it sounds despicable to you, I daresay . . . but I swear it wasn't like that . . . I work for my living . . . I earn . . .'

'Try and describe exactly what happened.'

'Where shall I begin?'

'At midday, let's say.'

'We had lunch together. She's a marvellous cook . . . We were sitting over by the window . . . She was expecting someone, as always on a Wednesday . . . but not before five-thirty to six . . .'

'Who was it?'

'His name is François Paré. He's a man in his early fifties, head of a Department in the Ministry of Public Works . . . He's in charge of Waterways . . . He lives at Versailles . . .'

14

'Did he never arrive early?'

'No.'

'What happened after lunch?'

'We chatted.'

'How was she dressed?'

'In her dressing-gown . . . Except when she was going out, she always wore a dressing-gown . . . It was about half-past three when the bell rang and I took refuge in the cupboard . . . It's a sort of closet really . . . in the bathroom, not the bedroom . . .'

Maigret was beginning to find all this a little wearing.

'And what then?'

'I'd been in there about a quarter of an hour, when I heard a sound like a shot.'

'That would have been at about a quarter to four?'

'I imagine so.'

'So you rushed into the bedroom?'

'No . . . I wasn't supposed to be there . . . Besides, it might not have been a shot, but just a car or a bus backfiring.'

The whole of Maigret's attention was now focused on Florentin. He recalled that, in the old days, most of the tales he told were pure fantasy, almost as though he had been unable to distinguish between lies and truth.

'What were you waiting for?' Without realizing it, Maigret had addressed him as 'vous'.

'Why so formal? . . . Don't you see?'

Florentin looked hurt and disappointed.

'Sorry, no offence meant. What were you waiting for, there in the wardrobe?'

'It isn't a wardrobe, more of a large clothes closet. I was waiting for the man to go.'

'How do you know it was a man? You didn't see him, you say . . .'

Florentin looked stunned.

'I never thought of that!'

'Was it because Josée had no women friends?'

'As a matter of fact, I don't think she did . . .'

'Any family?'

'She came from Concarneau originally. I never met any of her family.'

15

'How did you know when the caller had gone?'

'I heard footsteps in the sitting-room, and the door opening and closing.'

'What time was that?'

'About four.'

'So the murderer was there about a quarter of an hour after he killed her?'

'I suppose he must have been.'

'When you went into the bedroom, where did you find her?'

'On the floor, next to the bed.'

'How was she dressed?'

'She was still wearing her yellow dressing-gown.'

'Where was she shot?'

'In the throat.'

'Are you sure she was dead?'

'There couldn't be any doubt about that.'

'What was the state of the room?'

'Much as usual . . . I didn't notice anything wrong.'

'Any drawers left open . . . papers scattered about?'

'No, I don't think so.'

'You mean you can't be sure?'

'I was too upset . . .'

'Did you call a doctor?'

'No. Seeing that she was already dead . . .'

'Did you ring the local police?'

'No . . . I . . .'

'You got here at five past five. What had you been doing since four o'clock?'

'To begin with, I was absolutely stunned . . . I just collapsed into an armchair . . . I couldn't understand it . . . I still can't . . . Then I realized that I was the one they'd be bound to suspect . . . especially as that cow of a concierge can't stand the sight of me.'

'Are you telling me that you sat there for the best part of an hour?'

'No . . . I don't know how long it was, but eventually I pulled myself together and went into a bistro, the Grand-Saint-Georges, and had three large brandies, one after another.'

'And then?'

'And then I remembered that you were now the Big White Chief of the C.I.D.'

'How did you get here?'

'I took a taxi.'

Maigret was furious, but his expression remained impassive. He went across to the door leading to the Inspectors' Duty Room, opened it, and looked uncertainly from Janvier to Lapointe, who were both at their desks. Finally, addressing Janvier, he said:

'Come in here a minute, will you? I want you to ring Moers at the lab, and ask him to join us in the Rue Notre-Dame-de-Lorette . . . What number?'

'Seventeen B.'

Each time his glance rested on his old school friend, Maigret's eyes hardened in an expression of impenetrable reserve. As Janvier was telephoning, he glanced at the clock. It was half-past five.

'What did you say his name was, the Wednesday visitor?'

'Paré . . . The civil servant . . .'

'In the ordinary way, you'd be expecting him to arrive at the flat about now?'

'That's right . . . He'd be due just about now . . .'

'Has he a key?'

'None of them have keys.'

'Have you a key?'

'That's quite a different matter. Don't you see, my dear fellow . . . ?'

'I'd rather you didn't address me as your dear fellow.'

'There, you see! Even you . . .'

'Let's be going.'

He grabbed his hat on the way out, and, as they descended the wide, greyish stone staircase, he refilled his pipe.

'What I want to know is why it took you so long to make up your mind to come and see me . . . And why didn't you get in touch with the local police? . . . Had she any money of her own?'

'I imagine so . . . Three or four years ago, she bought a house as an investment, in the Rue du Mont-Cenis, overlooking Montmartre.'

'Did she keep any money in the flat?'

'She may have done . . . I can't say . . . What I do know is that she distrusted banks.'

They got into one of the row of little black cars parked in the forecourt, with Janvier at the wheel.

'Are you saying that, all the time you were living with her, you never found out where she kept her savings?'

'It's the truth.'

He was hard put to it to stop himself from bursting out: 'Stop playing the clown, can't you!'

Was it pity that he felt for him?

'How many rooms are there in the flat?'

'Sitting-room, dining-room, bedroom, bathroom, and small kitchen.'

'Not to mention the clothes closet.'

'And the clothes closet.'

Weaving his way through the traffic, Janvier tried to pick up the threads from these snatches of overheard conversation.

'I swear to you, Maigret . . .'

It was something to be thankful for, that he did not address him as 'Jules'. Fortunately, it had been customary at the lycée for the boys to call one another by their surnames!

*

As the three men went past the glass-walled lodge, Maigret saw the net curtain over the door twitch, and caught a glimpse of the concierge. She was, in every sense, a huge woman, massively built and enormously fat. Her face was large, round and expressionless, and, staring at them, she resembled a larger-than-life statue or oil-painting.

The lift was cramped, and Maigret, crushed up against Florentin, found himself almost eyeball to eyeball with his old school friend. He felt thoroughly uncomfortable. What thoughts were, at this moment, passing through the mind of the confectioner's son from Moulins? He was making an effort to appear natural, even to smile, but was succeeding only in screwing up his face into a ludicrous grimace. Was he frightened, was that it?

Was he the murderer of Joséphine Papet? What had he been

18

up to during the hour that had elapsed before his arrival at the Quai des Orfèvres?

On the third floor, they crossed the lobby, and Florentin took a bunch of keys out of his pocket, as though it were the most natural thing in the world. The door of the flat opened on to a tiny entrance hall, and Florentin led them straight into the sitting-room. Maigret felt as though he had been transported back fifty years or more.

The elaborately draped curtains were of old rose silk, held back by heavy plaited silk cords. A faded, flowered carpet covered the parquet floor. There was a great deal of plush and brocade upholstery, a number of table-runners, and, on all the fake Louis XVI chairs, antimacassars of lace or embroidery.

Near the window stood a velvet-covered couch, piled high with crumpled cushions of every colour, as though someone had very recently been sitting there. On a pedestal table near by, there was a gilt table-lamp with a pink shade.

This, no doubt, had been Josée's favourite seat. There was a record-player within easy reach, a box of chocolates, and a handy pile of magazines and romantic novels. The television set stood facing the couch, in the opposite corner of the room.

The walls were papered in a pattern of tiny flowers, and here and there were landscape paintings crowded with fussy detail.

Florentin, who was watching Maigret closely, confirmed his impression:

'That's where she nearly always sat.'

'What about you?'

The antique dealer pointed to a shabby leather armchair, that looked entirely out of place in such a setting.

'That's mine. I brought it here for my own use.'

The dining-room was no less conventionally old-fashioned, and conveyed the same impression of over-crowded stuffiness. There were heavy, draped, velvet curtains over both windows, and dark green potted plants on the ledges.

The door to the bedroom was open. As Florentin seemed reluctant to go in, Maigret pushed past him. The body was stretched out on the carpet, not six feet from the door.

As so often happens, in such cases, the hole in the woman's

throat seemed much larger than might have been expected from a bullet wound. She had bled a great deal, but her face expressed nothing but pure astonishment.

As far as one could judge, she must have been a plump, kindly little woman, the sort normally associated with good home cooking, nourishing stews, and lovingly bottled preserves.

Maigret's glance travelled round the room, as though searching for something that appeared to be missing.

'There was no weapon as far as I could see . . .' His friend was quick to guess what he was looking for. 'Unless she's lying on it, which doesn't seem very likely.'

The telephone was in the sitting-room. Maigret was anxious to get the necessary formalities over and done with as quickly as possible.

'You'd better ring the Divisional Superintendent first, Janvier. Tell him to bring a doctor . . . After that, let the Public Prosecutor's office know . . .'

Moers and his staff of experts would be arriving any minute now. Maigret would have liked a few quiet minutes to himself. He went into the bathroom, and noted that all the towels were pink. There was a great deal of pink all over the flat. He opened the door of the clothes closet, which was a kind of short passage, leading nowhere. Here was more pink, a sugar-pink negligée and a summer dress of a deeper pink. Indeed, all the clothes hanging there were of pastel colours, mostly almond green and powder blue.

'There doesn't seem to be anything of yours here.'

'It would have made things a bit awkward,' murmured Florentin, more than a little put out. 'There were the others, you see . . . Ostensibly, she was living alone . . .'

Naturally! There was an old-fashioned flavour about this too: a succession of elderly 'protectors', who came once or twice a week, each unaware of the existence of the others, and fondly cherishing the illusion that he was 'keeping' her.

But had she really succeeded in keeping all of them in ignorance?

Returning to the bedroom, Maigret began poking about in various drawers. He found bills, underclothes, and a jewel box containing a few cheap trinkets.

It was six o'clock.

'The Wednesday caller ought to be here by now,' he remarked.

'He could have been and gone. If he rang and got no answer, he wouldn't have hung about, would he?'

Janvier came in from the sitting-room.

'The Superintendent is on his way, and the Deputy Public Prosecutor will be arriving shortly with the Examining Magistrate.'

In any inquiry, this was always the stage that Maigret most detested, with half a dozen of them sitting about staring at one another, while the police doctor knelt by the corpse, making his examination.

It was anyway a pure formality. The doctor could do no more than certify death. For the details, they would have to await the autopsy. As for the Deputy Public Prosecutor, he merely held a watching brief for the Government.

The Examining Magistrate was looking at Maigret as though seeking his opinion, whereas, of course, Maigret had, so far, not formed any opinion. As for the Divisional Superintendent, he was all impatience to get back to his office.

'Keep me in the picture,' murmured the Examining Magistrate. He was a man of forty, and must only recently have come to Paris.

His name was Page. He had worked his way up from an obscure provincial post, through most of the major provincial cities, to his present appointment in the capital.

Moers and his men were waiting in the sitting-room, where one of them was examining all likely surfaces for fingerprints.

When he had seen the official party off the premises, Maigret said to Moers: 'It's all yours. You'd better get on with photographing the body before the hearse arrives.'

Seeing that Florentin was minded to follow him out, he said:

'No, you stay here. Janvier, I'll leave you to interview the neighbours on this floor, and, if necessary, those on the floor above. You never know, they may have heard something.'

The Chief Superintendent, ignoring the lift, went down by the stairs. The house was old, but very well cared for. The crimson carpet was secured by brass stair-rods. All the door-knobs were highly polished, and beside the door of one of the flats was a gleaming brass plate, inscribed: 'Mademoiselle Vial. Corsets and foundation garments made to measure.'

The giantess of a concierge was still standing behind the glass door of the lodge, holding back the net curtain with the bloated fingers of her huge hand. As he put his hand on the door-knob, she moved back a pace, as though pushed, and he went in.

She looked at him with such a total lack of interest that he might have been an object rather than a person; nor did his official badge, when he produced it, evoke the slightest response.

'I take it you haven't heard?'

She did not reply, but her eyes seemed to ask, 'Haven't heard what?'

The lodge was spotlessly clean, with a round table in the middle, on which stood a cage with two canaries in it. The kitchen could be seen through a door at the far end.

'Mademoiselle Papet is dead.'

This at least did elicit some response. She did have a tongue, it seemed, though her voice was toneless, as blank as her face. But maybe she was not as indifferent as she appeared. Was not that very blankness possibly evidence of hostility? It was as though she looked out upon humanity through her wall of glass, hating all she saw.

'Is that what all the coming and going is about? There must be ten or a dozen people up there still, I should think.'

'What's your name?'

'I can't see what business it is of yours.'

'As I shall have to put a number of questions to you, I shall need your name to include in my report.'

'Madame Blanc.'

'Widow?'

'No.'

'Does your husband live here with you?'

'No.'

'Did he desert you?'

'Nineteen years ago.'

In the end, she condescended to sit down, in a huge armchair that must have been specially made for her. Maigret, too, sat down.

'Did you see anyone go up to Mademoiselle Papet's flat between half-past five and six?'

'Yes, at twenty to six.'

'Who was it?'

'The Wednesday regular, of course. I don't know their names. He's tall, going bald, and always wears a dark suit.'

'Was he up there long?'

'No.'

'Did he say anything when he came down?'

'He asked me if her ladyship had gone out.'

He had to draw the information out of her, a very little at a time.

'What did you say?'

'That I hadn't seen her.'

'Did he seem surprised?'

'Yes.'

It was exhausting, especially with that blank, fixed stare to contend with. Her eyes were as motionless as her gross body.

'Did you see him earlier in the day?'

'No.'

'Did you see anyone go up round about half-past three? Were you here then?'

'I was here, but no one went up.'

'Did you see anyone come down, round about four o'clock?'

'Not till twenty past four . . .'

'Who was that?'

'That fellow.'

'Whom do you mean by "that fellow"?'

'The one who was with you . . . I can't bring myself to call him by his name.'

'Joséphine Papet's real lover, you mean?'

That did bring a smile to her lips, a smile at once ironic and embittered.

'Did he speak to you?'

'I wouldn't even go so far as to open the door for him.'

'Are you quite sure no one else went up or came down between half-past three and four?'

Having already said so, she was not prepared to go to the trouble of repeating herself.

'Do you know your tenant's other friends?'

'Friends! Is that what you call them?'

'Visitors, then. How many of them are there?'

Her lips moved, as though in prayer. At last she said:

'Four, not counting that fellow.'

'Did any of them ever meet? Was there ever any trouble?'

'Not that I know of.'

'Are you in here all day, every day?'

'Except in the morning, when I go out to do my shopping, or when I'm cleaning the stairs.'

'Did you, personally, have any visitors today?'

'I never have any visitors.'

'Did Mademoiselle Papet go out much?'

'Usually at about eleven in the morning, just round the corner to do her shopping. Occasionally, she went to the cinema of an evening, with *him*.'

'What about Sunday?'

'Sometimes they went out in the car.'

'Whose car?'

'Hers, of course.'

'Did she drive?'

'No, he did.'

'Do you know where the car is now?'

'In a garage in the Rue la Bruyère.'

She did not ask him what had caused her tenant's death. She was as devoid of curiosity as of energy. Maigret looked at her with growing wonder.

'Mademoiselle Papet was murdered.'

'Well, it was only to be expected, wasn't it?'

'Why do you say that?'

'Well, with all those men . . .'

'She was shot almost at point-blank range.'

She nodded, but said nothing.

'Did she never confide in you?'

'She was no friend of mine.'

'In other words, you couldn't stand her?'

'I wouldn't go as far as that.'

It was becoming oppressive. Maigret mopped his brow, and made his escape. It was a great relief to be outside in the open air. The hearse from the Forensic Laboratory had just arrived. He would only be in the way while the men were bringing down the body on a stretcher. He decided to go across the road to the Grand-Saint-Georges, and have a half-pint of beer at the bar.

The murder of Joséphine Papet had not caused the faintest stir in the neighbourhood, not even in the house where she had lived for so many years.

He watched the hearse drive away. As he went back into the house, he saw the concierge standing watching him exactly as before. He went up in the lift, and rang the doorbell. Janvier let him in.

'Have you seen the neighbours?'

'Those that were at home. There are three flats to every floor, two overlooking the street and one the yard at the back. Mademoiselle Papet's nearest neighbour is a Madame Sauveur, an elderly woman, very pleasant, very well groomed. She was in the whole afternoon, knitting and listening to the radio.

'She heard a sound that might have been a muffled shot about mid-afternoon, but she thought it was a car or bus back-firing.'

'Didn't she hear anyone going in or leaving?'

'I checked that. You can't hear the door opening or shutting from her flat. It's an oldish building, and the walls are thick.'

'What about upstairs?'

'There's a couple with two children. They've been away in the country or at the sea for the past week ... The flat at the back belongs to a retired railway official ... He has his grandson living with him ... He didn't hear a thing.'

Florentin was standing at the open window.

The Chief Superintendent asked him:

'Was that window open earlier this afternoon?'

'I think so ... Yes.'

'What about the bedroom window?'

'No, I'm sure it wasn't.'

'How can you be so positive?'

'Because Josée was always most particular about keeping it shut when she had a visitor.'

Across from the bedroom window could be seen a spacious dressmaker's workroom, with a dress form covered in coarse canvas, mounted on a black plinth, and four or five teenage girls sewing.

Florentin, though making a visible effort to keep smiling, seemed uneasy. That fixed, forced smile reminded Maigret of the old days at the Lycée Banville, when, as often happened, Florentin was caught out mimicking a master behind his back.

'You won't allow us to forget we are descended from the apes, I see, Master Florentin,' the weedy little fair-haired man who taught them Latin used to say.

Moers and his men were going through the flat with a fine-tooth comb. Nothing, not so much as a speck of dust, escaped them. In spite of the open window, Maigret was feeling the heat. This case was not at all to his liking. There was something distasteful about it. Besides, he felt that he had been placed in a false position, and was finding it impossible wholly to banish the past from his mind.

He had completely lost touch with all his old school friends, and now here was one turning up out of the blue, in a predicament that was delicate, to say the least.

'Have you seen our piece of monumental masonry?'

Maigret looked puzzled.

'The concierge. That's what I call her. I shudder to think what she calls me.'

' "That fellow".'

'So I'm "that fellow", am I? What else did she say about me?'

'You're sure you've told me everything, exactly as it occurred?'

'Why should I lie to you?'

'You were always a liar. You lied for the fun of it.'

'That was forty years ago!'

'You don't strike me as having changed all that much.'

'If I had had anything to hide, would I have deliberately sought you out?'

26

'What else could you have done?'

'I could have made a run for it . . . I could have gone back to my flat in the Boulevard Rochechouart.'

'To wait there until I came the following morning to arrest you?'

'I could have left the country.'

'Have you any money?'

Florentin flushed crimson, and Maigret felt a twinge of pity for him. As a young boy he had been a kind of licensed jester, with his long clownish face, his jokes and his grimaces.

But, in an elderly man, the old mannerisms were no longer entertaining. Indeed, they were painful to watch.

'You surely don't imagine that I killed her?'

'Why not?'

'But you know me . . .'

'The last time I set eyes on you was twenty years ago, in the Place de la Madeleine, and that, if you remember, was our first meeting since we were schoolboys in Moulins.'

'Do I look like a murderer?'

'A man may be a blameless citizen one minute and a murderer the next. Up to the moment of his victim's death, he is a man like any other.'

'Why should I have killed her? We were the greatest of friends.'

'Just friends?'

'Of course not, but I rather past the age for a grand passion.'

'What about her?'

'I believe she loved me.'

'Was she jealous?'

'I never gave her cause to be . . . You still haven't told me what that old witch downstairs has been saying.'

Janvier was intrigued by the situation, which was unusual, to say the least. He was watching the Chief Superintendent closely, curious to see how he would handle it. Maigret was plainly hesitant and uneasy. For one thing, he seemed unable to make up his mind whether to address Florentin as 'tu' or 'vous'.

'She didn't see anyone go upstairs.'

'She's lying . . . Or else the man must have slipped past the lodge while she was in the kitchen . . .'

'She denies that she ever left the lodge.'

'But that's impossible! The man who killed her must have come from somewhere ... Unless ...'

'Unless what?'

'Unless he was in the house already.'

'One of the tenants?'

Florentin seized upon this suggestion eagerly.

'Why not? I'm not the only man in the building.'

'Was Josée friendly with any of the other tenants?'

'How should I know? I wasn't here all the time. I have my own business to attend to. I work for my living ...'

This statement had the unmistakable ring of falsehood. Florentin, who had spent his whole life acting some part or other, now saw himself in the role of breadwinner.

'Janvier, I'll leave you to comb the building from top to bottom. Call at all the flats. Talk to everyone you can. I'm going back to the Quai ...'

'What about the car?'

Maigret had never been able to bring himself to learn to drive.

'I'll take a taxi.'

And, turning to Florentin, he said:

'You come with me.'

'You're not arresting me, surely?'

'No.'

'What are you up to then? What do you want me for?'

'Just for a chat.'

Chapter Two

Maigret's original intention had been to take Florentin back with him to the Quai des Orfèvres, but, just as he was about to give the address to the taxi-driver, he changed his mind.

'What number Boulevard Rochechouart?' he asked Florentin.

'Fifty-five B. Why?'

'Fifty-five B Boulevard Rochechouart,' Maigret said to the taxi-driver.

It was no distance. The driver, annoyed at having been engaged for so short a journey, grumbled under his breath.

Sandwiched between a picture framer and a tobacconist-cum-bar was a narrow cobbled alley leading to two glass-fronted workshops, outside one of which stood a handcart. Inside the other, a painter was at work on a view of the Sacré-Coeur, which was no doubt intended for the tourist trade. Judging from the way in which he was dashing it off, he must have produced them by the dozen. He had long hair, and a pepper-and-salt beard, and wore a floppy bow tie of the kind favoured by pseudo-artists at the turn of the century.

Florentin got out his bunch of keys and unlocked the door of the workshop on the right. Maigret followed him inside, burning with resentment.

For Florentin had somehow contrived to tarnish his boy-hood memories. At the very moment when he had turned up at the Quai des Orfèvres, Maigret had been watching the fly that had settled so obstinately on the top left-hand corner of the report he was studying, and re-living his school days in Moulins.

What, he had wondered, had become of the other boys in his form? He had completely lost touch with all of them. Crochet, whose father had been a notary, had presumably taken over his practice by now. Orban, plump and good-natured, had, no doubt, achieved his ambition and qualified as a doctor. As for the others, they had probably settled in various towns all over France, or gone to live abroad.

Why, among them all, did it have to be Florentin to cross his path, and in such very disagreeable circumstances, at that?

He had a vivid recollection of the confectioner's shop, though he had seldom been in it. For some of the other boys, those with money to spare, it had been a meeting-place, where they ate ices and cakes in an atmosphere redolent of hot spices and sugar, surrounded by marble and gilt-framed mirrors. According to the discerning ladies of the town, a cake was not worth having unless it came from Florentin's.

Returning to the present, he found himself in a dark, dusty room, full of junk, with windows that looked as though they had never been cleaned, and which consequently let in very little light.

'I'm sorry about the mess . . .'

In the circumstances, for Florentin to call himself an antique dealer was worse than pretentious. God knows where he had got the furniture that was lying about the place, but it was all alike, old, battered, ugly, and quite worthless. The most that could be done with it was to repair the worst of the damage, and slightly improve its appearance with furniture polish.

'Have you been in this business long?'

'Three years.'

'And before that?'

'I was in exports.'

'What did you export?'

'A little of everything. Chiefly to the emergent countries of Africa.'

'And before that?'

It was a humiliating question. Florentin murmured uncomfortably:

'Oh! well, you know, this and that . . . I tried my hand at all sorts of things. I had no wish to spend the rest of my days in the shop in Moulins. My sister married a confectioner, and they are running the business now.'

Maigret remembered Florentin's sister, plump as a pigeon behind the snow-white shop counter. Had he not been just a little in love with her? She was fresh-faced and cheerful, like her mother, whom she closely resembled.

'Living in Paris, one has to be up to every trick. I've had my ups and downs . . .'

Maigret had known so many like him, up one minute, down the next, for ever promoting some marvellously profitable scheme, which, in the end, collapsed like a house of cards. Such men were always within a hair's breadth of arrest and imprisonment. Frequently, though they might try to touch you for a loan of a hundred thousand francs to build a seaport in some remote territory, they would gladly settle for a hundred francs, to avoid the indignity of being thrown out of their lodgings.

Florentin had been lucky. He had found Josée. If the workshop was anything to go by, it was evident that he could not be making a living out of selling furniture.

There was a door at the back. It was ajar. Maigret pushed it

30

open, to reveal a narrow, windowless annexe, bare except for an iron bedstead, a washstand and a rickety wardrobe.

'Is this where you sleep?'

'Only on Thursdays.'

Maigret could not now remember who the Thursday caller was, the only one privileged to spend the night in the Rue Notre-Dame-de-Lorette.

'Fernand Courcel,' volunteered Florentin. 'He and Josée were friends long before I came on the scene ... He's been coming to see her and taking her out for the past ten years ... He can't get away nowadays as much as he used to, but he still manages to find an excuse for spending Thursday nights in Paris ...'

Maigret was poking about in corners, opening hideous old cupboards, from which all the polish had been chipped and worn away. He was not at all sure what he was looking for, only that something was bothering him, some detail that had escaped him.

'You did say, didn't you, that Josée had no bank account?'

'Yes. At least, as far as I know.'

'You say she mistrusted banks?'

'That was part of it ... But mainly she didn't want anyone to know what she had, because of tax.'

Maigret came upon an old pipe.

'Do you smoke a pipe?'

'Not in her flat ... She disliked the smell ... Only when I'm here ...'

In one rustic-style wardrobe, there were some clothes, a blue suit, some shabby jeans, three or four shirts, espadrilles thick with sawdust, and one solitary pair of outdoor shoes.

The wardrobe of a squalid layabout. Joséphine Papet must have had money. Had she been mean with it, mistrustful of Florentin, who would not have hesitated to squander the lot, down to the last sou?

He had found nothing of interest, and almost regretted having come. After all he had seen, he was beginning to feel sorry for his old school friend. As he was making for the door, he caught sight of something wrapped in newspaper on top of a cupboard. He turned back, took a chair up to the cupboard, climbed on to it, and lifted down a square parcel.

Florentin's forehead was beaded with perspiration.

The Chief Superintendent removed the wrappings to reveal a biscuit tin, with the maker's name stamped on it in red and yellow. He opened it. It was tightly packed with bundles of hundred-franc notes.

'Those are my savings . . .'

Maigret stared at him blankly, as though he had not heard. He sat down at the work-bench to count the bundles of notes. There were forty-eight.

'Are you fond of biscuits?'

'I like one occasionally.'

'Have you another box like this?'

'Not at the moment, I don't think . . .'

'There were two, I noticed, of the same make in the flat in the Rue Notre-Dame-de-Lorette.'

'I daresay that's where I got it . . .'

He had always been a liar, either because he couldn't help himself, or just for the fun of it. He was for ever romancing, and the more unlikely the tale, the more barefaced the lies he told. This time, however, there was a great deal at stake.

'Now I see why you didn't get to the Quai des Orfèvres before five.'

'I couldn't make up my mind what to do . . . I was frightened . . . I knew suspicion was bound to fall on me . . .'

'You came here.'

He still persisted in denying it, but his self-confidence was ebbing fast.

'If you won't tell me, the painter next door will.'

'You must listen to me, Maigret.'

His lower lip was trembling. He seemed on the verge of bursting into tears. It was a distressing sight.

'I know I don't always speak the truth. I can't help myself. Don't you remember how I used to have you all in fits of laughter with the tales I made up to amuse you? But you've got to believe me now, I beg of you. I didn't kill Josée, and I truly was hiding in the clothes closet when it happened.'

He really was a pathetic sight, but then it should not be forgotten that he was also a born actor.

'If I had killed her, would I have come to you, of all people?'

'In that case, why didn't you tell me the truth?'

'I don't know what you mean. What truth?'

He was prevaricating, playing for time.

'At three o'clock this afternoon, this biscuit tin was still in the flat in the Rue Notre-Dame-de-Lorette. Isn't that so?'

'Yes.'

'Well, then?'

'Surely it's not so hard to understand . . . Josée had completely lost touch with her family . . . She only had one sister, married to a fruit grower in Morocco . . . They're rich people . . . I'm on my beam ends . . . so, when I saw her lying there, dead . . .'

'You took advantage of the situation to slope off with the loot.'

'That's a crude way of putting it, but just look at it from my point of view. After all, I wasn't doing any harm to anyone . . . And without her, I didn't know what was to become of me.'

Maigret looked fixedly at him, a prey to conflicting emotions.

'Come along.'

He was hot and thirsty. He felt utterly exhausted, and fed up with himself and everyone else.

As they emerged from the little alley, he hesitated for a moment, then propelled his companion into the tobacconist's shop that was also a bar.

He ordered two halves.

'Do you or don't you believe me?'

'We'll talk about it later.'

Maigret drank two half-pints, then set about looking for a taxi. It was the rush hour, and the traffic was at its worst. It took them half an hour to get to the Quai des Orfèvres. The sky was a uniform blue. It was oppressively close. All the café terraces were crowded, and there were men in shirtsleeves everywhere, carrying their jackets.

His office, from which the sun had by now retreated, was comparatively cool.

'Take a seat . . . Smoke if you feel like it.'

'Thanks . . . It's a very odd feeling, you know, to find oneself in a situation like this with an old school friend.'

'Don't I know it!' grumbled the Chief Superintendent, refilling his pipe.

'It's different for you.'

'Well . . .'

'You take a pretty low view of me, don't you? To you, I'm just a slob.'

'It's not for me to pass judgement. I'm trying to understand.'

'I loved her.'

'I see.'

'I don't pretend it was a grand passion. We didn't claim to be Romeo and Juliet . . .'

'I must confess I can't quite see Romeo skulking in a clothes closet. Was that a regular occurrence?'

'No, not more than three or four times. It was most unusual for any of them to call unexpectedly.'

'Did these gentlemen know of your existence?'

'Of course not!'

'Did you never meet any of them?'

'I knew them by sight. I couldn't help wondering what they looked like, so I hung about in the street, waiting for them to come out. I'm being perfectly frank with you, you see . . .'

'Have you never been tempted to try a little blackmail? They're all married men, I presume, fathers of families, and so on?'

'I swear to you . . .'

'You're altogether too ready to swear to anything. I wish you wouldn't.'

'Oh! Very well, but how else can I make you believe me?'

'By telling the truth.'

'I never resorted to blackmail.'

'Why not?'

'I was happy with things as they were. I'm not young any more. I've been a rolling stone long enough. All I wanted was a quiet life and a bit of security. It was restful being with Josée and she took good care of me.'

'Whose idea was it to buy a car? Yours?'

'No, we both wanted one. I may have been the first to suggest it . . .'

'Where used you to go on Sundays?'

'Nowhere in particular ... anywhere ... the Chevreuse Valley ... the Forest of Fontainebleau ... occasionally, though not so often, we'd have a day by the sea ...'

'Did you know where she kept her money?'

'She made no secret of it, as far as I was concerned. She trusted me. For heaven's sake, Maigret, what possible reason could I have had to kill her?'

'Suppose she was tired of you?'

'But she wasn't! Quite the opposite, in fact. The whole point of saving money was so that eventually we could set up house together somewhere in the country. Put yourself in my place ...'

Chief Superintendent or not, it was Maigret's turn to make a face.

'Do you possess a revolver?'

'She had one that she always kept in the drawer of her bed-side table. It was very old. I found it a couple of years ago in a chest I bought at an auction.'

'Was there any ammunition with it?'

'If you mean, was it loaded, yes, it was.'

'And you kept it at the Rue Notre-Dame-de-Lorette?'

'Josée was rather a nervous type. I thought it would reassure her to have it close at hand in the bedside table drawer.'

'It isn't there now.'

'I know ... I looked for it, too.'

'Why?'

'I realize it was stupid of me ... I've behaved like an idiot ... The trouble with me is that I just blurt everything out ... I should have rung the local police, and stayed put until they arrived ... I could have told them any old tale ... that I'd just arrived and found her dead.'

'I asked you a straight question and I want a straight answer. Why were you looking for the revolver?'

'To get rid of it ... I would have shoved it down a drain, or thrown it in the river. As it was my gun, I realized it was bound to get me into trouble.

'And how right I was, seeing that even you ...'

'So far, I haven't accused you of anything.'

35

'But the reason I'm here is that you don't believe a word I say . . . Am I under arrest?'

Maigret looked at him uncertainly. He appeared grave and anxious.

'No . . .' he said, at last.

He was taking a risk, and he knew it, but he had not the heart to do otherwise.

'Where do you intend to go from here?'

'I'll have to get a bite to eat, I suppose, and after that, I'll just go to bed.'

'Where?'

Florentin hesitated.

'I don't know . . . I suppose I'd better keep away from the Rue Notre-Dame-de-Lorette . . .'

Was he really so insensitive as to be in any doubt about it?

'Oh, well, it will just have to be the Boulevard Roche-chouart.'

In the narrow little windowless box at the back of the work-shop, where there were not even any sheets on the bed, but only a shabby, old, threadbare, grey blanket.

Maigret got up and went into the Inspectors' Duty Room. Lapointe was on the telephone. He waited until he had finished.

'I've got a man in my office, tall and thin, my age, but rather the worse for wear. He lives at the end of a little alley in the Boulevard Rochechouart, number fifty-five B . . . I don't know what he'll do when he leaves here, but I don't want you to let him out of your sight . . .

'See to it that there's someone to relieve you on the night shift . . .

'And arrange for someone else to take over in the morning.'

'Does it matter if he knows he's being followed?'

'Better not, but it's not all that important . . . He's as cunning as a wagon-load of monkeys, and he's sure to be on the look-out . . .'

'I'll see to it, sir . . . I'd better go and wait for him outside.'

'I shan't keep him more than another minute or two.'

As Maigret pushed open the door, Florentin stepped back several paces, looking thoroughly uncomfortable.

'So you were listening?'

Florentin hesitated, then the corners of his wide mouth twitched in a rather pathetic smile.

'What would you have done in my place?'

'You heard, then?'

'Not everything . . .'

'I'm having you tailed by one of my inspectors . . . I warn you that if you make any attempt to shake him off, I'll put out an all-stations call, and you'll find yourself under lock and key.'

'You've no call to speak to me like that, Maigret!'

Much as the Chief Superintendent would have liked to tell him to stop addressing him in that familiar way, he had not the heart to do so.

'Where were you planning to go?'

'When?'

'You knew that there would be an investigation, and that you were bound to be a suspect. It wasn't very sensible of you to hide the money where you did . . . Presumably you intended to move it somewhere safer as soon as you got the chance? . . . Had you already decided to come to me?'

'No . . . my first thought was to go to the local police.'

'You didn't consider leaving the country before the body was found?'

'It did cross my mind.'

'What stopped you?'

'I realized it would look like an admission of guilt, and I'd be laying myself open to extradition, so, on second thoughts, I decided to go to the local police . . . and then, suddenly, I remembered about you . . . I'd seen your name in the papers, often. You're the only one in our form to have become almost a celebrity.'

Maigret was still contemplating his old school friend with an air of perplexity, as though he represented an insoluble problem.

'You have the reputation of not being taken in by appearances. It's said that you have a way of keeping at a thing until you get to the bottom of it . . . so I was hoping you'd understand . . . I'm beginning to think I was mistaken . . . You believe I'm guilty, and you might as well admit it.'

'I've already told you, I haven't made up my mind one way or the other.'

'I shouldn't have taken the money. I did it on impulse. It didn't even occur to me to take it until I was actually on my way out.'

'You may go.'

They were both on their feet. Florentin hesitated, as though about to hold out his hand. Perhaps in order to forestall him, Maigret got out his handkerchief and mopped his face.

'Shall I be seeing you tomorrow?'

'Very likely.'

'Good-bye, Maigret.'

'Good-bye.'

He did not stand at the door to watch him go down the stairs, with Lapointe at his heels.

For no very precise reason Maigret was displeased with himself. With himself and everyone else. Up to five o'clock, things had jogged along at an agreeably indolent pace. He had enjoyed his day. Now it was spoilt.

The reports were still there on his desk, demanding his attention. The fly had disappeared, affronted perhaps at his defection.

It was half-past seven. He dialled the number of his flat in the Boulevard Richard-Lenoir.

'Is that you?'

It was what he always said. Absurd, really. As if he didn't recognize his wife's voice by now.

'Won't you be in to dinner?'

He so often wasn't, that she took it for granted that this was what he was ringing to say.

'As a matter of fact, I will . . . What are we having? . . . Good . . . Good . . . In about half an hour.'

He went into the Duty Room. Most of the inspectors had gone. He sat at Janvier's desk, and scribbled a message on his pad, for him to ring him at home as soon as he got back.

He was still feeling vaguely uneasy. There were a number of puzzling features about this case, and the fact that Florentin was, in some sense, an old friend didn't make things any easier.

And then there were the others, middle-aged men of some

standing, each with a life of his own, regular habits, and a stable family background.

Except for one day a week! Except for those few furtive hours in Joséphine Papet's flat.

Tomorrow, the newspapers would be full of the story, and they would all shake in their shoes.

He ought to go up to the attics, to Criminal Records, and find out how Moers was getting on. With a shrug, he stood up and took his hat from its hook.

'See you tomorrow.'

'Good night, sir.'

He fought his way through the evening crowds as far as the Châtelet, and there joined the queue waiting for his bus.

*

As soon as he came in, Madame Maigret could see that he had something on his mind, and he read the unspoken question in her glance.

'A wretched business!' he grumbled, as he went out to the bathroom to wash his hands.

He took off his jacket, and loosened his tie a little.

'I was at school with the fellow, and now he's up to his neck in this ghastly mess. And frankly, I can't see anyone having the slightest sympathy for him in his predicament!'

'What is it, a murder?'

'A shooting . . . the woman is dead.'

'What motive? Jealousy?'

'No, not if he did it.'

'Is there any doubt about it?'

'Let's eat.' He sighed, as though he had had more than enough of the subject.

All the windows were open, and the room was bathed in the golden light of the setting sun. There was chicken with tarragon, which Madame Maigret cooked to perfection, garnished with asparagus tips.

She had on a cotton housecoat printed all over with little flowers. It was one of several that she was fond of wearing at home. He felt tonight that it enhanced the domestic intimacy of their dinner together.

'Will you have to go out again?'

'I don't think so. I left a message for Janvier to ring me.'

Just as he was digging his spoon into his half-melon, the telephone rang.

'Hello, yes . . . Oh! It's you, Janvier . . . Are you at the Quai? . . . Anything to report?'

'Very little, sir . . . First of all, I went into the two shops on the ground floor . . . You remember, there's a lingerie shop on the left . . . Chez Éliane . . . Very fancy stuff . . . the sort of thing you usually only find in Montmartre . . . Apparently the tourists are crazy about it.

'It's owned by two girls, one dark, one fair, and they seem to spend most of their time watching the comings and goings in the building. They had no difficulty in recognizing Florentin and the dead woman from my description . . . She was a customer of theirs . . . though she didn't go in for any of the fancy stuff.

'According to them, she was a charming woman, even-tempered, always ready with a smile . . . Very much the little housewife . . . extremely neat in her person, and very kind-hearted.

'They knew about her and Florentin, and they thought a lot of him, too. He struck them as quite the gentleman . . . a gentleman down on his luck was how they put it.

'They saw Josée go out with the Wednesday visitor one evening, but they didn't think any the worse of her for that . . .'

'François Paré, do you mean? The Ministry of Public Works man?'

'I presume so . . . Anyway, that's how they found out about his weekly visits. He always arrived in a black Citroën, punctual almost to the minute, except that he could never find anywhere to park . . . And, invariably, he came armed with a box of fancy cakes.'

'Do they know about the other men, too?'

'Only the Thursday one . . . He was the very first . . . He's been coming to the Rue Notre-Dame-de-Lorette for years . . . Some time in the distant past, they think, he actually lived in the flat for several weeks . . . They call him Fatty . . . He has round, pink cheeks, like a baby, and pale, protuberant eyes . . .'

'Almost every Thursday, he took her out to dinner and the theatre ... In the ordinary way, he would have spent tomorrow night in the flat ... Quite often, he didn't leave until lunch-time the following day.'

Maigret consulted his notes.

'That would be Fernand Courcel of Rouen ... He has an office in Paris, Boulevard Voltaire ... What about the others?'

'They didn't mention them, but they're convinced Florentin is the one she was deceiving.'

'And what else?'

'Next, I went into the shoe shop opposite, Chaussures Martin ... It's a dark, narrow little place ... You can't see into the street, because of the window display, though there is a glass door, if you should happen to be looking out ...'

'Go on ...'

'The flat on the left on the first floor belongs to a dentist ... He doesn't know a thing ... Josée went to him for treatment about four years ago ... a filling ... she had three appointments ... On the right, there's an old couple who are practically housebound ... The husband used to work for the Banque de France, I don't know in what capacity. They have one married daughter, who comes to see them every Sunday, with her husband and two children ...

'Then there's the flat overlooking the courtyard ... It's empty at present. The tenants, a man and wife, have been in Italy for the past month. They're both in the catering trade.

'On the second floor there's the woman who makes corsets. She has two girls working for her ... None of them have ever heard of Joséphine Papet.

'Across the way there's a woman with three children, all under five ... She's got a voice like a foghorn, and no wonder, considering the row those kids make.

' "It's disgusting," she said, "I've written to the landlord about it. My husband was against it, but I wrote all the same ... He's scared stiff of making trouble ... Carrying on like that in a respectable house, with children about! ... It was a different man almost every night ... I got to know which was which by the way they rang the bell ...

' "The one with the limp always came on Saturdays, straight after lunch . . . You could tell him by his walk . . . Besides, he always jabbed at the bell four or five times in quick succession. Poor fool, he probably thought he was the only one." '

'Were you able to find out anything more about him?'

'Only that he's a man of about fifty, and always came by taxi.'

'What about *Le Rouquin*?'

'He's a new boy . . . He put in his first appearance only a few weeks ago. He's younger than the others, thirty to thirty-five, and it seems he takes the stairs four at a time . . .'

'Has he a key?'

No, none of them had except Florentin . . . According to my informant on the second floor, he's just a high-class pimp . . .

' "I'd rather have those you see round about the Pigalle any day," she said. "They at least are taking a risk . . . And anyway, they're not fit for any other sort of work . . . But he looks as if he's seen better days, and seems to be a man of some education." '

Maigret could not help smiling. He rather regretted not having interviewed the tenants himself.

'There was no answer from the flat opposite, so I went up to the fourth floor, and there I walked straight into the middle of a family row.

'The husband was yelling at the top of his voice: "If you don't tell me where you've been and who with . . ."

' "Surely, I've a perfect right to go out and do my shopping, without having to give you a detailed account of every shop I've been into! What do you expect me to do, get a certificate from the manager wherever I go?"

' "You don't expect me to believe you spent the whole afternoon buying a pair of shoes! Who were you with? Answer me, will you!"

' "I don't know what you are talking about."

' "You must have gone to meet someone. Who was it?"

'Frankly, I thought I'd better make myself scarce,' commented Janvier.

'There's an old woman living opposite. It's amazing the number of old people there are in that district. She could tell me nothing. She's pretty deaf, and the flat smells of stale food.

'As a last resort, I had a go at the concierge ... She just stared at me with those fish-eyes of hers, and I couldn't get a thing out of her ...'

'Nor could I, if that's any consolation ... except that, according to her, no one went up to the flat between three and four o'clock.'

'Is she quite sure?'

'So she says ... She also says that she was in the lodge the whole time, and that no one could have gone past without her seeing them ... That's her story, and it's my belief she'll stick to it, even on oath.'

'What shall I do next?'

'Go home. I'll see you tomorrow in the office.'

'Good night, sir.'

Maigret, his melon still untasted, scarcely had time to put the receiver down when the telephone rang again. This time it was Lapointe. He seemed excited.

'I've been trying to get through to you for the last quarter of an hour, sir, but it was engaged the whole time. Before that, I tried the Quai ... I'm speaking from the tobacconist's on the corner ... There have been developments, sir ...'

'Go on.'

'Before we were even out of the building he knew he was being tailed. He actually turned round and winked at me as we were going down the stairs ...

'Outside I followed about three or four yards behind him ... When we got to the Place Dauphine, he seemed to hesitate, and then went towards the Brasserie Dauphine ... He looked at me as though he expected me to catch him up, and when I didn't, he came up and spoke to me.

' "Look here, I'm going in for a drink ... I don't see any reason why you shouldn't join me, do you?"

'I had a feeling that he was taking the mickey. He's a bit of a clown, isn't he? I said I didn't drink on duty, so he went in alone. I watched him gulp down three or four brandies, one after the other ... I'm not quite sure how many.

'When he came out, having satisfied himself that I was still there, he gave me another wink, and started off towards the

Pont-Neuf. The streets were very crowded at that hour, and the cars were jammed nose to tail, with every other driver leaning on his horn . . .

'We walked in single file as far as the Quai de la Mégisserie, and then, suddenly, he pulled himself up on to the parapet and jumped into the Seine! It all happened so quickly that only those few people nearest to him saw him do it.

'He came up within no more than a couple of yards of a boat made fast to the bank . . . By that time there was quite a crowd gathered . . . Then something almost comical happened . . . The owner of the boat took hold of a long, heavy boathook and held it out to Florentin, who grabbed hold of the hook end, and allowed himself to be hauled in like a fish!

'By the time I had scrambled down the bank and reached the boat, Florentin was on dry land, with a police constable bending over him.

'The whole place was swarming with spectators by then . . . You'd have thought that something really serious had happened.

'I decided I'd better keep out of it, in case there were any reporters about, who might be curious as to what I was doing there . . . So I kept watch from a distance . . . I hope I did the right thing . . .'

'You did very well . . . Besides, I can assure you that Florentin was never in any danger . . . We used to go swimming together in the Allier as boys, and he was far and away the best swimmer in the school . . . What happened next?'

'The boatman gave him a tot of rum, not realizing that he'd already had three or four brandies . . . and then the police constable marched him off to the station at Les Halles.

'I didn't go in, for reasons I've already explained . . . I presume they took his name and address, and asked him a few questions . . . When he came out, I was having a sandwich in the bistro opposite the Police Station, and I don't think he saw me . . . He looked a sorry sight, I must say, wrapped in an old police blanket they'd lent him . . .

'He took a taxi back to his place . . . He changed into dry clothes . . . I could see him through the workshop window . . . He caught sight of me as he came out, and treated me to another wink, and made a comic face at me for good measure. Then he walked as far as the Place Blanche, where he went into a restaurant . . .

'He got back here half an hour ago, and bought a paper, and the last I saw of him, he was stretched out on his bed, reading it.'

By the time he had heard the whole story Maigret was looking quite stunned.

'Have you had any dinner?'

'I had a sandwich. I see they sell sandwiches in here, so I shall probably have a couple more before I leave . . . Torrence will be relieving me at two in the morning.'

'Good luck to you,' said Maigret, with a sigh.

'Shall I ring you again if anything further happens?'

'Yes, no matter how late it is.'

He had almost forgotten about his melon. It was dusk by now. He ate the melon over by the window, while Madame Maigret cleared the table.

One thing was certain. Florentin had had no intention of committing suicide. It is virtually impossible for a strong swimmer to drown in the Seine, least of all in the middle of June, with the Quais swarming with people, and within a few feet of a conveniently moored boat!

Why, then, had his old friend jumped into the water? To create the impression that he was being driven to distraction by the unfounded suspicions of the police?

'How is Lapointe?'

Maigret could not help smiling. He knew very well what his wife was getting at. She would never ask him point blank about his work, but there were times when she was not above angling for information.

'He's in the best of health, which is just as well, because he's got several more hours ahead of him pounding the pavement at the end of a little alley in the Boulevard Rochechouart.'

'All on account of your old school friend?'

'Yes, he's just been making a spectacle of himself by jumping off the Pont-Neuf into the Seine.'

'You mean he tried to commit suicide?'

'No, I'm quite sure he had no such intention.'

What possible reason could Florentin have for drawing attention to himself in that way? Did he just want to get his name in the papers? Surely not, but then, where Florentin was concerned, anything was possible.

'Shall we go out for a breath of air?'

The street lights in the Boulevard Richard-Lenoir were all switched on, although it was not yet dark outside. They were not the only couple taking a quiet stroll, enjoying the cool of the evening after a hot day.

At eleven, they retired to bed. Next morning, the sun was shining, promising another hot day. Already, a faint smell of tar rose from the streets, a smell characteristic of Paris in mid-summer, when the road surfaces seem almost to melt in the heat.

Maigret found a huge pile of mail waiting for him in his office, which all had to be dealt with before he could get down to his report. The morning papers mentioned the murder in the Rue Notre-Dame-de-Lorette, but gave no details. Maigret reported to his Departmental Chief with a brief summary of the facts, as far as he knew them.

'Has he confessed?'

'No.'

'Have you any real evidence against him?'

'Only pointers.'

He saw no reason to add that he and Florentin had been at school together. As soon as he got back to his office he sent for Janvier.

'One thing we know for certain, Joséphine Papet had four regular visitors. We have the names of two of them, François Paré and Courcel. I shall see them myself this morning. I'll leave the other two to you. Question as many people as you like, the neighbours, the tradesmen, anyone else you can think of, but I want their names and addresses before the day is out.'

Janvier could not help smiling. Maigret knew as well as he did that it was an almost impossible assignment.

'I'm relying on you.'

'Very good, sir.'

Next Maigret rang though to the Police Surgeon. Alas, it was no longer his dear old friend Doctor Paul, whose greatest pleasure in life had been to take him out to dinner and regale him, throughout the meal, with a detailed account of his autopsies.

'Have you recovered the bullet, doctor?'

By way of reply, the doctor began reading from the report that he was in the middle of writing. Joséphine Papet had been in the prime of life, and had enjoyed excellent health. All her organs were sound, and it was plain that she had been exceptionally fastidious in her personal habits.

As to the shot, it had been fired at a range of between eighteen inches and three feet.

'The bullet was on a slight upward trajectory when it lodged in the base of the skull.'

Maigret could not help thinking of the tall figure of Florentin. Was it possible that he had fired the shot sitting down?

He put the question to the doctor.

'Could she have been shot by someone sitting down?'

'No, the angle of entry wasn't steep enough for that. A slight upward trajectory, I said ... I've sent the bullet to Gastinne-Renette for an expert opinion ... If you ask me, I don't believe that bullet was fired from an automatic weapon, but more probably from an old-fashioned cylinder-revolver.'

'Was death instantaneous?'

'Within half a minute at most, I'd say.'

'So nothing could have been done to save her?'

'Absolutely nothing.'

'Thank you, doctor.'

Torrence was back in the Inspectors' Room. He had been relieved by Dieudonné, who was new to the job.

'What's he been up to?'

'He got up at half-past seven, shaved, had a cat's lick, and went out in his slippers to the tobacconist's on the corner for breakfast. He had two cups of coffee, and two or three croissants. Afterwards, he went into the phone box. Presumably, he intended to make a call, but, after some hesitation, he came out without doing so.

'He turned round several times to see if I was watching. I don't know what he's like normally, but, at the moment, he seems listless and depressed ...

'He went to the newspaper kiosk in the Place Blanche, and

bought several papers. Then he just stood there in the street, glancing through a couple of them.

'After that, he went back indoors ... Then Dieudonné arrived and took over, and I came back here to report to you.'

'Didn't he speak to anyone?'

'No ... Well, not unless you count the painter, who turned up while he was out buying the papers. I don't know where he lives, but he certainly doesn't sleep in his studio ... When Florentin got back he called out: "How's tricks?"'

'And the painter replied: "Fine". Then he gave me an old-fashioned look. He must be wondering what on earth we're up to, keeping watch in relays at the top of the alley. He was still peering out, when Dieudonné took over from me.'

Maigret took his hat off its hook, and went out into the forecourt. In the ordinary way, he would have taken an inspector with him, and driven off in one of the row of black cars parked in front of the building.

Today, however, he preferred to walk. He crossed the Pont Saint-Michel, making for the Boulevard Saint-Germain. He had never before had occasion to set foot in the Ministry of Public Works. He looked in bewilderment from one to another of the many staircases, each marked with a different letter of the alphabet.

'Can I help you?'

'I'm looking for the Department of Inland Waterways.'

'Staircase C, top floor.'

There was no lift that he could see. The staircase was as dingy as his own at the Quai des Orfèvres. On each floor the various offices leading off the corridor were signposted with black arrows.

On the third floor, he found the sign he was looking for. He pushed open a door marked: *Enter without knocking.*

It led into a large room, where four men and two girls were working at desks, behind a barrier.

The walls were covered with old, yellowing maps, just as in the classrooms of the lycée in Moulins.

'Can I help you?'

'I'm looking for a Monsieur Paré.'

'What name, please?'

He hesitated. Very likely the Head of the Department of Inland Waterways was a man of impeccable character, and he had no wish to compromise him in the eyes of his staff. On reflection, he decided not to produce his card.

'My name is Maigret.'

The youth, frowning, took a closer look at him, then, with a shrug, turned and disappeared through a door at the back of the room.

He was soon back.

'Monsieur Paré will see you now,' he said, ushering Maigret into an inner room.

Maigret saw, coming forward to greet him, an elderly man of dignified bearing, though somewhat overweight. With formal ceremony he invited Maigret to be seated.

'I was expecting you, Monsieur Maigret.'

There was a morning paper lying on his desk. He lowered himself gently into the chair behind the desk, and laid his arms along the arms of the chair. There was a touch of ritual solemnity in the way he did this.

'I'm sure there is no need for me to tell you that, as far as I'm concerned, this is a very unpleasant situation.'

He was not smiling. He had the air of a man who seldom smiled. He was self-possessed, a little pompous, the sort who would weigh his words carefully before speaking.

Chapter Three

The office was very much like the one Maigret had occupied before Police Headquarters were modernized. There, on the mantelpiece, was a black marble clock identical with the one in his present office. Maigret wondered if it was as unreliable as his.

The man himself was as impassive as the clock. He was very much the senior civil servant, a combination of self-possession and caution. It must have been a deep affront to his self-esteem to find himself suddenly in the hot seat.

His features were undistinguished. The sparse brown hair was carefully combed to hide an incipient bald patch, and his little toothbrush moustache was too black to be natural. He had well-cared-for white hands, covered with long, fine hairs.

'It was good of you to come yourself, Monsieur Maigret, and spare me the indignity of a summons to Police Headquarters.'

'I'm as anxious as you are to avoid any unnecessary publicity.'

'I noticed that the morning papers gave little more than the bare facts.'

'Had you known Joséphine Papet long?'

'About three years ... It gives me an odd feeling, you know, to hear you use her full name ... I've always known her as Josée ... As a matter of fact, it wasn't until several months after we met that I learned what her surname was ...'

'I understand ... How did you meet her?'

'It happened quite by chance. I'm fifty-five, Superintendent. I was fifty-two at the time, and it may surprise you to know I had never before been unfaithful to my wife.

'This, in spite of the fact that, for the past ten years, my wife has been a sick woman. She suffers from a psychiatric disorder, which has strained our relationship a good deal.'

'Have you any children?'

'Three daughters. The eldest is married to a shipowner in La Rochelle. The second is a schoolteacher in a lycée in Tunis. The youngest is also married. She lives in Paris, in the XVIth *arrondissement*. I have five grandchildren in all, the oldest of whom is nearly twelve. As to my wife and myself, we have lived in the same flat in Versailles for thirty years. As you see, most of my life has been wholly uneventful, very much the life you would expect a conscientious civil servant to lead.'

He spoke deliberately, choosing his words with care, as a prudent man should. There was not the faintest hint of self-mockery in his manner, and his face remained expressionless. Had he ever been known to burst out laughing? Maigret doubted it. Even his smile was probably no more than a twitch of the lips.

'You asked me where I met her ... Occasionally, when I leave the office, I stop for a drink in a brasserie on the corner of the Boulevard Saint-Germain and the Rue de Solférino ... I did so on that day . . . It was raining . . . I can still see the rain streaming down the windows.

'I sat in my usual corner, and the waiter, who has known me for years, brought me my glass of port . . .

'There was a young woman at the next table. She was writing a letter, and having trouble with the café pen. She was using violet ink. There wasn't much left in the bottle, and what there was was reduced almost to a paste.

'She was a respectable-looking young woman, soberly dressed in a good navy-blue suit . . .

'She called out to the waiter: "Is this the only pen you have?"

' "I'm sorry, madam," he said, "but nowadays most of our customers use their own fountain pens."

'I took mine from my pocket, and held it out to her. It was more or less a reflex action.

' "Allow me," I said.

'She took it, with a grateful smile. And that's how it all started. She had almost finished writing her letter. She was drinking tea.

'As she gave me back my pen, she asked: "Do you come here often?"

' "Almost every day," I said.

' "I like these old-fashioned brasseries, where most of the customers are regulars. They have atmosphere."

' "Do you live in this district?"

' "No, I have a flat in the Rue Notre-Dame-de-Lorette, but I'm quite often in this part of the world." '

His expression, as he described this first meeting, was as artless as a child's.

'So you see, it was pure chance that we met. She wasn't there the following day, but the day after that she was back, sitting at the same table. She smiled at me.

'There was something about her, her manner, her expression, an air of gentle serenity. One felt one could trust her.

'We exchanged a few words. I told her I lived at Versailles, and I seem to remember that I mentioned my wife and daughters. She came to the door, and watched me get into my car and drive away.

'It may surprise you to know that things went on in this way for a month or more. Some days she wasn't in the brasserie, and I always felt a pang of disappointment when I didn't see her.

'I had come to look upon her, as a friend, nothing more. It was just that, with my wife, I always had to weigh every word. She was so apt to take things amiss, and then there would be a scene.

'Before my daughters left home, it was all very different. There were always noisy, cheerful young people about, and, in those days, my wife was energetic and high-spirited. You can't imagine what it's like to go home to a vast, empty flat, and be watched from the minute you're in the door by a pair of eyes, full of anguish and mistrust . . .'

Maigret, having lit his pipe, held out his tobacco pouch.

'No thanks. I gave up smoking years ago. Please don't imagine I'm making excuses for myself.

'I am on the committee of a charitable organization which meets every Wednesday. One Wednesday I skipped the meeting and went back with Mademoiselle Papet to her flat.

'By then she had told me quite a lot about herself, including the fact that she lived alone on a modest income inherited from her parents. She had repeatedly tried to get some sort of job, she said, but without success.'

'Did she ever talk about her family?'

'Her father, who had been an officer in the regular army, was killed in the war when she was only a child. She lived in the provinces with her widowed mother until she grew up. She had one brother.'

'Did you ever see him?'

'Only once. He was an engineer, and he travelled a good deal. One Wednesday I arrived early, and he happened to be there, and she introduced us.

'He was distinguished-looking, a good deal older than she was. He's no fool. He recently patented a process for eliminating the toxic gases in exhaust fumes.'

'Is he tall and thin, with light grey eyes and an unusually mobile face?'

François Paré looked surprised.

'Do you know him?'

'I've met him. Forgive me for asking, but did you give Josée much money?'

The Head of the Inland Waterways flushed and averted his eyes.

'I'm in the fortunate position of being comfortably off, more than comfortably off. I was left two farms in Normandy by a brother of my mother's. I could have retired years ago, except that I shouldn't know what to do with myself if I did.'

'Would it be fair to say that you were supporting her?'

'Not exactly . . . I saw to it that she didn't have to watch every penny, and perhaps enabled her to enjoy a few small extra comforts . . .'

'You only saw her once a week, on Wednesdays?'

'It was the only day I had an excuse for spending the evening in town . . . My wife grows more jealous and possessive with every year that passes . . .'

'I take it she doesn't go so far as to spy on your movements?'

'No . . . She hardly ever goes out . . . She's so thin that she can scarcely stand up . . . She's seen innumerable doctors, but they all say it's hopeless.'

'Did Mademoiselle Papet lead you to believe that you were her only lover?'

'It's not a word either of us would ever have thought of using . . . although, in the sense that our relations were intimate – I won't deny that – I suppose we were lovers . . .

'But that wasn't the real bond between us . . . It was more that we were both lonely people, trying to put a good face on things . . . I don't quite know how to put it . . . We talked the same language . . . We were able to open our hearts to one another . . . In other words, we were friends.'

'Were you jealous?'

He started, then gave Maigret a hostile look, as though he resented the question.

'I have taken you into my confidence. I've told you that she was the first and only woman in my life, other than my wife . . . You know that I'm not a young man . . . I haven't attempted to hide the fact that I set very great store by our relationship . . . I looked forward with eager impatience to those Wednesdays.

You might even say I lived for Wednesday evening ... It was our time together that made life endurable for me ...'

'In other words, you would have been shattered to learn that she had another lover?'

'Of course ... It would have been the end ...'

'The end of what?'

'Of everything ... Of the happiness I had known for the past three years ... a modest enough share, in a lifetime ...'

'You say you only met her brother once?'

'Yes.'

'And you didn't suspect anything?'

'What was there to suspect?'

'Did you never meet anyone else in the flat?'

He gave a ghost of a smile.

'Just once, a few weeks ago. As I got out of the lift, I saw a youngish man leaving the flat.'

'A man with red hair?'

He stared at Maigret in amazement.

'How did you know? Well, anyway, if you know that, you must also know that he's an insurance agent. I must confess I followed him, and saw him go into a bar in the Rue Fontaine ... I got the impression that he was a regular there ...

'When I asked Josée about him, she didn't seem in the least embarrassed.

'She just said: "He keeps pestering me to take out a life assurance policy. This is the third time he's called. But what use would such a policy be to me? I have no dependants ... I must have his card somewhere ..."

'And she began opening drawers and searching through them, and she did, in fact, find a visiting card in the name of Jean-Luc Bodard, of the Continentale, with offices in the Avenue de l'Opéra. It's not one of the larger companies, but it has an excellent reputation ... I spoke to the personnel manager, and he confirmed that Jean-Luc Bodard was one of their agents.'

Maigret was puffing reflectively at his pipe. He was playing for time, painfully aware of the distasteful task ahead.

'I take it you went to the flat yesterday?'

'Yes, just as usual ... I was a little late. I had to see the Permanent Under-Secretary, and it took longer than I expected

'. . . I rang the bell, and was surprised to get no reply . . . I rang again, and then knocked, but there was still no answer . . .'

'Did you speak to the concierge?'

'That woman gives me the creeps . . . I never go near her if I can help it . . . I didn't go straight home . . . I dined alone in a restaurant at the Porte de Versailles . . . Officially, I was supposed to be at my committee meeting . . .'

'When did you first learn of the murder?'

'This morning, as I was shaving . . . I was listening to the news on the radio . . . It was just a bare announcement, no details . . . I didn't see it in the papers until after I got here . . . I'm absolutely shattered . . . I can't understand it . . .'

'You weren't there, by any chance, between three and four yesterday afternoon?'

He replied with some bitterness:

'I see what you're getting at . . . I never left the office yesterday afternoon . . . My staff will confirm that, though, naturally, I should much prefer to have my name kept out of it . . .'

Poor man! He really was shattered, torn between grief and anxiety. His Indian summer, with all that it had meant to him, had come to a sudden and shocking end, yet he was still very much concerned to preserve his reputation.

'I realized that you were bound to find out about me from either the concierge or Josée's brother, if he's in Paris . . .'

'There was no brother, Monsieur Paré.'

He frowned, in angry disbelief.

'I'm terribly sorry to have to disillusion you, but you'll have to know the truth some time. The real name of the man who was introduced to you as Léon Papet it Léon Florentin . . . It's an odd coincidence, but he and I were schoolboys together at the lycée in Moulins.'

'I don't understand . . .'

'No sooner were you out of Joséphine Papet's flat, than he was letting himself in with his key . . . Did she ever give you a key?'

'No . . . I never asked for one . . . It wouldn't have occurred to me . . .'

'He practically lived in the flat . . . but when visitors were expected, he made himself scarce . . .'

'Did you say visitors, in the plural?'

He was very pale, and sat rigid in his chair, as though turned to stone.

'There were four of you, not counting Florentin.'

'What do you mean?'

'I mean that Joséphine Papet was being kept, more or less, by four separate admirers ... One of them, she knew long before you met ... In fact, many years ago, he practically lived in the flat for a time ...'

'Have you seen him?'

'Not yet.'

'Who is he?'

In spite of everything, François Paré still believed that there must be some mistake.

'His name is Fernand Courcel. He and his brother own a ballbearings factory in Rouen, with head offices in Paris, Boulevard Voltaire ... He's about your age, and a good deal overweight ...'

'I find it hard to believe.'

'His day was Thursday. He was the only one privileged to spend the night in the flat.'

'This isn't a trap, by any chance?'

'How do you mean?'

'I don't know. One hears that the police sometimes resort to devious methods. All you've said seems so utterly incredible to me ...'

'There was also a Saturday visitor ... I know very little about him, except that he has a limp ...'

'What about the fourth man?'

He was putting a brave face on it, but he was gripping the arms of his chair so tightly that his knuckles showed white.

'The insurance agent whom you saw coming out of the flat. He's generally known as *Le Rouquin*, on account of his red hair.'

'He is a genuine insurance agent. I checked up on him myself.'

'Being an insurance agent doesn't stop a man from also being the lover of an attractive woman.'

'I don't understand ... You never knew her ... If you had,

56

you would have found it just as impossible to believe ...
I never met anyone like her. She was so sane, so serene, so unas-
suming ... I have three daughters, so I should know something
about women ... I'd have trusted her with my life, more than
any one of my children ...'

'I'm sorry to have to disillusion you.'

'I take it you're quite sure of your facts?'

'If you wish, I can arrange for Florentin to tell you himself.'

'I absolutely refuse to meet that man, or, indeed, any of the
others ... If I understand you, Florentin was what is known
as her "steady"?'

'More or less ... He's tried his hand at most things in his
time, and never succeeded at anything ... In spite of which, he
has a kind of fascination for women ...'

'He's almost as old as I am.'

'Yes, just a couple of years younger ... But he has one great
advantage over you ... He's available at all times of the day
and night ... Besides, he's never serious about anything. He
takes each day as it comes, and lives entirely according to the
whim of the moment.'

Paré was a very different case. He bore the burden of a conscience, a sense of guilt. He took life with deadly seriousness. It
showed in every line of his face, in his every gesture.

It was almost as though he carried on his own shoulders the
whole responsibility of his department, if not of the entire ministry. Maigret found it hard to imagine him in the company of a
woman like Josée.

Fortunately for him she had been of an equable disposition.
No doubt she had been one of those women who could sit,
smiling and nodding for hours at a stretch, while a man, embittered by misfortune, unburdened himself of all his misery.

Maigret was beginning to form a clearer picture of her. She
was nothing if not practical, and she knew the value of money.
She had bought herself a house in Montmartre, and had had
forty-eight thousand francs salted away. Very likely, given time,
she would have acquired a second, and possibly even a third
house.

There are some women for whom houses are the only hard

currency, as though nothing in life has any real substance but bricks and mortar.

'Did you never think that she might come to a tragic end, Monsieur Paré?'

'Never for an instant ... She seemed to me the very embodiment of stability and security ... Everything about her, her life, her home ...'

'Did she tell you where she came from originally?'

'From Poitiers, if I remember rightly ...'

A wise precaution, telling each of them a different story.

'Did she strike you as a woman of some education?'

'She had her *baccalauréat*, and had worked for a time as secretary to a lawyer.'

'Did she mention the name of the lawyer?'

'She may have done ... I don't remember.'

'Had she never been married?'

'Not to my knowledge ...'

'Were you not surprised by her taste in reading?'

'She was sentimental, rather naïve, really. It's not surprising that she enjoyed romantic novels. But she was the first to laugh at her own foibles.'

'I don't want to distress you more than is absolutely necessary ... but there is one thing I must ask you ... Think back ... Try to remember everything you can ... You never know ... the most trivial detail, a few words spoken at random, something that may seem to you of no importance, could provide us with a clue ...'

François Paré levered his heavy frame out of the chair. He seemed uncertain whether or not to offer his hand to Maigret.

'I really can't think of anything ...'

He hesitated, then, his voice suddenly toneless, asked:

'Did she suffer much, do you know?'

'According to the police surgeon, death was instantaneous.'

Maigret saw his lips move, presumably in silent prayer.

'Thank you. I very much appreciate your discretion in this matter. I'm only sorry we could not have met in happier circumstances.'

'So am I, Monsieur Paré.'

Phew! No sooner was he on the stairs, than Maigret took a

deep breath. He felt as though he had just emerged from a tunnel, and was much in need of the fresh air of the daylight world.

Although his interview with the Head of Inland Waterways had not yielded any tangible results, or told him anything which could be immediately useful, it had enabled him to form a clearer picture of the young woman herself.

Had she entrapped all her patrons by means of a letter written with a faulty pen in a brasserie frequented by a prosperous class of customer, or had her meeting with Paré been genuinely accidental?

The first of her lovers, as far as was known, had been Fernand Courcel. She must have been twenty-five at that time. What had she been doing before that? Maigret could not imagine her, with that well-bred air of hers, loitering on the pavements round about the Madeleine or the Champs-Elysées.

Perhaps she really had been secretary to some lawyer or other?

There was a light breeze in the Boulevard Saint-Germain, causing a faint tremor among the leaves of the trees. Maigret savoured the morning air as he walked along. Turning off into a little side street leading to the Quais, he noticed a bistro with a pleasantly old-fashioned air. There was a lorry parked in front of it, from which crates of wine were being unloaded.

He went in and, resting his elbows on the zinc counter, asked:

'Where do you get your wine?'

'From Sancerre. I come from those parts myself, and I get my supplies from my brother-in-law . . .'

'I'll have a glass.'

It was dry, yet at the same time fruity. The bar counter was made of good old-fashioned zinc, and there was sawdust on the red-tiled floor.

'The same again, please.'

Joséphine, it seemed, had been a purveyor of dreams. What a very odd calling! He had three more men to see, three more of her lovers.

François Paré would not find it easy to replace her. Who else would listen to the outpourings of his sad old heart? Florentin had been driven back to his workshop in Montmartre, to doss down on a miserable bed in a windowless cubby-hole.

Better get on to the next one! He sighed as he went out of the bistro, and made his way to the Quai des Orfèvres.

Another illusion to be destroyed, more dreams to be shattered!

*

Having reached the top of the stairs, Maigret, making his way down the long corridor of Police Headquarters, paused automatically to look into the glass-walled waiting-room, always jocularly referred to by the inspectors as 'the aquarium'.

Much to his surprise, he saw, sitting in two of the uncomfortable green velvet armchairs provided, Léon Florentin in company with a stranger, a smallish man, running to fat, with a round face and blue eyes, unmistakably one who appreciated the good things of life.

At present, however, he seemed distressed. Florentin was speaking to him in an undertone, and every now and then, as he listened, he dabbed his eyes with a handkerchief, which was crumpled into a ball in his hand.

Across the room, ignoring them, and absorbed in the racing page of a newspaper, was Inspector Dieudonné.

Maigret passed by unnoticed. As soon as he got to his office, he rang the bell for old Joseph, who appeared almost at once.

'Has anyone been asking for me?'

'Two men, sir.'

'Which of them got here first?'

'This one, sir.'

He handed Florentin's card to Maigret.

'And the other one?'

'He arrived about ten minutes later ... He seemed very upset ...'

The stranger, it turned out, was Fernand Courcel, of the firm of Courcel Frères, manufacturers of ballbearings in Rouen The card also gave an address in the Boulevard Voltaire.

'Which will you see first?'

'Bring in Monsieur Courcel.'

He sat down at his desk, with a brief glance through the oper window at the glittering sunlight outside.

'Come in . . . Please sit down.'

The man was smaller and fatter than Maigret had at first supposed, yet there was something attractive about him, an infectious vitality and unforced goodwill.

'You don't know me, of course, Chief Superintendent . . .'

'If you had not come here this morning, Monsieur Courcel, I should have called on you in your office.'

The blue eyes widened in surprise, but there was no hint of fear in them.

'You know?'

'I know that you and Mademoiselle Papet were very close friends, and that it must have been a terrible shock this morning when you heard the news on the radio or read it in the paper.'

Courcel's face crumpled, as though he were about to burst into tears, but he managed to control himself.

'I'm sorry . . . I'm absolutely shattered . . . She was much more than a friend to me . . .'

'I know.'

'In that case, there isn't much I can tell you, because I've no idea what could possibly have happened . . . She was the kindest, the most discreet of women . . .'

'Do you know the man who was talking to you in the waiting-room?'

It was hardly possible to imagine anyone less like a captain of industry. The owner of the ballbearings factory stared at him in astonishment.

'Didn't you know she had a brother?'

'When did you first meet him?'

'About three years ago . . . Soon after he got back from Uruguay.'

'Had he been there long?'

'Haven't you interviewed him?'

'I'd like to hear what he told you.'

'He's an architect. He was out there on a government contract to build a new town.'

'You met him in Joséphine Papet's flat?'

'That's right.'

'Did you, on that occasion, arrive unexpectedly early?'

'To tell you the truth, I don't remember.'

He was taken aback by the question. He frowned, and Maigret noticed that his eyebrows, like his hair, were very fair, almost white. This colouring, combined with his delicate pink-and-white complexion, gave him the appearance of a chubby baby.

'I don't quite see what you're getting at.'

'Did you ever see him again?'

'Three or four times . . .'

'Always in the Rue Notre-Dame-de-Lorette?'

'No . . . He came to see me in my office . . . He had a scheme for developing the coastline between Le-Grau-du-Roi and Palavas as a luxury seaside resort, with hotels, smart villas, bungalows, and so on . . .'

'And he thought he might interest you in the project?'

'That's right . . . There was a lot to be said for it, I must admit . . . I don't doubt that it will be a success. Unfortunately, I have no capital of my own. My brother and I own the business jointly, and I can't act independently of him . . .'

'So you weren't able to help him at all?'

He flushed, much taken aback by Maigret's manner.

'I lent him a few thousand francs, just to enable him to register the plans.'

'Do you know if the plans were, in fact, registered? Did he send you copies?'

'As I told you, I wasn't interested.'

'Was that the only time he touched you for a loan?'

'I don't care for your way of putting it, but no . . . He came to see me again last year . . . It's always the same with any far-reaching project . . . There are bound to be problems and difficulties . . . His office in Montpellier . . .'

'Is that where he lives?'

'Yes, didn't you know?'

They were at cross-purposes the whole time, and Fernand Courcel was beginning to show signs of impatience.

'Look here, why not have him in and ask him yourself?'

'All in good time.'

'You seem to have it in for him, for some reason.'

'Not at all, Monsieur Courcel . . . In fact, I may as well tell you that he's an old school friend of mine . . .'

The little man took a gold cigarette case out of his pocket and opened it.

'May I smoke?'

'Please do . . . How many times did you lend him money?'

He thought for a moment, then said:

'Three times . . . On the last occasion, he had left his cheque-book at home . . .'

'What was he saying to you, out there in the waiting-room?'

'Must I answer that?'

'You would be well advised to do so.'

'It's such a painful subject . . . Oh, well!'

He sighed, stretched out his little legs, and drew deeply on his cigarette.

'He is entirely in the dark as to his sister's finances . . . So am I, as it happens, but then it's no business of mine . . . He's invested every penny he owns in this project of his, so, naturally, he's short of ready cash for the time being . . . He asked me to contribute to the funeral expenses . . .'

Maigret smiled broadly. This really was rich! Courcel was outraged.

'Forgive me . . . but you'll soon see why I can't help smiling. First of all, I'm bound to tell you that the real name of the man you know as Léon Papet is Léon Florentin. His father was a confectioner in Moulins, and he and I were at school together at the Lycée Banville.'

'You mean, he isn't her brother?'

'No, my dear sir, he is not. He is not her brother, nor even her cousin, but that doesn't alter the fact that he was living with her . . .'

'You mean . . .?'

He had sprung to his feet, as though stung.

'No!' he exclaimed. 'It's not possible. Josée was incapable . . .'

He was pacing up and down the room, dropping his ash all over the carpet.

'You must remember, Chief Superintendent, that I have known her for ten years . . . In the early days, before I was married, we lived together . . . It was I who found the flat in the Rue Notre-Dame-de-Lorette, and I spent a great deal of time and care decorating and furnishing it to suit her tastes.'

'She was about twenty-five at that time, wasn't she?'

'Yes, and I was thirty-two. My father was still alive then, and my brother Gaston was running the office in Paris. So I was left with a good deal of time on my hands . . .'

'Where and how did you meet?'

'I knew you'd ask me that, and I realize how it must look to you . . . I met her in a night-club in Montmartre, the Nouvel Adam . . . It doesn't exist any more . . .'

'Did she just take her turn with the other girls?'

'No, she was a hostess, so she didn't have to entertain just anyone . . . only if she was specifically asked for . . . I found her sitting alone at a table . . . She was wearing a very simple black dress, and almost no make-up . . . She looked sad, I thought, and rather shy, so much so that I hesitated for a long time before going up to speak to her.'

'Did you spend the whole evening with her?'

'Naturally . . . She told me all about her childhood . . .'

'Where did she say she grew up?'

'La Rochelle . . . Her father was a fisherman . . . He was drowned at sea . . . She had four younger brothers and sisters . . .'

'And her mother? Dead too, I've no doubt . . .'

Courcel glared at him furiously.

'Do you wish me to go on? If so . . .'

'Do forgive me . . . but, you see, it's all a pack of lies.'

'You mean she didn't have four brothers and sisters?'

'No, and it wasn't in order to bring them up that she was working in a cabaret in Montmartre. That was her story, wasn't it?'

He returned to his chair and sat, staring at the floor. Then, after some hesitation, he said:

'I find it hard to believe . . . I was passionately in love with her . . .'

'And yet you got married.'

'Yes, I married a cousin . . . I felt the years were slipping by, and I wanted children.'

'You live in Rouen?'

'Most of the week, yes.'

'But not Thursdays . . .'

'How do you know?'

'On Thursdays you took Josée out to dinner and then to a theatre or cinema, and spent the night in the flat in the Rue Notre-Dame-de-Lorette.'

'That's right ... When I married, I intended to break it off, but I found I couldn't.'

'Did your wife know?'

'Of course not!'

'What about your brother?'

'I had to take Gaston into my confidence ... Supposedly, I paid a weekly visit to our Marseilles office ...'

With quite touching candour, the little man added:

'He says I'm an idiot ...'

Maigret just managed to suppress a smile.

'When I think that only in the last few minutes, I almost burst into tears when that man ...'

'Florentin wasn't the only one ...'

'What are you insinuating?'

'I give you my word, Monsieur Courcel, that if she had died in any other way, I would have spared you this. But she was murdered. It is my duty to find the man who killed her, and that can't be done without bringing the truth out into the open.'

'Do you know who shot her?'

'Not yet ... There were three men, besides yourself and Florentin, who visited her regularly.'

He shook his head, as though, even now, he could not believe it.

'There were times when I almost made up my mind to marry her ... If it hadn't been for Gaston, it's more than likely that ...'

'Wednesday was the day of a senior civil servant ... He didn't spend the night in the flat ...'

'Have you seen him?'

'This morning.'

'Did he admit it?'

'He was perfectly open about his visits, and the nature of his relationship with Josée.'

'How old is he?'

'Fifty-five ... Did you ever see a man with a limp, if not in the flat, then perhaps in the lift?'

'No.'

'There was a man with a limp ... middle-aged. I'll find him soon enough, if one of my men hasn't done so already ...'

'Who else?' He sighed, clearly feeling that the sooner he knew the worst, the better.

'A man with red hair, a good deal younger than the rest of you. He's not much over thirty, and he's an insurance agent.'

'I take it you never knew her when she was alive?'

'That is so.'

'If you had, you'd understand how I feel ... You'd have thought she was as honest as the day, so frank and open as to be almost childlike ... I could have sworn ...'

'Were you supporting her?'

'It was a hard job to persuade her to take a penny ... She wanted to work in a shop, selling lingerie or something of the sort ... But she wasn't strong ... She was subject to fits of giddiness ... She was always reproaching me for being too generous ...'

He was suddenly struck by a thought that had not, up to then, occurred to him.

'What about the others? Did they ...?'

'I'm afraid so, Monsieur Courcel ... Three of you, at least, were keeping her. I don't know about the redhead yet, but it won't be long before I do. The civil servant whom I saw this morning, at any rate, certainly was ...'

'But what did she do with the money? She had such simple tastes ...'

'For a start, she bought a house in the Rue du Mont-Cenis. And furthermore, after her death, forty-eight thousand francs in cash were found in the flat ... Now, I'm afraid I must ask you to try and take a grip on yourself and think back ... I won't ask you where you were between three and four yesterday afternoon ...'

'I was in my car on the way from Rouen. I drove through the Saint-Cloud tunnel, and must have come out the other end at about a quarter past three ...'

He pulled himself up sharply, and stared at Maigret in blank astonishment.

'You can't mean you suspect me!'

'I don't suspect anyone. It's a purely routine question ... What time did you get to your office?'

'I didn't go straight there ... I stopped off for a minute or two at a bar in the Rue de Ponthieu, to place a bet on a horse. ... I go there regularly ... It wasn't, in fact, until about a quarter past five that I got to the Boulevard Voltaire ... Nominally, my brother and I are partners ... I spend a couple of days a week at the factory, and I have an office and a secretary in the Boulevard Voltaire ... but, in practice, they could perfectly well manage without me ...'

'Does your brother not resent having to carry such a large share of the burden?'

'Quite the contrary. The less I do, the happier he is ... That way, he's the boss, don't you see?'

'What make is your car, Monsieur Courcel?'

'A Jaguar convertible ... I've always had a convertible ... My present one is pale blue ... Do you want the number?'

'That won't be necessary.'

'When I think that not only Josée but her so-called brother ... what did you say his name was?'

'Florentin. His father made the best cakes in Moulins.'

He clenched his little fists.

'Don't distress yourself. Unless events take an unexpected turn, your name will be kept out of it. You may rest assured that I will treat all you have said in the strictest confidence ... Is your wife of a jealous disposition?'

'I dare say she is, in a mild way. She suspects me of kicking over the traces once in a while, in Marseilles or Paris ...'

'Has there ever been anyone, apart from Josée?'

'Occasionally ... I suppose, like most other men, I'm intrigued by the unknown.'

He looked about him for his hat, then remembered that he had left it in the waiting-room. Maigret went with him, fearing that he might be tempted to attack Florentin.

Florentin looked at them glumly, obviously in some trepidation as to what Courcel's reaction would be.

When the little captain of industry had gone, Inspector Dieu-donné, who had stood up when Maigret came into the waiting-room, asked:

'Shall I report to you now, sir?'

'Has something happened?'

'No. After he'd had breakfast in the bistro on the corner, he went back to his room and stayed there until 9.30, when he left to come here by Métro. He asked to see you. Soon after, the other gentleman arrived. They shook hands and talked. I didn't hear what they said . . .'

'Thanks. That will be all for today.'

Maigret beckoned to Florentin.

'Come with me.'

He ushered him into his office, shut the door, and gazed at him reflectively for a considerable time. Florentin, meanwhile, kept his eyes resolutely lowered, and his long, bony frame, slumped in a chair, was limp, seeming almost on the point of disin-tegration.

'You're a worse scoundrel even than I thought.'

'I know.'

'What possessed you to do a thing like that?'

'I'd no idea I should run into him here . . .'

'What have you come here for?'

He raised his head and gave Maigret an anguished look. It was pitiful.

'Guess how much money I have in my pocket.'

'What's that got to do with it?'

'I assure you, it has everything to do with it. All I have left in the world is a fifty-centime piece . . . There isn't a shop or restaurant or café in the neighbourhood willing to give me credit . . .'

This time it was the Chief Superintendent who looked stag-gered, just as his fat little visitor had done a short while before.

'Have you come here to ask me for money?'

'Who else can I turn to, in my present predicament? I've no doubt you told that pompous ass Paré that I wasn't really Josée's brother . . .'

'Naturally.'

'So you robbed him of all his illusions, did you? I bet it shook him!'

'Be that as it may, he has a cast-iron alibi. Yesterday, between three and four, he was in his office.'

'And to think that when I saw that little runt coming into the waiting-room, I thought to myself that there was still hope for me!'

'The funeral expenses! Aren't you ashamed of yourself?'

Florentin shrugged.

'When one has had cause to be ashamed as often as I have ... Mind you, I guessed he'd tell you about it ... But, as I got here first, there was just a chance that you might hear my story before he got his oar in ...'

Maigret stood up and went over to the window. He drank in the fresh air as though it were nectar. Florentin watched him in silence.

'What will happen to the forty-eight thousand francs?'

Maigret gave a violent start. It really was almost inconceivable that, at a time like this, Florentin should still be thinking about Josée's money.

'Can't you understand that I'm absolutely destitute? Look, there's no point in trying to deceive you ... It's true, I do occasionally sell a piece of furniture for a few hundred francs ... but the antique business was only a front ...'

'I realized that.'

'Well, then, just until I get on my feet ...'

'What do you intend to do?'

'If necessary, I'll sign on as a porter in Les Halles.'

'I must warn you that you won't be able to leave Paris.'

'So I'm still under suspicion?'

'Until we get the man who did it ... Do you really know nothing of the man with the limp?'

'Even Josée didn't know his surname ... She called him Victor ... He never mentioned a wife or children ... She had no idea what he did for a living ... He was prosperous-looking. He wore good suits and hand-made shirts ... Oh! and there's one other thing I've just remembered ... Once, she told me, when he took out his wallet, she saw his railway season ticket. It was a Paris–Bordeaux ticket ...'

Here, at least, was something for his men to work on. Surely, there could not be all that many Paris–Bordeaux season tickets?

'I'm doing my best to be helpful, you see . . .'

Maigret, taking the hint, got out his own wallet and extracted a hundred-franc note.

'You'd better make it last.'

'Are you keeping a tail on me?'

'Yes.'

He opened the door to the Inspectors' Room.

'Leroy.'

He gave the necessary instructions, and, this time, could see no way of avoiding shaking the hand of his old school friend when it was held out to him.

Chapter Four

It was three o'clock, and Maigret was standing at the open window, hands in his pockets, pipe clenched between his teeth, in an attitude familiar to all who knew him.

The sun was shining and the sky was a cloudless blue dome, yet it was raining in diagonal streaks, and the large, widely dispersed raindrops formed black patches on the ground where they fell.

The door opened behind him.

'Come in, Lucas,' he said, without looking round.

He had sent him up to the attics of the Palais de Justice to find out from Records whether Florentin had any previous convictions.

'Three convictions, Chief. Nothing very serious.'

'Fraud?'

'The first conviction – that was twenty-two years ago – was for passing a dud cheque. At that time he was living in a furnished flat in the Avenue de Wagram. He was a fruit importer in those days, and he had an office in the Champs-Elysées. He got a suspended sentence of six months . . .

'Eight years later, he was convicted on charges of fraud and misappropriation. By then, he had moved to a small hotel in Montparnasse. This time he had to serve his prison sentence . . .

'Five years ago, another dud cheque . . . Described as being of no fixed address . . .'

'Thanks.'

'Is there anything else I can do?'

'You'd better go to the Rue Notre-Dame-de-Lorette, and have a word with the shopkeepers. Janvier has already taken statements from them, but I want you to ask them a specific question. I want to know whether any of them saw a light-blue Jaguar convertible parked outside the building or in a near-by street between three and four yesterday afternoon. You'd better inquire at the local garages as well.'

Left to himself, he stood looking out of the window, frowning. Moers's men had failed to come up with anything of interest. Joséphine Papet's fingerprints were all over the flat, which was only to be expected.

There were, however, no prints on any of the door handles. They had all been carefully wiped off.

Florentin's prints, too, were everywhere, including the clothes closet and the bathroom, but there were none on the drawer of the bedside table, which the murderer must have opened to get at the revolver.

The Chief Superintendent had been struck, from the first, by the scrupulous cleanliness of the flat. Joséphine Papet had neither maid nor daily woman. He could imagine her in the mornings, with a scarf tied round her head and the radio playing softly, going from room to room, dusting and cleaning with meticulous thoroughness.

He was wearing his most surly expression, which meant that he was dissatisfied with himself. The truth was that he had an uneasy conscience.

If he and Florentin had not been schoolboys together in Moulins, would he not, by now, have applied to the Examining Magistrate for a warrant for his arrest?

It was not that he and the confectioner's son had ever been close friends, exactly. Even in their school days, Maigret had had reservations about him.

Florentin had always been good for a laugh, and had often risked punishment just for the sake of a bit of fun.

But had there not been a touch of defiance, even aggressiveness, in his attitude?

He didn't give a damn for anyone, and would mimic the tics and mannerisms of the teachers with cruel accuracy.

He had had a ready wit, but was quick to take offence if ever one of his quips failed to raise a laugh.

Had he not even then, been teetering on the borderline? Had he not begun to see himself as, in some sense, set apart? That was, perhaps, the reason why his witticisms had often jarred.

He had grown to manhood and come to Paris, where he had alternated between periods of semi-respectability and darker phases, during one of which he served a prison sentence.

But he had never admitted defeat. He still had an air about him, a kind of innate elegance, even in a threadbare suit.

He was a born liar, scarcely aware that he was lying. He always had told lies, and never seemed disconcerted when he was found out. It was as though he were saying:

'Well, it was a good story, anyway! Too bad it didn't work.'

No doubt he had, in his time, haunted Fouquet's and other smart bars in the Champs-Elysées, not to mention cabarets and night-clubs. Such places give a man a false sense of well-being.

Fundamentally, Maigret suspected, he was insecure. His clowning was, in reality, just a defence mechanism, a mask, behind which was concealed a sadly inadequate personality.

He was a failure, typical of his kind, and, what was worse and more painful, an ageing failure.

Was it pity that was preventing Maigret from arresting him? Or was it rather that he simply could not believe that anyone as sharp as Florentin would, had he actually been guilty, have left so many clues pointing to himself?

Take the matter of Josée's savings for instance. He had removed the biscuit tin to his own workshop, wrapped in that day's newspaper. Surely, he could have found a safer hiding-place than the miserable hovel in the Boulevard Rochechouart, where, as he must have known, the police could not fail to search?

Then there was that lapse of time after the shot, when he had stayed hidden in the clothes closet. A whole quarter of an hour!

Was it fear that had kept him there, fear of meeting the murderer face to face?

And why had he chosen to go straight to Maigret, when the obvious course was to report to the local police?

There was certainly a strong enough case to justify Maigret in arresting him. Even the recent appearance on the scene of the young man known as *Le Rouquin* told against him, for here surely was a real threat to Florentin's security, a younger man who might well succeed in ousting him from the cushy billet on which he depended for his very life.

Janvier knocked at the door, came in without waiting for an answer, and collapsed into a chair.

'We've got him, sir, at last!'

'The man with a limp?'

'Yes ... I've lost count of the number of phone calls I've made, including half a dozen to Bordeaux. I almost had to go on my knees to the Railways Board, to get them to give me a list of season-ticket holders ...'

He stretched out his legs, and lit a cigarette.

'I hope to heaven I've got the right man! I don't know whether I've done the right thing, but I've asked him to come and see you ... He'll be here in a quarter of an hour ...'

'I'd rather have seen him on his own ground.'

'He lives in Bordeaux. When he's in Paris, he has a suite in the Hôtel Scribe. It's almost next door to his office in the Rue Auber.'

'Who is he?'

'If my information is correct, he's a man of some standing in Bordeaux. He has a house on the river in Les Chartrons, which is where all the old-established families live. As you'd expect, he's a wine grower in a big way, exporting mainly to Germany and the Scandinavian countries ...'

'Have you seen him?'

'I've spoken to him on the telephone.'

'Did he seem surprised?'

'He was very snooty at first . . . he asked me if this was some kind of joke. When I assured him that I really was from the C.I.D., he said he couldn't imagine what business the police could possibly have with him, and that we'd better keep out of his hair if we didn't want trouble . . . So I told him it was to do with what had happened in the Rue Notre-Dame-de-Lorette.'

'How did he take it?'

'There was a long silence, then he said:

' "When does Chief Superintendent Maigret want to see me?"

' "As soon as possible."

' "I'll come to the Quai des Orfèvres as soon as I've been through my mail."

'His name is Lamotte,' Janvier added, 'Victor Lamotte . . . If you like, I'll ring the C.I.D. in Bordeaux while he's with you, and see if there's anything more they can tell me.'

'Good man.'

'You don't seem too happy . . .'

Maigret shrugged. Wasn't it always so, at this stage of an inquiry, before the case had really begun to take shape? After all, Florentin apart, he had never even heard of any of these people until yesterday.

This morning, he had interviewed a chubby little man who, though quaint, had not struck him as being a person of much character. If Courcel had not had the good fortune to be born the son of an industrialist, what would have become of him? Probably he would have been a commercial traveller, but there was really no telling. He might have ended up like Florentin, part parasite, part crook.

Joseph announced the visitor, and ushered him in. The man, as expected, had a pronounced limp. To Maigret's surprise, he had snow-white hair and a flaccid face. He looked sixty.

'Come in, Monsieur Lamotte . . . I'm sorry to have put you to the trouble of coming here . . . I hope you had no difficulty in parking your car in the forecourt?'

'I leave all that to my chauffeur.'

Naturally! He would have a chauffeur and, no doubt, in Bordeaux, a whole retinue of servants.

'I presume you know what I want to see you about?'

'The inspector mentioned the Rue Notre-Dame-de-Lorette. I couldn't quite make out what he was getting at.'

Maigret was seated at his desk, filling his pipe. His visitor sat opposite him, facing the window.

'You knew Joséphine Papet . . .'

The man hesitated for a considerable time before replying.

'How did you find out?'

'As you are no doubt aware, we have our methods and sources of information. If we had not, the prisons of this country would be standing empty.'

'I don't quite see the relevance of that last remark. You're surely not insinuating . . .?'

'I'm not insinuating anything. Have you seen a newspaper this morning?'

'Certainly. I read the papers, like anyone else.'

'You must, therefore, be aware that Joséphine Papet, commonly known as Josée, was murdered in her flat yesterday afternoon. Where were you at that time?'

'Not in the Rue Notre-Dame-de-Lorette, at any rate.'

'Were you at your office?'

'At what time?'

'Let's say between three and four.'

'I was taking a walk in the Grands Boulevards.'

'Alone?'

'What's so strange about that?'

'Do you often go for solitary walks?'

'Regularly, when I'm in Paris, for an hour in the morning, from ten to eleven or thereabouts, and again for an hour in the afternoon. My doctor will tell you that he has urged me to take regular exercise. Until recently, I was a good deal overweight, and it was putting a strain on my heart.'

'You realize, don't you, that that leaves you without an alibi?'

'Do I need one?'

'As one of Josée's lovers, yes.'

If this was news to him, he showed no sign of it. Looking perfectly composed, he asked:

'Were there many of us?'

There was a tinge of irony in his voice.

'Four, to my knowledge, not counting the man who lived with her.'

'So she had a man living with her, did she?'

'If my information is correct, your day was Saturday. I may say that each of the others had a specific day too.'

'I'm a creature of habit. I lead a very regular life. Every Saturday, after my visit to the Rue Notre-Dame-de-Lorette, I catch the Bordeaux express, which gets me home well before bedtime.'

'Are you married, Monsieur Lamotte?'

'Yes, married, with a family. One of my sons is in the business with me. He's in charge of our warehouse in Bordeaux ... Another represents the firm in Bonn, and travels a good deal in the north ... My daughter and son-in-law live in London, with their two children ...'

'How long have you known Joséphine Papet?'

'Four years or thereabouts.'

'What did she mean to you?'

Condescendingly, not without a hint of contempt, he replied:

'She provided relaxation.'

'In other words, you had no real affection for her?'

'Affection is rather too strong a word.'

'Perhaps I should say liking.'

'She was a pleasant companion, and I believed her to be discreet. So much so that it surprised me that you were able to track me down ... May I ask who put you on to me?'

'To begin with, all we knew about you was that you called on Saturdays, and that you had a limp.'

'A riding accident, when I was seventeen ...'

'You have a railway season ticket ...'

'Ah! I see ... Find the limping man with the Paris–Bordeaux season ticket!'

'There's one thing that puzzles me, Monsieur Lamotte. Staying at the Hôtel Scribe as you do, you are surrounded by bars where you could meet any number of attractive women of easy virtue ...'

The man from Bordeaux, determined not to be ruffled, answered equably, though not without a touch of con-

76

descension. After all, Les Chartrons, where he lived, was the Faubourg Saint-Germain of Bordeaux, the domain of ancient and noble families.

As far as Lamotte was concerned, Maigret was a policeman like any other. Policemen, of course, were necessary to protect the rights and property of honest citizens, but this was the first time he had ever come into direct contact with this class of person.

'What did you say your name was?'

'It's of no importance, but, if you must know, it's Maigret.'

'To begin with, Monsieur Maigret, I am a man of regular habits. I was brought up to believe in certain principles which are, perhaps, scarcely fashionable nowadays. I am not in the habit of frequenting bars. It may seem strange to you, but I have not set foot in a bar or café in Bordeaux since my student days.

'As to receiving a woman of the sort you have in mind in my suite at the Scribe, you surely must see that it would scarcely be the thing, and besides, it's risky . . .'

'Blackmail, do you mean . . .?'

'For a man in my position, there is always the risk . . .'

'Yet you visited Josée once a week in the Rue Notre-Dame-de-Lorette?'

'A much less precarious arrangement. You must see that, surely?'

Maigret's patience was wearing thin.

'All the same, you must admit you knew precious little about her.'

'What do you expect? Or perhaps you think I should have asked you to make inquiries on my behalf?'

'Where did you first meet her?'

'In the restaurant car.'

'Was she going to Bordeaux?'

'No, she was returning to Paris . . . We happened to be sitting opposite one another at a table for two . . . She seemed a very respectable sort of woman . . . When I passed the breadbasket across to her, I remember, she looked at me as though I had taken a liberty . . . Later it turned out that we had seats in the same compartment.'

'Had you a mistress at that time?'

'Don't you think that's rather an impertinent question? Anyway, I can't see what it can possibly have to do with your present inquiries.'

'You don't have to answer if you would rather not.'

'I have nothing to hide ... I did have a mistress, a former secretary. I had set her up in a flat in the Avenue de la Grande Armée. Just a week before I met Josée, she announced that she was going to be married.'

'In other words, there was a vacancy to be filled . . .'

'I don't care for your tone, and I'm not sure that I feel inclined to answer any more questions.'

'In that case, I may have to detain you longer than you may find convenient.'

'Is that a threat?'

'Just a warning.'

'I'd be within my rights in refusing to answer questions except in the presence of my lawyer, but it hardly seems worth the trouble. Carry on.'

He was now very much on his dignity.

'How long had you known Josée when you first went to the Rue Notre-Dame-de-Lorette?'

'About three weeks, maybe a month . . .'

'Did she say she had a job?'

'No.'

'Did she claim to have independent means?'

'A modest allowance from one of her uncles.'

'Did she tell you where she came from, originally?'

'Somewhere near Grenoble.'

Joséphine Papet, it seemed, had been, like Florentin, a compulsive liar. She had invented a different family background for each of her lovers.

'Did you make her a generous allowance?'

'That's a most indelicate question!'

'Nevertheless, I should be glad if you would answer it.'

'I gave her two thousand francs a month in an envelope, or rather, I should say, I left it discreetly on the mantelpiece.'

Maigret smiled. It took him right back to his very early days in the Force, when there were still to be seen, about the Boulevards, elderly gentlemen in patent-leather shoes and white gaiters, ogling the pretty women through their monocles.

Those were the days of furnished mezzanine flats and kept women, women not unlike Joséphine Papet, good-natured, warm-hearted and discreet.

Victor Lamotte had not fallen in love. His life was centred on his family in Bordeaux. He was at home, not in the Rue Notre-Dame-de-Lorette, but in his austere family mansion, from which he ventured forth once or twice a week, to stay at the Hôtel Scribe and attend his office in the Rue Auber.

Nevertheless, he too had felt the need of a refuge, where he could drop the oppressive mask of respectability, and open his heart to a woman. And was not Josée just the woman with whom a man could safely relax, without fear of unpleasant repercussions?

'Did you know any of her other "protectors"?'

'You would hardly expect her to introduce us!'

'There might have been an accidental encounter. You could have come face to face with one of them leaving the flat, say.'

'As it happens, I didn't.'

'Did you ever take her out?'

'No.'

'What about your chauffeur? Did he wait outside?'

He shrugged. Evidently he thought Maigret somewhat naïve.

'I always took a taxi.'

'Did you know she'd bought a house in Montmartre?'

'It's the first I've heard of it.'

He was at no pains to conceal his total lack of interest in her personal affairs.

'What's more, forty-eight thousand francs in notes were found in her flat.'

'I daresay some of it was mine, but, don't worry, I shan't ask for it back.'

'Were you distressed to learn of her death...?'

'To be honest with you, no. Millions of people die every day...'

Maigret stood up. He had had enough. If this interview were to go on any longer, he would be hard put to it to conceal his disgust.

'Don't you want a signed statement from me?'

'No.'

'Am I to expect a summons from the Examining Magistrate?'

'I can't answer that, at present.'

'If it should come to a trial . . .'

'It will.'

'Always supposing you get the murderer.'

'We'll get him.'

'I'd better warn you that I shall take steps to keep my name out of it . . . I have influential friends . . .'

'I don't doubt it.'

Whereupon the Chief Superintendent stumped over to the door, and held it wide open. As he was going out, Lamotte turned back as though intending to say something by way of leave-taking, but then, apparently thinking better of it, went off without a word.

That was three of them dealt with! There still remained *Le Rouquin*. Maigret was in a foul temper, and felt he must give himself a little time to cool off. He went back to his desk and sat down. It had stopped raining some time ago. A fly – perhaps the same one that had haunted him the previous day – flew in through the window, and settled on the sheet of paper on which he was idly doodling.

Abruptly, he woke up to the fact that his wandering pencil had formed a word:

Premeditation.

Unless Florentin had done it, premeditation seemed unlikely. The killer had come to the flat unarmed. Undoubtedly, he was a familiar visitor, since he knew that there was a revolver in the bedside table drawer.

Was it not possible that he had intended all along to make use of it?

Assuming, for the sake of argument, that Florentin really had been hiding in the clothes closet, and was telling the truth, what reason could the intruder have had for hanging about in the bedroom for a full quarter of an hour, especially in view of the fact that, as he moved about the room, he would have had to step back and forth across the body repeatedly?

Had he been searching for the money? If so, why had he not found it, since all he would have had to do was force a very flimsy lock?

Letters? A document of some sort?

Which of them needed money? Not François Paré, the civil servant, nor tubby little Fernand Courcel. Still less the high and mighty Victor Lamotte.

Any one of them, on the other hand, might well have reacted violently to attempted blackmail.

As usual, he was back to Florentin, Florentin, whom the Examining Magistrate would certainly have ordered Maigret to arrest, had he been fully informed of the facts.

*

Maigret had hoped that an opportunity of questioning Jean-Luc Bodard, known as *Le Rouquin*, would not be long delayed, but the inspector who had been sent to find him returned with a disappointing report.

The young insurance agent was out on his rounds, and was not expected back till the evening.

He lived in a small hotel, the Hôtel Beauséjour, in the Boulevard des Batignolles, and took his meals in the restaurant.

Maigret was fretful, as always when he felt something was amiss with the case he was working on. He was uneasy and dissatisfied with himself. He could not bring himself to settle down to the paperwork cluttering up his desk. He got up, went across to the door leading to the Inspectors' Duty Room, and opened it.

'Lapointe,' he called. 'Come along. I need a car.'

It was not until they were driving along the Quai that he said grumpily: 'Rue Notre-Dame-de-Lorette.'

He had the feeling that he had overlooked something important. It was as though the truth had brushed past him, and he had failed to recognize it. He spoke not a word the whole way there, and bit so hard on his pipe that he cracked the ebonite stem.

'Come in when you've parked the car.'

'To the flat?'

'No, the lodge.'

There was something about the huge bulk and stony eyes of the concierge that haunted him. He found her exactly where she had been the previous day, standing at the door, holding back the net curtain. He had to push the door open before she would let go of it and step back.

She did not ask him what he wanted, but just glared at him disapprovingly.

Her skin was very white, unhealthily so. Was she just mentally deficient, a harmless 'natural', such as one used to come across in country districts in the old days?

It was beginning to get on his nerves, seeing her standing there in the lodge, motionless as a pillar.

'Sit down,' he said brusquely.

Unruffled, she shook her head.

'I asked you a number of questions yesterday. I am now going to repeat them, and, this time, I warn you that, unless you tell the truth, you may find yourself in serious trouble.'

She did not stir, but he fancied he detected a flicker of derision in her eyes. It was quite obvious that she was not afraid of him. She was afraid of no one.

'Did anyone go up to the third floor between three and four yesterday?'

'No.'

'Or any of the other floors?'

'One old woman, for the dentist.'

'Do you know François Paré?'

'No.'

'He's a tall man, heavily built, in his fifties, balding, with a black moustache . . .'

'I may have seen him.'

'He always came on Wednesdays at about half past five. Did he come yesterday?'

'Yes.'

'At what time?'

'I'm not sure. Before six.'

'Was he upstairs long?'

'He came down straight away.'

'Did he say anything to you?'

'No.'

82

She answered like an automaton, her face set, her stony eyes fixed unwaveringly on Maigret, as though she suspected him of wanting to trap her. Was she capable of loyalty, of lying to protect someone else? Was she aware of the significance of her testimony?

It was a matter of life and death to Florentin, for if, as she claimed, no one had entered the building, then his whole story was a tissue of lies: the ring at the doorbell, the unexpected visitor, the dash for cover in the clothes closet. There were no two ways about it; if she was telling the truth, Florentin had been the one to fire the shot.

There was a tap on the glass door. Maigret went to let Lapointe in.

'This is one of my assistants,' he explained. 'I repeat, think before you speak, and say nothing unless you're sure of your facts.'

Never before in her life had she been called upon to play so important a part, and, no doubt, she was thoroughly enjoying it. For here was the Head of the Criminal Investigation Department almost pleading for her help, something which, surely, she could not have hoped for in her wildest dreams?

'You say François Paré came into the building shortly before six. Had you not seen him at all earlier in the day?'

'No.'

'You're quite sure that, if he had been in, you couldn't have missed seeing him?'

'Yes.'

'But there must be times when you're in your kitchen, and can't see the entrance.'

'Not at that hour.'

'Where is the telephone?'

'In the kitchen.'

'Well, then, if it was ringing . . .'

'It didn't ring.'

'Does the name Courcel mean anything to you?'

'Yes.'

'How do you come to know Monsieur Courcel by name, and not Monsieur Paré?'

'Because he almost lived here at one time . . . About ten years ago, he often spent the night up there, and he and the Papet woman went out a lot together.'

'Did you find him friendly?'

'He would always pass the time of day.'

'You seem to prefer him to the others.'

'He had better manners.'

'I believe he still spends the night here sometimes, usually on a Thursday?'

'That's no business of mine.'

'Was he here yesterday?'

'No.'

'Would you recognize his car?'

'Yes, it's blue.'

Her voice was flat and toneless. Lapointe seemed very much struck by this.

'Do you know the name of the man with the limp?'

'No.'

'Has he never been into the lodge?'

'No.'

'His name is Lamotte . . . Did you see him yesterday?'

'No.'

'Nor the man with red hair, whose name is Bodard?'

'No. I didn't see him either.'

Maigret would have liked to shake the truth out of her, as one shakes coins out of a money box.

'What you're saying, in other words, is that Léon Florentin was alone up there with Joséphine Papet the whole time?'

'I didn't go up to see.'

It was infuriating.

'You must see that, if you're telling the truth, there's no other explanation.'

'There's nothing I can do about it.'

'You can't stand Florentin, can you?'

'That's my business.'

'One would almost think you were determined to get your own back on him.'

'You can think what you like.'

There was something wrong somewhere. Maigret could feel it. Maybe she really was as stolid as she seemed. Possibly she could not help her monotonous voice. Perhaps she had always been a woman of few words. Even so, there was a jarring note somewhere. Either she was deliberately lying, for some reason best known to herself, or she knew more than she was telling.

Of one thing there was no doubt. She was very much on the defensive, striving to anticipate and prepare for the questions to follow.

'Tell me, Madame Blanc, has anyone been trying to intimidate you?'

'No.'

'If you know Joséphine Papet's murderer, and he has threatened reprisals if you talk . . .'

She shook her head.

'Let me finish . . . You would do well to ignore his threats. If you talk, we shall arrest him, and you will be safe from him. If not, you are running a grave risk that he may decide, at any time, that you would be better out of the way . . .'

She looked at him with a faintly mocking expression. What did it mean?

'Few murderers will hesitate to kill a witness who knows too much for their peace of mind . . . I could tell you of dozens of cases . . . And there's another thing, unless you take us into your confidence, we can't protect you . . .'

Maigret's hopes rose.

It was not so much that she was beginning to look almost human, as that he thought he detected a faint tremor, an almost imperceptible softening of her expression, at any rate a hint of indecision.

He held his breath anxiously for a second or two.

'What have you to say to that?' he prompted at last.

'Nothing.'

He had reached the end of his tether.

'Let's go, Lapointe.'

Outside in the street, he said:

'I'm almost certain she knows something . . . I can't help wondering if she's really as stupid as she looks.'

'Where are we going next?'

He hesitated. The next step should really have been to question the insurance agent. Failing that, he was not sure what he wanted to do. At last he said:

'The Boulevard Rochechouart.'

Florentin's premises were locked up. The painter, who was at his easel in the doorway of the neighbouring workshop, called across to them:

'There's no one there.'

'Has he been out long?'

'He's been gone since this morning, and he didn't come back for lunch. Are you police?'

'Yes.'

'I thought so ... Ever since yesterday, there's been someone on the prowl hereabouts, and he's followed wherever he goes ... What's he done?'

'We don't know for sure that he's done anything.'

'In other words, he's a suspect?'

'If you like.'

He was the kind of man who wanted nothing better than to have someone to talk to. It must have been lonely for him most of the time.

'Do you know him well?'

'He stops by for a chat occasionally.'

'Does he get many customers?'

The painter gave Maigret a broad grin.

'Customers? For one thing, I can't imagine where they'd come from ... Whoever would think of looking for an antique shop, if you can call it that, down a miserable little alley like this?

'Besides, he's hardly ever in ... When he does come, it's mostly just to hang up a sign saying "Back soon" or "Closed until Thursday".

'He does, from time to time, spend a night in the cubby-hole, I believe.

'At least I presume he does, because sometimes I see him shaving when I arrive in the morning ... I have lodgings in the Rue Lamarck, myself.'

'Did he ever talk about himself?'

The painter worked with rapid brush-strokes. No doubt, he had painted the Sacré-Coeur so often that he could have done it blindfold. Without pausing in his work, he considered Maigret's question.

'He couldn't stand his brother-in-law, that's for sure.'

'Why not?'

'Well, according to him, if his brother-in-law hadn't cheated him, he wouldn't be where he is now ... His parents, it seems, had a prosperous business, I can't remember exactly where ...'

'In Moulins.'

'You may be right ... When the father retired, the daughter's husband took over the business ... The agreement was that he should make over a share of the profits to Florentin ... However, after the father died, he never got another sou ...'

Maigret was thinking of the laughing, rosy-cheeked girl who used to stand behind the white marble counter. It seemed to him, in retrospect, that perhaps his visits to the shop, infrequent though they were, had been chiefly on her account.

'Did he borrow money from you?'

'How did you know? Never very large sums ... The fact is, I've never had much to spare ... Twenty francs, now and again ... Once or twice, but not often, as much as fifty ...'

'Did he pay you back?'

'He always said he would pay me back next day, but, actually, it was usually a day or two later ... What's he supposed to have done? You're Chief Superintendent Maigret, aren't you? I recognized you at once. I've often seen your picture in the papers ...

'If you're taking a personal interest in him, it must be something pretty serious. Murder is it? Do you suspect him of having killed someone?'

'I just don't know.'

'If you want my opinion, I don't think he's capable of murder ... he's not the sort ... Now, if you were to say he'd been ... well ... careless over money ... But even then, maybe it isn't altogether his fault ... He's always full of schemes, you know, and I'm sure he genuinely has faith in them ... Some of them aren't half bad either! It's just that he gets carried away, and is apt to fall flat on his face ...'

'You don't happen to have a key to his workshop, do you?'

'How did you know?'

'I just thought you might have.'

'Of course, it's only once in a blue moon that a customer

turns up, but it has been known to happen ... That's why he leaves a key with me ... He only has a few bits and pieces to sell, and I know what he wants for them.'

He went indoors, opened a drawer, and returned with a massive key.

'I don't suppose he'll mind . . .'

'You've no need to worry about that.'

For the second time, Maigret, assisted by Lapointe, searched the workshop and annexe with meticulous care and thoroughness. A sweetish smell pervaded the narrow little annexe where Florentin slept, that of some brand of shaving soap unfamiliar to Maigret.

'What are we looking for, sir?'

Crossly, Maigret replied:

'I've no idea.'

*

'The blue Jaguar doesn't seem to have been anywhere near the Rue Notre-Dame-de-Lorette yesterday. The woman who runs the dairy near by knows it well by sight.

' "It's always parked just across the street on Thursdays," she said, then as an afterthought: "That's odd! Today is Thursday, and I haven't seen it ... The owner is a little fat man ... I hope nothing has happened to him!" '

This was Janvier, making his report.

'I also inquired at the garage in the Rue La Bruyère ... I had a look at Joséphine Papet's car while I was at it ... It's a Renault, two years old. It's in very good condition, and has only done twenty-four thousand kilometres ... Nothing in the boot ... A Michelin Guide, a pair of sun-glasses and a bottle of aspirin tablets in the glove compartment ... I hope we'll have better luck with the insurance agent.'

Janvier, sensing that the Chief Superintendent was still a good deal at sea over the case, assumed a guileless expression, and waited in tactful silence for his comments.

In the end, however, he was forced to ask: 'Are you having him up here?'

'He's not expected back at his hotel until this evening. It might be a good idea, if you went round there tonight, say at about eight ... You may have a long wait ... Anyway, as soon as he gets there, give me a ring at home.'

It was past six. Most people had already left. Just as Maigret was reaching for his hat, the telephone rang. It was Inspector Leroy.

'I'm in a restaurant in the Rue Lepic, sir. He's just ordered dinner. I'll take advantage of the opportunity, and have mine here too. We spent the afternoon seeing an idiotic film in a cinema in the Place Clichy. As it was a continuous programme, we made a proper meal of it, with me sitting just behind him, and saw it twice round ...'

'Did he seem on edge?'

'Not in the least ... Every now and then, he turned round and winked at me ... If I'd given him the slightest encouragement just now, he'd have invited me to sit at his table ...'

'I'll send someone along to the Boulevard Rochechouart shortly, to relieve you.'

'There's no hurry ... This isn't exactly a taxing assignment ...'

'Janvier, I leave it to you to lay on a relief ... I don't know who is available ... And don't forget to ring me as soon as the redhead gets back to his hotel ... It's the Beauséjour ... Keep out of sight as far as you can ...'

Maigret stopped for a drink at the bar in the Place Dauphine. A depressing day on the whole, and the worst of it had been his meeting with Victor Lamotte.

No, perhaps not the worst, he must not forget his exchange with the concierge.

'Charge it to my account.'

Several of his colleagues were playing *belote* in a corner of the café. He waved to them as he went out. When he got home, he made no attempt to hide his ill-humour. It would have cut no ice with Madame Maigret if he had. She knew him too well.

'When I think how much simpler it would be!' he grumbled, hanging up his hat.

'What?'

'To arrest Florentin. Anyone else, in my place, wouldn't hesitate. If the Examining Magistrate knew just half of what I know, he'd send me off to arrest him here and now.'

'What's stopping you, then? Is it because you used to be friends?'

'Not friends,' he corrected her, 'schoolmates.'

He filled the meerschaum pipe that he never smoked except at home.

'Anyway, that's not the reason . . .'

He did not seem very sure himself what the true reason was.

'Everything points to him . . . Almost too much so, if you see what I mean . . . And I can't stand that concierge.'

She repressed a strong inclination to burst out laughing. To hear him talk, one would have thought that his dislike of the concierge was a major factor in his reluctance to arrest Florentin!

'It's virtually impossible to imagine anyone nowadays leading the kind of life that girl led . . . As for her gentlemen callers, with their regular visiting hours, it's almost beyond belief!'

He was thoroughly fed up with the lot of them, starting with Joséphine Papet, who ought to have known better than to let herself be murdered. And Florentin was no better, scattering incriminating evidence right, left and centre. Then there were Paré, with his neurotic wife, and the fat little ballbearings tycoon and, worst of all, the insolent cripple from Bordeaux.

But the most maddening of them all was the concierge. He could not get her out of his head.

'She's lying . . . I'm certain she's lying, or at least that she's got something to hide . . . But she'll never be made to talk . . .'

'You haven't touched your food.'

There was an *omelette aux fines herbes*, succulently moist, but Maigret had not even noticed it. To follow, there was a salad flavoured with garlic *croûtons*, and finally, ripe, juicy peaches.

'You shouldn't take it so much to heart . . .'

He gave her a preoccupied look.

'How do you mean?'

'It's almost as though you were personally involved, as though it concerned a member of your own family.'

This touched a chord in him, and made him realize how

absurdly he had been behaving. He felt suddenly relaxed, and was even able to muster a smile.

'You're right . . . but I can't help it, somehow . . . I can't stand being played for a sucker . . . And someone in this case is doing just that, and it's burning me up . . .'

The telephone rang.

'You see!'

It was Janvier, to tell him that the insurance agent had just got back to his hotel.

Next on the agenda: *Le Rouquin*. Maigret was about to put the receiver down, when Janvier added:

'He's got a woman with him.'

Chapter Five

The Boulevard des Batignolles, with its double row of trees, was dark and deserted, but at the end of it could be seen the brilliant illuminations of the Place Clichy.

Janvier, the red glow of his cigarette piercing the darkness, came forward out of the shadows.

'They arrived on foot, arm-in-arm. The man is shortish, especially in the leg – a very lively character. The girl is young and pretty . . .'

'You'd better be off home to bed, or your wife will have it in for me.'

A familiar smell greeted Maigret in the dim, narrow entrance, for it was in just such a hotel, the Reine Morte in Montparnasse, that he had stayed when he had first come to Paris. He had wondered which dead queen the hotel had been named after. No one had been able to tell him. The proprietor and his wife had come originally from the Auvergne, and had militantly enforced the ban on cooking in the bedrooms.

It was a smell of warm sheets, and of people living in close proximity to one another. A fake marble plaque beside the entrance bore the legend: *Rooms to let. Monthly, weekly or daily terms. All home comforts. Bathrooms*. He might have been back in the Reine Morte, where the proudly advertised bathrooms had numbered one to each floor, so that it was impossible to get near them without queuing.

Seated at a roll-top desk in the office, with the bedroom keys on a board facing her, was a woman with tow-coloured hair, in dressing-gown and slippers. She was making up the accounts for the day.

'Is Monsieur Bodard in?'

Without looking up, she replied, in a somewhat unfriendly tone:

'Fourth floor. Number sixty-eight.'

There was no lift. The stair carpet was threadbare, and the higher he climbed, the more pronounced the smell. Room number 68 was at the end of the corridor. Maigret knocked at the door. There was no reply at first. Then, when he had knocked for the third time, a man's voice called out irritably:

'Who's there?'

'I'd like a word with Monsieur Bodard.'

'What's it about?'

'I should prefer to state my business in private. There's no need for the whole hotel to hear what I have to say.'

'Can't you come back another time?'

'It's rather urgent.'

'Who are you?'

'If you'll just open the door a crack, I'll tell you.'

There was a sound of creaking bed springs. The door opened a little way, and there appeared a tousled head of curly red hair, surmounting the blunted features of a boxer. Maigret could see that the man was naked, though he was doing his best to use the door as a shield. Without a word, Maigret produced his badge.

'Do I have to come with you?' asked Bodard, showing no sign of apprehension or anxiety.

'I want to ask you a few questions.'

'The fact is, I'm not alone . . . I'm afraid you'll have to wait a few minutes . . .'

The door slammed shut again. Maigret could hear voices, and the sound of people moving about. He went down the corridor and sat on the stairs to wait. It was a full five minutes before the door of number 68 was opened again.

'You can come in now.'

The sheets on the brass bed were rumpled. Seated at the dressing-table was a dark girl, tidying her hair. Maigret felt as though he had gone back thirty-five years, so strongly did the room recall those of the Reine Morte.

The girl was wearing nothing but a cotton dress and sandals. She seemed out of humour.

'You want me to go, I suppose?'

'I think you'd better,' replied the man with red hair.

'How long will you be?'

Bodard looked inquiringly at Maigret.

'About an hour?'

The Chief Superintendent nodded.

'You'd better wait for me in the brasserie.'

With a malevolent look, she inspected Maigret from head to foot, then grabbed her handbag and went out.

'I'm sorry to have called at such an inconvenient time.'

'I wasn't expecting you so soon. I thought it would take you at least two or three days to track me down.'

He had not bothered to do more than slip on a pair of trousers. He was still naked from the waist up. His shoulders and chest were broad and powerful, with well-developed muscles, which made up for his lack of stature. His feet too were bare, and Maigret noticed that he had unusually short legs.

'Please sit down.'

He himself sat on the edge of the rumpled bed. Maigret took the only armchair. It was exceedingly uncomfortable.

'I presume you've seen the papers?'

'I should think everyone has, by now.'

He seemed a good sort. Apparently, he bore his visitor no ill will for breaking in on his *tête-à-tête*. There was an easy good nature about him. He would always be ready to make the best of things, if the expression of his clear blue eyes was anything to go by. He was not the worrying kind, nor the sort to take a tragic view of life.

'So you really are Chief Superintendent Maigret? I imagined you as much fatter ... And I certainly wouldn't have expected anyone so exalted to be going around knocking on people's doors ...'

'There are times when it's necessary.'

'I realize, of course, that you've come about poor Josée ...'

He lit a cigarette.

'Have you arrested anyone yet?'

Maigret smiled at this reversal of roles. It was he who should have been asking the questions.

'Was it the concierge who put you on to me? What a monstrous creature! She's more like a monument than a woman. She reminds me of one of those marble figures on tombs. She sends a shiver down my spine ...'

'How long have you known Joséphine Papet?'

'Let me think ... We're in June, aren't we? ... It was the day after my birthday, so it must have been April the nineteenth ...'

'How did you meet her?'

'I called at her flat. I called at all the flats in the building that day. It's my job, if you can call it a job. You know: "I'm an insurance agent and I represent so-and-so"!'

'I know ...'

'Each one of us has a round of three or four blocks, and we spend our whole time knocking on doors and trying to drum up business ...'

'Can you remember what day of the week it was?'

'A Thursday ... I remember because, as I said, the previous day was my birthday, and I had a filthy hangover ...'

'Was this in the morning?'

'Yes, about eleven.'

'Was she alone?'

'No, there was a man with her, a bit of a layabout, very tall and thin. He said to the woman:

' "Well, I'd better be going."

'He gave me a good, hard look, and then he left.'

'You sell life assurance, I believe?'

'Accident policies as well, oh! and savings-linked insurance. That's a fairly new gimmick, and it's not going too badly ... I haven't been in the job very long. Before that, I was a waiter in a café.'

'What made you change?'

'That's just it, I felt like a change ... I used to be a fairground barker . . . You have to have the gift of the gab for that, even more than in insurance, but insurance is more respectable . . .'

'Were you able to interest Mademoiselle Papet . . . ?'

'Not in the sense you mean.'

He chuckled.

'How then?'

'Well, to begin with, she was in her dressing-gown, with her hair tied up in a scarf, and the vacuum cleaner was pulled out into the middle of the room . . . I went into my usual patter, and all the time I was talking I was sizing her up . . .

'She wasn't all that young, of course, but she was a tidy little armful, and I had the feeling that she quite fancied me . . .

'She told me she wasn't interested in a life policy for the very good reason that she had no one to provide for. She had no idea what would become of her money in the end, she said.

'I suggested that she should take out an annuity to mature when she was sixty, or, better still, an accident and illness policy.'

'Did she show any interest?'

'She wouldn't commit herself, one way or the other. So, as usual, I made an all-out play for her . . . I can't help myself . . . It's just the way I'm made . . . Sometimes there's a scene and I get my face slapped, but it's worth a try, even if it only comes off one time in three . . .'

'Did you bring it off with her?'

'I'll say!'

'How long have you known the young woman who was here just now?'

'Olga? Since yesterday.'

'Where did you meet her?'

'In a self-service store . . . She's a shop assistant in the Bon Marché . . . Don't ask me if she's any good . . . You interrupted before I got a chance to find out . . .'

'How often did you see Joséphine Papet, after that first time?'

'I wasn't counting . . . Ten or a dozen times, perhaps.'

'Did she give you a key?'

'No. I rang the bell.'

'Did she fix any special day for your meetings?'

'No, she just told me that she was never there at week-ends. I asked her if the grey-haired man was her husband. She assured me he wasn't . . .'

'Did you ever see him again?'

'Yes, twice . . .'

'Did you ever speak to him?'

'I don't think he liked me much . . . Each time, he just gave me a dirty look, and sloped off . . .

'I asked Josée who he was. She said:

' "Don't bother your head about him . . . He's rather pathetic really. He reminds me of a stray dog . . . That's why I took him in . . ."

' "All the same, you go to bed with him, don't you?" I said.

' "What else can I do? . . . I don't want to hurt his feelings . . . There are times when I'm almost afraid he'll commit suicide." '

As far as Maigret could judge, Bodard spoke with unfeigned sincerity.

'Was he the only man you ever saw in her flat?'

'I never saw any of the others . . . We had a pre-arranged signal . . . If she had anyone in the flat when I rang, she would open the door just a crack, I would say that I was selling insurance, and she would say she wasn't interested, and shut the door on me.'

'Did the occasion ever arise?'

'Two or three times.'

'Any particular day of the week?'

'There you have me . . . Wait a minute though, I've just remembered, one of the times it was a Wednesday.'

'What time of day?'

'Round about four or half past, I think.'

Wednesday was Paré's day. But the Head of Inland Waterways had told him that he had never got to the Rue Notre-Dame-de-Lorette before half past five or six.

'Did he see you?'

'I don't think so. She only opened the door a crack.'

Maigret gazed at him intently. He seemed preoccupied.

'What do you know about her?'

'Let me think . . . Occasionally, she would let fall a hint about

96

this or that . . . I seem to remember she told me she was born in Dieppe.'

So she had not bothered to lie to the man known as *Le Rouquin*. The Divisional Superintendent had telephoned to Dieppe to inquire about next of kin in connection with the funeral arrangements, and was informed that thirty-four years ago, in Dieppe, a daughter, Joséphine, had been born to Hector Papet, deep-sea fisherman, and Léontine Marchaud, housewife. As far as was known, there was no one left of the family in the town.

Why should she have told the truth to Bodard, when she had lied to all the others, inventing a different tale for each of them?

'She worked for a time in a night-club, until she took up with a man she met there, a very respectable man, an industrialist. He set her up in the flat, and lived with her for several months . . .'

'Did she tell you where her money came from?'

'More or less . . . She gave me to understand that she had several rich friends who visited her from time to time.'

'Do you know their names?'

'No . . . But she would say things like: "The one with the limp is getting to be a bit of a bore . . . If it wasn't that I'm a little scared of him . . ." '

'Did you get the impression that she really was frightened of him?'

'She was never altogether easy in her mind. That's why she kept a revolver in her bedside table drawer.'

'Did she show it to you?'

'Yes.'

'So she wasn't afraid of you?'

'You must be joking! Why should anyone be afraid of me?'

Why indeed? There was something so very likeable about him. His whole appearance was somehow reassuring, curly red hair, blue, almost violet eyes, stocky body and short legs. He looked younger than his thirty years, and would probably never lose his impish charm.

'Did she give you presents?'

He got up, went over to the chest of drawers, and took out a silver cigarette case.

'She gave me this.'

'What about money?'

'Well, really!'

He was affronted, almost angry.

'I don't mean to be offensive. I'm only doing my job.'

'I hope you put the same question to her tame scarecrow!'

'Florentin, do you mean?'

'I didn't know his name was Florentin ... I mean the one who had no objection to being kept by her.'

'Did she talk to you about him?'

'I'll say she did!'

'I was under the impression that she was very fond of him.'

'I daresay she was, to begin with ... She liked having someone about the place ... someone she could talk to ... who would put up with anything ... who didn't matter. Most women like to keep a pet, but usually it's a dog or a cat or a canary, if you see what I mean ...

'Mind you, that character, Florentin, or whatever his name is, went a bit too far ...'

'In what way?'

'When she first met him, he gave himself out to be an antique dealer ... He was down-and-out, but was expecting to come into a fortune any day ... In those days, he really did spend some of his time buying and doing up old furniture ... But, as time went by, he got more and more into the habit of doing nothing ...

'It was always the same old story: "When I get the two hundred thousand francs owing to me ..."'

'And then he'd touch her for fifty francs or so.'

'If she didn't care for him, why didn't she throw him out?'

'Well, you see, she was really very sentimental. In fact, they don't come that sentimental any more, except in romantic novels. Look! I told you how it all started, didn't I? Well, she wasn't exactly a kid any more, was she? In fact, she'd had a good deal of experience, one way and another. All the same, when it was over, she burst into tears!

'I couldn't make it out. I just sat up in bed and stared at her. Then she said, between sobs:

' "How you must despise me ... !"'

'I mean to say, you come across that sort of thing in old books, but it was the first time I'd ever actually heard a woman talk like that . . .

'That Florentin fellow had her sized up all right . . . He knew how to tug at the heartstrings . . . Whenever things looked like getting sticky, he'd turn on the sentiment like a tap . . . They used to have the most heartrending scenes . . . sometimes he'd storm out, swearing that he would never come back, that she would never hear of him again, and then she'd go chasing after him to some hovel or other in the Boulevard Rochechouart, where I believe he shacks up . . .'

There was nothing very surprising to Maigret in this character-sketch of his old school friend. It was just the way Florentin had behaved when threatened with expulsion from the lycée. The story went – and it had not seemed too far-fetched at the time – that he had literally grovelled at the feet of the head-master, declaring, between sobs, that the disgrace would kill him.

'On another occasion, he took the revolver from the bedside table drawer, and made as if to shoot himself in the temple . . .

' "I shall never love anyone but you . . . You're all I have left in the world."

'D'you get the picture? For hours, sometimes for days, after one of these scenes, he'd have her just where he wanted her . . . Then, as his self-confidence returned, so did her doubts . . .

'But if you ask me, the real reason she didn't throw him out was because she dreaded being left on her own, and there was no one to take his place . . .'

'And then she met you.'

'Yes.'

'And she saw you as a possible successor?'

'I think so . . . She used to ask me if I still had many girl-friends, and sometimes she'd say: "You do like me a little, don't you?"

'She didn't exactly throw herself at me . . . It was more subtle than that, just a hint here and there:

' "I suppose I must seem an old woman to you."

'And when I protested, she'd say:

' "Well. I am five years older than you are, and a woman ages more quickly than a man ... It won't be long before I'm a mass of wrinkles ..."

'Then she'd return to the subject of the antique dealer:

' "You'd think he owned me," she said. "He wants me to marry him." '

Maigret gave a start.

'She told you that, did she?'

'Yes. And she went on to say that he wanted her to invest in a bar or small restaurant somewhere round about the Porte Maillot ... She owned a house, you know, and had quite a bit of money saved, too ...

'He had it in for me, apparently, and always referred to me contemptuously as Ginger or Shorty.

' "Sooner or later," he used to say, "he'll be leading you by the nose." '

'Tell me truthfully, Bodard, did you go to the Rue Notre Dame-de-Lorette at any time yesterday afternoon?'

'I see what you're getting at, Chief Superintendent ... You want to know if I've got an alibi ... Well, I'm sorry to say, haven't ... For a time I gave up seeing other girls, for Josée' sake, though I must admit, it wasn't easy ... But yesterday morning, I signed up an old gent of sixty-five for a hefty policy ... He was looking anxiously to the future ...

'The older they are, the more they worry about the future ...

'Well, the sun was shining, and I'd treated myself to the best lunch that money could buy, so I decided to go on the prowl ...

'I made for the Grands Boulevards and went into a few bar ... It was a bit of a frost to begin with, but then I met up with Olga, that's the girl you saw ... She's waiting for me in a brasserie three doors down the street ... I ran into her at about seven ... Otherwise, I've no alibi ...'

With a laugh, he asked:

'Are you going to arrest me?'

'No ... But to get back to Florentin, are you saying that, in the past few weeks, his position had become precarious?'

'I'm saying that, if I'd wanted to, I could have stepped into his shoes, but as it happened I had no wish to.'

'Did he know?'

'He sensed that I was a possible rival, I'm sure of that ...
He's no fool ... Besides, Josée must have dropped a hint or
two ...'

'Surely, in the circumstances, if he'd wanted to get rid of
anyone, you would have been the obvious choice?'

'You'd have thought so ... He couldn't have known that I'd
made up my mind to say no, and that I was already gently easing
my way out ... I can't stand snivelling women ...'

'Do you think he killed her?'

'I've no idea, and, anyway, it's no concern of mine. Besides, I
know nothing about the others ... Any one of them might have
borne her a grudge for one reason or another ...'

'Thank you.'

'Don't mention it ... I say, old man, I don't feel like getting
dressed ... Would you mind awfully, on your way out, giving
the dolly the green light? Tell her, I'm waiting for her up
here ...'

Never in his life before had Maigret been asked to undertake
such an errand, but the request was made with such engaging
artlessness that he had not the heart to refuse.

'Good night.'

'I hope it will be!'

He had no difficulty in finding the brasserie, which was full of
regulars, playing cards. It was an old-fashioned place, and the
lighting was poor. Seeing Maigret making straight for the only
young girl in the room, the waiter smiled knowingly.

'I'm sorry I was so long ... He's waiting for you up
there ...'

She was so taken aback that she could find nothing to say. He
left her there, gaping, and had to walk all the way back to the
Place Clichy before he could find a taxi.

*

Maigret's feeling that the Examining Magistrate, Judge Page,
had only recently come to Paris, proved to be correct. His
office, one of those not yet modernized, was on the top floor of
the Palais de Justice. There was an archaic atmosphere about it,
reminiscent of the novels of Balzac.

His clerk was working at an unstained deal kitchen table, to the top of which a sheet of brown paper had been fastened with drawing-pins. His own office, which could be seen through the open communicating door, was bare of furniture, though cluttered with files piled up on the floorboards.

Before coming up, the Chief Superintendent had taken the precaution of ringing through, to make sure that the judge was free, and willing to see him.

'Have this chair ... It's the best we've got, or perhaps I should say, the least dilapidated ... The pair to it collapsed last week under the weight of an eight-stone witness ...'

'Do you mind if I smoke?' Maigret asked, lighting up.

'Please do.'

'All our inquiries have so far failed to locate anyone related to Joséphine Papet. She can't be kept indefinitely at the Forensic Laboratory ... It may take weeks, or even months, to discover some second or third cousin ... Don't you think, in the circumstances, Judge, that the best thing would be to make arrangements for the funeral without further delay?'

'As she was not without means ...'

'That reminds me, I deposited the forty-eight thousand francs with the Clerk of the Court, because I wasn't too happy about keeping it locked up in my office.

'With your permission, I'll get in touch with a firm of undertakers right away.'

'Was she a Catholic?'

'According to Léon Florentin, who lived with her, she wasn't. At any rate, she never went to Mass.'

'Have the account sent to me ... I'm not quite sure what the procedure is ... Make a note of it, Dubois ...'

'Yes, sir.'

The moment Maigret had been dreading had come. He had not attempted to stave it off. On the contrary, he himself had asked to see the judge.

'You must have been wondering why I haven't let you have an interim report. The truth is that, even now, I'm far from sure I'm on the right track.'

'Do you suspect the man who lived with her? What's his name again?'

'Florentin ... All the evidence points to him, and yet I still have the gravest doubts ... It all seems too easy, somehow ... Besides which, by an odd coincidence, he and I were at school together in Moulins ... He's by no means a fool, in fact, I should say that he had all his wits about him, rather more than most ...

'Admittedly, he's a failure, but that's because of a flaw in his personality ... He resents all authority and is totally incapable of self-discipline ... As I see it, he lives in a fantasy world, a kind of imaginary puppet theatre, in which nothing and no one is to be taken seriously ...

'He has a police record ... Dud cheques ... Fraud ... He did a year's stretch in prison ... But, in spite of it all, I still don't believe him capable of committing murder ... Or at any rate, he's incapable of bungling it ... If he'd done it, he would have taken very good care to cover his tracks ...

'All the same, I'm keeping a round-the-clock watch on him.'

'Does he know?'

'He takes it as a compliment, and makes a point of turning round in the street every so often, to wink at the man on his tail ... He always was the clown of the form ... You must know the type ...'

'There's one in every school.'

'The trouble is that, in a man of fifty, that sort of behaviour is no joke any longer ... I've tracked down Joséphine Papet's other lovers ... One is a highly placed civil servant with a neurotic wife ... The other two also are men of standing and considerable wealth ... One lives in Bordeaux, the other in Rouen ...

'Needless to say, each of these men imagined himself to be the only one privileged to visit the flat in the Rue Notre-Dame-de-Lorette ...'

'Have you undeceived them?'

'I've done more than that ... I have arranged, this morning, for each of them to receive a personal summons to a meeting in my office at three o'clock this afternoon.

'I have also summoned the concierge to attend, because I'm quite sure in my own mind that she's hiding something. I hope, by tomorrow, to have definite news for you.'

A quarter of an hour later, Maigret was back in his office, instructing Lucas to make arrangements for the funeral. Then, taking a note out of his wallet, he murmured:

'Here, see that there are some flowers on the coffin.'

The sun had been shining brilliantly for days, and today was no exception, but a high wind had suddenly blown up, causing the trees outside to rock violently, and making it impossible to have the window open.

No doubt all those who had been summoned to the forth-coming meeting were shaking in their shoes. Little did they know that Maigret was even more uneasy than they were. True, it had been something of a relief to unburden himself to the Examining Magistrate, but he was still very much a prey to conflicting emotions.

There were two people constantly in the forefront of his mind. One, needless to say, was Florentin, who, it almost seemed, had piled up evidence against himself out of sheer mischief. The other was that old witch of a concierge, who haunted him like a nightmare. As far as she was concerned, he was taking no chances. Knowing that she was quite capable of ignoring his summons, he was sending an inspector to fetch her.

Realizing that it would be best to put the case out of his mind for the time being, he settled down grudgingly to his neglected paperwork, and soon became so immersed in it, that when next he looked up to see the time, he was surprised to find that it was ten to one.

He decided not to go home for lunch, and rang his wife to tell her so. Then he strolled across to the Brasserie Dauphine, and sat down in his usual corner. Several of his colleagues were there having a drink at the bar, as well as a number of people he knew, from other departments.

The proprietor himself came over to take his order.

'There's *blanquette de veau*. How will that do?'

'Fine.'

'And a carafe of our special rosé?'

He lingered over his meal, soothed by the low murmur of voices, which was punctuated by an occasional burst of laughter. As usual, the proprietor brought him a small glass of Calvados, 'on the house', with his coffee, and he made it last until it was time to go back to his office.

At a quarter to three, he went into the Inspectors' Duty Room to fetch some chairs, which he set out in a semi-circle facing his desk.

'I don't want any slip up, Janvier. You're to go and fetch her, and then take her into a room by herself, and keep her there until I send for you.'

'I'm not sure I'll be able to fit her into the car all in one piece!' retorted Janvier jocularly.

The first to arrive was Jean-Luc Bodard. He was in high good humour. At the sight of the row of chairs, however, he frowned.

'What's this, a family reunion, or a council of war?'

'A bit of both.'

'You don't mean you're bringing together all . . . ?'

'Just so.'

'Well, it suits me all right, but how do you think the others will take it? You'll get a few old-fashioned looks, I shouldn't wonder.'

And indeed the next comer, ushered in by old Joseph, having looked round the room, turned to Maigret with an expression of unhappy distaste.

'I came in response to your summons, but I wasn't told . . .'

'You're not the only person concerned, I'm afraid, Monsieur Paré. Take a seat, won't you?'

As on the previous day, he was dressed all in black. He held himself stiffly, and was more strung up than he had been in his own office. He kept darting anxious glances at the young man with red hair.

There followed an awkward pause lasting two or three minutes, during which no one spoke a word. François Paré had taken the chair nearest the window, and sat with his black hat balanced on his knees. Jean-Luc Bodard, wearing a loud check sports jacket, was watching the door as though, as far as he was concerned, the others couldn't come soon enough.

The next to arrive was Victor Lamotte, very much on his dignity. Furiously he turned on Maigret:

'What's this? A trap?'

105

'Please be seated.'

Maigret, ignoring the undercurrents, was playing the gracious host, faintly smiling, imperturbable.

'You've no right to . . .'

'You will have every opportunity of complaining to my superiors in due course, Monsieur Lamotte. Meanwhile, I'd be obliged if you would take a seat.'

Florentin was brought in by an inspector. The set-up was no less of a surprise to him than to the others, but his reaction was a loud guffaw.

'Well, I must say . . . !'

He looked Maigret straight in the eye, and gave him an appreciative wink. He thought he knew every trick in the book, but this was beyond everything!

'Gentlemen,' he said, bowing with mock solemnity to the assembled company.

He sat down next to Lamotte, who at once shifted his chair as far away from him as possible.

The Chief Superintendent looked at the time. The chimes of three o'clock sounded, and a few more minutes went by before Fernand Courcel appeared in the doorway. What he saw was such a shock to him that he spun round, as though minded to take to his heels.

'Come in, Monsieur Courcel . . . Sit down . . . We're all here now, I think . . .'

Young Lapointe was seated at one end of the desk, ready to take down in shorthand anything of interest that might be said.

Maigret sat down, lit his pipe and murmured:

'Please smoke if you wish.'

The only one to do so was the young man with red hair.

Maigret looked with interest from one to another. They were an ill-assorted bunch. In a sense, they fell naturally into two groups. In the first group were Florentin and Bodard, whom Josée had truly loved, and who were now engaged in sizing each other up. They represented, in effect, age and youth, the old and the new.

Did Florentin know that the young man with red hair could have ousted him, had he so wished? If so, he did not appear to

106

bear him any grudge. If anything, he seemed rather to approve of him.

In the second group were the three men who had visited the Rue Notre-Dame-de-Lorette in pursuit of an illusion. Their plight was much the more serious.

This was the first time that they had ever met, and yet not one of them deigned so much as to glance at the others.

'Gentlemen, you can be in no doubt as to why you are assembled here. You have all been good enough to answer my questions separately, and I, in my turn, have given you the true facts of the situation, as far as I knew them.

'There are five of you present, every one of whom has, for a longer or shorter period, known Joséphine Papet intimately.'

He paused for an instant. No one stirred.

'Apart from Florentin and, to a limited extent, Bodard, none of you knew of the existence of the others. That is so, is it not?'

The only response was from Bodard, who nodded. As for Florentin, he looked as though he was enjoying himself hugely.

'The fact is that Joséphine Papet is dead, and that one of you killed her.'

Monsieur Lamotte half-rose from his seat and began:

'I protest . . .'

To judge from his expression, he was near to storming out of the room.

'Kindly keep your protests until later. Sit down. So far, I have accused no one. I merely stated a fact. All but one of you deny having set foot in the flat between three and four on Wednesday afternoon . . . Not one of you, however, can establish an alibi . . .'

Paré raised his hand.

'No, Monsieur Paré, yours won't do. I sent one of my men to have another look at your office. There is a second door, leading on to a corridor. You could have gone out that way without anyone seeing you. What's more, if any of your staff had gone into your office and found it empty, they would naturally have assumed that you had been called away by the Permanent Under-Secretary . . .'

Maigret relit his pipe, which had gone out.

'Obviously, I can hardly expect one of you to stand up and confess his guilt. I am simply telling you what is in my mind. I am convinced not only that the murderer is here in this room, but also that there is present someone who knows who he is, and who, for some reason that escapes me, is keeping that knowledge to himself.'

He looked from one to another of them. Florentin's eyes were turned towards the group in the middle, but it was impossible to tell whether his attention was fixed on anyone in particular.

Victor Lamotte was staring intently down at his shoes. He was very pale, and his face seemed all hollows and shadows.

Courcel, poor man, was trying to smile, but all he could manage was a pathetic little grimace.

Bodard was looking thoughtful. It was clear that he had been much struck by Maigret's last remark, and was trying to sort things out in his own mind.

'Whoever killed Josée must have been well known to her, since she received him in her bedroom. But Josée was not alone in the flat . . .'

This time, they all looked at one another, and then, with one accord, turned to stare uneasily at Florentin.

'You're quite right . . . Léon Florentin was there when the doorbell rang, and, as he had been forced to do on other occasions, he took refuge in the clothes closet . . .'

Maigret's old school friend was making a valiant effort to maintain his air of unconcern.

'Did you hear a man's voice, Florentin?'

He addressed him as 'vous', but, on this occasion, at least, Florentin could scarcely object.

'You couldn't hear much in there, just a murmur of voices . . .'

'What exactly happened?'

'I'd been there about a quarter of an hour when I heard a shot.'

'Did you rush into the bedroom to see what was the matter?'

'No.'

'Did the murderer leave at once?'

'No.'

'How long was he in the flat after the shot?'

'About a quarter of an hour.'

'Did he take the forty-eight thousand francs from the drawer of the desk?'

'No.'

Maigret saw no necessity to disclose that it was Florentin himself who had made off with the money.

'The murderer must have been looking for something. Every one of you, I presume, must have had occasion to write to Josée, if only to cancel an appointment, or to keep in touch while you were away on holiday.'

Once more, he looked from one to another. They shifted uneasily, crossing or uncrossing their legs.

He was now concentrating his attention on the three solemn-faced men who had most to lose in terms of family, position and reputation.

'What about you, Monsieur Lamotte, did you ever have occasion to write to her?'

'Yes,' he muttered under his breath. He was barely audible.

'The social world in which you move in Bordeaux has changed very little with the times, I fancy. If my information is correct, your wife is a very rich woman in her own right and, according to the scale of values accepted in Les Chartrons, comes from a family even more distinguished than your own. Have you ever been threatened with exposure by anyone?'

'I simply cannot permit . . .'

'And you, Monsieur Paré, did you ever write to her?'

'Yes, as you suggested, when I was on holiday . . .'

'You are, I believe, in spite of your visits to the Rue Notre-Dame-de-Lorette, very much attached to your wife . . .'

'She's a sick woman . . .'

'I know . . . And I'm sure you would go to great lengths to spare her the anguish . . .'

Paré clenched his teeth. He seemed on the verge of tears.

'And now, Monsieur Courcel, what about you?'

'I may have scribbled a note to her once or twice . . .'

'Which, I'm sure, would leave no one in any doubt as to the

nature of your relations with Joséphine Papet ... Your wife is younger than you are, and of a jealous disposition, I daresay ...'

'What about me then?' broke in the redhead, making a jest of it.

'You could have had an altogether different reason for wanting to get rid of her.'

'Not jealousy, at any rate,' he protested, and turned to the others as if for moral support.

'Josée could have told you about her savings. You may have known that she didn't deposit her money in a bank, but kept it in the flat ...'

'If so, then surely I would have taken it?'

'Not if you were interrupted while you were still searching for it.'

'Do I look as if I'd do a thing like that?'

'Most of the murderers I've met have looked very much like anyone else ... As to the letters, you could have taken them with the intention of blackmailing the signatories ...

'Because the letters have vanished, all of them, possibly including some from people we haven't even heard of. You'd expect most women, by the age of thirty-five, to have accumulated quite a volume of correspondence ... But there was nothing in Joséphine Papet's desk except bills. Every single one of your letters, gentlemen, has been spirited away, and by one of you ...'

They were all so anxious to appear innocent, that none of them succeeded in looking anything but thoroughly guilty.

'I am not inviting the murderer to stand up and confess. I shall simply remain here in the confident hope that, within the next few hours, the man who knows who murdered Josée will come to see me ...

'All the same, that may not be necessary ... There is still one witness missing, and that witness also knows who the murderer is ...'

Maigret turned to Lapointe.

'Fetch Janvier, will you?'

There was a long pause, during which not a sound was heard. The five men held their breath, scarcely daring to move. Suddenly, the room felt very hot. When at last Madame Blanc made her entrance, resembling more than ever a piece of monumental sculpture, the effect was electric.

She was wearing a dress of spinach green, with a red hat perched on the very top of her head, and the handbag she was carrying was almost as big as a suitcase. She stood for a moment, framed in the doorway, her face stony, her expressionless eyes darting from one to another of those present.

When she had taken them all in, she turned her back on them, and it was all Janvier could do to prevent her from leaving. For a moment, it looked as if they might come to blows.

In the end the woman gave way, and came into the room.

'I still have nothing to say,' she announced, glowering malevolently at Maigret.

'I think you know all these gentlemen?'

'I'm not being paid to do your job for you. Let me go.'

'Which of these men did you see going towards the lift or the stairs, between three and four in the afternoon on Wednesday?'

Then a strange thing happened. This stubborn, stony-faced woman was unable to prevent her lips from twitching in a faint ghost of a smile. All of a sudden, she was looking distinctly smug, there was no doubt about it. It was almost as though she had won a victory.

They were all looking at her. Maigret was watching them, hoping to detect signs of special anxiety in one of their faces. But he could not tell which of them was most affected. Victor Lamotte was pale with suppressed fury. Fernand Courcel, in contrast, was very flushed; Maigret had noticed his rising colour for some minutes past. As for François Paré, he was simply overwhelmed with shame and misery.

At last Maigret spoke.

'Do you refuse to answer?'

'I have nothing to say.'

'Make a note of that, Lapointe.'

She shrugged and, still with that enigmatic glint of triumph in her eyes, said contemptuously:

'You can't frighten me.'

Chapter Six

Maigret stood up, looked at each of them in turn, and concluded:

'Gentlemen, I'm grateful to you all for coming here. It is my belief that your time has not been wasted, and I have no doubt that I shall be hearing from one of you very shortly.'

He cleared his throat.

'In conclusion, for those who are interested, I am now in a position to inform you that the funeral of Joséphine Papet will take place tomorrow morning. The hearse will set out from the Forensic Laboratory at ten o'clock.'

Victor Lamotte, still fuming, was the first to go. He did not even glance at the others, and, needless to say, took no leave of the Chief Superintendent. No doubt his chauffeur-driven limousine was waiting for him below.

Courcel hesitated a moment, then, with a nod, went out. François Paré, as though he scarcely knew what he was saying, murmured:

'Thank you . . .'

Le Rouquin was the only one to offer his hand. He bounded to Maigret, exclaiming appreciatively:

'You certainly don't pull your punches!'

Florentin alone hung back. Maigret said to him:

'You wait here a minute . . . I shan't be long.'

He left Lapointe, who had not moved from his seat at the end of the desk, to keep an eye on him, and went into the Inspectors' Room next door. Torrence was there, a bulky figure seated at his typewriter, transcribing a report. He typed with two fingers, and applied himself to the task with intense concentration.

'I want the house in the Rue Notre-Dame-de-Lorette watched . . . See to it at once, will you? I want the names of everyone who goes in or comes out . . . If any one of the men who have just left my office turns up, he's to be followed inside.'

'Is something worrying you?'

'I'm quite sure the concierge knows more than is good for her. I don't want her to come to any harm.'

'What about Florentin? Same drill?'

'Yes. I'll let you know when I've done with him.'

He went back to his office.

'You can go, Lapointe.'

Florentin was standing at the window, hands in his pockets, looking very much at home. He was wearing his usual expression of ironic detachment.

'I say, you didn't half rattle them! I've never enjoyed myself so much in all my life!'

'Is that so?'

For it had not escaped Maigret that there was something very forced about this display of high spirits.

'The one who really took my breath away was the concierge ... Talk about getting blood out of a stone! Do you really think she knows?'

'I hope so, for your sake.'

'What do you mean?'

'She maintains that no one went upstairs between three and four ... Unless she changes her mind, I shall have no choice but to arrest you, because if what she says is true, you're the only person who could have done it.'

'What was the point of the confrontation?'

'I was hoping one of them would panic.'

'Aren't you concerned that I might be in danger, too?'

'Did you see the murderer?'

'I've already told you I didn't.'

'Did you recognize his voice?'

'No. I've told you that too.'

'Then what have you got to worry about?'

'I was in the flat. Thanks to you, they all know that now. The murderer can't be sure I didn't see him.'

Casually, Maigret opened a drawer in his desk, and took out the packet of photographs that Moers had sent down to him from Criminal Records. He glanced through them, and handed one to Florentin.

'Take a look at that.'

The confectioner's son from Moulins, assuming an air of

bewilderment, examined the photograph carefully. It was of a corner of the bedroom, showing the bed, and the side-table with its drawer half-open.

'What am I supposed to be looking for?'

'Doesn't anything strike you?'

'No.'

'Remember your first statement . . . The door bell rang . . . You bolted into the clothes closet . . .'

'It's the truth.'

'Very well, let's assume, for the sake of argument, that it is. According to you, Josée and her visitor barely paused in the sitting-room, and went straight on through the dining-room into the bedroom . . .'

'That's right.'

'Let me finish. Also according to you, they were together in the bedroom for nearly a quarter of an hour before you heard the shot.'

Florentin, frowning, examined the photograph again.

'That photograph was taken very soon after the murder . . . Nothing in the room had been touched . . . Look at the bed . . .'

A little colour rose in Florentin's wasted cheeks.

'Not only has the bed not been turned down, but there isn't so much as a dent or a crease on the counterpane.'

'What are you getting at?'

'I'll tell you! Either the visitor merely wanted to talk to Josée, in which case they would have stayed in the sitting-room, or he came for some other purpose. And since the condition of the bed suggests that it wasn't the usual purpose, perhaps you can tell me what in actual fact they were doing in the bedroom?'

'I don't know . . .'

Maigret could almost see his mind ticking over, as he thought up plausible answers.

'Just now, you mentioned letters . . .'

'Well?'

'Maybe he came to ask for his letters back . . .'

'Are you suggesting that Josée would have refused to give them to him? Do you think it likely that she would have tried to blackmail a man who was making her a generous monthly allowance?'

'They could have gone into the bedroom for the usual reason, and then quarrelled ...'

'Listen to me, Florentin ... I have your statements by heart ... I felt from the very beginning that there was something wrong somewhere ... Did you take those letters as well as the forty-eight thousand francs?'

'I swear I didn't ... If I had surely you'd have found them, just as you found the money. If I'd had the letters, I'd have hidden them in the same place.'

'Not necessarily ... It's true that you were frisked to make sure you hadn't got the revolver, but you weren't searched. I know you're an excellent swimmer, don't forget, and I also know that you took a sudden dive into the Seine ...'

'I was fed up with everything ... I realized that you suspected me ... And besides, I'd just lost the only person in the world who ...'

'I'd be obliged if you'd spare me the crocodile tears.'

'When I jumped off that parapet, my only thought was to end it all ... It was just a foolish impulse ... One of your chaps was on my tail ...'

'Just so.'

'What do you mean by that?'

'Suppose that, when you hid the money on top of the wardrobe, you'd momentarily forgotten about the letters, which were still in your pocket? You couldn't take the risk of their being found in your possession. How could you have explained them away?'

'I don't know.'

'You realized that a constant watch would be kept on you from then on. But if you were to jump into the Seine, ostensibly in a fit of despair, you could easily get rid of the incriminating papers ... They only needed to be weighted with a pebble or something of the sort, to sink safely to the bottom.'

'I never had the letters.'

'I agree, that's one possibility. If true, it would certainly explain what the murderer was doing in the flat during the quarter of an hour after the shot. But there's another thing that's worrying me ...'

'What am I being accused of now?'

115

'The fingerprints . . .'

'I daresay mine were all over the flat, but what do you expect?'

'That's just it, there were no fingerprints in the bedroom, neither yours nor anyone else's. Now we know you opened the desk to get at the money. And presumably the murderer opened at least one drawer when he was looking for the letters . . . At any rate, he can't have spent a quarter of an hour in the room without touching anything . . .

'Which can only mean that, after he'd gone, all the smooth surfaces, including the door handles, were wiped – by you.'

'I don't understand . . . I did no such thing . . . Who's to say that someone didn't sneak in and do it after I'd left? There was plenty of time, while I was on my way to the Boulevard Roche-chouart, or coming to see you at the Quai des Orfèvres.'

Maigret did not reply. Noticing that the wind had dropped, he went over and opened the window. There followed a long silence, then Maigret said very quietly:

'When did your notice expire?'

'What notice? What on earth are you talking about?'

'Your notice to quit the flat . . . to part from Josée . . . in other words, to get out . . .'

'There was never any question . . .'

'Oh yes, there was, and well you know it . . . you were be-ginning to show your age and, what's more, you were becoming greedy . . .'

'I suppose that swine of a redhead told you that?'

'What does it matter?'

'It couldn't be anyone else. He's been oiling himself into her good graces for weeks.'

'He has a job. He works for his living.'

'So do I.'

'Your so-called antique business is only a front. How many pieces of furniture do you sell in a year? Most of the time there's a "Closed" sign on your door.'

'I have to be out and about, buying.'

'No . . . Joséphine Papet had had about as much as she could take . . . For want of anything better, she was planning to install Bodard in your place.'

'It's his word against mine.'

'I know you of old, Florentin. Your word isn't worth *that* . . .'

'You have got it in for me, haven't you?'

'Why should I "have it in for you", as you put it?'

'You always did, even in Moulins . . . My parents owned a prosperous business . . . I always had money to spend . . . But what was your father? Just a sort of upper servant on the Château de Saint-Fiacre estate . . .'

Maigret flushed, and clenched his fists. He could have hit him, for, if there was one thing he could not tolerate, it was a slur on his father's name. Maigret senior had, in actual fact, been steward of the estate, with responsibility for twenty or more farms.

'You're despicable, Florentin.'

'You asked for it.'

'The only reason I'm not having you locked up here and now is because I haven't yet got the tangible evidence I need. But it won't be long now, I promise you . . .'

He strode across to the door of the Inspectors' Room, and flung it open.

'Which of you is in charge of this scoundrel here?'

Loutrie stood up.

'Keep close up behind him, and when he gets home, mount guard at the door. You can arrange a rota among yourselves.'

Florentin, realizing that he had gone too far, looked very much abashed.

'I apologize, Maigret . . . I lost my head . . . I didn't know what I was saying . . . Put yourself in my shoes . . .'

The Chief Superintendent maintained a grim silence, and kept his eyes averted as Florentin went out. Almost immediately after he had gone, the telephone rang. It was the Examining Magistrate wanting to know the outcome of the confrontation.

'It's too early to say,' explained Maigret. 'It's rather like dragging a pond. I've stirred up a lot of mud, but I can't tell yet what may come up . . . I've arranged the funeral for ten tomorrow morning.'

A number of newspapermen were hanging about in the corridor. He was unusually short with them.

'Are you on the track of the killer, Chief Superintendent?'

'There's more than one track.'

'And you're not sure which is the right one?'

'Just so.'

'Do you think it's a *crime passionel*?'

It was on the tip of his tongue to say that there was no such thing, because that, more or less, was what he believed. In his experience, a lover scorned or a woman slighted was more often driven to murder by hurt pride than by thwarted passion.

That evening, he and Madame Maigret sat watching television and sipping their little glasses of raspberry liqueur, from the bottle sent to them by his sister-in-law in Alsace.

'What did you think of the film?'

He almost said:

'What film?'

Certainly he had been watching the screen. There had been a lot of movement and bustle and agitation, but if he had been asked to summarize the plot, he could not have done it.

Next morning, with Janvier at the wheel of the car, he arrived at the entrance of the Forensic Laboratory just before ten.

Florentin, looking taller and thinner than ever, was standing on the edge of the pavement with a cigarette dangling from his lips. Beside him was Bonfils, the inspector who had relieved Loutrie.

Florentin gave no sign of having seen the police car draw up. He just stood there with hunched shoulders, utterly dejected, as though he would never again be able to look the world in the face.

The hearse was at the door, and the undertaker's men wheeled the coffin over to it on a hand cart.

Maigret opened the rear door of the car.

'Get in!'

And, turning to Bonfils:

'You can go back to the Quai . . . I'll look after him.'

'Are we ready?' inquired the undertaker's man.

They set off. In the rear mirror, the Chief Superintendent caught sight of a yellow car, which seemed to be following them. It was a cheap, much battered, little open two-seater. Above the windscreen Jean-Luc Bodard's mop of red hair was clearly visible.

They drove in silence towards Ivry, and almost the entire length of the great, sprawling cemetery. The grave was in one of the new extensions, where trees had not yet had time to grow. Lucas had not forgotten to order flowers, as Maigret had asked him, and the young man with red hair had also brought a wreath.

As the coffin was being lowered from the hearse, Florentin buried his face in his hands, his shoulders shaking. Was he really weeping? Not that it meant anything. He had always been able to shed tears to order.

It was to Maigret that the undertaker's man handed the spade, for him to shovel the first sods of earth into the grave. A few minutes later, the two cars were starting up for the journey back.

'The Quai des Orfèvres, sir?'

Maigret nodded. Florentin, in the back of the car, still did not say a word.

When they reached the forecourt of the Quai des Orfèvres, Maigret got out of the car, and said to Janvier:

'You'd better stay with him until Bonfils comes down to take over.'

From the back of the car came an anguished cry:

'I swear to you, Maigret, I didn't kill her!'

Maigret merely shrugged, and walked away slowly, through the glass doors, towards the staircase. He found Bonfils in the Inspectors' Duty Room.

'I've left your customer downstairs ... He's all yours.'

'What shall I do if he insists on walking side-by-side with me?'

'That's up to you, only don't lose sight of him.'

To his surprise, when he went into his office, he found Lapointe waiting for him. He looked worried.

'I've got bad news, sir.'

'Not another murder?'

'No. The concierge has vanished.'

'I gave orders that she should be kept under close watch!'

'Loutrie rang through half an hour ago. He was almost in tears ...'

He was one of the oldest inspectors in the Force, and knew every trick of the trade.

'How did it happen?'

'Loutrie was mounting guard on the pavement opposite the building, when she came out. She had no hat on, and was carrying a shopping-bag.

'She didn't even look round to see if she was being followed. First, she went into the butcher's, and bought an escalope ... They seemed to know her there ...

'Still without looking round, she went on down the Rue Saint-Georges, stopping to go into an Italian grocer's. While she was in there, Loutrie stayed outside, pacing up and down.

'When, after a quarter of an hour or more, she hadn't reappeared, he began to get worried, and went into the shop. It's very long and narrow, and there's another entrance at the back, opening on to the Square d'Orléans and the Rue Taitbout. Needless to say, the bird had flown.

'After he'd spoken to me, Loutrie went back to resume his watch on the building. As he said, there was no point in trying to search the whole district ... Do you think she's done a bunk?'

'I'm quite sure she hasn't.'

Maigret was back at the window, looking out on to the chestnut-trees, and listening to the birds twittering in the branches.

'She didn't murder Joséphine Papet, so why on earth should she try to escape? Especially as she took nothing with her except her shopping-bag, not even a hat!

'She must have been going to meet someone ... I rather suspected she might, after the confrontation yesterday ...

'I was convinced from the start that she had seen the murderer, either when he arrived or when he left, or both ...

'Suppose that, as he was leaving, he saw her there with her nose pressed against the glass, and those extraordinary eyes of hers, staring at him ...'

'I see what you mean!'

'He knew that she was bound to be subjected to questioning. And he, remember, was a regular visitor to Joséphine Papet's flat, and therefore known to the concierge.'

'Do you think he used threats?'

'Threats would cut no ice with a woman of that sort. You saw what she was like yesterday afternoon ... On the other hand, I can't see her being able to resist a bribe ...'

'If she's already had money out of him, why the disappearing trick?'

'Because of the confrontation.'

'I don't understand.'

'The murderer was here in this room ... She saw him ... She had only to say the word for him to be arrested ... But she preferred to say nothing ... It's my belief that she suddenly woke up to the fact that her silence was worth a great deal more than she had been paid ...

'So she decided, this morning, to raise her price ... but she couldn't do much about it with a police inspector at her heels ...

'Get me the hall porter at the Hôtel Scribe.'

As soon as he was through, Maigret grabbed the receiver.

'Hello! Hôtel Scribe? Is that the hall porter? Chief Superintendent Maigret speaking ... How are you, Jean? ... The children all well? ... Good ... Splendid ... I'm interested in one of your regulars, name of Lamotte, Victor Lamotte, yes. I presume his suite is booked by the month? ... Yes, that's what I thought ...

'Put me through to him, will you? ... What's that? ... Did you say yesterday? ... The express to Bordeaux? ... I thought he always stayed until Saturday night ...

'Has anyone been asking for him this morning? You haven't by any chance had an inquiry from a very fat woman, shabbily dressed, carrying a shopping-bag?

'No, I'm perfectly serious ... You're quite sure? ... Oh! well, thanks all the same, Jean.'

He knew the hall porters of all the big hotels in Paris, some ever since they had joined the staff as page-boys.

The Blanc woman had not gone to the Hôtel Scribe, and even if she had done so, she would not have found the wine-grower there.

'Get me his office in the Rue Auber.'

He was determined to leave nothing to chance. The offices in the Rue Auber were shut on Saturdays, but there was one member of the staff in the building, catching up on a backlog of work. He had not set eyes on the boss since two o'clock the previous afternoon.

'Try the offices of Courcel Frères, Ballbearings, in the Boulevard Voltaire.'

No reply. Here, on Saturdays, there was not even a caretaker on duty.

'Try his home in Rouen . . . Don't breathe the word "police", I just want to know if he's in.'

Fernand Courcel occupied the whole of an old house on the Quai de la Bourse, a stone's throw from the Pont Boieldieu.

'May I speak to Monsieur Courcel, please?'

'He's just gone out. This is Madame Courcel speaking . . .'

She had a pleasant, youthful voice.

'Can I take a message?'

'Do you know when he'll be back?'

'He'll be in for lunch . . . We've got people coming . . .'

'I take it he only got back this morning?'

'No, last night . . . Who is that speaking?'

In view of Maigret's injunction, Lapointe judged it wiser to ring off.

'He's just gone out . . . He got back last night . . . He's expected home for lunch . . . They've got people coming . . . His wife sounds charming . . .'

'That only leaves François Paré . . . Try his number in Versailles . . .'

Here, too, a woman's voice answered. She sounded tired and fretful.

'Madame Paré speaking.'

'Is your husband available, please?'

'Who is that?'

'A member of his staff,' said Lapointe, telling the first lie that came into his head.

'Is it important?'

'Why do you ask?'

'Because my husband is in bed . . . When he got back last night, he wasn't feeling well . . . He had a very restless night, so I thought it best to keep him in bed today . . . He works too hard for a man of his age . . .'

The inspector, sensing that she was about to hang up on him, hastily came to the point:

'Has anyone been asking for him this morning?'

'What do you mean?'

'Has anyone called to see him on business?'

'No one at all.'

Without another word, she rang off.

Florentin and *Le Rouquin* had been at the cemetery at the time of Madame Blanc's disappearance, and she had not been in touch with any of the other three suspects.

*

Madame Maigret, sensing that he had enough on his mind already, decided that he was not to be worried further until he had eaten his lunch. It was not until she had poured out his coffee that she ventured to ask:

'Have you seen the paper?'

'I haven't had time.'

There was a morning paper on an occasional table in the sitting-room. She went to fetch it, and handed it to him.

He read the banner headline:

THE MURDER IN THE RUE NOTRE-DAME-DE-LORETTE

And below, two somewhat more informative sub-titles:

> *Mysterious gathering at the Quai des Orfèvres*
> *Chief Superintendent Maigret baffled*

He gave a groan, and went off to fetch his pipe before settling down to read the story.

'Yesterday's edition of this paper carried the full story of the murder committed in a flat in the Rue Notre-Dame-de-Lorette.

'The victim was a young, unmarried woman, Joséphine Papet, occupation unknown.

'We venture to suggest that the killer was probably one of several men who had enjoyed the favours of the murdered girl.

'In spite of the stubborn silence of the Criminal Investigation Department, we are given to understand that a number of persons were summoned to the Quai des Orfèvres yesterday, to attend a meeting which was in the nature of a confrontation. Among those present, we are told, were several men of standing and influence.

'Our attention has been drawn to the fact that one of the

123

suspects, in particular, was in the flat at the time of the murder, and the question arises: Is he the guilty man, or merely a witness to the crime?

'It is a source of some embarrassment to Chief Superintendent Maigret, who is personally in charge of the case, that the man in question, Léon F . . . . . , is an old school friend.

'Can this be the reason why, in spite of the evidence against him, the man is still at large? It seems hard to credit . . .'

Maigret, grinding his teeth, crushed the paper up into a ball.

'Idiots!' he muttered.

Was it possible that one of his own inspectors had in all innocence committed an indiscretion, led on by the wily gentlemen of the press? He was all too familiar with the methods of newspapermen. They would certainly have left no stone unturned. There was no question but that they must have interviewed the concierge, and it was not unlikely that she had been a good deal more forthcoming with them than with the police.

There was also the bearded painter, Florentin's next-door neighbour in the Boulevard Rochechouart.

'Does it matter so much?'

He shrugged. If the truth were known, the only effect of the article was to make him more than ever reluctant to act precipitately.

Before leaving the Quai, he had received the ballistics report from Gastinne-Renette. This confirmed the opinion of the police surgeon. The bullet was enormous, of twelve-millimetre calibre. There were very few in existence, and it could only have been fired from an obsolete revolver of Belgian make, which would not be obtainable from an ordinary gunsmith.

The writer of the report had commented that it would be impossible to fire such a weapon with any degree of accuracy.

There was no doubt that the murder weapon was the old gun from Josée's bedside table. Where was it now? It would be a waste of time to search for it. It could be anywhere, in the river, in some drain or other, on a rubbish dump, or in a field in the country.

What could have possessed the murderer to remove so compromising an object, instead of leaving it where it was?

124

Possibly, in his haste to get away, he had not had time to remove all trace of fingerprints.

If that were so, then he would not have had time, either, to wipe his fingerprints from the surfaces he had touched in the flat.

Yet the fact remained that all the surfaces in the bedroom, including the door handles, had been wiped clean.

Was it, therefore, to be concluded that Florentin was lying, when he claimed that the murderer had stayed in the flat for a quarter of an hour after the shot had been fired?

Was it not more likely that Florentin himself had wiped away the prints?

Whatever Maigret's line of reasoning, it always led back to Florentin. He was the obvious suspect. But the Chief Superintendent distrusted the obvious.

All the same, he was ashamed of himself for allowing Florentin so much latitude. It almost smacked of favouritism, he felt. Had he not, perhaps, been unconsciously influenced by a sort of loyalty to his own youth?

'It's perfectly ridiculous!' he exclaimed aloud.

'Were you really such friends?'

'I should have said not ... I used to find all that clowning rather irritating.'

He did not mention the fact that he used sometimes to go into the shop just to catch a glimpse of Florentin's sister. It almost made him blush, even now.

'See you later.'

She put up her face to be kissed.

'Will you be in to dinner?'

'I hope so.'

He had not noticed that it had started to rain. His wife caught him up on the stairs, and gave him his umbrella.

He boarded a bus on the corner of the Boulevard, and stood on the platform, swaying with the motion of the vehicle, and gazing absently at the people hurrying to and fro along the pavements. What queer cattle human beings were, ready to break into a run at the slightest provocation! Where did they think they were going? What was all the rush for?

'If I'm no further forward by Monday, I'll put him under

lock and key,' he promised himself, as a sop to his conscience.

He put up his umbrella, and walked from the Châtelet to the Quai des Orfèvres. The wind was blowing in squally gusts, driving the rain full into his face. This was what he used to refer to as 'wet water' when he was a child.

No sooner was he in his office than there was a knock at the door, and Loutrie came in.

'Bonfils has taken over from me,' he said. 'She's back.'

'What time did she get in?'

'Twenty past twelve . . . I saw her coming down the street, as cool as you please, carrying her shopping-bag . . .'

'Was it full?'

'A good deal fuller and heavier than it was this morning . . . She didn't even deign to look at me as she went past. I think she was trying to needle me. She made straight for the lodge, and took down the sign saying: "Concierge at work on staircase".'

Maigret paced back and forth between the window and the door at least half a dozen times. Then, abruptly, he halted. He had come to a decision.

'Is Lapointe there?'

'Yes.'

'Tell him to wait for me. I won't be a minute.'

He took a key from his drawer, the one that opened the communicating door between his department and the Palais de Justice. He made his way down several long corridors and up a dark staircase to the Examining Magistrate's offices. He knocked at the door.

Most of the offices in this part of the building were empty and silent. He was not very hopeful of finding Judge Page still at work on a Saturday afternoon.

'Come in,' said a voice, sounding a long way off.

Maigret found the judge, covered in dust, in the little window-less room adjoining his office, struggling to get things into some sort of order.

'Would you believe it, Maigret, there are documents here, two years old or more, that have never been filed. It will take me months to clear up the mountain of papers left behind by my predecessor.'

'I've come to ask you to sign a search warrant.'

'Just give me time to wash my hands.'

The nearest washbasin was at the far end of the corridor. Maigret warmed to him. A thoroughly decent, conscientious chap.

'Any new developments?'

'I've had trouble with the concierge. That woman knows a great deal, I'm sure of it . . . Yesterday, when I had them all together, she was the only one who didn't turn a hair. What's more, I believe she's the only one, apart from the murderer himself, who knows who did it.'

'Why won't she talk? Is it just because she looks upon the police as her natural enemies?'

'I don't think that would be enough to keep her quiet, considering the risk . . . It wouldn't have surprised me if the killer had tried to get rid of her . . . In fact, with that possibility in mind, I've put a watch on the building . . .

'It's my belief that she's been paid to keep her mouth firmly shut, though I don't know how much . . .

'As soon as the crucial importance of her evidence was brought home to her, she must have realized that she hadn't been paid enough . . .

'So this morning she gave my inspector the slip with all the cunning of a professional . . . She set the scene first by going into the butcher's, so that my man naturally assumed that she was just doing her ordinary shopping, and then she went into the grocer's . . . He, of course, suspected nothing, and waited outside for her, for a quarter of an hour, only to discover that the shop had two entrances, and that she'd slipped out by the back way.'

'Do you know where she went?'

'Florentin was with me at the cemetery at Ivry, and so was Jean-Luc Bodard . . .'

'Did she call on any of the others?'

'Well, she certainly didn't see any of them. Lamotte went back to Bordeaux yesterday on the evening express . . . Courcel is in Rouen, and was giving a luncheon party. As for Paré, he's in bed ill, and his wife is worrying about him, for a change . . .'

'Whose name do you want on the search warrant?'

'Madame Blanc . . . the concierge . . .'

The judge went over to his clerk's table, and took a warrant from the drawer. He filled it in, signed and stamped it.

'I wish you luck.'

'Thanks.'

'Incidentally, don't worry your head about all that stuff in the papers . . . No one who knows you . . .'

'Most kind of you.'

A few minutes later, he was driving away from the Quai des Orfèvres, with Lapointe at the wheel. The traffic was heavy, and everyone seemed even more in a hurry than usual. It was always the same on a Saturday. In spite of the rain and the wind, they couldn't wait to get out of town, onto the motorways, into the country.

For once in a way, Lapointe had no trouble in parking. There was a convenient space just across the road from the house. The lingerie shop was shut. The shoe shop was still open, but there was no one in it. The proprietor was standing in the doorway, gloomily watching the rain pouring down.

'What are we looking for, sir?'

'Anything we can make use of, but chiefly money.'

For the first time, Maigret found Madame Blanc sitting down inside the lodge. She was wearing a pair of steel-rimmed spectacles on the end of her bulbous nose, and reading the early edition of the afternoon paper.

Maigret went in, followed by Lapointe.

'Have you wiped your feet?'

And as they did not reply, she muttered:

'What do you want this time?'

Maigret handed her the search warrant. She read it through carefully, twice.

'I don't know what it means. What are you going to do?'

'Search.'

'You mean you're going to go through all my things?'

'I do apologize!'

'I'm not sure I oughtn't to get a lawyer.'

'If you do, it will only suggest that you have something to hide . . . Keep an eye on her, Lapointe, and see that she doesn't touch anything.'

128

Against one wall of the lodge was a Henri II-style dresser. The top half was a cupboard with glass doors, in which were displayed some tumblers, a water-jug, and a pottery coffee set decorated in a bold flower-pattern.

In the right-hand drawer there were knives, forks and spoons, a corkscrew, and three napkin rings of various shapes and sizes. The cutlery had once been silver-plated, but was now so worn that it looked more like brass.

The left-hand drawer proved more interesting. It was stuffed with papers and photographs. One of the photographs was of a young couple, presumably Monsieur and Madame Blanc, though she was scarcely recognizable. It must have been taken when she was about twenty-five. Although, even at that age, she was plump, no one could have foreseen that she would grow into the huge mountain of flesh that she was today. As for Monsieur Blanc, at whom she was actually smiling in the picture, his chief distinguishing feature was a fair moustache.

Neatly folded in an envelope was a list of the tenants, with the rents they paid, and, under a stack of postcards, a post-office savings book.

It went back many years. At the beginning, the sums deposited were small, ten or twenty francs at a time. Later, she had got into the habit of saving fifty francs a month regularly, except for January, when the annual tips from the tenants raised the sum to between a hundred and a hundred and fifty francs.

The total amounted to eight thousand, three hundred and twenty-two francs, and a few centimes.

There were no very recent entries. The last was a fortnight old.

'Much good may it do you!'

Ignoring her, he went on with his search. In the lower half of the dresser there was a dinner service, and, beside it, a pile of folded check tablecloths.

He lifted the velvet cloth draped over the round table, to see if there was a drawer underneath, but he found none.

To his left there was a television set on a table. He opened the drawer of the table, but found nothing except a few bits of string, and some nails and drawing-pins.

He went into the room at the back, which served a double purpose as kitchen and bedroom. The bed stood in an alcove, concealed by a shabby curtain.

He began with the bedside table and found, in the drawer, a rosary, a prayer book and a sprig of rosemary. For a moment, he could not imagine what the rosemary was doing there, then he remembered the custom of sprinkling aromatic herbs with holy water as a sign of family mourning, and could only suppose that she had kept it in memory of one of her parents.

It was hard to think of that woman as ever having been a wife to anyone, but, undoubtedly, she had once been somebody's child, like everyone else.

He had known others like her, men and women, whom life had so hardened that they had almost been turned into monsters. For years now, she had been confined, by day and by night, to these two dark, airless rooms, with scarcely more freedom of movement than she would have had in a prison cell.

As for any communication with the outside world, she saw no one except the postman, and the tenants going in and out.

Every morning, regardless of her weight and swollen legs, she had to clean out the lift, and sweep the stairs from top to bottom.

And if, tomorrow or the next day, she should no longer be able to work, what then?

And here he was, harassing her. He felt ashamed of himself. He opened the door of the little refrigerator. Inside was half an escalope, the remains of an omelette, two slices of ham and a few vegetables, no doubt those she had bought that morning.

On the kitchen table stood a half-bottle of wine. It only remained now for him to search the cupboard. Here he found nothing but underclothes and dresses, a corset and a pair of elastic stockings.

It was painful to him now to have to continue the search, but he was unwilling to admit defeat. She was not the woman to be fobbed off with promises. If anyone had bribed her to keep her mouth shut, he must have paid her there and then, in cash.

He went back into the lodge and, on seeing him, her eyes flickered, revealing a twinge of anxiety that she was unable to hide.

It was enough to tell him that there was nothing for him to find in the kitchen. Very slowly, he surveyed the lodge. Where was it that he had failed to look?

He made a sudden dive for the television set, on top of which were stacked a few periodicals. One of these was devoted to radio and television programmes, with accompanying articles and photographs.

No sooner had he picked it up than he knew that he had won.

It fell open of its own accord at the place where she had slipped in three five-hundred franc and seven hundred franc notes.

Two thousand two hundred francs. The five-hundred franc notes were brand new.

'I'm entitled to my savings, aren't I?'

'I've seen your post-office book, don't forget.'

'What of it? Who says I have to put all my eggs in one basket? I might find myself needing ready money at any time.'

'Two thousand two hundred francs isn't exactly petty cash!'

'That's my business. Just try making trouble for me, and see where it gets you . . .'

'You're a good deal cleverer than you make yourself out to be, Madame Blanc . . . I have a shrewd suspicion that you were expecting me today, search warrant and all . . . If you had deposited the money in the post office, the transaction would have been entered in your book, and I could not have failed to be struck by the unusually large sum, and the date . . .

'You could have put the money in a drawer or a cupboard, or have sewn it into your mattress, but no – have you by any chance read the works of Edgar Allan Poe? – you chose to slip the notes between the pages of a magazine . . .'

'I'm not a thief.'

'I'm not suggesting that you are. In fact, I don't believe you asked for this money. It's my opinion that the murderer, seeing you at the door of the lodge as he was going out, came in and offered it to you, before you even knew that a murder had been committed in the building . . .

'There was no need for him to volunteer any explanation . . .

He had only to ask you to forget you had seen him on that occasion ...

'You must have known who he was, otherwise he would have had nothing to fear from you ...'

'I have nothing to say.'

'Yesterday, when you saw him in my office, you realized that he was a very frightened man, and that the person he was afraid of was none other than yourself, you being the only one in a position to give him away.

'It didn't take you long to work out that a man, especially if he is rich, probably values his liberty a good deal higher than two thousand two hundred francs. So you decided to seek him out this morning, and see how much more you could get.'

As on the previous day, her lips twitched in a faint ghost of a smile.

'You found no one there ... You had forgotten that today was Saturday.'

The expression of the woman's bloated face, at once stubborn and enigmatic, did not change.

'I'm saying nothing. Beat me up if you like ...'

'I'd rather not, thank you. We shall meet again. Let's go, Lapointe.'

And the two men went out, and got into the little black car.

Chapter Seven

Sunday was a gloomy day, with a glimmer of pale sunlight filtering through the massed banks of cloud. In spite of this, they followed the crowds streaming out into the country for the day.

When they had first bought the car, it had been their intention to use it only for going to and from their little house in Meung-sur-Loire and for touring on holiday. They had, in fact, been to Meung three or four times, but it was really too far to go there and back in a day. There was no one to look after the house in their absence, which meant that Madame Maigret barely managed to dust around, and prepare a scratch meal, before it was time to leave.

It was about ten in the morning when they set out.

They had agreed that it would be best to keep off the motorways.

Unfortunately, thousands of other Parisians had come to the same conclusion, and the little country roads that ought to have been so delightful were as crowded as the Champs-Elysées.

They were looking for an attractive little inn, with an appetizing bill of fare. They knew from long experience that most of the wayside inns were always full to overflowing, and that those which were not served digusting food, but this did not deter them from trying again, Sunday after Sunday.

It was the same as with the television set. When they had first bought it, they had vowed that they would only look at programmes that really interested them. At the end of a fortnight, Madame Maigret had taken to laying the table in such a way as to enable them both to face the screen while they were eating.

They did not bicker in the car, as so many married couples do. All the same, Madame Maigret was very tense at the wheel. She had only recently passed her driving test, and was still lacking in self-confidence.

'Why don't you pass them?'

'There's a double white line.'

On this particular Sunday, Maigret scarcely said a word. He sat slumped in his seat, puffing at his pipe, his eyes fixed on the road ahead, glowering. In spirit, he was in the Rue Notre-Dame-de-Lorette, reconstructing the events leading up to the death of Joséphine Papet in as many different ways as he could think of.

He considered each hypothetical reconstruction in turn, having built it up with great attention to detail, even to the extent of inventing appropriate dialogue. Then he tested its validity from every angle. Each time, just when it was beginning to seem impregnable, some flaw would appear, and he was back where he started.

It was like trying to solve a chess problem, with the people involved as the pieces, which could be moved here or there to produce this or that result.

Time and again, he set up the problem, rearranging the pieces in different positions, sometimes removing one or more pieces, sometimes bringing new ones into play.

They stopped for lunch at an inn. The food was no better and no worse than that to be had at any railway-station buffet. The only difference was the size of the bill.

They set out for a walk in the woods, but were discouraged by mud underfoot and a steady downpour of rain.

They got home early, to a dinner of cold meat and Russian salad. Maigret was so restless that his wife suggested they should go to the cinema, which they did.

At nine o'clock sharp on Monday morning, he was in his office. The rain had stopped, and the sun, though not very bright, was shining.

The reports of the inspectors who had taken it in turn to keep watch on Florentin were on his desk.

Florentin had spent the Saturday evening in a brasserie in the Boulevard de Clichy. This, it seemed, was not one of his usual haunts, as no one there appeared to recognize him.

He had ordered a half-pint, and taken it over to a table, next to a party of four regulars, who were obviously old friends, and who were immersed in a game of *belote*. He had sat for some time with his elbow on the table and his chin in his hand, following the game in a desultory way.

At about ten, one of the card-players, a weedy little man, who had been chattering away ceaselessly the whole evening, suddenly said:

'I'm sorry, you fellows, but I'll have to be going ... Her ladyship will roast me alive if I'm late home, especially as I'm going out fishing tomorrow.'

The others pressed him to stay, but to no avail. When he had gone, they had looked about them for someone to make up the four.

One of them had asked Florentin, in a strong southern accent: 'Do you play?'

'I'll join you with pleasure.'

Thereupon he had moved over to the vacant seat at the table and stayed there, playing *belote* until midnight, while poor Dieudonné, whose shift it was, sat gloomily slumped in a corner.

And Florentin, always the gentleman, had stood drinks all round, thus making a substantial dent in the hundred francs that Maigret had given him.

134

He had gone straight home from the brasserie and, with a final conspiratorial wink at Dieudonné, had retired to bed.

He had slept late, and had not gone into the tobacconist's for his breakfast of croissants dipped in coffee until after ten. Dieudonné, by that time, had been relieved by Lagrume, and Florentin had looked him up and down with interest, as much as to say: 'This is a new one on me!'

Lagrume was the gloomiest of all the inspectors, and not without reason, as he never seemed to be without a cold for more than a couple of months in the year, besides which he was afflicted with flat feet, which gave him endless trouble, and caused him to walk in a most peculiar way.

From the tobacconist's, Florentin had gone into a betting shop, where he had invested in a ticket for the Tote treble, after which he had sauntered off down the Boulevard des Batignolles. He had gone past the Hôtel Beauséjour without so much as a glance. There was no reason to suppose that he knew that *Le Rouquin* lived there.

He had lunched in a restaurant in the Place des Ternes, then, as on the previous Friday, had gone into a cinema.

What was to become of this tall, thin man with the expressive, indiarubber face, when the Chief Superintendent's hundred francs were exhausted?

He had not met a single person he knew. No one at all had tried to get in touch with him. He had gone into a self-service bar for his dinner, and then straight home to bed.

As to the Rue Notre-Dame-de-Lorette, there was nothing of any interest to report from there either. Madame Blanc had emerged from the lodge only to sweep the stairs and put out the dustbins.

Some of the tenants had attended Mass, others had gone out for the day. All in all, it had been a boring and frustrating day for the two inspectors on watch outside in the street, which on a Sunday had been virtually deserted.

Maigret was devoting this Monday morning to rereading all the reports on the case, in particular those of the police surgeon, the ballistics expert, Moers and Criminal Records.

Janvier, after a discreet knock on the door, came in, looking fresh, cheerful and ready for anything.

'How do you feel, sir?'

'Rotten.'

'Didn't you enjoy your day out?'

'No.'

Janvier could not help smiling. He was well acquainted with this mood, and, as a rule, it was a good sign. It was Maigret's way, when he was working on a case, to soak everything up like a sponge, absorbing into himself people and things, even of the most trivial sort, as well as impressions of which he was perhaps barely conscious.

It was generally when he was close to saturation point that he was at his most disgruntled.

'How did you spend the day?'

'We went to my sister-in-law's, my wife and I and the kids ... There was a fair in the market-place, and the children spent a small fortune shooting at clay pigeons ...'

Maigret got up and started pacing the room. A buzzer sounded summoning Heads of Departments to the weekly conference for the exchange of information.

'They can perfectly well get along without me,' grumbled Maigret.

He was in no mood to answer the questions that his Chief would undoubtedly ask, nor to give him advance warning of his plans, which were anyway somewhat nebulous. He was still feeling his way.

'If only that frightful woman could be made to talk!'

The huge, phlegmatic concierge was still in the forefront of his mind.

'There are times when I regret the abolition of third-degree methods. I'd like to see just how long she'd hold out.'

He didn't seriously mean it, of course. It was just his way of letting off steam.

'What about you? Have you any ideas?'

Janvier never liked it when Maigret asked him pointblank for his opinion. Somewhat hesitantly, he ventured:

'I think ...'

'Come on, out with it! You think I'm barking up the wrong tree, is that it?'

'Not at all. It's just that I have a notion that Florentin knows

136

even more than she does ... And Florentin is in a much weaker position ... He's got nothing to look forward to ... If he's able to pick up a few sous here and there by loafing around Montmartre, he'll be lucky ...'

Maigret looked at him with interest.

'Go and fetch him.'

As he was leaving, Maigret called him back.

'And you'd better pick up the concierge from the Rue Notre-Dame-de-Lorette at the same time, while you're about it. She'll raise Cain, but take no notice, use force if necessary ...'

Janvier smiled. He could not quite see himself coming to blows with that great battering-ram of a woman, who was at least twice his weight.

Soon after he left, Maigret was on the telephone to the Ministry of Public Works.

'I'd be obliged if you would put me through to Monsieur Paré.'

'Hold on, please.'

'Hello! Is that Monsieur Paré?'

'Monsieur Paré isn't in today ... His wife has just rung through ... He's not at all well ...'

Maigret rang off, and dialled the Versailles number.

'Madame Paré?'

'Who's speaking?'

'Chief Superintendent Maigret. How is your husband?'

'Not at all well ... The doctor has just left ... He's afraid he may be on the verge of a nervous breakdown.'

'It wouldn't be possible for me to talk to him, would it?'

'The doctor recommends complete rest.'

'Does he seem worried? Has he asked to see the newspapers?'

'No ... He's just withdrawn into himself ... I can scarcely get a word out of him ...'

'Thank you.'

Next he rang the Hôtel Scribe.

'Is that you, Jean? Maigret here ... Is Monsieur Victor Lamotte back from Bordeaux yet? ... So he's left for his office already, has he? ...Thanks.'

He dialled the number of Lamotte's office in the Rue Auber.

'Chief Superintendent Maigret speaking. Would you put me through to Monsieur Lamotte, please?'

There was a great deal of clicking on the line. Apparently it was necessary to go through a whole hierarchy of subordinates to get to the great man himself.

At long last, a voice said dryly:

'Yes?'

'Maigret here.'

'So I was told.'

'Will you be in your office all morning?'

'I really can't say.'

'I'd be obliged if you'd stay there until you hear from me again.'

'I'd better warn you that, if I'm summoned to your office again, I shall have my lawyer with me this time.'

'You'll be perfectly within your rights.'

Next, Maigret tried the Boulevard Voltaire, but Courcel had not yet arrived.

'He never gets in before eleven, and sometimes he doesn't come in at all on a Monday. Would you care to speak to the assistant manager?'

'No, that's all right.'

Pacing up and down the room with his hands behind his back, and glaring from time to time at the clock, Maigret once again reviewed all the possibilities that he had considered in the car on the previous day.

He eliminated each in turn, until only one was left. This, subject to the tying up of a few loose ends, provided the answer.

Looking more than a little shamefaced, he opened the cupboard in which he always kept a bottle of brandy. It was not intended for his own use, but as a restorative, to be produced in case of need, as when, for instance, someone he was questioning collapsed after making a confession.

He could not claim to be in a state of collapse. It was not he who was going to have to make a confession. All the same, he took a long swig straight out of the bottle.

Having done so, he felt thoroughly ashamed of himself. Once more, he glanced impatiently at the clock. Then, at long last, he heard footsteps in the corridor, and a voice raised in furious anger, which he recognized as that of Madame Blanc.

He crossed to the door, and opened it.

Florentin, though visibly uneasy, attempted, as usual, to laugh it off.

'I'm beginning to look on this place as quite a home from home!'

As for the woman:

'I'm a free citizen, and I demand . . .' she thundered.

'Take her away and lock her up somewhere, Janvier . . . You'd better stay with her, but take care she doesn't scratch your eyes out.'

And, turning to Florentin:

'Take a seat.'

'I'd rather stand.'

'And I'd rather you sat down.'

'Oh! well, if you insist . . .'

He made a face, just as he used to in the old days, after an altercation with one of the masters, trying to restore his self-esteem by raising a laugh.

Maigret went into the other room to fetch Lapointe. He had been present at most of the earlier interviews, and was familiar with all the details of the case.

Taking his time over it, the Chief Superintendent filled his pipe, lit it, and gingerly pressed down the smouldering tobacco with his thumb.

'I take it, Florentin, that you have nothing to add to your statement?'

'I've told you all I know.'

'No.'

'It's the truth, I swear it.'

'And I know it's a pack of lies, from start to finish.'

'Are you calling me a liar?'

'You always were a liar. Even at school . . .'

'It was only for a laugh . . .'

'Agreed . . . But this is no laughing matter.'

He looked his old school friend straight in the eye, with a very grave expression, in which there was something of contempt and also something of pity. But probably more of pity than contempt.

'What's to become of you?'

Florentin shrugged.

'How should I know?'

'You're fifty-three.'

'Fifty-four . . . I'm a year older than you are. I had to repeat in the sixth form.'

'You're getting a bit past it . . . It won't be easy to find another Josée.'

'I shan't even try.'

'Your antique business is a flop . . . You have no skills, no training, no professional experience . . . And you're too seedy to work the confidence racket any longer . . .'

It was cruel but it had to be said.

'You're a miserable wreck, Florentin.'

'Everything always went sour on me . . . I know I'm a failure, but . . .'

'But you won't admit defeat, will you? You're still hoping . . . what for, for heaven's sake?'

'I don't know . . .'

'Right. That's settled then. And now the time has come for me to take a weight off your mind.'

There was a long pause, during which Maigret looked searchingly into the face of his old school friend. Then he came out with it:

'I know you didn't kill Josée.'

Chapter Eight

It came as much less of a surprise to Florentin than to Lapointe. He shot up in his seat, aghast, with his pencil poised in mid-air, and gaped at his chief.

'But that doesn't mean you've got anything to crow about. Your conduct has been far from blameless . . .'

'But you yourself admit . . .'

'I admit that, on that one point, you've told the truth, which, I must confess, is more than I'd have expected of you . . .'

'I can explain . . .'

140

'I'd rather you didn't keep interrupting. On Wednesday last, probably round about a quarter past three, as you say, someone rang the doorbell of the flat . . .'

'You see!'

'Oh! Do shut up . . . As usual, not knowing who it might be, you made a bolt for the bedroom . . . As you and Josée were not expecting any callers, you listened . . .'

'I take it that one or other of her lovers did occasionally change the time of his visit?'

'In that case, they would always telephone . . .'

'Didn't they ever turn up unexpectedly?'

'Very rarely.'

'And on those rare occasions, you hid in the clothes closet. On Wednesday, however, you were not in the clothes closet but in the bedroom . . . You recognized the voice of the caller, and you took fright . . . Why? Because you realized that it wasn't Josée he had come to see, but you.'

Florentin froze . . . It was clear that he simply could not make out what process of reasoning had led his old school friend to this conclusion.

'I have proof, you see, that he went up to the flat on Wednesday . . . Because the gentleman in question, having just committed a murder, panicked and tried to buy the concierge's silence with the sum of two thousand two hundred francs, which was all he had on him at the time . . .'

'But you yourself have admitted that I'm innocent!'

'Of the murder . . . But that isn't to say that you weren't indirectly the cause of it . . . If one can talk in terms of morality where you're concerned, one could say that you were morally responsible.'

'I don't understand.'

'Yes you do.'

Maigret stood up. He never could sit still for long. Florentin followed him with his eyes, as he paced up and down the room.

'Joséphine Papet had fallen in love with someone new . . .'

'You surely don't mean *Le Rouquin*?'

'Yes.'

'It was just a passing fancy . . . He'd never have agreed to her terms . . . living with her, skulking in cupboards, keeping out of the way when necessary . . . He's young . . . He can get all the girls he wants . . .'

'That doesn't alter the fact that Josée was in love with him, or that she'd had enough of you . . .'

'How do you know? You're only guessing.'

'She said so herself.'

'Who to? Not to you. You never saw her alive.'

'To Jean-Luc Bodard.'

'And you really believe every word that fellow says?'

'He had no cause to lie to me.'

'What about me, then?'

'You faced the risk of a longish prison sentence . . . probably as much as two years, having regard to your previous convictions.'

Florentin took this more calmly. Although he had not realized just how much Maigret had discovered about his past, he had heard enough to be prepared for the worst.

'To get back to the Wednesday caller . . . The reason you were so badly shaken when you recognized his voice was that, some days or weeks earlier, you had attempted to blackmail one of Josée's lovers.

'Needless to say, you picked on the one who seemed to you the most vulnerable, in other words the one who set the greatest store by his reputation. You raised the subject of his letters . . .

'How much did you get out of him?'

Florentin hung his head, looking very sorry for himself.

'Nothing.'

'You mean, he wouldn't play?'

'No, but he asked for a few days' grace.'

'How much were you asking for?'

'Fifty thousand . . . I needed at least that . . . I wanted to make a clean break, to get right away, and start life afresh elsewhere . . .'

'So I was right. Josée was trying to ease you out as gently as possible.'

'Maybe she was . . . She certainly wasn't the same, any more . . .'

'Now you're beginning to talk sense. Keep it up, and I'll do my best to see that you're let off as lightly as possible in the circumstances.'

'Would you really do that for me?'

'What a fool you are!' muttered Maigret in an undertone, not intending Florentin to hear. But he did hear, and flushed crimson to the roots of his hair.

It was no more than the truth. There were literally thousands of people like him living in Paris, subsisting on the border-line of crime by more or less openly exploiting the naïvety or cupidity of their fellow-men.

Such people were always full of grandiose schemes, the realization of which was thwarted only by the lack of a few thousand or a few hundred thousand francs.

Most of them managed, in the end, to cheat some mug out of his money. And then there would follow a brief spell of prosperity, of fast cars and expensive restaurants.

When the money was spent, they were back where they started, and the whole laborious process would begin again. And yet, scarcely one in ten of such people ever saw the inside of a corrective training establishment or a gaol.

Florentin was the exception. All his schemes had come to nothing, and the last had proved the most disastrous of all.

'Now, will you tell the rest of the story, or would you rather I did?'

'I'd rather leave it to you.'

'The visitor asks to see you. He knows you are in the flat, because he's made it his business to find out from the concierge. He is unarmed. He's not of a particularly jealous disposition, and he has no wish to kill anyone . . .

'All the same, he is in a highly excitable frame of mind. Josée, nervous on your account, denies that you are in the flat, and claims to have no idea where you are.

'He goes into the dining-room, making for the bedroom. You retreat into the bathroom with the intention of hiding in the closet.'

'But I never got that far.'

'Right . . . He marches you back into the bedroom.'

'Shouting at the top of his voice that I was despicable, beneath contempt,' interposed Florentin, bitterly. 'And with her there, listening.'

'She knows nothing about the blackmail business . . . She doesn't understand what's going on . . . You tell her to keep out of it . . . But, in spite of everything – because you feel it's your last chance – you still cling to the hope of getting that fifty thousand francs . . .'

'I'm not sure of anything any more . . . It was all so confused . . . I don't think any of us quite knew what was happening . . . There was Josée, pleading with us to calm down . . . The man was in a furious temper . . . I'd refused to give him back his letters. When he saw that I meant it, he pulled open the bedside table drawer, and grabbed the revolver . . .

'Josée began screaming . . . I admit, I was scared, too . . .'

'So you took shelter behind her?'

'I swear to you, Maigret, that it was sheer accident that she was hit . . .

'You could see the man didn't know the first thing about handling firearms . . . He kept waving the gun about . . . I was actually on the point of giving him back his blasted letters, when it went off . . .

'He looked utterly stunned . . . He made a queer little gurgling noise in his throat, and bolted out of the room.'

'Had he still got the revolver?'

'I presume so . . . At any rate, when I looked for it, it had gone . . . As soon as I bent down to look at Josée, I knew she was dead . . .'

'Why didn't you call the police?'

'I don't know . . .'

'I do . . . You were thinking about the forty-eight thousand francs she kept in a biscuit tin, the tin you wrapped in newspaper and took back to your workshop . . . Incidentally, it was very careless of you to use that day's morning paper . . .

'As you were leaving, you remembered the letters, and stuffed them in your pocket . . .

'At last, you had riches within your grasp . . . For the man whom you had blackmailed by threatening to expose an affair with a woman had now committed a murder . . .'

'What on earth put that idea into your head?'

144

'The fact that you removed the fingerprints on the furniture and door handles. It wouldn't have mattered if your prints had been found – even you never attempted to deny that you were in the flat. No, it was the other man's prints that you were anxious to get rid of, because once he was identified and caught, he could be of no further use to you.'

Maigret returned to his chair, sat down heavily, and refilled his pipe.

'You went back to your place, and hid the biscuit tin on top of the wardrobe ... For the time being, you forgot about the letters in your pocket. Then, suddenly, you thought of me, your old school friend, who would surely protect you, at least from rough handling ... You always were something of a physical coward ... Remember? ... There was that kid Bambois ... As I recall, he only had to threaten to twist your arm to have you shaking in your shoes ...'

'Now, you're being cruel.'

'Look who's talking! If you hadn't been such a louse, Josée would be alive today.'

'I'll never forgive myself, as long as I live.'

'That won't bring her back ... Anyway, it's entirely between you and your conscience. You came here with every intention of leading me up the garden path, but you'd scarcely opened your mouth before I realized there was something wrong somewhere.

'I had the same feeling in the flat ... The whole set-up was phony. It was as though I'd been handed a tangled ball of string, but couldn't find the end that would help me straighten it out.

'Of all the people concerned in this case, the concierge intrigued me most. She's a great deal tougher than you are.'

'She never could stand the sight of me.'

'Any more than you could stand the sight of her. By keeping her mouth shut about the caller, not only did she stand to gain two thousand two hundred francs, but she had you just where she wanted you. As to your dive into the Seine, that was sheer folly. If it hadn't been for that, I might never have thought of the letters ...

'It was clear from the start that you had no intention of drowning. No one who could swim as you can would attempt

145

suicide by throwing himself off the Pont-Neuf when it was crawling with people, knowing, moreover, that he would hit the water within a few feet of a boat moored to the bank.

'You suddenly remembered those letters in your pocket ... One of my men was close on your heels ... At any moment, you might be searched ...'

'I never dreamed you'd guess ...'

'It's my job, and I've been at it thirty-five years,' muttered Maigret.

'The secret is never to let oneself be taken in,' he added, and went out to have a word with Lucas.

When he came back into his office, he found all the stuffing knocked out of Florentin. He was just a long, lean husk of a man, with hollowed cheeks and sunken eyes.

'Am I right in thinking that I shall be charged with demanding money with menaces?'

'That depends ...'

'On what?'

'On the Examining Magistrate ... And, to some extent, on me ... Don't forget that, by obliterating the fingerprints, you were obstructing the police, and laying yourself open to a further charge of being an accessory after the fact ...'

'You wouldn't do that to me, surely?'

'I'll have a word with the judge ...'

'I could probably survive a year or, at most, two in gaol, but if it's a question of being shut up for years, then I'll have to be carried out feet first ... I have heart trouble, as it is ...'

No doubt he would do his utmost to be allowed to serve his sentence in the infirmary of La Santé Prison. And this man had once been the boy Maigret had known in Moulins, who had kept them all in fits of laughter. He could always be relied on to brighten up a dull lesson, with the whole class egging him on.

And they always had egged him on, knowing how much he delighted in thinking up new practical jokes, and displaying himself in an infinite number of different guises.

The clown ... there had been that time when he had pretended to drown in the Nièvre. They had spent a quarter of an hour searching for him, and found him, at last, hiding in a clump of reeds to which he had swum under water.

146

'What are we waiting for?' he asked, suddenly anxious again.

It was certainly a relief to him to have got it over, but he was by no means confident that his old friend might not, even now, have a change of heart.

There was a knock at the door, and old Joseph came in and handed a visiting card to Maigret.

'Show him up ... And go and ask Janvier to bring in the woman.'

He would have given anything for a long, cool, glass of beer, or even another nip of brandy.

'Allow me to introduce my lawyer, Maître Bourdon.'

One of the leading lights of the legal profession, a former President of the French Bar, whose name had been put forward for membership of the Academy.

With icy dignity, Victor Lamotte, dragging his foot a little, crossed the room and sat down. He scarcely glanced at Florentin.

'I presume, Chief Superintendent, that you have good and sufficient reasons for insisting on the presence of my client here today? I understand that on Saturday last, also, he was summoned to attend a meeting here, and I should warn you that, on my advice, he reserves his position as to the legality of those proceedings ...'

'Won't you sit down, Maître?' said Maigret tersely.

Janvier propelled Madame Blanc into the room. She seemed much agitated. Then she caught sight of the lame man, and froze.

'Come in, Madame Blanc. Please sit down.'

She had been taken completely unaware, or so it seemed.

'Who is that?' she asked, pointing to Maître Bourdon.

'Your friend Monsieur Lamotte's lawyer.'

'Have you arrested him?'

Her protuberant eyes seemed more prominent than ever.

'Not yet, but I intend to do so in a moment. Do you identify him as the man who, on Wednesday last, came down from Mademoiselle Papet's flat, and paid you two thousand two hundred francs to keep your mouth shut?'

She was silent, her lips pressed together in a straight, hard line.

'You were very ill-advised to give her that money, Monsieur Lamotte. So large a sum was bound to put ideas into her head.

147

It didn't escape her that if her silence was worth that much to you before she had even asked for anything, its real value was probably higher . . .'

'I haven't the least idea what you're talking about.'

The lawyer was frowning.

'Let me explain how I arrived at the conclusion that it was you, rather than any of the other suspects, who were guilty of murder . . .

'I have kept Madame Blanc under observation for several days. On Saturday, she managed to shake off the inspector who was following her, by going into a shop and slipping out through the back entrance . . . Her intention was to see you and demand more money . . . The matter, you see, was pressing, as she had no means of knowing how long it would be before you were arrested.'

'I certainly didn't see this woman on Saturday.'

'I know . . . But that's not the point . . . What matters is that she set out with the intention of seeing you . . . There were three of you, each with your regular days. François Paré's was Wednesday, Courcel's Thursday night to Friday morning . . . Jean-Luc Bodard had no set day . . .

'Most businessmen from the provinces who spend part of the week in Paris return home on Saturday. You did not, because you had an arrangement to spend Saturday afternoons with Mademoiselle Papet . . .

'The concierge was aware of this, of course, which is why she went to see you that day . . . She didn't foresee that, as you no longer had anything to keep you in Paris on Saturdays, you would go back to Bordeaux on the Friday night . . .'

'Ingenious,' remarked the lawyer, 'but a bit flimsy as evidence to put before a jury, don't you think?'

The concierge, silent and motionless, seemed to fill the room with her huge presence.

'I agree, Maître, but I am not relying on that alone . . . This gentleman here is Léon Florentin . . . He has made a full confession . . .'

'I was under the impression that he was the chief suspect.'

Florentin, shoulders hunched, hung his head, feeling that he would never again be able to look anyone in the face.

'He is not the murderer,' retorted Maigret, 'but the intended victim.'

'I don't understand.'

But Lamotte understood. He started violently in his chair.

'It was at him that the gun was levelled in a threatening gesture, designed to secure the return of certain compromising letters . . . Monsieur Lamotte, however, is a very bad shot, and, what's more, the weapon was unreliable . . .'

The lawyer turned inquiringly to his client:

'Is this true?'

He had not been prepared for this turn of events. Lamotte did not answer but, instead, glowered savagely at Florentin.

'It may help your case, Maître, to know that I am not convinced that your client fired the shot intentionally. He is a man accustomed to getting his own way, and when he meets with resistance he's liable to lose his temper. On this occasion, unfortunately, he had a gun in his hand, and it went off . . .'

This time, the man with the limp was really shattered. With a dazed expression, he stared at Maigret.

'I must ask you to excuse me for a moment. I shan't be long.'

Maigret went through to the Palais de Justice, and made his way up through the maze of corridors, as he had done the previous Saturday. He knocked at the Examining Magistrate's door, and went in to find him at his desk, immersed in a bulky file. His clerk was in the annexe, carrying on the work of restoring order.

'It's all over!' announced Maigret, collapsing into a chair.

'Has he confessed?'

'Who?'

'Well . . . that fellow Florentin, I presume.'

'He hasn't killed anyone . . . All the same, I shall require a warrant for his arrest . . . The charge is demanding money with menaces.'

'And the murderer?'

'He's waiting in my office in company with his lawyer, Maître Bourdon.'

'I can see trouble ahead! He's one of the most . . .'

'Don't worry, you'll find him most accommodating. I

wouldn't go so far as to say that it was an accident, but there are a number of extenuating circumstances . . .'

'Which of them . . .?'

'Victor Lamotte, the man with the limp, wine-grower of Bordeaux, respected member of the exclusive community of Les Chartrons, where such matters as dignity and rank, not to mention moral rectitude, are not to be trifled with . . .

'I'll devote this afternoon to completing my report, and I hope to be able to let you have it by the end of the day . . . It's almost lunch-time and . . .'

'You're hungry, I expect.'

'Thirsty!' admitted Maigret.

A few minutes later, he was back in his office, where he handed over to Lapointe and Janvier the warrants signed by the Examining Magistrate.

'Take them up to Criminal Records for the usual formalities, and then escort them to the cells.'

Janvier, pointing to the concierge, who had risen to her feet, asked:

'What about her?'

'We'll attend to her later . . . In the meantime, she'd better go back to the flats . . . The lodge can't be left unattended for ever.'

She looked at him without expression. Her lips moved, and a little hiss escaped her, as when water is splashed on hot coals, but she did not speak. At last she turned towards the door, and went out.

'I'll see you later, you two, in the Brasserie Dauphine.'

It was only afterwards that he realized how thoughtless it had been of him to toss off this invitation to his men in the presence of those other two, who were about to be deprived of their liberty.

Five minutes later, standing at the bar of the familiar little restaurant, he gave his order:

'A beer . . . In the tallest glass you can find.'

In thirty-five years, he had not set eyes on a single one of the boys who had been his schoolmates at the Lycée Banville.

And when, at last, he did, of all people it had to be Florentin!

Épalinges,
24 June 1968

Big Bob

**Translated from the French by
Eileen M. Lowe**

Chapter One

I was not at Tilly that Sunday. Taking advantage of the children being with their grandmother, my wife and I had accepted an invitation to spend the weekend with some friends who own an estate on the outskirts of the forest of Rambouillet. It had been a hot and sultry day, with storms threatening and even a few heavy drops of rain towards the end of the afternoon.

I must have glanced at the newspaper, at home, on the Monday morning, but if I don't particularly remember reading any information about Dandurand, it is because it only occasioned a few lines under the heading of news items.

It was after ten o'clock and I was examining a patient in my consulting room when Lulu telephoned me.

'It's you, Charles?'

I did not recognize her voice straight away, although I know it well. Lulu did not wait for my reply before adding:

'Bob is dead.'

Now I knew who was speaking. Nevertheless, the news took me so much by surprise, it was so unforeseen, that I frowned and murmured as if to gain time:

'Are you there, Lulu?'

I continued right away:

'When did it happen?'

'Yesterday morning at Tilly. *They* say it is an accident.'

'Where is he?'

'Here.'

I looked at the patient whose chest I was sounding and who was covering himself up with a towel.

'I'll be there just as soon as I can get away.'

'That's not why I called you. I thought perhaps you might not have read the paper.'

I can't say what bothered me. A woman whose husband has

just died suddenly, when nothing gave warning of his death, does not necessarily speak in her normal voice. Generally, Lulu's was full and rather hoarse. It always seemed to be joking, about to burst into laughter. It was a coarse voice, but so full of vitality that it was difficult to resist its good humour.

Now, the voice I had just heard was impersonal and neutral, without any trace of emotion, as if Lulu were fulfilling a task or a duty in announcing the news, and she hung up without giving me time for a word of sympathy.

Later I learned that she had spent part of the morning telephoning like this to all their friends, repeating in a monotonous tone of voice:

'Bob is dead.'

She was recording a fact, no more, as if the presence of the body, a few yards away from her, were not enough to convince her of the reality of the fact.

I often went to Tilly with my wife and the two boys. Even when they were still babies we used to go there, although not regularly. That is why it is easy for me to reconstruct the events of the Saturday evening and of the Sunday.

I know the millstream, as the regular visitors call it, in its remotest recesses, I mean the stretch of the Seine between the lock at Citanguette, downstream, and the lock at Vives-Eaux, six kilometres upstream. There are no important towns or villages on the banks, and the *Beau Dimanche*, kept by the Fradins, is about the only place with any life in it.

The Dandurands arrived there on the Saturday evening at half past seven, as on nearly every Saturday, for Lulu will never agree to close her shop before six. Sometimes she stays open until eight o'clock on week-days, as her clients know, and I have often seen Lulu get up from the table during dinner, on hearing the door-bell ring.

'It's little Mademoiselle Bovy coming for her hat,' she would say.

She spoke about them as friends, and it wasn't unusual for her to invite them into the back-room to take coffee or a little dessert with us.

Mademoiselle Berthe, her chief employee, was there when the shop closed. She is always there too, whenever we dine with the

Dandurands, and is looked upon as one of the family. She must be between forty-five and fifty, nearer fifty than forty-five. She is lean and swarthy, with a long thin nose, so chilly that, summer and winter alike, she wears woollen underclothes which give her a peculiar smell.

I suppose that, in her own mind, she is something like the household's guardian-angel. Bob's angel or Lulu's?

Replying to my questions, a few days later, she murmured:

'I can't say that I noticed anything special. Monsieur Bob was out nearly all afternoon. I imagine he went to Justin's for a game of *belote*.'

This is a small café-bar where the same people meet regularly. It is at the corner of the Place Constantin-Pecqueur, within a stone's throw of the shop, and here Bob used to play cards with the people of the district.

'What time did he come back?'

'About five-thirty. The *patronne* was in the bedroom, packing their suitcase.'

The two women use the informal '*tu*' when speaking to each other but, when Mademoiselle Berthe talks about Lulu, even to intimates, she always refers to her as the '*patronne*'.

'Did he seem preoccupied?'

'He was whistling.'

Bob always came back home whistling, whistled too as he strode about the streets.

'What happened?'

'Nothing. The *patronne* changed her dress and asked him if he wasn't going to put on a clean shirt. He answered that, in any case, he would change when they got to Tilly.'

The Dandurands' friends know the premises as well as their own homes. At the back of the shop is a large room they call the studio, which also serves as dining-cum-living-room. During the day, from three to five employees – according to the season – work there, and three long tables are always piled high with hats, pieces of fabric, ribbons and artificial flowers. When it is time to eat, a corner of one of the tables is cleared and covered with a checked cloth. The dimly lit kitchen is on one side, the bedroom on the other, and I never remember seeing any of the doors shut.

On Saturday afternoons, only Mademoiselle Berthe works.

155

The others have time off. As it was hot that Saturday, I'd like to bet that Lulu was just wearing a slip, for she's fat and suffers from the heat, so there are always rings of sweat on her dresses. Perhaps the word fat is misleading. Since she is extremely small, she appears to be stouter than she really is. I would rather call her plump, and some of her friends compare her to a peach. She has the bloom of one. Once, when we'd only known each other a few weeks, Bob asked me:

'Don't you think my wife is luscious?'

You could never tell whether he was joking or not.

'What did he do from five-thirty to six?'

'Nothing out of the ordinary. He may have teased me from time to time, so as not to lose the habit. I remember he helped himself to a glass of white wine and asked if I'd like one.'

This was one of his everlasting jokes. Mademoiselle Berthe didn't drink, hated the smell of wine but, year after year, Bob had never failed to offer her a glass when he poured one out for himself. She was not annoyed with him, in fact she would have missed it if a day had passed without his teasing her.

'You know what he was for dragging his big body from one room to another, without ever settling down anywhere.

' "You've got the car out?" the *patronne* asked him. He said he had, and, at the time, was busy attaching a small fish, made of wood or something, to a metal thread.'

'You don't know whether he'd bought it that day?'

'How can I tell?'

'Had you seen this fish in the house before?'

She couldn't tell me. Nor could Lulu, when I asked her the same question. Strange as it may seem, this has its significance at any rate in my eyes.

For fifteen years, to my knowledge, and even a little longer the Dandurands have stayed more or less regularly at the *Beau Dimanche* at Tilly. Before that, they used to stay somewhere on the banks of the Marne, on the Nogent side.

The clientèle of the two places is very different. At Nogent quite near Paris, you find mostly lovers who go and fool about at the water's edge, and dance, far into the night, in a huge dance-hall, vulgar and noisy. At Tilly, you meet hardly any but peace-loving folk. Many are married and take their children there. There are nearly always mothers knitting under the elms, at the water's edge, while their husbands are fishing.

At the beginning, the Fradins' inn only took in anglers, who would hire a boat or leave their own in Léon Fradin's care. When canoes first appeared on the Seine, young couples discovered the millstream and it wasn't long before a few small sailing craft were tacking about on it.

Up to the Sunday before 27 June, the Dandurands belonged to what one might call the canoe-set; that means they'd spend hours, on Sunday, gliding with the stream in their little boat of varnished mahogany. It was in perfect harmony with Bob's temperament, which seconded, at every turn, Alphonse Allais's dictum:

'Man is not made to work. Experience proves that it wearies him.'

At the *Beau Dimanche*, there are those who get up before dawn to go fishing and whom you hear frantically working away in the half light at engines that refuse to start, and those whom you never see leaving their rooms before ten o'clock to order a glass of dry white wine in lieu of breakfast.

The Dandurands belonged firmly to the second category; you could even call them its champions from the almost ostentatious way they came down last.

This was only true until the previous Sunday, which was the opening Sunday of the fishing season. The night before, instead of playing cards under the trees, where midges encircle the lamps hanging from their branches, while a few couples danced to the gramophone, Bob, with the help of Monsieur Métenier, had set a line for the pike. Then from five o'clock in the morning, in the stern of his boat, he trolled slowly from one lock to the other.

I was there that Sunday, reading on the terrace, and I saw him pass five or six times, stripped to the waist, a handkerchief over his head by way of a hat. Not far away, my wife was chatting with Lulu, and I can still hear the latter explaining:

'It took him all of a sudden. I'll be surprised if it lasts. In the first place, he just can't get up early. Next, he can never go for long without feeling what he calls an "alarming thirst", and demanding a glass of cool white wine.'

I hasten to say that I have never seen Bob really drunk. Neither have I seen him go beyond a certain time without helping himself to 'a drop of white', as he called it. Lulu didn't take exception to this. On the contrary, she herself enjoyed a drink and, at times, it made her lively and amusing.

What had persuaded Bob, from one day to the next, to transfer from the lie-abed group to that of the anglers? I was trying to find the answer to this by asking questions in every quarter. The first Sunday, of course, he hadn't caught a single fish, and had disembarked, a little before midday, with his back and neck burnt red from the sun, announcing that he had an 'alarming thirst'.

When I questioned Monsieur Métenier, he took time to reflect, for he isn't a man to speak rashly.

'He seemed to me genuinely interested in pike fishing. I have seen others, like him, come to it late in the day, and be all the more enthusiastic about it. I showed him how to weight the line in such a way that the devon – no doubt you know that's the name given to an artificial fish – floats neither too near the bottom, nor too near to the surface. Actually, the right depth varies according to the time of day, the place, the temperature, the state of cloud, according to many more factors still, but, in one lesson, I could only give him a general idea of the subject.'

'You don't know whether, some time between the two Sundays, he bought a new devon?'

Monsieur Métenier, who manages a fairly important machine-tool business near the Boulevard Richard-Lenoir, unfortunately couldn't tell me.

'I only remember saying that his own wasn't bad, that it was a good standard model, but, later on, when he had passed the beginner's stage, he would need quite a large variety.'

I also spoke to John Lenauer, who is not a fisherman but a lie-abed and who, like Bob, helps to make up the group of *belote* players.

I think I've already said that the Dandurands left the shop in the Rue Lamarck, a few houses away from the Rue Caulaincourt, at six o'clock on the Saturday. It was Lulu who locked up and made certain the door was secure. Mademoiselle Berthe stayed on the edge of the pavement watching them leave in their open car.

They cut right across the town to take the Fontainebleau road and turn left straight after Prigny. John Lenauer saw them arrive at the *Beau Dimanche* at about half past seven and, since he, too, always suffers from an 'alarming thirst', he led Bob to the bar while Lulu went upstairs to unpack.

'I didn't find him any different from other Saturdays,' said John, who is an Englishman with a French mother, and who works in Paris in the Cunard Offices. 'We had two or three drinks.'

'Or four or five?'

'Four perhaps.'

I am assured that John never touches a drop before six o'clock in the evening on working days. At Tilly, he starts on the white wine as soon as he wakens, and I always saw him with bright eyes and vacant gaze, a mocking smile at the corner of his mouth.

'Bob,' he went on, 'was a true friend, if ever there was one!'

At the *Beau Dimanche*, we breakfast and dine on the terrace at the water's edge. There are no parasols, but handsome elms provide shade and, in the evenings, lamps are lit in them. A sudden shower of rain is a catastrophe, in more ways than one, for a rush to the house overcrowds the dining-room, which is not big enough to hold everyone.

It didn't rain that Saturday, and it was mild. Bob shook hands to left and right, cracked a few of his favourite jokes and set off towards the annexe, where he and his wife occupy the same room, on the first floor, that they've had for years. One doesn't enjoy much privacy there, living, as it were, in sight of everyone else. The staircase is inside, and both the doors and windows of the rooms open on to a kind of balcony which takes the place of a corridor.

As he had promised in Paris, Bob changed into khaki drill trousers and his bright red weekend shirt, while Lulu got into black woollen slacks which emphasize the shape of her plump bottom.

I asked Lulu what they had talked about. She replied:

'Nothing that I can remember. I think he was whistling.

Then, from down below, Olga called to us that it was our turn.'

Olga is one of the waitresses. She was referring to their turn for a dinner-table for, on Saturday evenings, one eats in relays.

'We settled ourselves down with the Millots and Mado.'

Habitués also. Millot is a dentist in the Bastille district. They are both young, very much in love. I think perhaps they first met at the *Beau Dimanche*, where they used to come even before they were married, and now they have a nine-year-old daughter, Mado. They've bought a sailing-boat, a Star, spend their Sundays on board and, although they are friendly with everyone, you see them very little in either of the groups.

Millot told me:

'Bob was gay, as always.'

'Did he talk about fishing?'

'He gave us an amusing impersonation of Monsieur Métenier giving him a lesson the week before.'

Monsieur Métenier is a native of Cantal and has retained its accent.

Bob added: 'If fate willed me to catch a pike tomorrow it would make him ill, for he has strong arguments to prove that it would be against all the rules. According to him, you need a few months apprenticeship before you can begin to understand how to weight a line, then another season to enable you to judge where the fish's hide-out is, and finally, if you have any talent . . .'

This was exactly Bob, who must have ended his monologue with one of his favourite expressions:

'*Devastating!*'

He used to come out with this nearly as often as his famous 'alarming thirst', and with the same gravity.

'*Devastating!*'

If my wife and I had not gone to Rambouillet, there's no doubt the Dandurands would have had dinner with *us* that evening, for little Madame Millot was always rather afraid that Bob might tell a risqué story, or utter a coarse word in front of Mado. This never happened. He had an ironic way of stopping short at the very moment one imagined he was forgetting the little girl's presence, and he always cast an impish glance at her mother, absolutely delighted at her fears.

'*Devastating!*' he would conclude.

Since, from now on, he belonged to the anglers' set, he should have gone to bed early, as *they* did. At the *Beau Dimanche* this is the cause of a minor war, becoming more bitter each year. Several times it has almost brought about the exodus of one group of the clientèle. The fishermen complain that they are prevented from sleeping in the evenings by the playing of the gramophone, by loud voices on the terrace and in the garden, and finally by the sound of taps running late at night. For their part, the others grumble about the outboard motor engines starting their sputtering even before sunrise.

That Saturday, Bob did not go and seek advice from Monsieur Métenier. No one saw him getting his line ready, or cleaning his engine, as the others were busy doing all along the landing stage. Dinner over, it was he who suggested to John Lenauer:

'What about playing fifteen hundred up?'

They appealed to Riri, who works for an insurance company in the Rue Lafitte. At Tilly, he wears a seaman's jersey, and the white beret of the American Navy cocked over one ear. Since they couldn't find a fourth, Lulu played with them, in a corner of the terrace, and the game was still going on at midnight when Madame Fradin came to stop the gramophone, to which two or three couples were still dancing.

A detail strikes me when speaking of Riri. Lean and lanky, like a stray dog, he can't be much more than twenty-four or -five. He's still a youngster. Now John Lenauer is well over thirty and, although he's married, leads a bachelor's life; his wife lives in London, where she also works for Cunard, and they only see each other for a few days of the year during the holidays.

At the time of his death, Bob was approaching forty-nine and Lulu, who has never disguised the fact, is exactly three years younger. They were both born on 27 July, and it used to amuse them very much to exchange greetings on the same day.

What surprises me is that the difference in age between the Dandurands and one set of their friends has never struck me until now. At Tilly, they belonged to all groups equally, but I remember them more often with younger people than with those of their own age. At the Rue Lamarck, where one rarely found them alone, and where sometimes, at eleven o'clock at night, fifteen or more people were busy drinking in the studio-living-room, you would see couples under thirty and young girls in their teens mixing with people like the painter Gaillard, who is well over sixty, and almost a fixture there, or like Rosalie Quéven, an elderly neighbour who tells fortunes and reads the coffee grounds.

I asked John:

'Did he win?'

'As always.'

I have seldom seen Dandurand lose at *belote*. Since he plays every day, for at least two or three hours, his skill is devastating. All the same, a certain amount of luck enters into the game. Now, in his long and extremely supple fingers the cards seemed to be bewitched. Sometimes, as a challenge, he would call without even consulting his hand, especially if his opponents were grousers.

'I take!'

And the next moment, he would find in his hand the cards needed to follow suit. I wouldn't go so far as to say that this angered Lulu. She was never really angry with him. On these occasions, however, she would look at him frowningly. I don't know exactly what she was thinking, but she must have been a bit annoyed at his almost childish way of defying fate, and perhaps at his persistent good luck. I fancy that, if he had been capable of turning up poor cards and being beaten hollow, she'd have been almost relieved.

I must admit that he seemed to be making fun of people. He would say casually to the player on his left, just as if he himself could see through the cards:

'Your king of spades, please.'

And sure enough the other was obliged to surrender his king.

He didn't play for high stakes, more often than not for drinks. If he had wanted to, he could have made a living at *belote*, become a kind of professional, like those one meets in the small bars around Montmartre and elsewhere. He was quite content to win some Championship or other of the XVIIIth *arrondissement* every year, or nearly so.

'You had a lot to drink?' I asked Lenauer, once more.

'Two bottles of white wine.'

It was no quantity for four people, especially when Bob and John were among the four.

'He went to bed straight after the game?'

'Lulu went first and put the light on in their room. I can see her now, like a shadow-show, pulling her sweater over her head.'

'He didn't say anything to you at the time?'

John seemed to ponder, answered with a certain surprise:

'As a matter of fact, he did. It had gone out of my head. As he left, he said:

' "You're a good chap!"

'I am practically certain that, when his back was already turned, he added:

' "*Devastating!* There are masses of good chaps!" '

I insisted:

'There was no quarrelling during the game?'

No. That was a silly question.

The lamps outside were extinguished. I know there was a moon that evening because, at Rambouillet, we stayed up late, chatting with our friends in the park and listening to the crickets. The Seine flowed idly on, and the moon shone into the room where Lulu was undressing.

'He went up to join her.'

John sleeps in the room directly underneath, on the ground floor, and you can hear everything from one floor to the next.

'They talked for a long time?'

'Just the time it takes to get ready for bed. I heard Lulu say:

' "Sh! You'll waken Monsieur Métenier."

'I didn't see Bob again. In the morning I heard nothing.'

No more had Riri, who went, as usual, to sleep on board Yvonne Simart's house-boat, moored a hundred yards away from the inn. No one gossips about them. He and Yvonne, who is eight years older than he is, never behave in public in any way that might reveal their intimacy, don't even use the familiar '*tu*' to one another, as is the custom at Tilly. When she leaves the *Beau Dimanche*, where she has her meals, she says good night to him just as she does to the others. Nearly always, he remains

163

standing the last, doubtless considering it his duty as a gentleman to behave like this; and only then, in his seaman's dress, which emphasizes his gangling gait, does he make his way towards the boat's gangway.

Actually, it is rather like a small barge with a kind of little wooden house built on to it; it comprises two narrow cabins, a third which serves as lounge-cum-dining-room, and a plunge board.

Yvonne Simart, daughter of Admiral Simart, sleeps on board with her friend Laurence, a buxom girl of her own age; they are both sales-girls in a fashion-house in the Avenue Matignon.

Like everyone else, Laurence must know. Just by counting the bedrooms and guests, it is obvious that there isn't room for Riri at the inn.

Invariably, Riri only waits for the lights to go out before crossing the plank which serves as a gangway and, as Laurence gets up early, you see him roaming around outside from dawn. With Léon Fradin he is the only one, in the mornings, to watch the fishermen leave, and to give them a hand sometimes when an engine refuses to start.

Lulu was vaguely conscious of her husband getting up, but didn't waken altogether.

'I believe he kissed my forehead and I rubbed his unshaven cheek.'

Riri saw him going downstairs, a sweater tied around his neck on top of his red shirt. As yet, there was only one boat underway and the sun hadn't risen.

'I noticed that his cheeks were as rosy as a child's just pulled out of bed. He remarked on the cold, even shivered, and had to pull on the cord four or five times before getting the engine going.'

It was one of those duraluminium engines, one and a half horse power, that you fix in the stern of a canoe.

'He made two turns opposite the inn.'

'Looking up at his bedroom window?'

'I don't know what he was looking at. The water was covered with a smoke-like mist. He sped upstream, half the boat thrusting up out of the river.'

'You saw him cast his line?'

'I don't think he did. It didn't strike me. He was standing motionless, one hand on the rudder. At least, if he did start to fish, it must have been higher up when I was no longer looking at him. Monsieur Métenier, who was overhauling his boat, growled:

' "It does happen, once in a while, that *they* catch something!" '

I have already said that I am familiar with the millstream. Almost the whole of the right bank, quite a steep hillside, is thickly wooded, with, here and there, a red roof making a splash of colour in the green. The left bank, on the other hand, is a low-lying mass of reeds for lovers to push their boats into.

The pike anglers, who troll their lines from one lock to the other, with their engines ticking over, are a minority. The roach and chub fishermen are far more numerous. They moor their boats to pegs set a few yards from the bank and, sitting in deck-chairs, they remain motionless for hours, sometimes the whole day long. It is one of Léon Fradin's duties to go during the week, and put ground bait down in those spots for his visitors. He has the ways of a poacher and, year in year out, wears a gamekeeper's corduroy suit.

Fradin, his moustache, always damp from his habit of chewing it, told me:

'When he left, there were at least five fishermen settled down like this between their stakes, beginning with Monsieur Raismes, who got up at four o'clock to go and moor his boat at the foot of the quarry.'

Monsieur Raismes, a man of about fifty, manager of the Ministry of Public Works, is accounted the finest chub fisherman at Tilly. He saw the canoe go past. He even signed to Bob to give him a wider berth so as not to startle the fish. No, he hadn't the impression that Dandurand's line was in the water. Besides, if he had fished, he'd have been handling his craft more slowly. He was, just then, roughly two kilometres from the weir, and seemed to be making straight for it. An empty canal-boat, sailing up the Seine, emitted two hoots to give notice of approach to the lock. The ones that belong to a fleet or a big company are generally lying motionless the length of the bank on Sundays. But there are always a few motor-boats, piloted by their owners, cruising up and down that day.

The bargee must have seen Bob close-to, as he passed him. In fact, it seems they waved to each other. And Bob, in so far as it is possible to judge, was living his last ten minutes.

I wasn't able to question the bargee, who must be far away by this time, somewhere on the Saône or on the eastern canals. It was Monsieur Raismes who saw them wave to each other.

For the rest, there remains practically no evidence. The lock-keeper at Vives-Eaux thinks he remembers the sound of an outboard motor-engine while he was operating the sluice-gates, but he didn't take any notice of it because there was nothing unusual about it.

'My hands were cold. You would never have believed it had been so hot the night before and that it was going to be just as hot that day. I left the lock for a second to go and drink the cup of coffee I was preparing when the emptying warning came. I even asked the bargee if he'd like one. He answered that he'd just had some. You know how it is.'

'You didn't look towards the weir?'

Even if he had looked, he wouldn't have seen anything. Below the weir, in fact a dozen yards away from it, right in the middle of the stream, lies a small island. It is overgrown with brushwood which partly obstructs the view.

The noise was coming from the other side.

'The engine stopped?'

'Probably. When the boat moved away, I heard nothing more.'

The lock-keeper had gone back inside.

A few minutes later, a fisherman, who doesn't stay at the *Beau Dimanche* because he has a shanty of his own in the mill-stream, spotted the canoes not far from the island, in the eddies of the weir.

'Something was preventing it from following the current, as if it were caught at the bottom. At first, I told myself that it was a boat that had cut adrift, somewhere upstream, and had leapt the weir. This happens now and again. I had my line in the water and I wasn't unduly perturbed to begin with. At some stage, as I was turning close to the canoe, it struck me, I don't know why, that something odd was going on. I drew in my line.

Then I recovered the canoe by one of its points and it glided for a second with my boat, but in fits and starts, as if something were holding it back. A man I don't know, who was fishing from the bank, shouted to me to ask if I needed any help. I shook my head.'

'How long did all that take?'

'Five minutes perhaps. It's difficult to judge. A kind of curtain-cord was steeping in the water, stretched taut – sometimes amateur canoeists make use of such a line, fastened to a massive stone or cast-iron weight, to moor themselves in mid-current. I tugged. It broke away in the river-bed. I began to drift, continuing to tug on the cord, and it wasn't long before I saw an arm emerge, an arm that seemed to be waving to me.'

The man, scared stiff, dropped everything. His name matters little. He is a cabinet-maker from Puteaux, father of four children. He gave no more thought to the angler on the bank, who was gesticulating and, his hands cupped around his mouth, was shouting heaven knows what to him. He headed for the lock, no doubt because a lock-keeper is something of an official and wears a uniform cap.

'Down there . . . near the canoe . . . a drowned man . . .'

If more rapid action had been taken, would Bob be dead? It appears that he had only gone overboard five minutes before the cabinet-maker first noticed the canoe. One must not be misled by the arm movements, for the current often makes drowned people look as if they are gesticulating.

The lock-keeper took a boat-hook with him and, strangely enough, probably without thinking, a life-buoy.

On the other bank, the fisherman, powerless to help, was still shouting words they couldn't catch.

They tugged on the curtain-cord. Bob's body appeared, the pullover still tied around his neck, his red shirt clinging to him, the cord wound twice around his right ankle.

To the end of the rope was secured a leaden weight of five kilos, hexagonal in shape, like those used in the shops.

The lock-keeper, who, he assured me, has fished out a good dozen drowned people, living or dead, in the course of his career, said awkwardly, as if it were a subject he didn't care to touch on:

'I knew him well. He often came to the lock to beg a drop of white wine.'

'You think the cord was wound round his leg when he threw the weight into the water?'

First of all, there wasn't any reason for Dandurand to moor right in the middle of the current. His line was on the bottom of the canoe, and didn't seem to have been lowered into the water at all. Then, even if his engine had stopped without his wanting it to, he would have waited to be carried a little lower down, into calmer waters, before examining it.

'For a cord to be wound once round, that's happened before,' the lock-keeper said to me gravely. 'I saw a bargewoman dragged into the water of the lock like that just as she was casting a mooring-rope. But twice round . . .'

This conversation took place in his home. He opened an oak sideboard, its doors embellished with lead-lights, to take out a bottle of marc and fill two small thick-based glasses.

'To his health!' he said, lifting his glass to the level of his eyes, and staring at the colourless liquid.

After wiping his lips, he added:

'He had a taste for that too.'

Chapter Two

I was about to leave my consulting-room to visit the Rue Lamarck when I was detained by an emergency, a neighbour's kid who had gashed his hand with a kitchen knife. I had to put in three stitches, his mother crying all the time because he'd have the scar for life.

I was finishing the dressing when my wife knocked discreetly at the door communicating with the private part of the flat.

'You're alone?' she asked, in her usual whisper.

'I'll just be two more minutes.'

I knew she was standing behind the door. I could have heard her breathing. When I opened it she was holding the daily paper in her hand.

'You've seen the news?'

I should have left it to her to tell me.

'Bob Dandurand is dead,' I answered, as I tidied up my instrument case, for I intended making one or two calls on my way back from Montmartre.

'It says in the paper that he was drowned, yesterday morning, at Tilly.'

'Lulu telephoned me.'

'How is she?'

'It's difficult to say. She seemed calm. I'm going over there.'

'You don't think I ought to go with you?'

'I wouldn't advise it this morning; it would be better if you went this afternoon or tomorrow.'

My small black 6 C.V., the dirtiest in the district, because I never find time to have it washed, was parked at the edge of the pavement where it stays most nights. We have lived in the Rue Notre-Dame-de-Lorette, opposite the Place Saint-Georges, for fifteen years. A few shop-keepers from the bottom of the street and from the Rue des Martyrs come to consult me, but by far the biggest part of my practice is made up of dancers, dance hostesses, even a few professional prostitutes, all good sorts, from the Place Blanche and the Place Pigalle. That's why you find more people in my waiting-room in the afternoons than in the mornings. And now that the boys are nine and a half and eleven years old, my wife is trying to persuade me to move from the district.

'You should realize, Charles, that they are at an age when they are beginning to understand things.'

I turn a deaf ear, but I foresee a serious discussion on this subject, one day or another.

It was about midday when I got out of my car opposite Lulu's pale blue boutique, and I didn't fully realize that Bob was dead until I saw the lowered shutters – on one of them a black-edged card, which I didn't read. The wood-panelled door was ajar, so I only had to push it. I don't know how many people were standing between the two shop-counters, six or seven at least, neighbours and tradeswomen of the vicinity, as far as I could judge.

In the studio-cum-dining-room I found more people still, and my first impression was that everyone was talking at once. I looked about for Lulu who, as always, was the smallest present, and, as soon as she saw me, she threw herself into my arms.

We both spoke at the same time, uttering such trite phrases that we were mutually embarrassed, and as we looked at each other, I said:

'I'm late.'

While she, for her part, was saying:

'It's kind of you to come.'

Did she think, as I did, that, if Bob had been alive, he would have watched us with eyes sparkling with malice, letting fall from one corner of his mouth, because from the other hung an eternal cigarette:

'*Devastating!*'

Lulu went on:

'You'd like to see him, Charles?'

This time the bedroom door was shut. Lulu opened it noiselessly. The undertakers hadn't come yet to fit out the mortuary chapel; all the same, the atmosphere was none the less funereal already, with the drawn curtains, the candles burning on either side of the bed and, at the foot, a few bouquets, the first ones, bought by women neighbours from the small hand-carts.

I wondered where Lulu had found the prie-Dieu at which Mademoiselle Berthe was kneeling, a rosary twined around her skinny fingers. No doubt it had been lent to her by some old church-hen living in the house.

'What do you think of him, Charles?'

The body hadn't stayed in the water long enough to have taken on the horrifying appearance of most of the drowned.

'You'd swear he was smiling, wouldn't you?'

There was a sprig of boxwood and some holy water on a table covered with a white cloth. I made the ritual gestures. Another woman, extremely old, was standing in a corner, murmuring prayers.

When we went out on tiptoe, Mademoiselle Berthe followed us, sighing, as if it were only with reluctance that she was leaving Bob's body. It was strange as we went through the door to be welcomed, so near to the dead, by the familiar smell of good cooking. One of the employees was, in fact, preparing a ragoût. There were two of them near the stove, and we could see two glasses and two opened bottles on a table.

Gaillard, the painter, was sitting in a corner, purple-faced as usual, his eyes watery, hands trembling. I didn't speak to him immediately, and can't remember what I said to him later on. It isn't important, and I don't think he has many lucid moments. Medically speaking, he is an almost perfect specimen of a drunkard in his final stages, wherein he no longer needs to eat, and the extraordinary thing about it is that a man can go on for so long. When I come to think of it, I'm not sure of what I've just said regarding lucidity. Often, when people, believing him past understanding, have levelled cruel or ironic remarks at him, I've seen Gaillard's eyes grow hard and his teeth clench.

Someone I don't know separated Lulu and me; he had just come in, so she took him to see the body. Then it was that Mademoiselle Berthe touched my arm.

'She hasn't said anything to you yet?' she asked me, in a church-whisper.

We were in a corner, out of the way, behind a table on which were piled up all the hats that had been lying around.

'What about?'

'They shouldn't have spoken to her as they did. What good did it do them to let her believe it was an accident?'

I knew practically nothing yet about what had happened at Tilly.

'It wasn't an accident?'

She shook her head, looking me straight in the eyes. She was more drawn than Lulu, her lips pale, her complexion yellow, and I automatically caught hold of her wrist to take her pulse.

'It's only tiredness,' she murmured. 'Neither of us has slept. The police talked too much. Too much or too little. Now, she is eating her heart out, because she realizes what lies behind their questions.'

'Suicide?'

She nodded, and her chin began to tremble. I don't know what her normal pulse-rate is, very likely below average. Just then, it registered hardly more than 55.

'You should take a mouthful of alcohol.'

It was useless to insist. Nothing I could say would be of any

171

help. Better to question her to bring out what was rankling in her mind.

'They don't know why?'

'They know nothing. It seems so unaccountable!'

Like everyone else, I exclaimed:

'He was always so light-hearted!'

Again it's one of those things you say without thinking. I noticed she was looking at me with some surprise, as if to reproach me for it. If I'd had to interpret that look it would have meant:

'You too!'

Didn't she agree with Bob's friends and all who knew him? Wherever he went, he was the life and soul of the party; faces lit up just at the sight of him.

'You don't know if he was ill?' the old maid was asking me now.

I didn't know. I had often, in the course of an evening or a weekend, recommended some cure or other to Bob for a sore throat or a minor ailment, but he had never set foot in my consulting-room. This is the case with many of my friends, and I can understand that a kind of diffidence might prevent them from laying their small woes before a man they meet afterwards on different ground.

Lulu wasn't shy like that. She often came to consult me. Formerly, when there were five or six friends in the house, she would say to me under her breath:

'Can you spare a minute, Charles?'

Bob would watch us, knowing what it was about. On these occasions, she would close the bedroom door, settle herself on the edge of the bed, her skirt lifted right above her hips.

'It's my belly again, Charles. I'm scared that one day I'll have to have everything taken away.'

She'd already had womb-trouble before she was twenty, and this preyed on her mind. She was more afraid of an operation than of a serious illness, tuberculosis, for instance.

As far as I know, Bob himself was in as good health as a man of his age could be, leading the life he led. He only became aware that he had a stomach two or three years ago, and that white wine was putting it severely to the test. After every meal, often between meals, he would take a huge dose of bicarbonate

172

of soda. I had tried to dissuade him, without being unduly insistent. I had taken him a gastric dressing with a kaolin base, but he preferred the bicarbonate which gave him more immediate relief.

I inquired of Mademoiselle Berthe:

'He was seeing a doctor?'

'I'm not sure. I think so.'

'What makes you think so?'

'I couldn't say. Little things . . .'

She turned her head away. Perhaps she realized that she was thus admitting having studied Bob more attentively than his own wife.

I shook hands with Riri, who had just arrived, and whom one is always surprised to see in town clothes. A butcher came in, still in his apron, and, like everyone else, kissed Lulu on both cheeks. One of the employees asked me:

'She really must eat, doctor, mustn't she?'

'Yes, indeed she must,' I said.

I was on the point of leaving, without finding any way of talking to Lulu again, when she was in front of me. Right away she began to squeeze my arm so hard that I could feel her nails through my sleeve.

'Tell me, Charles, you who knew him so well, why should he have done that?'

And as I cast about for an answer:

'Do you think it was because of me?'

She wasn't crying. She was living on her nerves, so tense that she seemed unconscious of it.

'And to think that, all my life, I believed I was making him happy!'

If you had stuck a needle in her arm, she probably wouldn't have felt anything. This notion reminded me that I had my case with me.

'Is there some place where I could give you an injection, Lulu?'

'An injection for what?'

'Just a sedative.'

'I don't want to sleep.'

'I promise you won't sleep.'

'Sure?'

She looked about her, made her way to the kitchen.

'Come in here.'

The two employees were still there. Lulu shut the door, watched me preparing the syringe, lifted up her dress on one side. One of the girls, the one who calls herself Adeline – because she considers this a more poetic name than her own, which is Jeanne – started to cry.

'Poor kid!' murmured Lulu, still as if in a waking dream. 'This has been a shock to her too. You wouldn't like to give her an injection?'

'I don't think it's necessary. What's needed, just now, is less of a crowd, fewer comings and goings in the house.'

'Can I help it if people come?'

Perhaps I was wrong, after all. All this bustle was saving her from having to face up to the harsh reality.

As we came out of the kitchen, Lulu said to me, in a low voice, indicating Adeline with a slight nod:

'You know that Bob and she . . .?'

I nodded.

'I have never been jealous. So long as he was happy . . .'

Just when I was about to pass into the crowded studio, it seemed to me that Adeline caught my eye as if to convey a message. I am not certain of this. I promised myself I'd speak to her at the next opportunity.

Lulu continued:

'Bob's sister telephoned that she'd come this afternoon.'

As she spoke, she was rubbing the place on her thigh where she'd had the injection.

'Bob's sister?'

'You didn't know he had a sister? She's married to a solicitor from the Péreire district, and he used to go and see her once or twice a year. She's on holiday in Dieppe with her children. Her husband, who stayed behind in Paris, telephoned the news to her and she rang me up at once. She's on her way by car.'

I was just leaving when once more I came upon Mademoiselle Berthe whom I suspected of waylaying me deliberately.

'You've given her a tranquillizer?'

174

'Yes. By the way, when were you told about all this?
'Yesterday evening, at about seven o'clock. I was at home.'

She lives in a flat about three houses away. They joked about it sometimes. Bob claimed that she was so skinny because she spent her nights polishing floors. In front of the door, he revealed, were two pairs of felt undersoles that you had to skate about on so as not to dull the gleaming surface.

'One pair for her and one for the chance visitor!'

'And suppose there are two visitors?'

'They got off with hopping on one leg.'

Mademoiselle Berthe went on telling me, still in a whisper, what had happened the evening before. She hadn't seen the ambulance bringing back the body, for her windows overlook the courtyard. It was her concierge who had noticed it and gone up to warn her.

For about an hour, there had been a confused coming and going, not too much, however, because it was a Sunday and most of the neighbours had not yet come back from the country.

'We stayed alone with him all night.'

I looked towards the bedroom:

'It's you who arranged . . .'

'Yes,' she said, adding as she closed her eyes:

'I did the laying out.'

There's a question I would have liked to ask her, that I shall ask her one day, perhaps, unless I ask Lulu, which would be much easier. For it's true that Lulu isn't jealous, never has been, at any rate since I've known the ménage. At Tilly, Bob had a number of adventures, always the easy kind, of no importance, and generally short-lived. All the couples' friends knew this, and also that he would often join one or other of the employees in their rooms. Adeline, the latest comer, barely twenty years old, was among them. She had an attractive, but not particularly pretty face.

Where did Mademoiselle Berthe fit in, with her forty-five or fifty years, her long thin nose and woollen underwear? It was obvious that she was consumed with a love for Bob that she hardly made any effort to hide. What kind of love? It's more difficult to say. And I wouldn't be surprised to learn that

Dandurand, out of charity, perhaps also because he found it quaint – '*devastating!*' he must have said – had paid a short visit, every now and then, to the felt-slipper flat.

This would explain nothing. It is merely one of the traits of Dandurand's character. If it is so, Lulu knows about it and will answer my question.

What upset me most, just then, was the thought of the two women spending the night laying out the dead man, and arranging the room around him, the candles, the table with its white cloth and the sprig of boxwood in the holy water.

It wasn't until much later that I found out what had happened beforehand, throughout the Sunday.

The lock-keeper, with the help of the cabinet-maker, who had given the alarm, had first hoisted the body onto the bank then, for a quarter of an hour, the lock-keeper had tried artificial respiration while his companion was phoning the police station.

It wasn't long before two policemen on bicycles arrived, and one of them recognized Bob, whom he'd often seen on the millstream although he didn't know him by name.

'Isn't he the one who was always gliding up and down in a canoe with a plump little wife?'

'His name is Dandurand,' said the lock-keeper.

'They're staying with the Fradins, aren't they?'

The body was not carried into the house, but laid on the lock tiles and covered over with a piece of canvas.

At eight o'clock, the telephone rang at the *Beau Dimanche*, and Madame Fradin answered it.

'Hello, Madame Blanche? Sergeant Jovis here. Is there a Madame Dandurand staying with you?'

'She's still asleep, why?'

'It was her husband who left this morning in a canoe?'

'Monsieur Bob, yes. Something has happened to him?'

'He's been drowned.' The police sergeant pronounced the word 'drowned' in the local way.

'It would be better if you went yourself and woke his wife, so that she can come and identify him. In the meantime, I'll telephone the lieutenant, at Melun.'

John Lenauer wasn't up. Two or three couples, among them the Millots, and their daughter, were breakfasting on the terrace. Riri, his hands in his pockets, his white cap aslant over his ear, was wandering around the front room where the bar is.

'You wouldn't like to come with me, Monsieur Riri? I have to tell poor Madame Dandurand that her husband has just died.'

He would have followed without thinking. She thought better of it.

'As she's still in bed, perhaps it's better for me not to go in there with a man.'

Since then, I've talked about it to Madame Fradin, whom the local people and the guests call Madame Blanche. Unexpected though it may seem of Léon Fradin's wife – he himself is a kind of brute – she was brought up in a convent and, behind the inn counter, she has kept its manners, including something of its way of dressing. Moreover, their daughter, in her turn, is at the convent and, in the summer, is sent away to relatives in the Cher in order to spare her all contact with the turbulent life of the *Beau Dimanche*.

'The door wasn't locked. My heart was beating so violently that I stayed outside for a time before pushing it. She didn't hear me come in. She was sleeping, with one arm stretched across the place where you could still see the hollow her husband had left. I called:

' "Madame Lulu! Madame Lulu!"

'At first she made a movement as if to chase a fly away. Unlike the majority of women, she looks younger when she's asleep, and she pouts like a little girl. She sat up suddenly, stark naked, then seeing me, crossed her hands over her breast, and inquired:

' "What time is it?"

' "Eight o'clock."

'It was obvious that she couldn't make out why I was there, and I didn't know how to set about telling her. No doubt my face showed that I was bringing bad news for, leaping out of bed and hurling herself upon me, she cried out:

' "It's Bob, isn't it?"

'I nodded.

' "He's hurt?"

'I didn't have time to open my mouth. She uttered such a cry

177

that they heard her in nearly all the rooms and even as far as the terrace.

' "He's dead!"'

'Could I deny it? Then she clung to me, her nails digging into my wrists, and wailed:

' "It's not true! It's not true! Say it's not true! Where is he? I want to see him!"'

'I believe that, if I hadn't stopped her, she would have rushed outside just as she was, without a stitch on. I handed her the black slacks and sweater I found on a chair. Automatically, she looked about for her brassière and put it on, even ran a comb through her hair while I was explaining:

' "He's at the Vives-Eaux lock. I don't know how the accident happened. The sergeant didn't have time to tell me."'

'Riri was waiting for us at the foot of the stairs.

' "I'll drive you," he suggested. "You have the key of the car?"'

' "I don't know where Bob put it."'

' "It doesn't matter. I'll take John's car. He always leaves his key in."'

'In spite of everything, I managed to make her drink a cup of coffee before leaving. The guests were looking at her, hardly daring to go near. I can understand them. You don't know what to do on occasions like that. It was Riri who grabbed a bottle of rum from a shelf and poured her out a glassful. She evidently didn't realize what she was drinking, for it made her cough and spill some of it down her sweater.

'I didn't see them again all morning, neither her nor Riri. Monsieur John – when he got up at last – he was the only one to have heard nothing – went off in a borrowed car.

'All three came back here at about two o'clock for lunch. It seems they had to go as far as Melun where the body was taken first.'

'They had lunch here?'

She said they had, and that that was all she knew. After the meal, Lulu had piled all her things and Bob's into the suitcase, and John drove her to Melun. She doesn't drive, so she couldn't use her own car.

I learned practically nothing from Riri. Despite his having

178

the face and bearing of a young hooligan, he is surprisingly tactful where women are concerned.

'Lulu is a good sort!' was all he would say. 'As for the lieutenant, I'd a good mind to knock his face in.'

'Why?'

'Because of the questions he asked.'

The police lieutenant, whom I don't know, believed right
away that it was suicide rather than an accident. It appears that,
in the afternoon, one of his men, using Bob's canoe, the curtain-
cord and the five-kilo weight, threw this into the water in every
conceivable manner, without the cord getting caught round his
ankle, one single time, in the same way as it had wound itself
around Dandurand's.

At ten o'clock in the morning, the lieutenant had already had
the body taken to the Melun Barracks, where he'd called in the
medical expert. Did he have some idea at the back of his mind?
Was he considering the possibility of a crime? If so, the evidence of those who saw Bob leaving the *Beau Dimanche* and of
those who saw him going past on the millstream in the stern of
his boat must have undeceived him.

I don't believe, like Riri, that he is a kind of sadist, but rather
a scrupulous type, one of those men who seek perfection in the
minutest detail. He is in daily contact with all kinds of people.
Lulu smelled of drink. With her close-fitting black slacks, her
soiled sweater, her hurriedly combed hair, darker at the roots
because she dyes it, he must have taken her for what she isn't.

John Lenauer heard some of his questions in the office at the
police station, where the lieutenant sat down without inviting
the others to do the same. Twice, John had intervened furiously, and it had ended by his being sent out of the room. The
policeman had even inquired of Lulu:

'He's your lover?'

Before that, he had wanted to know whether she had quarrelled with Bob the night before, if he had a mistress, how much
money he earned as publicity agent of a little known magazine
for which he'd been working for two years.

'What was he doing before that?'

'He was a representative for a boot and shoe factory.'

'In Paris?'

'Yes.'

'He was sacked?'

'No.'

'Why did he change his job?'

'Because he'd had enough of it.'

'He often changed jobs?'

'Whenever he felt like it.'

'In short, if I am to understand aright, it is you, with your hats, who keeps the pot boiling?'

'I bring in my share.'

'The bigger share?'

'Not always.'

This was all the more cruel in that the lieutenant wasn't far wrong. In the thirteen or fourteen years I've known him, Bob Dandurand has had twenty different jobs, and it wasn't always of his own accord that he left them. He never succeeded in taking seriously the tasks that the need to earn his living imposed on him.

'You never reproached him?'

'Reproach him for what? I hadn't anything to reproach him with.'

A 'good sort', Riri had said about her and, coming from him, the compliment really meant something. She had defended herself valiantly, or rather she had valiantly defended her Bob against the police officer's insinuations. Had she convinced him? That's another story.

'What did he drink in the course of yesterday evening?'

'Some wine.'

'How many glasses?'

'I didn't count them.'

'He drank a great deal?'

In his way, he too was looking for a reason for a death that no one was able to explain to him. What he wanted was the simple truth in black and white.

'Was he drunk when he went to bed?'

Her teeth clenched, eyes glaring, she replied:

'I have never seen him drunk.'

'He spent a lot of his time in bars?'

The medical expert, after examining the body, must have told him that Dandurand was an alcoholic which, in the medical sense, was true.

'Had he any debts? Do you know if he had any enemies?'

Then, once more, he had insisted on knowing if Bob had any mistresses, she herself any lovers.

When, at last, he was tired of asking fruitless questions, she had requested permission to take the body away.

'Come and see me this afternoon. First of all, I must make a report to the public attorney.'

The latter was spending the day with friends near Corbeil, and it had taken some time to get in touch with him by telephone. When finally, towards four o'clock, the formalities had been completed, the lieutenant had announced:

'It is up to you to find an ambulance to take him away, unless you would prefer the mortuary van.'

This had taken almost another hour, for there wasn't an ambulance free right away. Lulu had got into it with her husband's body, refusing to let Riri and John accompany her. The Parisians were beginning to return home after the weekend, and, on the Fontainebleau road, cars were moving at a snail's pace, the traffic having been jammed for more than a quarter of an hour owing to a car accident on the Juvisy road. A motor-cycle policeman had even talked of requisitioning the ambulance for a casualty and only gave up the idea at the sight of the dead man.

No one has ever told me, but I am sure there was no dancing that evening on the terrace at the *Beau Dimanche*.

'What does she say?' my wife asked me when I got back from Lulu's at lunch-time on the Monday.

'What would you have her say? It appears that Bob committed suicide.'

'*Him?* You believe that?'

'Indeed I must. It seems certain.'

'Why should he have done that?'

'No one has any idea.'

What does one know about others, after all, when one doesn't know very much about oneself? I remember that, as I ate my chop, I stared so intently at my wife that, rather ill at ease, she inquired:

'What are you thinking about?'

For want of a better answer, I murmured:

'About nothing. About everything.'

Actually, a quite definite thought had just occurred to me. Suppose it were my body, instead of Bob Dandurand's, that had just been dragged out of the Seine, below the weir at Vives-Eaux, what would Madeleine have replied to the question she had just put to me?

'Why should he have done that?'

I tried to imagine her answers, those of my friends, of my patients, of all who are in more or less regular contact with me and are convinced that they know me.

I had cold shivers at the sudden realization that I was alone in the world.

Chapter Three

The concierge, with the help of the old church-hen of the prie-Dieu, organized everything. It seems that both are crazy about a curate in the parish whom they alert the moment anyone in the house falls ill, so that a tenant can't take to his bed without finding the priest at his side.

I have never discussed the matter with Dandurand, but I know he didn't attend Mass, and that Lulu wasn't a practising Catholic either.

When my wife went to the Rue Lamarck, on the Monday afternoon, the Abbé Doncoeur was there, taller and heftier than everyone around him, arguing with Lulu, while a printer waited for the final wording of the funeral-cards. I received mine at midday on the Tuesday. The four employees had buckled to to write the addresses. The card announced the burial for the Wednesday at ten o'clock, with the Absolution at the church of Saint-Pierre in Montmartre. Had the Abbé Doncoeur asked his bishop for a dispensation, or did the fact that there was no absolute proof of suicide suffice to open the doors of the church to Dandurand's body?

Something Lulu said to me later makes me think that she let herself be persuaded without too much difficulty.

'I think he too would have preferred the usual rites and ceremonies to take place, if only for his family's sake.'

When I made my way to the Rue Lamarck with my wife, at a quarter to nine the next morning, I knew scarcely anything about the Dandurand family. Bob never made any allusion to it, no more than to his reasons for settling down in Montmartre. At most, he would sometimes recall his quite unsuccessful attempt as a song writer, in a cabaret near the Place Blanche.

I have seldom seen a more glorious summer's day. The sun was as dazzling as on the previous days, with a heavenly breeze stirring the foliage of the trees and the light dresses of the women with the same delicious tremor. A crowd of people was standing in front of the house of the deceased; the door was draped in black, and the mortuary chapel had, in the end, been set up in the shop, making it unrecognizable.

I knew many faces by sight. Men and women of the neighbourhood were there, customers of Lulu's also, and men Bob met regularly in the bistros and played cards with. Justin, the *patron* of the café in the Place Constantin-Pecqueur, was wearing a black suit and starched shirt; he was so spotless, so consequential, shook so many hands as he stood outside on the pavement that he appeared to be the central figure of the ceremony.

On the Monday, I had wondered where Lulu would sleep for the two nights preceding the funeral, because Bob's body was still in the bedroom. There was, in fact, a couch against one of the walls in the studio, but it was hard and narrow, and I knew that she wouldn't be left by herself in the flat.

When I spoke to my wife about it, she said:

'It is all arranged. She is going to Mademoiselle Berthe's.'

Without thinking, I exclaimed:

'But there's only one bed.'

'Two women can sleep in the same bed, can't they?'

All the same it embarrassed me. I tried to picture them both in the spinster's over-polished rooms, while Bob was left all alone at the back of the shop. I couldn't see Lulu, used to sleeping with her husband, bumping into Mademoiselle Berthe's skinny body during the night. I experienced the same kind of uneasiness at the funeral; something indefinable struck me, I don't know exactly what, a curious mixture of respect for tradition and lack of conventionality.

The funeral-cards, the mortuary chapel, the Absolution in the church, that's all part of convention. Not the body abandoned for two nights behind closed shutters, nor other details almost impossible to quote because each in itself is unimportant. For instance, when I went into the house to pay my last respects before the coffin, Lulu wasn't in the mortuary chapel. I half-opened the studio door, as one might slip into the wings of a theatre, as an intimate. I caught her standing in front of a mirror, with one of her employees fitting a little black and white hat on to her head. She looked weary, but less than I would have expected, and it didn't prevent her from keeping an eye on everything.

'The hearse has come?' she inquired anxiously.

'Not yet.'

'It will be here in three minutes. You've seen the crowd in the street, Charles?'

More often than not I have seen Lulu dressed in light colours, winter and summer alike, apart from the black slacks she wore – I can't think why – at Tilly. For the first time, I was seeing her all in black. Her dressmaker must have made the dress for the occasion and, making the heat an excuse, had chosen a very light, dull satin.

'You're quite sure, Louise, that I don't need something white around my neck?'

And Louise, her second assistant, replied through a mouthful of pins:

'It would kill the white in the hat.'

The hairdresser had called too, or Lulu had been to her. Her hair was a more pronounced red than usual. She was naturally auburn but, ever since I have known her, she's been dyeing it a coppery blonde. Since she has gone on deepening the colour a little more year after year, today it has reached an almost flaming red.

There was a drink placed handy on a table. It probably wasn't she who had asked for it. Someone must have said to her:

'Keep up your strength. You'll have need of it shortly.'

She asked:

'Is his sister still there?'

That was how I learned that the tall, distinguished-looking woman I had seen in the half-light of the mortuary chapel was Bob's sister. She had made less impression on me than the children accompanying her, especially the young man, about twenty years old, who is so like Bob that, during the Absolution, I couldn't take my eyes off him. I was expecting, quite unreasonably, to see children of the same age as mine, and here were a tall young man and a young girl who seemed to be a little disconcerted at discovering a new world.

Pétrel, the barrister husband, was not at the Rue Lamarck. He joined the cortège en route, and wormed his way to the front near his wife. He is a small, spare man, turning grey, and wears the rosette of the Legion of Honour. He too has a certain distinction.

Less than his wife and children, however. Bob's sister was also in black, but her dress was in such a different class from Lulu's as to render the latter's embarrassingly vulgar.

I didn't take much notice of her daughter, who has the banality of what is known as a well-brought-up young girl.

I always come back to the young man, Jean-Paul, as I learned later. Did he have the chance of meeting his uncle during one of the rare visits the latter made to the Boulevard Péreire? Didn't Dandurand contrive to meet his sister privately? In the first instance, it must have been disturbing for both of them to meet face to face, more alike than most fathers and sons. It would have been interesting to compare their attitudes. Bob had assimilated himself to Montmartre to such a pitch that he had acquired its slightest mannerisms and affected its slang, as well as a casual off-handedness which, at the Boulevard Péreire, could only be considered counterfeit.

Jean-Paul, on the contrary, possessed a polished ease of manner, barely tempered by a hint of shyness. He was as tall as his mother and, throughout the ceremony, looked after her with a lover's thoughtfulness.

Most of the regular guests from Tilly were there, including Léon Fradin in black; black tie on white shirt, hands the colour of baked earth.

Just when the cortège was about to form, there had been, as there always is, some hesitation. Lulu, naturally, went to take her place behind the hearse, while the master of ceremonies, whom she hadn't given time to accompany her, drove Madame Pétrel and her children.

Had the two women talked to each other in the house? I know nothing about it yet. Actually, on the Monday afternoon, when she had come from Dieppe, while the confusion was at its height, Madame Pétrel had gone straight up to Lulu, whom she had recognized, either from photographs Bob had shown her, or from the description he'd given of her.

'I am his sister,' she had said to her.

Once inside the room, she had remained standing for about ten minutes, meditating; there were no tears, she didn't say a word, while Lulu neither knew what to do, nor where to put herself. Only as she was leaving did she murmur:

'You will let me know the date and the hour of the ceremony.'

On the morning of the funeral, she hadn't spoken to anyone, except to three gentlemen whom Lulu didn't know, two of them elderly and one very ancient whom the others greeted deferentially.

Just when the hearse was about to move off, Lulu had turned round, embarrassed perhaps to find herself at the front with her husband's family. She had made a sign to someone behind me and, since there was no response to her appeal, she had gone to look for Mademoiselle Berthe and had obliged her to sit beside her.

Our small party consisted of John Lenauer, Riri, little Madame Millot whose husband couldn't come, and finally Léon Fradin joined us.

I don't know how many there were in the cortège, I estimate it at about three hundred at least for, when I turned round, I could see the street black with people for more than a hundred yards.

We went slowly up the Avenue Junot, people saluting us as we passed, then the hearse threaded its way down the narrow streets of the Butte, and it wasn't long before it reached the Place du Tertre.

This, despite the early morning hour, was already thick with parasols, the tables under them spread with red-checked cloths. A car, crammed with foreigners, had parked opposite one of the terraces, and a tall, blonde girl in shorts was taking photographs.

The rural constable of the Commune Libre was there, with his light blue tunic, his drum and képi. He knew Bob well, and they must often have had a drink together. I don't know whether he had dressed up for the occasion, but the fact remains that, as the coffin was entering the church, he drew himself up stiffly like a soldier on parade and beat the drum.

If all the women went into the church, many of the men stayed outside, most of them making a bee-line for the nearest bars.

Lulu and Mademoiselle Berthe stood alone on one side of the coffin, the Pétrels on the other.

Lulu had certainly been wrong to have her hair tinted the day before the funeral; her dressmaker, too, had been ill-inspired in choosing a dress style as clinging as the Tilly slacks. Was it the contrast between the black silk and the sunshine? I don't know, but Lulu had never seemed to me so naked; she gave the impression of having nothing on at all but her dress.

The church doors had been left open, so that the noises from outside mingled with the organ-music and liturgical chants. The Abbé Doncoeur was officiating. He was so tall, muscular, powerful that, on him, the soutane and surplice seemed like fancy-dress. A little while ago, in the street, he strode like a footballer, behind the cross an altar boy was carrying, bawling out verses at the top of his voice, and looking the passers-by full in the face as if challenging them.

The sunshine outside merged pleasantly into the shadowy light inside the church, and, in the freshness prevailing under the arches, gusts of warm air circulated, bearing the odours of the city.

The men who stayed out on the Place du Tertre went back in for the Offertory.

Only the family, with the Abbé Doncoeur and his acolyte, went to the cemetery in the motor-hearse since, for want of space in Montmartre cemetery, Bob was to be buried at Thiais.

187

Those hearses always make me think of charabancs. Lulu insisted on Mademoiselle Berthe getting in with her. She seemed to be looking for someone, and I'm sure that, if there had been more room, she would have summoned her three other employees.

The same confusion arose as at the departure from the Rue Lamarck. Parties were re-formed. Some made their way quite openly to the tables outside, where a flower-girl offered her wares. We were all together again, my wife, John Lenauer, Riri and Madame Millot, and John was talking of standing us a drink when I noticed Adeline, alone on the edge of the pavement and looking in my direction.

I had left my car in the Rue Caulaincourt, for I had two calls to make before going back home. I said to my wife and the others:

'I'm leaving you now.'

'You won't have a quick one?'

I answered with a shake of the head. Adeline had started to walk towards the Rue du Mont-Cenis steps. I caught up with her in a few strides. If she had something to tell me, I was giving her the opportunity.

'You're going back to the Rue Lamarck?' I inquired.

'No. We're not working this afternoon. I'm going back home, to the Rue Clignancourt.'

'You live with your parents?'

She looked at me in surprise, almost with reproach:

'Even if I wanted to, it would be difficult. They live in Finistère.'

She was less youthful when she was speaking, as if her voice were too mature for her body and face. After a few steps in silence:

'It's all over,' she sighed, in the way one states a fact.

People were overtaking us. We were not walking quickly, and she was swinging her handbag at arm's length, like the young girls you see strolling along with a lover. I nearly asked:

'What's all over?'

But I could understand her state of mind. With grave face, she was following her own train of thought.

'I suppose it *is* certain he committed suicide?'

'As certain as it can be in such a case.'

'It's odd,' she murmured then.

I had a feeling she wanted to go on, but was hesitating. By way of encouragement, I questioned:

'When did you see him for the last time?'

Giving her words a special emphasis, she answered:

'On Saturday afternoon.'

So that was her secret. I had wondered how Bob had spent that afternoon, which was his last. Mademoiselle Berthe had told me he'd probably played cards at Justin's.

Still trying to help, I said:

'At home?'

She nodded, adding, after a silence:

'I live in lodgings and I entertain whom I choose. He came to see me quite often, especially on Saturday afternoons. The *patronne* knows. She has never been jealous.'

'Did she know about last Saturday?'

'She hasn't spoken to me about it. Because of what happened the next day at Tilly, I thought I was right not to say anything to her.'

'He stayed with you a long time?'

'He never stayed long.'

'He was in love with you?'

She shrugged her shoulders, surprised at such a question coming from me.

'I don't count any more than the others. He would take his pleasure, light a cigarette, and that was all. I don't hold it against him. I'd rather it happened like that, without complications.'

I was sure there was something she still hadn't told me, something she was longing to say.

'He behaved just as he did the other times?'

'More or less. At first, the difference didn't strike me. When he arrived he would begin by joking, and he'd be joking again as he left.'

'He didn't do so last Saturday?'

'Not in the same way. He seemed more ardent than usual. Just as he was getting out of bed, he exclaimed:

' "It's crazy!"

189

' "What's crazy?" I asked him. "Making love to me?"

'He gave a queer laugh.

' "No. Don't take any notice. You're a good kid. And, after all, you deserved something better."

' "I deserved something better than you?"

' "I'm talking to myself as old men do."

'He was whistling as he dressed. It's a habit that has always irritated me. Then he lit a cigarette and offered me one. I had stayed stretched out on the bed, for I intended going to sleep when he'd gone. I got the impression that he was anxious to talk before leaving, but couldn't find the words.

' "When all's said and done," he began, "the world is full of people who . . ."

'As he stopped, I insisted:

' "Who what?"

' "Nothing. It's too complicated. It's no use thinking."

'He came up to the bed and, before kissing me, looked me slowly up and down from head to foot. His expression was so different from his usual one that I was rather scared.

' "Lulu's a decent kid too," he sighed. "But you, you're still quite young . . ."

' "Young with the bloom gone!" I joked.

'That seemed to anger him. Then he saw that I was making fun of him and of myself. He was usually the first to laugh at everything, especially at things that don't make others laugh, at what others respect. Meeting a priest in the street, I've heard him wisecrack as he swept off his hat:

' "Greetings, Priestling!"

'Now, because of my joke, I saw his eyes darken. They were light eyes, you remember, of a grey-blue you rarely see in a man, but at times they could turn into the dark grey of a storm-cloud.

'It didn't last. Instead of kissing my mouth, he put his lips to my forehead. I'm sorry now that this should have made me laugh. If I had known, I would never have said, because of that kiss:

' "So long, Daddy!"

'Was he really angry or not? I only saw his back as he crossed to the door. He went out without turning round, just stopped on

190

the staircase to relight the cigarette he'd allowed to go out.

'I badly needed to talk to someone about it. Now it's done. Even on Monday, when you came to the Rue Lamarck, I fancied you were making an effort to understand. I am almost certain he had an idea at the back of his mind and that, when he came into my room, his decision had already been taken.'

She turned towards me and looked at me with insistence.

'You can understand the effect it had on me?'

I believed I understood, though she didn't explain. She was the last woman Bob had held in his arms. As he entered that furnished room, he was fully aware that he was about to make love for the last time. I also would swear he had worked out all the details. He had not acted, on the Sunday morning, in a moment of despondency, nor on a sudden impulse.

Having made up his mind to die, he tried to devise a way of doing so decently. It was in character. He must have envisaged every kind of suicide in his search for the one that would make his death seem accidental.

Did he care about the opinion of his sister and the people of the Boulevard Péreire? I don't know. I don't think so. It was for Lulu that he set the stage, so that she wouldn't know.

He never had any inclination for fishing, and he was not the man to get up at four or five in the morning out of sheer exuberance. Pike-fishing provided him with a plausible excuse to be alone in the canoe when the mill-race was almost deserted. If he had wound the rope around his ankle with one turn only, instead of two, I am convinced that no one, not even the police lieutenant, would have raised the question of suicide.

We were standing at the corner of the Rue Caulaincourt and the Rue du Mont-Cenis, Adeline and I, and most of the people who passed were still mourners.

'He knew,' she said, looking at the pavement, 'and for all that, he was in my bed. I think it's going to be some time before I let a man take me in his arms again.'

Her lower lip was swelling as if she were on the verge of tears. I took hold of her elbow.

'As time goes on, you will forget,' I told her, only half believing it myself.

Certain pictures of Bob would come back to her probably

more than once, and would spoil what might have been pleasant moments.

It was only just when I was about to leave her that she resolved to unburden herself, modifying, with an ironic smile, whatever might be sentimental in the words:

'If he had shown himself as he was, instead of always acting the clown, I could have fallen in love with him.'

That phrase struck me. It often comes back to my mind when I think of Bob Dandurand. After all, Adeline's attitude is not without some analogies to my own reactions.

I have never compared him specifically to a clown but, as long as Bob lived, I never took him very seriously either. Among all those who associated with the Dandurands at Tilly, or in the back of the shop in the Rue Lamarck, were there many who did take him seriously? One would be inclined to attach more importance to Lulu's words and opinions than to his.

In a city like Paris, where four million human beings live side by side, ceaselessly rubbing shoulders, the word friend hasn't quite the same meaning as elsewhere.

For me, Bob was a friend, like John Lenauer is, like Gaillard, in much the same way as the Millots are friends, in that they have invited us to dine or to play bridge two or three times. But we know practically nothing about any of them, as they really are, beyond what they themselves want us to know.

Few people have as many friends of this kind as the Dandurands, for heaps of reasons, in particular because they always kept open house, so you were sure to find company there, at no matter what time of day. It is more unusual than it seems – when one has a free hour – to be able to say off-hand:

'We'll go to so-and-so's.'

They were hardly ever away, in actual fact never. You didn't get the impression of intruding. There was nothing to dirty, nothing to spoil. You didn't disturb anyone in their work or their enjoyment. Bob's invariable greeting was:

'*A drop of white?*'

Sometimes, in rush periods, the girls used to work late in the evening, and the fact that they were surrounded by a chattering or even teasing crowd didn't disturb them in the least.

Here, in a sense, was neutral ground, like a café, but a café

192

where each was free to act and speak as he pleased, with the certainty of shocking no one.

I have met there people belonging to very different social classes, a police-court magistrate among others, small, rotund and bald-headed. He was sitting shyly in a corner, never moved from there throughout the evening, happy to be held captive in an atmosphere of idle relaxation.

Perhaps Bob deliberately tried to create this atmosphere, at times coming out with an extravagant bit of nonsense, a turn of phrase that anywhere else would be considered sacrilegious, or again a coarse word which, uttered by him, in his own house, made no one blush.

Not so long ago, I began to wonder how my wife and I had found our way to the Rue Lamarck, and I had to rack my brains to remember. Shortly before the war we had stopped by chance at the *Beau Dimanche*, and developed the habit of going back there quite regularly when the weather was fine. If Madame Blanche had not exactly taken us under her wing, and if she wasn't yet calling me Monsieur Charles, she was, nevertheless, beginning to look upon us with a favourable eye. She certainly didn't reserve the same room for us every Saturday – a favour granted only to those who'd been going there for years – but she always found somewhere to put us at the last minute.

This was before our sons were born. I recall the looks my wife used to give me, as we sat outside in the evening, when chance set us down not far from the table where the Dandurands, John, Riri and Yvonne Simart were gathered, as well as a few others who stopped coming, later on.

Bottles of wine circulated at a breath-taking speed, and Bob and John vied with each other in playing the craziest and most outrageous practical jokes.

We were asleep, one Saturday night, when there was a hesitant knock on the door. In my pyjamas, and without putting the light on, I opened it to find Bob, also in pyjamas, standing there in the moonlight.

'I believe you're a doctor,' he murmured, in an embarrassed way.

I had never seen him embarrassed until then, and I didn't think he could be.

'My wife is ill. She's been having dreadful attacks of pain for the last hour and, now, she's at the end of her tether.'

Even then they occupied the room in which, on Saturday, he spent his last night.

'I know it isn't fair to disturb a doctor on holiday, but I wondered . . .'

I didn't have my medical kit with me. I merely put on my dressing-gown and followed him. Lulu, naked under the sheet, was white-lipped, her face streaming with sweat, and she was clutching her lower abdomen with both hands.

'You've had pains like this before?'

She nodded, her eyes imploring me to put an end to her suffering. I felt her abdomen to make sure there was no question of appendicitis, and I was beginning to palpate the liver when she said to me, through almost clenched teeth:

'That's not it.'

She had already been examined then under the same circumstances, and she knew what these gestures implied.

'I'm going to have a miscarriage,' she concluded, casting a look of distress at her husband.

I asked him to go and find a hot water bottle, and I suppose he wakened Madame Fradin. After that I sent him to Corbeil, in his car, with a prescription. The pains were not continuous, they came in waves, almost like the pains of childbirth, only more violent. During respites, Lulu talked to me, as she would have talked to anyone at all, for reassurance and distraction.

'This is the fifth time, Doctor. The last time, the doctor warned me that, if it happened again, I might die.'

'You won't die this time, I promise you.'

'Certain?'

'Which doctor told you that?'

She mentioned one of my colleagues who has his consulting-rooms in the Rue Lepic.

'He wanted me to warn my husband so that he could make sure it didn't happen again.'

'Your husband refused to take precautions?'

'I didn't tell him.'

'Why?'

She was shaken with fresh spasms. During the next inter-mission, I asked:

'Do you want to have a child?'

She answered yes, but it wasn't a decided yes. If it was one of her justifications, it couldn't be the only one.

'Is your husband very anxious to have any?'

'He has never talked about it.'

I thought I understood and I hadn't the courage to insist. She was looking at me intensely, watching for my reactions. I'm convinced she knew that I had guessed and was grateful to me for saying nothing about it.

Since that night, she has had complete confidence in me. Bob came back with the medicines I had prescribed, and these at least enabled me to alleviate the pains. He seemed glad to find me at his wife's bedside, holding her hand, and to get a smile from her.

Two weeks later, we belonged to the group we had con-sidered so boisterous, and in the autumn, we dined for the first time at the Rue Lamarck, together with Gaillard, the painter.

The following spring, Lulu had another miscarriage, less dangerous, and again went to see her doctor in the Rue Lepic.

Bob Dandurand asked me:

'He's a good doctor?'

'I have nothing against him.'

He looked at me with extreme seriousness, and murmured:

'Thank you.'

A year later, Lulu came to my consulting room to tell me she was pregnant once again.

'Do you mind taking me as a patient?'

After examining her, I had been obliged to tell her that, in all probability, her pregnancy would end like the previous ones.

'I'm used to it now. Whenever it happens, it's a bad time to get through but, afterwards, I don't think about it any more.'

'It's also a big risk to take.'

'I know.'

This has happened four times since then, to my knowledge. The second time, on account of certain complications, I had to make her go into a clinic, where she stayed for three weeks. When she came out she didn't weigh forty kilos, and was so thin that, with her less than average stature, she looked like a little girl.

'It doesn't matter, Charles. I'm going to eat twice as much as I usually do, and I'll soon be back on my feet.'

When I tried to talk to her like her doctor from the Rue Lepic, she shrugged her shoulders, saying:

'It wouldn't be worthwhile being his wife any more!'

Mine, I don't suppose, was ever aware of this professional side of our relationship. She only knows that Lulu, like many women, has certain disorders requiring the attention of a doctor, every now and again.

That's why, perhaps, had I listened to her, we'd have met the Dandurands less frequently. She is easily put out, especially since we've had the children, and tends to lead a more conventional life. Jokes which used to make her laugh, only a few years ago, now occasion no more than a frown, and Montmartre, which amused her at first, is beginning to frighten her.

Now that Bob is dead, I am expecting her to supply me with good reasons for spacing out our visits to the Rue Lamarck, and even for severing the connection altogether.

*

When I went back to my car, the pavement in the Rue Lamarck was deserted.

The furnishers had finished taking down the black hangings embroidered with silver tears. The shop shutters, painted sky-blue, were lowered, with the funeral notice still on the left one.

I went to Justin's bar, for I was thirsty. He hadn't changed, merely taken off his jacket and tie, and rolled up the sleeves of his excessively white shirt. He was wearing purple braces.

'What will you have?' he inquired in the voice he must have used in the morning to offer his condolences. 'Drinks are on me today.'

I asked for a sweet vermouth. I don't know why, when what I really wanted was a white wine. A few workmen in overalls were standing in front of the zinc counter.

'I'm really glad he had such a fine funeral. Did you hear the drum?'

The hearse should have reached Thiais by now. There in the

196

sunshine stretch the graves as far as the eye can see, planes from Orly droning above them in a cloudless sky.

'It's going to be hard for her,' sighed Justin, clinking his glass against mine. 'There are not ten men like him in the whole of Montmartre.'

'He came here last Saturday?'

'About four o'clock. He stayed long enough to play fifteen hundred points with Hubert, the young couple and me, in this corner, see, behind the door.'

That was after he left Adeline.

'He didn't say anything special?'

'He was his usual self. The only thing is that, although he won, as he nearly always does, he insisted on standing his round.'

'Why?'

'He didn't say, and no one insisted.'

I suddenly realized that the men in the small bars he frequented had for Bob – Big Bob as they called him – a respect that, as a rule, was only given grudgingly by such people.

'I can't get it out of my head that he was ill, that he knew it, and that he didn't want to condemn his wife to nursing him for years.'

'He was seeing a doctor?'

'He didn't say so. For some time now, he has had a strange way of looking at himself in the glass, the one behind the bottles. When a man of his kind begins to study himself in the mirror, believe me, it's not a good sign.'

I was struck by the truth of his remark. I catch myself looking into the same mirror, which is old and greyish, giving a scarcely flattering likeness.

'He often did this?'

'It must have been often, or I wouldn't have noticed it. He was approaching the age when one begins to have worries. I maintain that men go through the same difficult periods as women, towards forty-five or fifty and, if I may judge by what I've had to put up with from the *patronne* . . .'

He filled my glass up without asking me.

'I expect they'll have lunch at an inn out towards the cemetery. There is one where the food isn't bad. I've driven customers there two or three times.'

He clinked his glass against mine once more.

'To Bob's health!'

Then, leaning on the wet counter:

'You saw his sister?'

I nodded.

Madame Pétrel had impressed him and the whole district had noticed it.

'I always suspected that he wasn't just anyone. One afternoon, I had a well-known barrister here who stops occasionally for a drink. They began to discuss matters that are beyond my understanding and I saw right away that Monsieur Bob knew as much about them as the other.'

His wife came out of the kitchen, grey hair coiled into a bun, stomach well in advance:

'It's time you went and changed, Justin. Where have you put your cuff-links?'

He had dropped them into a glass behind the counter, and turned to wink at me as he went off.

Chapter Four

It was so hot the next day that the schools were closed. In the streets, where there wasn't a breath of air, you saw men carrying their jackets over their arms, patches of sweat darkening the backs of the women's dresses; life in Paris was reduced to dead slow, and the buses seemed to stick to the softened tarmac so that the smell of it caught in your throat. What impressed me most, was the policemen on duty at the Place Clichy. He had spread out his handkerchief behind his képi to protect his neck, like the infantrymen do when they're in the field.

Towards four o'clock, at the most stifling moment of the day, I happened to be within a stone's throw of Lulu's shop, so I decided to stop there for a minute or two.

From the outside, the house had recovered its everyday look; there were a few smartly coloured hats in the window and, by comparison with the burning heat of the street, it was almost cool in the back of the shop which, the day before, had been draped in black.

The studio too was back to normal with, however, a difference so slight that I hesitate to mention it. I remember glancing towards the bedroom door. A ray of sunshine fell across the bed which was littered with two or three dresses, some women's underwear, stockings, an elastic girdle. I understood when it became quite obvious to me that two of the employees had hardly anything on under their overalls, while Adeline had nothing on at all beneath a red wrapper of Lulu's that was too short for her.

It might have happened when Bob was alive, but not quite in the same way. It's difficult to explain. Lulu was in a slip, which isn't unusual and, through the nylon, you could see her brassière and her pants with a roll of fat bulging over them.

Lulu has always been utterly lacking in modesty, not brazenly, almost without realizing it, and certainly without any depravity. Once, on the terrace at the *Beau Dimanche*, at cocktail time, a flying ant crawled inside her blouse and I can see her now, lifting out a pink breast, with the same natural and noble gesture as a woman feeding her baby, to make sure she hadn't been bitten. It had nothing in common with the flagrant immodesty of Yvonne Simart, for instance, who would spend days on end, lying stark naked in the sun, on the bridge of her boat and, when someone came on board, merely covered her sex with a strip of towel. By the end of June, she was already as brown as a Hindu.

Only Mademoiselle Berthe was dressed normally, in black from head to foot, as if it were she who was in mourning; and old Rosalie Quéven – the one who tells fortunes and reads the coffee grounds – had flopped into the one and only arm-chair, her eyes red-rimmed as usual.

There were no bottles of white wine on the table, but a jug of lemonade, with lemons cut in two and lumps of ice floating in it.

Lulu's first words were:

'How are you, Charles?' She had used the familiar '*tu*'. She was working on a hat, and corrected herself at once:

'I'm sorry, Charles. I've seen so many people during the last few days that I no longer know whom I'm addressing intimately and whom I'm not.'

'That's all right.'

Her voice was hoarse and I asked if her throat was sore.

'A bit. That's what the lemonade's for.'

In Bob's time too, there was always a fairly free and easy atmosphere in the studio. But when he was alive, old Quéven would not have sat in the arm-chair as if in her own home, and she certainly wouldn't have taken her shoes off to massage her swollen feet. And I wonder if Lulu would have lent one of her négligées to Adeline.

One felt that they were anxious to catch up with the work that had accumulated.

'Won't you sit down, Charles?'

'I'm not staying long. I just called for a second, between two visits.'

'A propos, you don't know anyone who's looking for a second-hand car? Fradin brought ours back from Tilly for me, yesterday. I'm not going to learn to drive at my age, and there's no point in paying the garage for nothing. I would rather sell it privately than put it in the hands of a second-hand dealer who would give me practically nothing for it.'

'No one comes to mind immediately, but . . .'

'There's no hurry. If I haven't found anyone by next week, I'll put an advertisement in the paper.'

As a matter of fact, she hadn't any use for the car. It was natural for her to get rid of it. Was I shocked by this because Bob had only been buried the day before, or because she sounded so business-like?

This brought to mind something that hadn't yet occurred to me. Lulu no doubt wouldn't be spending weekends at Tilly any more. It isn't practicable to go there by train, first on account of the timetables, second because there are still two good miles to walk from the station. Someone like John would be glad to take her there in his car, and to bring her back, but I suspected that, for her, the *Beau Dimanche* already belonged to the past.

I let a week go by before going back to the Rue Lamarck.

One evening, after dinner, when the boys were in their room studying for their exams, I said to my wife:

'I'm going to drive round to Lulu's.'

My words were hardly an invitation for her to accompany me, and she realized this.

'Ah!' she said, at first.

Then, after a rather ominous silence:

'She's phoned you?'

'No.'

'I thought perhaps she was ill and had asked you to go and see her.'

'The last time I was down there, I didn't think she was at all well.'

To reassure my wife, I took my bag with me, to give my visit a somewhat professional look. All the same, I know she was displeased, and that this will crop up again. I left my bag in the car and knocked at the door beyond which I could see a light in the studio.

Not Lulu, but Mademoiselle Berthe opened the door to me and greeted me with:

'What a nice surprise! The *patronne* will be pleased to see you.'

The flat was so quiet that I was quite taken aback. Lulu was sitting before a table on which were playing cards, a bottle of Benedictine and two glasses.

'Come in, Charles. As you see, I am teaching Mademoiselle Berthe to play *belote* for two.'

She was the one wearing the red wrapper this evening. She obviously hadn't combed her hair since morning so it was straggly; the day-long sweat had made the powder on her face patchy, which gave it an older, wearier look.

'A glass of white wine?'

I shook my head.

'Benedictine? Incredible as it may seem, Berthe is beginning to get a taste for it, so we treat ourselves to a drop every night.'

What did she read in my look that made her frown? I saw a shadow, almost of fear, pass over her face. Her voice changed, as she inquired:

'It's wrong?'

'Why should it be wrong?'

'I don't know. There are times when I fancy people are watching me, ready to criticize. I'm not used to it yet.'

Used to being a widow? I suppose that's what she meant to say, but she didn't go into details. She was talking too much, as if she were afraid of silence.

'You know that Berthe has agreed to come and live with me?'

'She has given up her flat?'

'She's keeping it on, of course, but just goes now and again to do an hour's polishing.'

I cast a glance at the bedroom door. There was still only one bed in it. There was no space for another. Mademoiselle Berthe had sat down in front of her cards as if she were just waiting for me to go so as to get on with the game. I had never dreamed that one day she would be playing *belote* as she sipped a liqueur. She'd be taking up smoking next! Wasn't it even more astonishing to see her usurping Bob's place in Lulu's bed?

'Your throat?'

'It's much better. I applied wet compresses. How is your wife?'

'Well, thank you.'

I had come with an ulterior motive – to ask a few questions about Bob – and it embarrassed me to do this in the presence of the old maid.

'We are going to the cemetery together on Sunday to take some flowers. I've ordered an elegant and simple tombstone.'

She went to look for the sketch the mason had drawn for her on the back of a bill.

'What do you think of it? Do you think he'd have liked that?'

I lied to my wife when I went home.

'I'm worried about her health. She is letting herself go. I'll need to call on her from time to time, to make sure she looks after herself.'

Was my wife taken in? Did she think I had designs on Lulu?

I went back to the Rue Lamarck, a few days later, and this time I had gone out after dinner because I genuinely had a patient to visit.

The two women were playing cards and had visitors, La

Quéven again, and the old painter, Gaillard, who was rambling on in a slurred voice. I only stayed for a few minutes. As she took me back through the shop, Lulu whispered:

'You look cross?'

'Not at all.'

'Is it on account of Mademoiselle Berthe?'

'I assure you, Lulu . . .'

'I couldn't bear to spend the night alone.'

'I can understand that.'

I shook her hand warmly to reassure her and, at the last minute, she planted a kiss firmly on both my cheeks.

'Shall I see you soon?'

'Yes.'

'Promise?'

I kept my word when my wife and children went to Fourras for the holidays. I only leave Paris for eight or ten days during August, as it is more and more difficult to find a locum, and every year I lose a few patients because of this.

I was right in thinking that Lulu would not be going to the *Beau Dimanche* any more. I met John one evening in the Place Clichy.

'How's Lulu?' he inquired.

'I haven't seen her for a few days.'

'I went to the shop last Saturday to suggest taking her to the *Beau Dimanche*. I can understand her having no great desire to go there, but I think she's being influenced by that bedbug who's living with her.'

Sadly, John added:

'She's no longer the same Lulu as in Bob's time.'

That must have been the opinion of most of the habitués of the Rue Lamarck for, on two evenings, several days apart, I found the two women alone there. It's true it was holiday time and most of our friends were at the seaside or in the country.

I did manage to talk to Lulu alone, but it required patience. I had arrived at about nine o'clock. For nearly an hour, we chatted idly about one thing and another, with long silences, and I could tell that the bedbug, as John called her, was longing to go to bed. She makes a habit of going early, and of getting up one of the first in the district, even before the milk is delivered.

203

Lulu understood, without needing any sign from me, and we dragged out the conversation as if we had no intention of bringing it to a close. At last, at half past ten, Mademoiselle Berthe got up and, with her prim look, said to Lulu:

'You won't object if I go to bed?'

She was hoping, in this way, to turn me out, but I pretended not to hear.

'Good night, Doctor. She's tired out, and I don't think it is good for her to go to bed late.'

We both smiled as the bedroom door was shut with a sharp click and, a little later, we could hear the old maid talking to herself in an undertone, as she undressed.

'She's jealous,' said Lulu in a low voice.

'Of me?'

'Of everyone who comes here. Before, she was jealous of Bob, and spent her life torturing herself. Now that she has taken possession of the house . . .'

With a gesture, she seemed to dismiss an unwanted thought.

'Let's think no more about it. All the same, it is better than starting out of my sleep, all alone in the middle of the night. What did you want to say to me?'

She had caught me off my guard.

'Nothing special. I've thought about Bob a great deal these last few days.'

'So have I.'

'When I saw his sister, his nephew and niece at the funeral, I realized that I only knew about one part of his life.'

She had understood and she didn't interrupt me until I was on the point of excusing my curiosity.

'I knew quite well you wanted to ask me some questions. You just can't make out why he killed himself, can you?'

The word demanded some effort on her part, but she uttered it.

'All day long I ask myself the same question. At times I think I've almost found the answer, then everything becomes muddled again. He was always light-hearted. You know that.'

'When you were alone also?'

'He was just the same when we were alone as when there was

a crowd, so much so that, sometimes, I longed to tell him not to put himself out so for me. It's unusual in a man. Most women grumble about their husbands being charming to everyone else but them.'

'He hadn't changed latterly?'

'Except perhaps to become more tender. Quite often, for instance, he would call me his little girl.'

That made me think of Adeline.

'Perhaps I made a mistake at the very beginning, when I agreed to go and live with him, but it came about in such a way that I didn't realize what was happening to me. And, in any case, at that time, I didn't know any better. I was a really poor girl, do you know, Charles?'

She looked at the bedroom door, thinking like me that Mademoiselle Berthe might have her ear glued to it.

'It's all the same to me. There are plenty of people who know where I come from, and I'm not ashamed of it. I was born at Saint-Martin-des-Champs, a village six miles from Nevers. My name is Poncin. My father was a road-mender and, when he lost his job, because of drink, he helped out on the farms.'

She went to look in a drawer for three photographs she wanted to show me. They had been so badly taken that all the faces looked askew. The man sat with folded arms, staring straight ahead, while his wife had her two hands resting flat on her knees. Their six children surrounded them, four girls and two boys.

'We would have been seven if the last one hadn't died soon after birth.'

'Your mother is still alive?'

'She lives in the same house in Saint-Martin, and we send her a little money every month. I don't really know how old she is now. I would have to work it out. In any case, she must be over eighty. But I'm boring you.'

'No.'

'It's strange those stories should interest you. It's a long time since I talked about my family.'

She went into details about what had become of each one of them. Her eldest brother, Henri, was a policeman in Aurillac, had four children, and one of his daughters had just been married. Another was a hairdresser in Marseilles. One of his daughters, Huguette, had married a Monsieur Longlois and they kept a café at Nantes.

'Those are the successful ones,' she concluded. 'Mireille, who is two years younger than me, was for a long time in a brothel at Béziers and now lives in Algiers, where it seems she has set up in business on her own account. It's *her* my mother talks about most in her letters, because she sends her the most money. As for Jeanine, my elder by a year, the very fat one in the photograph, she has never married and has spent her whole life as a chambermaid in the same hotel at Nevers. She had two children years ago, and handed them over to my mother to bring up. When I met Bob, I was, more or less, of the same type as those two.'

If Mademoiselle Berthe had been listening for a time behind the door, she had gone back to bed, for it was from that direction he heard her coughing to manifest her impatience.

'Cough away, old girl!' murmured Lulu, smiling at me. Then to me:

'You really don't want anything to drink?'

'No, thank you.'

'Do you want me to go on?'

She looked at the alarm clock standing on the mantelshelf:

'I was forgetting your wife isn't in Paris.'

She had guessed that my wife would not have approved of my staying so late at the Rue Lamarck.

'How old were you when you left your village?'

'I came to Paris when I was fifteen. In families like mine, girls are sent into service before they've taken their lower certificate. At thirteen, I was already nursemaid to the children of a chemist in Nevers. At fifteen, a family in the town, who went to live in Paris, took me with them. You must know the rest of the story, for you're not a doctor for nothing. The extraordinary thing is that two years passed without anything whatever happening to me. Then my employer, who was in the Administration, was sent to the south. I stayed behind, I had five or six jobs one after the other. And, at nineteen, I was practically on the streets.'

'Was it then you met Bob?'

'Not straight away. Nearly two years later, in 1930. I was

living, at that time, in the Latin Quarter, sometimes with one student, sometimes another. It might last a month, or only a fortnight.'

I didn't hesitate to ask:

'You'd already had your first miscarriage?'

'You can call it abortion, since it's the truth. I nearly died from it, and the medical student who helped me was so terrified that he threatened to commit suicide. I've come across his name in the papers since then, for he's now a celebrity.'

'You were in love with him?'

'Neither with him, nor with any of the others.'

She was sincere.

'I believe, in my heart of hearts, I didn't approve of that. I did it out of sheer necessity. One day in July, just as the exams were starting, I was sitting outside the Harcourt, in the Boulevard Saint-Michel, with a friend. He was a Rumanian student who was going back to his own country for the long vacation. July and August were difficult months for me to get through, and I was sometimes driven to accosting tourists on the Grands Boulevards. I was even arrested once, and I still wonder by what miracle I got away with it. I looked so young, in those days, that the police inspector before whom we had to line up took pity on me. You don't mind if I pour myself a drop?'

As she sat down again she questioned:

'I'm not shocking you?'

'Not in the least.'

'Admit that you had your suspicions about all this?'

'I did.'

'Now I'll tell you how I met Bob, though no one called him that yet. As I said, I was sitting with my Rumanian ouside the café. It was at the end of the afternoon and there were a lot of people about. A tall young man passed close to us, hatless, with reddish blonde hair and light grey eyes. His eyes struck me right away, and also the fact that his clothes might have been chosen to match them; his suit was of the same grey, his tie, even his socks. He stopped a moment to shake my companion's hand, only favoured me with a blank stare, and made his way towards the bar. He wasn't at all the Bob you knew; he was more like his nephew whom you saw the other day.

' "Who's that?" I asked my friend.

' "He interests you?"

' "He has unusual eyes."

My Rumanian smiled, turned round to the bar where his pal was busy drinking, alone, both elbows on the counter, like a man determined to get drunk.

' "Wait for me a second."

'I watched them as they talked together in an undertone. Bob turned several times to look at me, seeming to hesitate. In the end, he paid for his drink and, without enthusiasm, followed the Rumanian, shrugging his shoulders.

' "May I introduce Robert Dandurand, who is sitting his Law Finals tomorrow?"

'In my case, the introduction was much simpler. He merely said:

' "Lulu."

'For half an hour they paid no attention to me, except to offer me a cigarette now and again, as they discussed their professors and fellow students. Then the Rumanian, glancing at his watch, got up.

' "It's time I left. Finish your drink quietly and try not to argue!"

'I never saw him again. At the beginning, Dandurand had the glum expression of someone who's been lured into a trap.

' "You've known him for a long time?" he asked me.

' "Three weeks."

' "He's an intelligent chap. I'd like to bet he will be Prime Minister of his country one day."

'He was crossing and uncrossing his legs, as if he were ill at ease, and it was then I noticed his socks.

' "If you have something better to do, don't worry about me. I know you have an important exam tomorrow."

'I had no idea what was going on in his mind, and it had nothing to do with me. Even then he had a way of slightly curling his upper lip that made him look as if he were mocking other people and himself.

' "Your first name is Robert?"

' "Yes."

' "Has no one ever called you Bob?"

' "No. Why?"

208

' "Because I think it suits you."

'I know it was a silly thing to say, but I had to say something.'

As she told me this, Lulu smiled at me with such humility that I all but took her hand, angry with myself for judging her so harshly during the past weeks. The bedroom door half opened; Mademoiselle Berthe poked her head through, her hair in curling pins:

'It is none of my business, Doctor, but it does seem that in the interests of her health . . .'

'Go back to bed,' Lulu told her, 'I'm coming right away.' And, behind the closed door, the old maid began muttering to herself again.

'You see! I'm no longer allowed to go to bed when I please. I so much wanted to talk.'

'You're bound to obey her?'

'If I don't go, she'll sulk all day tomorrow, never opening her lips. Once already, last Sunday, we were on our own from morning till night without exchanging a single word because I refused to go to Mass with her. In the end, she didn't go. I'll tell you the rest another time. I want you to know everything. You will see that Bob was much more complicated than he appeared, and perhaps you, who are a better judge of human nature than I am, will understand what happened to him. What I want you to know, however, from now onwards, is that I had nothing to do with the decision he took then. A kind of miracle came about. Isn't it a miracle that, from that very moment, from the second he sat beside me on a wicker chair outside the café Harcourt, we have never left each other, never spent a single night apart, except during the weeks I was at the clinic? Even when he went to see his father at Poitiers, he took me with him, and came back to me at the hotel at night time. Nevertheless, we weren't married.'

I had stood up, ready to go.

'Do you know in which year we were married, Charles?'

I had no idea. She had just told me they'd been living together since 1930.

'In 1939, three weeks after the declaration of war. The day after the declaration, Bob went off to get the banns published.

He was so much afraid he'd be called up before we could be legally married.'

'He was called up?'

'Two months later, as stretcher-bearer, and he was lucky enough to retreat as far as the Dordogne without falling into German hands. I was wrong a few minutes ago. During that period, of course, we did not sleep together, although I joined him several times in the Aisne, where he was billeted, and I reached Périgeux only five days after he did.'

We could hear Mademoiselle Berthe's dry cough.

'Good night, Charles. I won't keep you any longer.'

As she was shutting the door, she called out to me once more: 'Thank you!'

I didn't dare return to the Rue Lamarck too soon, for fear of giving the impression that I was going specially to find out the rest of the story. Now that Lulu had spoken about Poitiers, I discovered that Bob Dandurand was, more than likely, the son of Professor Dandurand who was, for a long time, Dean of the Faculty of Law, and author of a Treatise on Philosophy still used in all the Universities.

Throughout the years, it had never occurred to me that there was any connection between the old Professor and Lulu's husband. I had only to leaf through a University directory to learn that Gérard Dandurand, who retired during the war, died in 1950 at the age of seventy-five.

Did Bob go to Poitiers for the funeral service? Did he take his wife, and did he join her in the hotel for the night? The contrast between the Pétrel party and the crowd that attended Bob's burial was more understandable now. The three personages who had paid their respects to Bob's sister were obviously friends of the family, and the old man who was greeted with deference must have been a Master at Law or a former professor.

I wouldn't like to give the impression that, during that time, I thought of nothing else all day long but Dandurand and Lulu. Despite the holiday period, my patients kept me fairly busy. I took advantage, moreover, of the fact that I was having my meals at a restaurant, to meet friends I rarely have the opportunity of seeing during the rest of the year, and among whom several, like myself, had wives and children in the country.

One Sunday, I took an old friend with me to Tilly. I had promised to show him a picturesque inn. It so happened that John was in England for a few days with his wife, and Riri had accompanied Yvonne Simart and her friend Laurence to Deauville, where their firm was putting on a fashion show. Apart from the Millots, there was hardly anyone there except the fishing-set, and you couldn't even say that the food was good.

'You knew Professor Dandurand of Poitiers?'

'His daughter married a friend of mine.'

'Pétrel?'

'That's right, a first-rate chap. Their son, Jean-Paul, is one of my daughter's chums.'

'Robert Dandurand was drowned five kilometres from here, just below the weir, only a few weeks ago.'

'A son of old Dandurand?'

'I believe so.'

'I didn't know he had a son. Accident?'

'Suicide.'

'His sister hasn't said anything to me about it. It's true the family is at Dieppe for the summer. They have a magnificent villa on the cliff there.'

'Do you think it would be possible for me to meet her when they return?'

'Nothing simpler. I've only to invite them to dinner with you and your wife. They will be back in Paris towards the middle of September.'

The following Wednesday, it so happened that I had a sick call to make right opposite Lulu's. It was three o'clock in the afternoon. She was in the shop with a customer and saw me through the window-glass, so I couldn't avoid going in. She indicated the studio by a glance, saying:

'I'll be there at once, Charles.'

I don't know why my eyes settled on Adeline, who was busy stitching together different coloured ribbons. She lifted her face with a look of surprise, either at seeing me suddenly in front of her, for I had come in quietly, or else at the expression on my face. It would be beyond me to say what that expression was, or even what I was thinking about. I must have smiled at her and she smiled back. This time, she was wearing her working dress.

Outside, it was raining cats and dogs. Mademoiselle Berthe said to me, as if in reproach:

'Aren't you going to sit down?'

I don't know what went on in my mind. The others had their backs turned. I could hear Lulu's voice as she was seeing her customer out. Looking hard at Adeline, I mouthed the word:

'Saturday?'

I repeated it twice:

'Sa-tur-day?'

She had understood, assented with a flutter of her eyelids. I only stayed a few minutes at the Rue Lamarck. In front of Lulu, I was rather ashamed of what I had just done. I promised her I'd come again the following evening but, when I got there the next day, there were four women playing *belote* and drinking Benedictine, including old Rosalie Quéven, whose pallid complexion and red-rimmed eyes are unpleasant to look at, and a woman who was introduced to me as Nouzon or Mouzon.

Lulu made it clear to me that she was dreadfully sorry and begged my forgiveness. I stayed just long enough not to give the impression of flight. It was only nine o'clock, and I had no desire to go home.

As I was starting my car up, I hesitated and, all of a sudden, headed for the Rue de Clignancourt. I told myself that there couldn't be so very many lodgings of the kind Adeline had described to me, and that perhaps she would be in.

As it happened, I chose the right building at the first attempt.

'Number 43, fourth floor,' said the Auvergnat who was standing in the office in his shirt-sleeves.

'Is she at home?'

He didn't deign to answer me.

The staircase and corridors were ill-lit. At the fourth floor, somewhat breathless, I was regretting coming. As I drew near the door marked 43, I heard a woman's voice and was about to turn back, concluding that there were people there. My mind registered the words, yet it seemed to me that the voice was not Adeline's and, in fact, a second later, she in her turn spoke.

Because someone was coming out of another room, and because I didn't know what attitude to adopt in the narrow corridor, I knocked

212

'Come in!'

Adeline was lying on the bed, in her pants and brassière; her friend, sitting in an arm-chair, her feet up on the sill of the open window, pulled her dress down over her knees.

'I was making a call in the street . . .' I mumbled.

I must have looked ridiculous. The two women exchanged glances. The friend stood still for a second in the middle of the room and said:

'In any case, I've got some stockings to wash.'

Adeline continued to observe me interestedly. Without getting off the bed, she said to me:

'Lock the door.'

When I turned round, she gave an amused smile.

'So you couldn't wait until Saturday?'

Even if I had been able to explain to her how the notion had come into my head, she wouldn't have believed me.

In the manner of one who knows the whys and wherefores, she added:

'Strange creatures, men!'

'What is your friend going to think?'

'That we're making love. Isn't that what you're here for?'

I was, of course, forced to agree.

Still without moving from the bed, arching her back, lifting her legs one after the other, she slipped off her pants and threw them on to a chair.

'Aren't you going to undress?'

She couldn't have been happy about her breasts, for she didn't take off her brassière.

At some stage, she gave a little laugh.

'Why are you laughing?'

'No reason. An idea that's just come into my head.'

She didn't say what it was, and when I got back to my car, three quarters of an hour later, I believe I was more dissatisfied with myself than I have ever been in my life.

Why not tell the whole story? In front of my house, I felt the seat of the car to take out my bag. I couldn't find it. I was certain I had taken it with me, so it must have been stolen while the car was parked in the Rue de Clignancourt. Fortunately I have a spare one. Nevertheless, I regret it because it's the one my mother gave me the day I passed my finals. I did not report it.

Chapter Five

I have thought a great deal about what happened to Adeline and myself and, were it not for my good old leather bag reddened by twenty years' service, I wouldn't regret having joined her in the Rue de Clignancourt. I have had other adventures, more or less avowable, but this one, it seems to me, happened at a time that was most likely to open my eyes. It is too soon yet to talk about it. I need time to sift my ideas. Different in appearance, and certainly in character, as the two women are, I can't help recognizing certain points of similarity between Adeline and Lulu, and then it's Bob I fancy I'm beginning to understand.

I'd had to write to my wife that my bag had been stolen but, far from mentioning anything about the Rue de Clignancourt, I told her it had happened while my car was parked near a restaurant in the Rue Drouot where we sometimes dine together. I even went there, as if to establish an alibi, and it was my wife I was annoyed with for this added humiliation.

Who knows? These considerations, seemingly superfluous, may perhaps be more intimately connected with Dandurand than one might think.

Two or three days later, it occurred to me to invite Lulu to have dinner with me in town, which is the best way for us to chat without being spied on by the exasperating Mademoiselle Berthe. Besides, I told myself it would do Lulu good to have a change of atmosphere for an evening, and I was already reaching for the telephone when I realized that I was going to create complications for myself. We've gone out together several times, the Dandurands, my wife and I. My wife would none the less consider it a lack of consideration towards her if I went out with Lulu alone, above all in her absence. I can hear her objection ever after:

'What do you suppose people will think?'

I gave up the idea. I have nearly always given in in circumstances like this and, on the rare occasions that I haven't done so, I've always regretted it in the end. I let several days pass before making my way to the Rue Lamarck. In the meantime, a letter from my wife asked if I had reported the theft to the police. She recalled to me the name of a police superintendent we'd met when visiting friends.

I went to Lulu's one Sunday evening, and I found the two women alone, Lulu reading magazines in one corner, Mademoiselle Berthe mending stockings in another.

Did Lulu notice my frown as I went into the studio? If so, I hope she didn't guess the reason for it. I'd already remarked, on a previous visit, that the smell of the house was changing. As old Quéven was there, I had ascribed the odour to her. I realized, today, that it wasn't the fortune-teller who was responsible, but probably Mademoiselle Berthe, perhaps Lulu also, who was letting herself go. I noticed, for instance, the black edges to her nails, and I thought I saw what looked like a tide-mark on her neck.

On this occasion, I accepted the white wine offered to me, for there were still a few bottles left from Bob's time. Lulu experienced a certain pleasure in serving me and, this time, took some also. The two women must have quarrelled that day, perhaps again because of Mass, for I sensed on both sides an accumulation of ill-temper and, after about twenty minutes, Lulu said, in a tone of voice I've seldom heard her use:

'You may go to bed, Berthe, since you're so anxious to.'

Stuffing her stockings and ball of wool into a workbasket, the latter retorted:

'Thanks for your permission. I understand perfectly.'

We watched her go and listened a moment to the old maid's enraged comings and goings in her room at the side.

'All the same, I have the right, once in a while, to speak to someone without a witness, don't you think so, Charles?'

I agreed, while she went on:

'What good deed have you done since you were here last?'

It was nothing more than an ordinary polite inquiry, but she suddenly recalled something and I saw a little gleam in her eyes. I took some time to reply and, then, I believe I actually

215

blushed, Adeline must have said something in the studio about the visit I'd paid her in her rooms. That's what Lulu remembered and, to rescue me from embarrassment, she went on:

'Still lots of sick people?'

I found out later that Adeline had, in fact, told in detail what had happened in her room. The result of her indiscretion was somewhat unexpected. Either I'm very much mistaken, or Lulu felt herself more on an equal footing with me. For her, as for very many people, a doctor is a being apart.

In spite of our years of friendly relationship, she had kept an instinctive respect for me which at times prevented her from letting herself go and showing me certain sides of her character.

It must have been a relief for her to realize that, after all, I am only a man like other men, who feels the need now and then to go and join a girl in her room and who, in these instances, shows himself to be as awkward and ridiculous as anyone else.

I don't hold it against Adeline, but it's in relation to the other employees that I find it embarrassing, and for some time I steered clear of the Rue Lamarck during the day.

This time, it's more difficult to repeat exactly what Lulu told me, first because she didn't take up her story at the precise point where Mademoiselle Berthe's ill-temper had interrupted her, but above all because she was no longer in the same frame of mind.

She seemed to me more listless, as if filled with an overwhelming despondency, as if she felt like telling everyone and everything to go to hell.

I'm using an expression on purpose that she made use of during the course of the evening. To hell with everything means, as far as I can make out, to have done with, once and for all, the thoughts that torment her, the questions she keeps asking herself about Bob and herself. It would be an overstatement to say that it meant to have done with Bob.

For weeks she trailed about the studio, from the studio to the bedroom and to the shop, with the same faces around her, the old maid developing into a kind of gloomy guardian angel.

'I don't go out any more, not even to do my shopping. Berthe attends to this for me, or sends the apprentice. I haven't put a pair of shoes on for two days.'

216

I regretted, in spite of my wife and any likely reproaches, not having invited her to the restaurant.

'After all, I'm beginning to believe there's some truth in the saying that you can't make a silk purse out of a sow's ear. It is always a mistake to leave one's own class and mix with people different from oneself.'

'You're not talking about Bob?'

'Why not?'

'You know very well, Lulu, that you've been happy together for twenty years.'

'Twenty-three.'

'You see!'

'If he'd been really happy he wouldn't have committed suicide. It's everyone's reaction, his sister's the first. I know it. I realized it by the way she was studying me. Even the butcher's wife, who said to me, patting my hands with her great moist paws:

' "It's not your fault, my girl. You have nothing to reproach yourself with. If he's done what he's done, it's because he's neurasthenic." '

'It isn't true. You know that.'

'But no, Lulu, I do not know it. He wasn't my patient. He never came to see me in my consulting room.'

She looked at me, unconvinced.

'Could he have become neurasthenic?'

For her, as for many others, it's a vague and at the same frightening word, and I wasn't risking much in replying:

'It isn't impossible.'

'I would like you to know, at all events, that I did nothing to persuade him to take me with him, even less to make him marry me, and it isn't I who've changed him. His family must think that I've turned him against them, and lured him into leading heaven knows what kind of life!'

'You told me, the other evening, how you had become acquainted outside one of the cafés on the Boulevard Saint-Michel.'

'At the Harcourt. With his well-pressed grey suit, his elegantly knotted tie, he looked like a young man of good family. Indeed, just like his nephew. His nephew resembles him to such

217

a degree that I nearly broke into sobs when I saw him and, for a second, I wondered if it was his son. Do you see what I mean ? You have a feeling that they are serious young people, whose parents have an assured position, and who don't mix with just anybody. They may be inclined to play about and have mistresses while they're students, but afterwards they will become persons of consequence who won't recognize you in the street.'

There was bitterness in her voice: she realized it, blushed, her eyes filled with tears and, changing her tone she said:

'I'm sorry, Charles. I'm becoming spiteful.'

She must have used the familiar '*tu*' several times that evening.

'What did your father do?' she questioned, point-blank.

Laughing, I replied:

'Baker, at Dijon.'

It was true and made her laugh too, for a second.

'It's myself I'm angry with. Or rather, there are days when I no longer know. I told you that he had to sit his Finals the next day. I wondered to see him hanging about brasseries, and it surprised me even more that in half an hour he'd ordered three apéritifs one after the other. He made me drink as many also, and I hadn't enough common sense to refuse.'

' "Aren't you afraid of not being very fit for your exam tomorrow?"

'I used "*tu*" to everyone in those days. I haven't changed so much. He must have made some reply, I've forgotten what, but I can still see him getting up and paying the waiter, as he said to me:

' "Anyway, let's begin by having dinner somewhere."

'He took me to the Rôtisserie Périgourdine, at the corner of the Boulevard Saint-Michel and the Quais, and we were on the first floor near a window. I can see again night closing in, lights springing up in the blueish twilight, increasing in brilliance in proportion as the figures of the passers-by darkened.

'At first I thought he was trying to dazzle me, for he ordered a choice dinner, nothing but expensive dishes, the finest wines.

' "You've known Constaninesco long?"

'I laughed.

' "Three weeks. I've told you so already."

'He was beginning to get tipsy, but he still knew what he was doing.

' "What is so devastatingly funny is that you should have come across me on this very day."

'Naturally, I asked him why.

' "You'll see! Or rather you'll see nothing, for nothing spectacular's going to happen. It'll be devastatingly all the same."

'It was already his favourite word, but he hadn't quite the same way of pronouncing it, and it seemed affected. He seemed strained the whole evening. Dinner over, he ordered armagnac in liqueur glasses, and it must have had some special significance for him which he didn't explain to me.

'Everything he did, everything he said had a kind of background of mystery, and once, when he looked at me banteringly, I suggested:

' "You're sure you're not a bit cracked?"

'There are some like that, especially when they're immature, who feel the need to act a part before the girls. I knew one who, after three or four glasses, began to undress himself on the Saint-Michel Bridge proclaiming that he was going to jump into the Seine.'

She stopped talking suddenly, turned pale, remembering that Bob had ended up in the Seine.

'I need a drink, Charles. May I?'

Why not? I poured her out a glass.

'It's wrong?'

'Why should it be wrong?'

'I don't know. I no longer know what to do or what to think. When I got up this morning, I had made up my mind to throw Mademoiselle Berthe out once and for all. I picked a quarrel with her and, a few minutes later, as she was threatening to leave, it was I who tearfully asked her pardon. I'm sure she hates me and that she too holds me responsible for Bob's death.'

She was forgetting to lower her voice and the old maid could hear her. I put my fingers to my lips.

'It's all the same to me. She knows what I think. When the bottle's empty, I'll go and get another out of the refrigerator, for I want to get as drunk as I was on the day I met him. He was drunk also. We were both drunk. We went into I don't know how many bars, and I can still see him getting red in the face when he knocked over the glasses belonging to two other drinkers. I guessed from this that he wasn't used to drinking and that he was forcing the pace.

' "You see, little girl," he explained with a degree of solemnity, "chance has ordained that you should share with me the most important night of my life."

'He was only four years older than me, and he was calling me "little girl" in a patronizing way.

' "By this time, four aged gentlemen are in bed, three with their wives, the other alone – for he is a bachelor – unless he has induced his cook to go to bed with him. Sh! . . ."

'I was laughing. He put his arm round my waist, and we staggered drunkenly into the middle of the deserted street, looking for another open bar.

' "Tomorrow, these four gentlemen will get up, will shave – four! I beg your pardon, three! the fourth is bearded! – and will make their way – the four! on foot, by bus or metro, towards the Law School with the precise object of putting a certain number of questions to a distinguished young man named Robert."

' "Robert *will* be in a fine state!"

' "Don't you understand that Robert won't be there?"

'You know how it happens, Charles? You've been a student, and you must sometimes have gone out with girls like me. After all the drink I'd had, I was feeling maternal, and I considered it was my sacred duty to prevent this young man of good family from doing some foolish action he'd regret for the rest of his life.

' "What will be the result?"

' "Nothing."

' "How, nothing?"

' "I shall be neither a barrister, nor an examining magistrate, nor a president of a tribunal."

' "What will you do?"

' "Anything at all."

'A taxi passed and he pointed to it with an emphatic gesture:

' "Taxi-driver, for instance? I know how to drive and I know the streets of Paris quite well."

' "And your parents?"

' "My mother is dead. As for my father, he's asleep a hundred yards from here, at the Hôtel d'Orsay, where he usually stays when he comes to Paris."

' "You're not from Paris?"

' "Poitiers, Vienne, 27 Rue des Carmélites. My father arrived on the 10.28 train and tomorrow morning he'll be prowling about the corridors of the Faculty where everyone will bow to him in passing, bleating:

' "*Monsieur le Professeur . . .*"

' "Your father's a Professor?"

' "In the Faculty at Poitiers."

' "Listen, Robert . . ."

'I was forgetting to call him Bob as I had done all evening.

' "Try to pay attention. Where do you live?"

' "And you?"

' "Nowhere. As far as I'm concerned, it's of no importance."

'It was true that I lived nowhere, as for the last few weeks I had slept in Constantinesco's hotel room where my belongings still were.

'I insisted:

' "Tell me where you live. You really must get to bed. You will try to make yourself vomit, then you will take some hot lemon and two aspirins and, tomorrow morning . . ."

'He began, right in the middle of the square, to lift me up and kiss my mouth, while I kicked my legs about to try and make him leave go. I've never felt so tiny beside a man.'

The recollection of Bob's great stature and her own small one started her crying and I handed her the clean handkerchief I always carry in the outside pocket of my jacket.

'How silly! It happened twenty-three years ago and just to speak of it overwhelms me with emotion as if I were still there.'

She stretched her hand towards her glass.

'May I?'

It was I who went looking for a second bottle in the refrigerator, where there were the remains of food on plates. Why did it distress me to see half a cutlet congealed in its own fat?

'We finished up in the bar at the Cupole. Keeping tight hold of his arm, I continued to lecture him and, for quite a time, he looked at himself in the mirror with a gloomy expression. I swear to you, Charles, that what I'm telling you is true. I even rummaged in his pockets in the hope of finding his key there, for it might have had the name of his hotel on it.

' "When you saw me coming into the Harcourt, little goose, it was half an hour after I had taken an irrevocable decision. I had made up my mind, so as to burn my boats for good and all, to get drunk in the quickest possible way."

' "Why are you doing this?"

'I can't recall all he said to me. He'd been obliged to leave me suddenly to make a rush for the lavatories, and I inquired of the barman:

' "Do you know him?"

' "This is the first time I've seen him. He's often like that?"

' "It's the first time for me too."

'When he came back, very much later, he looked ghastly, his eyelids as red and swollen as Rosalie Quéven's.

' "Let's go now," I said.

' "It's not worth it, although it wouldn't change anything even if we did."

' "Then, at least, drink a cup of black coffee."

'At the same time, I was winking at the barman who was already holding out a cup towards the percolator.

' "A cognac!" demanded Bob. "Two cognacs. In large glasses."

'He was beginning to scare me. The barman, too, must have been afraid he'd make a scene and preferred to serve him what he'd ordered. Afterwards, I can't remember under what pretext, we drank beer, then Cointreau.

'A phrase comes back to me that he kept repeating insistently: "But I give you my word of honour that you have nothing to do with it!"

'You believe me, Charles? You are convinced that I did everything possible to make him go to bed, to make him present himself for his exam?'

'I believe it, Lulu.'

'It doesn't seem beyond all probability?'

'Not to me.'

'You believe also that he had decided to give up his career like that?'

'He didn't give you any reason?'

'I've often tried to question him about it, but it displeased him. He would look at me then in a way I didn't like, at once tender and patronizing, as if I were only a little girl incapable of understanding certain matters.

' "Don't trouble yourself about that, my Lulu. I've done what I had decided to do, and I've never regretted it. The rest has no importance." '

'You've some cigarettes, Charles?'

She was smoking through sheer nervousness, threw her cigarette on to the floor almost at once and crushed it under her foot.

'What's got into me to upset myself over what's finished and done with? I didn't run after him. He was over twenty-one, was supposed to know what he was about. Heaven knows what would have happened to him if he'd fallen into any other hands but mine. I spent the rest of the night looking after him, even though I was just as sick as he was.'

It was strange to see this rebelliousness, which was so little in keeping with her character, rising and flaring up in her.

'You both went back to his rooms?' I questioned, to lead her back to another frame of mind.

'Rue Monsieur-le-Prince. Not in an hotel, but in a private house, where he had a complete flat, a beautiful bedroom, a drawing-room which served as a study, and a bathroom. Already, on the staircase, he'd nearly been sick. He was as he entered the room, and he called out angrily to me not to look at him. You know how it is, Charles? One minute he was throwing me out and the next he was begging me to stay. I found a gas-ring and made coffee. I took off his tie, his jacket, his belt, and I sat him on the edge of the bed to take his shoes off.

' "A rum night, eh?" he sniggered.

' "It'll be better tomorrow."

' "You've worked before?" '

She interrupted herself, looked straight at me, suddenly scar-let.

'I have to tell you this, if only this once, and I'd prefer it to be

223

between ourselves. That night, he said the cruellest thing anyone has ever said to me. I've never reminded him of it, although it has haunted me all my life. If, the next day, neither of us could recall all the details of the evening and the night, I am certain he remembered those words, that they must often have come back to his mind and that, each time, they caused him pain.

'He said . . .'

She gulped down a sob, before going on in a harder voice, almost challengingly:

'This is what he said:

' *"And you, you've worked before. I mean other than with your body?"*

'And I didn't protest. I didn't get on my high horse. I didn't begin to sob. Don't let anyone come and tell me, after that, that I deceived him about myself. I laughed. I took off my dress so that I wouldn't soil it washing the vomit off the carpet.

'That's how it happened. The people in the room above us began to knock on the floor to tell us to make less noise.

' *"It must be devastating!"*

'What? What did he mean? To work with one's body? I don't know. It's all the same to me. Sitting on the edge of the bed, still looking sick, he made me strip and, after studying me for a long time, all he found to say was:

' *"You're quite tiny."*

'I believe he added:

' *"Devastating!"*

'You see how romantic it was! I undressed him, and he couldn't even manage to urinate in the lavatory bowl. It didn't stop him trying to take me. The less successful he was the more insistent he became, and the people above were beginning to get angry.

'He finished by falling asleep. I stayed awake a long time, wondering if I wouldn't do better to go away. I decided to stay. There was an alarm-clock on the bed-side table and I set it for eight o'clock. It was then ten minutes to five. Day was breaking. At eight o'clock, I got up to go and prepare coffee. I didn't know what time his examination was, but I knew they usually took place at about ten o'clock. There was still time.

224

'When I woke him I put on my slip.

' "Bob! . . . It's time . . . It's eight o'clock."

'He half-opened his eyes, looked at me at first with surprise, as if he didn't remember me.

' "Why did you wake me?" he asked at last.

' "It's eight o'clock. Your exam . . ."

'It was then, Charles, that I really had proof that he'd taken his decision before meeting me. He had a hangover, he wasn't fully awake. His look was even so that of a man who knows what he's saying.

' "But, since I am not sitting the exam!"

' "But . . ."

' "Go to bed."

'He changed his mind when he smelled the coffee.

' "Give me a mouthful."

'He drank a cupful, resting on one elbow, and asked:

' "You were leaving?"

' "Why?"

' "You've put your slip on."

' "Are you positive there's no way of making you change your mind?"

' "About my exam? No, no, and no again! It's the last time I'll repeat it without getting angry. Now, go to bed or get out. The choice is yours." '

Lulu and I had nearly finished the second bottle. She continued:

'I got into bed; you know this as well as I do, since I'm here now. We went back to sleep. Very much later, I heard knocking on the door, and I shook Bob.

' "There's someone on the landing."

'He rubbed his eyes, swallowed a drop of cold coffee that was still at the bottom of the cup, and looked at the time.

' "It's my father," he announced calmly.

'The knocking must have been going on for three minutes, perhaps more, for I'm not sure that it woke me right away. Someone tried to turn the knob from outside, but I had locked the door the night before.

' "Robert!" A man's voice called.

'I saw that he was hesitating about answering.

' "I know you are in. The concierge heard you come back."

' "Yes, father."

' "Are you going to open the door to me?"

' "One second . . ."

'He was living his last moments as a little boy, and I saw him living them. Perhaps he was regretting then that I hadn't left. With feverish gestures, he pulled on his trousers and dressing-gown, for he'd gone to bed without pyjamas.

' "Through the other door . . ." he said.

'A door that led from the drawing-room to the landing. As for me, I was trying to dress as noiselessly as I could, with the idea of slipping away unnoticed.

' "There's someone in your bedroom?"

' "Yes, father."

' "A woman?"

' "Yes."

' "Is that why you didn't turn up for your examination?"

'It was eleven-thirty. I had only my dress to put on and I was counting on getting away holding my shoes in my hand.

' "That wasn't the reason," replied Bob, in a voice I have never heard since.

'Contrary to my fears, his father didn't get into a rage. His voice was all I ever knew of him and I was very taken with it. I've always fancied I'd have liked him. The door remained half-open between the two rooms.

'I got the impression that he was listening and I didn't dare to move another inch.

' "After much close thought, I have made up my mind to be neither a barrister, nor a magistrate. Please forgive me."

' "Why didn't you notify the Faculty?"

' "I was in the wrong."

' "Do you make a habit of getting drunk?"

' "I was drunk last night for the first time."

' "Do you know the woman in your room?"

' "Since yesterday at six-thirty."

' "You have nothing to say to me?"

' "Not today, except that I'm dreadfully sorry to disappoint you."

' "You will send your apologies to your professors?"

' "I will."

' "Your sister came to Paris with me, for I'd promised her that we would all three lunch at Foyot's to celebrate your success."

' "Tell her from me that I'm sorry."

' "When shall I see you?"

' "I'll come and see you at Poitiers as soon as I'm able to give you an explanation."

'They stayed silent for a time and it was too late for me to go away. I heard the door-knob being turned, then there was a slight cough.

' "Good-bye, my boy."

' "Good-bye, father."

'The door opened and closed again. Someone began to go slowly downstairs and, if I had dared, I would've rushed to the window to see Bob's father as he left the building.

'Bob didn't join me immediately. I was wondering what I ought to do when at last he appeared, calmer than I'd expected, a ghost of a smile on his lips. It was his smile, you know, but not yet quite the same as you knew. At that time, it still had a kind of trembling irritability and uneasiness about it.

'He looked in surprise at the shoes I was holding in my hand, took some time to understand.

' "Make some more coffee," he said. "Any more aspirin in the tube?"

' "Two."

' "Give them to me."

'He didn't ask me whether I hadn't as much need of them as he had.

' "Are you hungry?"

' "No."

' "I'm not either. We might as well stay in bed all day. There'll be time this evening to go out and dine."

'We made love and, while he slept afterwards, I stayed wide-awake, feeling sad. He slept until six o'clock.

'We took a bath one after the other, and this seemed to amuse him.

' "I don't know why," he announced suddenly, "but I've a frantic desire to eat snails."

'This made me laugh. We both began laughing, It seemed as if the last barrier between us had broken down. It was enough for us to look at each other, to say anything at all, to make us want to burst out laughing.

' "Where are your belongings?"

' "At your friend's place."

' "He's not my friend, just a fellow student."

'He suddenly gave me a suspicious look:

' "You love him?"

' "No."

' "You're infatuated?"

' "No."

' "You love me?"

'Laughingly, I answered no, and I was surprised at the seriousness with which he was watching me. I thought it was my duty to add:

' "I'm only joking."

'Dryly, he let fall:

' "No."

'Later he growled:

' "Let's go and eat some snails and look for your belongings." '

*

The door was flung open just when we were least expecting it, and we must have started as if we'd been caught red-handed. This time, Mademoiselle Berthe was not content just to put her head, bristling with curlers, through the half-opened door, but made a complete appearance, swathed in a frightful purple-coloured dressing-gown, her nostrils pinched with rage.

'I suppose you have made up your minds to spend the entire night exchanging filthy confidences?'

Lulu's nose trembled too, whitening at the tip, and red blotches sprang up on her face. At any moment, they were going to hurl themselves on each other, all claws unsheathed.

Lulu pulled herself together, merely replied in a flat voice:

'Precisely! I'll be another two hours yet.'

The other woman was so utterly dumbfounded that she withdrew as speedily as she had come in.

'You don't think she's going to leave?' I inquired, hearing

the opening and shutting of drawers in the bedroom.

'Don't count on it! It will be as difficult to get rid of her as to drown a cat.'

Mademoiselle Berthe must have heard, for Lulu hadn't bothered to lower her voice. Much to my astonishment, the comings and goings on the other side of the door ceased suddenly, the bed-springs creaked and complete silence reigned.

Chapter Six

I spent the last week of August and the first three days of September at Fourras, a few kilometres south of La Rochelle, where my wife used to go for holidays even as a child. I bathed twice a day in the sea, always slightly yellowish on account of its muddy depths. I ate the local fish-soup, oysters and clams. On days when it wasn't raining, I stayed stretched out for hours in a deck-chair, sometimes in the shade, sometimes in the sun, and, occasionally, I chanced a little money at boule in the evening at the Casino. In fact, I even played with my two sons now and again, but they only condescend to accept me as a partner to please me, ill-concealing their eagerness to join the boys and girls of 'the gang'.

Nearly every day, I hear talk of the stolen bag, which has ended by becoming a unique and irreplaceable object.

'You've seen the police superintendent, as I suggested in my letter?'

'I haven't had time.'

'And yet you haven't so many sick people in the month of August. How's Lulu?'

'Not too well.'

'She's worrying?'

'It's difficult to say. I don't find her quite herself. I'm afraid she's letting herself go.'

'You've seen her often?'

'Two or three times.'

'She still has her four employees?'

'Mademoiselle Berthe lives with her now.'

'Entirely?'

'Yes.'

'They sleep in the same bed?'

To be on the safe side, I changed the conversation, for from now on I have something to hide, something to reproach myself with, as my mother would say, looking at me distrustfully, and it isn't only the business of the bag stolen in the Rue de Clignancourt.

The fact is I went back to Adeline's, three times if I count the one when I didn't find her in her hotel, and one of the times it was like Bob, on a Saturday afternoon, the last Saturday spent in Paris before taking the train to Fourras.

If I were able to explain that, I would doubtless be in a position to throw light on one of the most obscure sides of human nature. Eyes half-closed on the noisy beach, vaguely watching the boys and semi-nude girls fooling about, I've several times asked myself the question, not because I feel remorse, but out of simple curiosity in relation to myself and others.

What drove me back to Adeline?

Seen through a doctor's eyes, hers is a small body, neither beautiful nor ugly, if anything rather unhealthy, lacking in red corpuscles, and the skin is pale and flabby, too transparent, the waist narrow, the ribs standing out, the pelvis wider than is usual at her age. She has pear-shaped breasts with dark nipples, the solidity of which makes me think of a goat's udder.

She hardly ever puts herself out for me and makes love rather badly, for the excellent reason that she only takes a moderate pleasure in it. She is more interested, during that time, in studying me than in co-operating, and I suspect her of behaving in the same way with all her partners.

Why does she consent? Why didn't she have a second's hesitation, neither the first time nor the two others? I've asked myself that question also. There is the fact, certainly, that it is a rather pleasant sensation. I'm none the less convinced that what interests her above all, is to obtain, if only for a few minutes, an undeniable importance.

I didn't warn her of my visits, which I only decided on each time at the last minute, almost reluctantly. Every time, she gave the same slightly ironic smile.

'It's you!'

The third time, she said:

'It's you,' using the familiar '*tu*'.

Then, as if it were amusing:

'Well then? So you've got the urge again?'

Inevitably I had been thinking about her, since I was there. I'd been obliged to upset the whole day's timetable. And it was her I'd chosen, for she is convinced that I have other opportunities, which is true.

Does she think she's pretty? It's immaterial. What counts, in her eyes, is that she is able to stir my senses, and it is all the more important because I'm a doctor, a man who all day long sees women in their private lives.

I'm quite certain that the more awkward I am as I draw near to her, the more pleased she is. It is my excitement she is waiting for instead of thinking of her own pleasure, the minute that, by a miracle which renews itself some millions of times a day, a woman's body becomes the only thing that matters to a man in the whole world.

Perhaps I am deceiving myself. In any case, she doesn't welcome me out of self-interest. I don't give her any money. On my second visit, I took her a box of chocolates which she put on the table without even looking at, and the next time I gave her a silk scarf in which she took as little interest.

But me? Why me? Not only me, but all the men who, I know, are in the same boat, even if they don't always admit it? It isn't curiosity on my part, for I have seen lots of others built like she is, better than she is, and I know their reactions and have lost interest. Whatever one may think of it, it isn't vice either, and besides that word doesn't exist in the medical vocabulary.

I wonder if, fundamentally, it isn't a reaction against society and its rules, a little the equivalent, for instance, of the well-fed man who has an open account with his butcher, who frequents the best restaurants, and who none the less goes hunting in order to kill, like the starving savage, urged by an instinct dating from the age of the cave-man. Isn't it significant that he has the heads of his victims stuffed and exhibits them on his walls, just as the American Indians carried their enemies' scalps on their belts?

Why should we not experience, also, from time to time, like a reversion to savagery, the nostalgia of copulation pure and simple, divested of the complicated trappings of legality, morality and sentimentality with which it has been surrounded?

I didn't pay court to Adeline. I didn't ask her for anything. She was in bed the first time, and merely slipped off her pants.

It mattered little to me, it matters little now, what she thinks of me, how she judges me, and if, when I'm gone, she calls her friend in to make fun of me.

At a time when society concedes so much importance to the most natural gesture of a man and a woman, and has raised up so many barriers around this gesture, on the fringe it has left, like a safety-valve, a few exceptions, a few Adelines.

I won't go so far as to pretend that when I took myself to the Rue Clignancourt I was protesting against society and avenging myself on it. There's nevertheless something of that about it. To escape from the rules for a few minutes, is to give oneself the right to act for once like an animal.

It doesn't explain Bob, I realize that. His case is more complicated. What I am going to say about the girl in red has no connection either with Bob and Lulu, nor directly with my visits to Adeline, and yet I instinctively involve her in my preoccupations.

I've watched this girl for hours playing volley-ball and beach games on the sand with the other young girls and young men. She wears a swim-suit as clinging as if it were made of rubber, bright red, and unquestionably hers is the most beautifully moulded female form in all Fourras, her flesh giving such an impression of ripeness that one feels tempted to touch it as one would handle a fruit.

Thanks to my sun-glasses, my wife couldn't tell what I was looking at as she recounted the tittle-tattle of the Casino where the women meet for tea, or talked to me about our children and other people's.

For three days, I lived intimately, as it were, with that lovely girl, until the time when, as we were coming out of the villa one evening, we met a little girl accompanied by her mother; it was the girl in red, now wearing a flowery cotton dress, and whom my wife greeted by the name of Martine.

'How old is she?' I inquired.

'Twelve. You wouldn't think so. She's big for her age.'

I blushed, and reproached myself the whole evening because, according to the rules of society, the rules of the game, I had been guilty in my mind. And I am well aware of the reactions I would have had, if I had been the little girl's father, with regard to another man, thinking as I had done.

One must believe that man wanted to live in a society since society exists, but also, for as long as it has existed, man has used a great deal of his energy and astuteness in fighting against it.

I wasn't losing sight of Bob and Lulu. It is in starting from them that I have got thus far, by heaven knows what round-about ways, in these rather muddled considerations. My wife's opinion is simple, final.

'I am convinced that Dandurand was a weakling. A decent chap, but a weakling. He let himself be sucked down little by little into the bohemian life of Montmartre and became a fail-ure like so many of them.'

'You believe that's why he killed himself, out of self-disgust and disgust at the life he was leading?'

'Why not? He was sufficiently well educated to be aware of his downfall.'

I didn't want to dispute this last word.

'How do you explain his waiting until he was forty-nine?'

'When you are younger you can still manage to create il-lusions, tell yourself that things may change. It's as he grew older that he became conscious of the emptiness.'

'You don't think he loved Lulu?'

'I'm not so sure. Some men prefer to stay with a woman rather than admit they've made a mistake. You'll agree that she wasn't the companion he should have had.'

I preferred not to answer. I betrayed you, my poor Lulu, but I hadn't the courage, on the sunlit beach where I was following with my eyes the manoeuvres of a small sailing-boat, to start a discussion which would have turned sour.

'After all,' I said, 'we could send her a postcard.'

'Who?'

'Lulu. It would please her.'

We both signed it. My wife's words about Bob's love for Lulu recalled a phrase of his that Lulu repeated to me. It was on the evening she had proved so explicit with Mademoiselle Berthe. She had declared, defiantly, that we'd be another two hours and, indeed, when I left, dawn was just breaking, and we had drained a third bottle of wine almost without realizing it.

The charm of that evening, or rather the charm of that close of night, was that Lulu no longer felt she had to talk against time. She had stretched out on the couch while I was seated in the arm-chair and she often remained silent for so long that, two or three times, I wondered if she had fallen asleep.

'We had been living together fully three weeks when he said to me, for no reason, just out of the blue:

' *"You know, when you've had enough of this you won't have to be embarrassed."* '

With a tearful emotional smile, Lulu added:

'I was foolish in those days. I sobbed my heart out. I thought he wanted to get rid of me. I even began to pack my case.'

'How did it end?'

'I can't remember. On the bed, probably.'

'You were still in the Rue Monsieur-le-Prince?'

'No. We only stayed there until the end of the month, because the rent was paid up. It was Bob who chose to go and live in a small hotel in the Boulevard des Batignolles, a stone's throw from the Place Clichy. He didn't look around any other districts. He seemed to have his own idea.'

'He was working?'

'No. Actually, he didn't need to. I learnt later on that his sister and he had inherited three farms from their mother in the Vienne, of which Bob was receiving half the income. He wouldn't have been able to live on it for long, but it enabled him to look around.'

'He still has a share in the three farms?'

I hadn't dared to say, he still *had* . . .

'Oh! No. Even when I first knew him, he was eager to get rid of them. Do you know why?'

I was beginning to have a suspicion, but I let her tell me.

'Because they prevented him from feeling a free man. He often declared that the money didn't count, that it had come into his hands by chance and that he was anxious to be rid of it.'

234

'He could have given it away.'

Lulu looked at me with stupefaction. I do believe that, at that moment, she almost lost confidence in me, for there is still some of the peasant in her.

'To whom?'

She was becoming almost aggressive.

'To anyone at all. To his sister, for instance.'

'It was his sister and his brother-in-law who bought his share when they married. The farms must still belong to them and heaven knows how much more they are worth now with the war and devaluation.'

'What did he do with the money?'

'He had spent some of it, for his sister had been advancing it. With the rest, he bought this shop.'

I had always wondered how their first years had been spent and it had intrigued me more since I'd known that Bob was Professor Dandurand's son.

'In short, you didn't stay long in the Latin Quarter?'

'He didn't like the Left Bank. He had chosen, as first port of call, one of the Paris squares, seething with life, on the fringe of the world of small shopkeepers, of manual workers and shop-assistants, in fact of bohemianism and dissipation.

'We had a little room on the fifth floor, with running water, and there was no lift.'

'What did he do all day?'

'We walked a lot. He never went out without me, but he never asked me where I wanted to go, nor if I was thirsty or tired. He had grown accustomed to my being there, and some-times he would stay silent for a whole hour, just as at other times he would talk at great length without taking any notice of my replies.

'We went into a great many bistros, the smallest and darkest, he loved the atmosphere, and he would listen to people talking at the counter, manual workers in overalls, shopkeepers of the neighbourhood who had come in for a quick drink. We had most of our meals in coffee-houses where the menu is written on a slate and the place always smells of fried onions.

'In the evening, in our room, he would start to write.'

'What was he writing?'

'He told me they were notes, but later he admitted it had to do with a novel.'

'He wanted to be a novelist?'

'He wanted to do something for himself, no matter what. He would have liked to describe Paris and its ordinary people as he saw them. One day, in a bar in the Place Blanche, he murmured:

' "I wouldn't mind working behind a bar counter like this."

'He was cross when I burst out laughing, but I had sincerely believed he was joking.

'Once, when we were in another bar in the district, where three masons were drinking red wine, he declared:

' "Theirs is one of the finest trades in the world. If I were not afraid of heights . . ."

'He used to read the small advertisements, cut some out and put them aside.'

'He never spoke about his family?'

'Only shortly before Feast Days, towards December 10 or 11. We had moved to a room in an hotel in the Rue Lepic, which he called the most humane street in the world. The first floor was reserved for what the proprietress called Casuals, that is the girls who, from three o'clock in the afternoon, used to take a client upstairs for a few minutes. Prostitution wasn't yet against the law. We knew them all by sight and, when it was particularly cold, Bob sometimes treated them to a grog at the corner of the street.

'He had bought a spirit stove so that we could prepare our meals in the room. It was forbidden, so one of us had to mount guard on the landing while the stove was alight, and afterwards we had to open the window wide to dispel the smell of cooking.

'He had given about fifty of the pages he'd written to be done by a typist who worked at home and whose white name-plate we had seen as we strolled along the Boulevard Rochechouart.

'Coming out of there, he'd announced:

' "We're going to Poitiers tomorrow."

' "Me too?"

' "You too."

' "You're not going to introduce me to your father?"

' "You'll wait for me at the hotel. I'll only be an hour or two."

'That surprises you, Charles. You have always known him joking and making others laugh. At twenty-four, that rarely happened. When it did, his pleasantries were either beyond me or seemed rather bitter.

' "Why don't you tell me what you're thinking about?"

' "Because I'm not thinking about anything."

' "There's no such thing as thinking about nothing."

' "Indeed there must be, since that's just what I'm doing."

'We caught the morning train to Poitiers and, as we came out of the station, he stopped in front of a jeweller's.

' "I nearly forgot my sister's birthday."

'He bought her a gold brooch, a bar without any ornamentation. Then, just as he was about to pay, he noticed a cheap ring with a pale-blue stone in a fancy setting and he bought that too, stopped the salesman from wrapping it up with the brooch, and held it out to me without looking at me.

' "It's for me?"

' "Yes."

'The miraculous part about it was that it fitted me. I still have it, but it's become tight, or rather it's my fingers that are podgy. One of these days I'll have it widened. It was the first present he'd made me. Then he took me to a hotel and only stayed a second to tidy himself and put a comb through his hair. I remember too that he used one of the towels to polish his shoes.

'He'd spoken of being away for an hour or two, and he came back after midnight to find me sobbing, face downwards on the bed, convinced that his family had succeeded in separating us for ever. I suppose I already loved him. I wonder now if I didn't love him the first day we met, on the terrace of the Harcourt. Is it possible, Charles?'

'Why not?'

'Then, perhaps he only said that to please me,' she murmured dreamily after a silence.

'Only said what?'

'It was years later, in this house. I'd just had a miscarriage

237

and was feeling depressed, especially as, every time, it made me ugly and for a while I was fit for nothing. In the evening we were sitting together just as we are now, which seldom happened.'

' "Do you think you love me, Bob?" I asked him seriously.

'He answered me with a spontaneity which gave me such joy:

' "Why, of course I do!'

' "Why?" I insisted.

' "That, my girl, I really don't know."

' "When did you begin to love me?"

'He was standing. He never remained sitting for long. It seemed as if he didn't know where to put his long legs. Looking at the floor, he thought it over:

' "You want to know the precise moment I realized it?"

' "Yes."

' "It was when, in the Rue Monsieur-le-Prince, my father had left me and, coming back into the room, I found you dressed, your hat on your head, your shoes in your hand. I was suddenly aware that I might have come back to an empty room and that I wouldn't even have known where to look for you."

'I didn't point out that he knew his friend's address to which I'd have had to go to fetch my belongings.

'I've often thought he spoke like that to please me. But since you believe it's possible . . .'

It annoyed or hurt Lulu, I felt, that Bob had said nothing to her about his meeting with his father and sister that night at Poitiers.

'She's pretty?' she'd asked him.

'Not bad.'

'Tall?'

'Nearly as tall as me.'

'How old is she?'

'Nineteen.'

'What's her name?'

'Germaine. Suppose we talk about something else.'

All she knew was, that he didn't look as if he had quarrelled with his father. Just as he was about to undress, he had glanced at his watch.

'A quarter past midnight. There's a train from Bayonne going through here at twenty past one. We've time to catch it. Get dressed.'

They had travelled third class, not so much for economy as because Bob wanted to.

I asked Lulu:

'You continued to travel third?'

'For some time. Later he preferred second.'

I was getting ready to leave when she begged:

'Stay a bit longer, Charles. It would do me so much good!'

It was then I knew that Adeline had talked, for Lulu added, with a knowing smile:

'Unless you have a rendezvous?'

I countered:

'Rue de Clignancourt?'

And she questioned without protest:

'She's kind?'

Adeline must have given her to understand that I was in love with her and spent my nights at her place. It's of no consequence.

'What's going to become of me, Charles?'

It is a question that's extremely difficult to answer. I pretended to be thinking it over.

'There are times when I feel guilty to be still alive. Do you know why I'm so afraid of staying by myself at night? It's because I always have the same dream. It still pursues me when I'm wide awake. I don't see Bob himself, but just a dim shape. Only his arm is alive, beckoning me to come. I seem to hear groaning, and I tell myself he's complaining that I'm staying here too long.'

'You must try to be reasonable, Lulu.'

'I try. When I go out, hoping to shake myself out of it, it's even worse, for there isn't a single street I haven't walked along with him, and that doesn't bring back a memory. I didn't know Montmartre, either, before I met him. We discovered it together, little by little.'

I let her cry her heart out and, as she bent her head forward, I noticed that her hair was becoming sparse.

'Even our friends were his, and they prove it by not coming here any more. Good old Gaillard, for instance, who, for a week now . . .'

'He's ill.'

'Are you sure?'

'He had to be taken to hospital urgently.'

'I must go and see him. What I'm telling you is the truth, Charles. I often get the idea that even my flesh doesn't belong to me any more, that it's Bob's, and has become useless. It's he who taught me the very words I use. He was the one who arranged everything I do from morning till night. What in heaven made him leave me?'

'He's never been ill?'

'He sometimes saw a doctor, like everyone else, if he had flu or tonsilitis, later on because of his stomach-aches, but you couldn't say he was ever really ill.'

'He hasn't consulted a doctor latterly?'

'In any case, he didn't say anything to me about it. Do you think that his health could have had anything to do with it?'

I hadn't got that far. I, too, was groping in the dark. She talked again about the fifty pages of the novel that Bob tore up without reading, the day the typist delivered the copy to him, then about the weeks he spent as curtain-raiser in a little cabaret in the Boulevard de Clichy. He didn't sing, merely recited a monologue of his own composition.

'I was in the hall the first night, right at the back because he'd warned me that it would embarrass him if he saw me. I didn't hear everything. Members of the audience were coming all the time he was talking. There was some applause, not much. When I joined him, he said:

' "They didn't laugh."

'And I, like an idiot, asked:

' "Were they supposed to?" '

I believe I must have dozed in my arm-chair, not for long, for when I came to my cigarette was still smouldering in the ash-tray. I took my hat from the table.

'You're leaving?'

'It's high time.'

'Thank you for coming, but you mustn't do it out of pity.'

It wasn't worth while going to bed so I drove right across Paris, where the first buses were beginning to fill the streets with their din. I spent some time meandering up and down the avenues of the Bois where I passed a few cyclists, and I finished up at Saint-Cloud on the Seine bank, in a bistro that was just opening its doors. The sun still had its pale freshness. A string of barges, smelling of tar, glided slowly by. I drank my coffee thinking about Bob, about his arm, the arm Lulu saw in her dreams. Had she been told that it was an arm that had emerged first when he was fished out of the Seine?

My wife said to me yesterday, as I wrapped myself in my beach robe when I came out of the water:

'The best thing for her to do would be to marry again.'

It took me a second or two, there on the beach, to realize that it was Lulu's fate she was deciding. Why should it be worrying her too? Did she feel that I was giving it far more thought than she would have wished?

'It's probably what she will do.'

Do I take it from that that my wife would marry again? The notion surprised me, because I'm accustomed to thinking of her as a mature person who has passed the age of certain things. With me it's normal because we are growing old together, but with someone else . . .

How strange! I'm convinced now, that if I were to die tomorrow, she would try to remarry. I can even guess the reason she'd give for it.

'For the children's sake, you understand . . .'

Bob would have exclaimed:

'*Devastating!*'

I didn't. Curious, I questioned:

'Why do you think that?'

'I don't know, except that she isn't the kind of woman to live without a man.'

'She loved Bob.'

'I know.'

The words were uttered in an odd tone of voice.

'I'll swear he loved her too,' I added.

'It's possible, Charles. I don't want to argue, and anyway where would that get us? You should take off your wet robe, and the sun will soon dry your swimming trunks.'

And I, would I marry again? It amused me to ask myself the question as I watched my wife knitting and counting the stitches in an affected manner. I'm not sure of the answer. I would be extremely sad, that's undeniable. I would miss Madeleine. For the children's sake, I'd have to engage a housekeeper for not under any circumstances would I send them to a boarding-school. I don't fancy I'd be tempted to marry Adeline, and it even seems to me that I'd have no great desire to go and see her any more.

The thought of it suddenly filled me with desire and I counted the days I still had to put in at Fourras.

'What are you thinking about?'

'One of my patients.'

I went home alone, by the night train, on September 3. The mornings on the coast were becoming fresh, with a golden mist shrouding the water until the warmth of the sun dispersed it.

I resumed my calls, my habits. Now that I had the opportunity, I no longer had any desire to take myself to the Rue Clignancourt and I wasn't over-anxious either to go and see Lulu.

I was content with telephoning her one morning when I'd finished my toilet and my breakfast, just before my consulting hour.

'You know how it is . . .'

'Your wife is well? The children?'

'Everyone is in excellent health. And you?'

'Not bad.'

'How's the morale?'

'I don't know. I've lost interest.'

I didn't like that answer.

'The bedbug's still with you?'

'Who?'

'Mademoiselle Berthe.'

'She's here.'

'Still the same?'

I got the impression that we were suddenly very far away from each other. We were reduced to making conversation. Lulu couldn't have been alone. She never is. The others were listening. Was it enough to account for the coldness of her voice?

'I'll come and see you one of these days.'

'It's kind of you.'

'Good-bye, Lulu.'

'Good-bye, Charles.'

Perhaps she is sorry for having spoken to me that night with such unreserved confidence. And yet, she didn't say anything she might have cause to regret. Or else is it simply that Mademoiselle Berthe has regained her influence over her?

I telephoned the hospital for news of Gaillard, expecting him to be dead. He'd been back for three days in his studio at the top of the Butte, and has resumed his daily round of the bistros. Once more he must be going to sit, every afternoon, in the studio at the Rue Lamarck to drink his drop of white, rambling on unintelligibly to the employees and making them burst into laughter.

I began to think again about . . . No! I don't want to go over that again. I suddenly recalled a phrase I'd read somewhere in Stendhal when I was still a student, and which I'd copied at the time into one of my exercise books because I found the words very profound:

Man accustoms himself to everything, except happiness and tranquillity.

In a word, it is the equivalent of the medico's sally: 'The healthy man is the sick man who is unaware of it.'

It matters little why that came into my head. I missed my wife and the children, particularly the children, during the week I still had to put in before their return. I met my colleague Martin Saucier, the one with a practice in Cochin hospital, and who knows Bob's sister and brother-in-law.

I purposely didn't mention them to him again. It's absurd. I get the impression, now, of having been in the sulks with Dandurand, as if I were annoyed with him for making me face up to some unpleasant truths. The widowhood of my wife, for instance, and her possible remarriage! It kept me awake one night, for half an hour, and I had to get up to take a phenobarbitone tablet.

If a man in good health, who considers himself normal and intelligent and who has spent more or less his whole life in the study of his fellow men, is reduced to creating imaginary difficulties so ridiculous, what is one to say of a Lulu plunged, in the twinkling of an eye, into a real tragedy?

'A propos, I've heard from Pétrel,' said Saucier, who never forgets anything. 'Their daughter has won some swimming contest or other. They're coming home on Saturday and my wife and I thought we would invite them to dinner the following week. Will your wife be back?'

'She's returning on Saturday also.'

'Will Wednesday suit you?'

'I don't want you to feel that you're obliged to . . .'

'But not at all! My wife will make a Brandade. The Pétrels are charming people, and I'm sure you will find them interesting.'

Now that I am up to my neck in this affair, there's no longer any escape for me. On Wednesday, then, I'll see the sister, her husband and the young man who is so like Bob.

I had only one call to make on the Saturday afternoon, and had no need to be at Montparnasse station until half past six.

All week, I kept saying to myself:

'I'll take advantage of this by going to see Lulu, for, once my wife is back, I'll have to space out my visits.'

I set out for the Rue Lamarck, went past the Place Constantin-Pecqueur and finally stopped in front of the dubious lodgings in the Rue Clignancourt.

The girl friend who was with her looked at me with a would-be mischievous smile and got up, murmuring:

'Well, I'm off.'

Adeline replied in the most natural way in the world:

'If you'd care to stay . . .'

Chapter Seven

The Sauciers live in a huge flat with windows overlooking the Luxembourg Gardens. They both belong firmly to the Left Bank, by conviction, as you might say. She was born there, a few hundred yards from the building they live in now and her father was a well-known doctor, Saucier being one of his pupils. Their son is in the army in North Africa, their elder daughter, who a year ago married a young intern in Cochin, has just had a baby, and the younger one will be another year receiving treatment in a Swiss sanatorium.

My wife and I were the first to arrive, and she immediately followed Charlotte Saucier into the kitchen where our hostess insists on preparing certain courses herself, for they keep a good table, and whenever they invite people to dine they are asked whether they like such dishes as Brandade, Coq au Vin, Perdrix aux Choux, Potée Lorraine. Saucier, on his part, goes down with due ceremony into the cellar to choose the wines he is going to bring to room temperature or to chill.

'How are you? A cigar?'

'Not before dinner.'

'Port?'

'I'll wait until . . .'

I was about to say that I'd wait until the other guests arrived when we heard the lift stopping on the landing. The Pétrels were accompanied by their son: their daughter was not with them and I didn't hear the explanation they gave of her absence. Madame Saucier and my wife went forward to greet them. We were all standing in the doorway of the drawing-room when Charlotte made the introductions.

It seemed to me that, as the young man shook hands, he looked at me with some insistence, as if he were racking his brains to find out where he'd seen me before, and a little later on I overheard the few words he spoke to his mother in an undertone.

Saucier was serving the wine. Pétrel came up to me and, to set the conversation going, asked:

'You're a specialist?'

'Mostly general practice.'

'It must be exhausting, but far more interesting.'

I said lightly:

'One sees all sorts of things.'

He wasn't as starchy as I had imagined when I saw him at the funeral. To be sure, he had the appearance and manners of a lawyer, and even of a lawyer of the XVIIth *arrondissement*, but, especially later on, he didn't seem to be so very narrow-minded and, on certain issues, such as the education of children, discussed while we were at table, his opinions were quite up to date.

I've no clear recollection of the rambling conversations we had before we sat down to table. The Sauciers' rooms are immense, high-ceilinged, with windows to the floor; the furniture is heavy, rich-looking, the general effect rather sombre. A portrait of Saucier hangs in the place of honour in the dining-room, just behind the seat occupied by the master of the house. When I teased him about this he replied – and I know it's a fact – that he had ordered the portrait to help a needy painter who promptly became a friend of the family and himself chose the position for his canvas.

Several times, I was conscious of Germaine studying me. Her son took part in the general conversation, without embarrassment or ostentation. Perhaps I'm wrong, but it seemed to me that he was talking especially for my benefit. His turns of phrase were respectful:

'Forgive me if I make so bold as to . . .'

It always has a strange effect on me to meet young men of his age who are my friends' sons. If my sons are so very much younger, it is because it was six years before we had any children, to our despair. Then the two boys were born one after the other, with scarcely more than a year between, with the result that they are sometimes taken for twins.

We went into a more homely room for coffee, where the men remained standing, and where Saucier, I'm convinced, contrived to put me closer to Germaine Pétrel. His task was not facilitated by my wife, who had embarked on a discussion with her and didn't intend letting her go. Charlotte, at a glance from her husband, came to the rescue and led my wife off to inspect something in another room.

It was Madame Pétrel who spoke to me first:

'You were a friend of Robert's, were you not?' she asked quite naturally.

'I suppose Saucier told you?'

'Yes, when he invited us for this evening. Besides, Jean-Paul recognized you as we came in.'

'I guessed as much.'

'He was indiscreet enough to whisper it to me.'

Her voice was warm and deep, and her black dress enhanced the beauty of her fine shoulders.

'You were at Tilly when it happened?'

'No. It so chanced that I didn't go to the *Beau Dimanche* that day.'

'I suppose there is no doubt whatever?'

'About it being suicide? In my opinion, no. I'll confess to you that I've questioned most of those who were there.'

'You liked Robert?'

'Very much.'

Someone had put a glass of liqueur in my hand and I didn't know what to do with it. It was she who got rid of it for me by placing it on an occasional table.

'You knew him well?'

'I knew him well, as he was during the last thirteen or fourteen years.'

'I loved him too,' she said, in a voice full of conviction. 'He was my only brother. When I was young, I thought he was the most wonderful man on earth.'

'You can't have been more than fourteen when he left Poitiers. You are five years younger than he is, aren't you?'

She smiled, saying:

'You are well-informed, but not quite accurate. I was seventeen when Robert left for Paris, for he read his first two years of Law at Poitiers.'

'It didn't embarrass him to study in a University where his father was a Professor?'

'That's the reason he continued his studies in Paris and my father agreed to this.'

'How did they get on together?'

She took time to reflect, chose her words:

'They had a tremendous respect for one another.'

'Their outlooks were different?'

'As they inevitably are between people of different generations. It wasn't that so much.'

She had no need to improvise. It was clear that she had given these matters a great deal of thought, and I suspected, knowing through Saucier that I would talk to her about her brother, that she had prepared certain replies, not in order to shine in conversation, nor to give me a favourable opinion of the family, but because she cared for the truth. She was very much concerned with accuracy, hesitated before each phrase, went back at times over the same ground to correct a detail or add a nuance.

'My father was clear-thinking, precise . . .'

It was the reputation he had left behind and his daughter was taking after him.

'Robert, on the contrary, never had one simple notion. Do you know what I mean? I never knew our mother, who died when Robert was eight years old. It seems it was her he resembled. At all events, it is what I often heard Aunt Augustine say. She brought us up.'

'She was your father's sister?'

'Yes. And a spinster.'

'Was she as cartesian as he?'

'She is still alive, in Poitiers, and occupies the first floor of a house in the Rue des Carmélites, which has remained in the family. She is a very old woman now, and father's death – he spent his last years alone with her – was a shock from which she hasn't completely recovered. One detail will give you an idea of her character. Do you know what she's been reading for the last year and a half as she sits, hour after hour, in her arm-chair by the window? The complete works of Voltaire, in a very early edition, most of the volumes of which have been annotated in the margin by my father.

'Some find her cold. I remember one of her favourite sayings when we were children:

'Justice is everything.'

I saw her make a slight sign and, turning my head, realized that it was to her son, who had held aloof.

'You may come over, Jean-Paul. Doctor Coindreau and I are talking about your uncle.'

She added for my benefit:

'My son adored his uncle. He hardly saw him more than once or twice a year but, nearly all the time Robert could spare at the Boulevard Péreire, they spent together.'

I was afraid she might hesitate to touch on certain topics in the young man's presence, but it was nothing of the kind.

248

'You wouldn't guess my brother's dream when he was seventeen. To become a priest in the Sahara. In his room there was a huge map of North Africa, a photograph of Père Foucould that he'd got hold of heaven knows how, and an ebony crucifix.'

'Your father put his foot down?'

'No. It is obvious that you never knew my father personally. He had very decided views, and he was convinced that they were right. He stated them forcefully, at times in a self-assertive way to which some people took exception. He was none the less as respectful of the opinions of others as he expected they should be of his. I don't think he ever tried to influence Robert. He merely watched him, at first with anxiety then with grief.'

'He didn't insist on his reading Law?'

'Certainly not. Robert reached his decision alone. This I know because, although I was only a little girl, he used to confide in me, more precisely to speak to me as he would have talked to himself.

' "*I shall never be a Père Foucould, after all,*" he would say, "*neither a good priest nor a good officer. At bottom, I lack the faith.*" '

I was watching Jean-Paul, as I tried to picture Bob at his age. Stirred by curiosity, I asked him:

'And what is your ambition?'

'The Navy!' he replied, so promptly and with so much ardour that I couldn't help smiling.

'I'm entering the Naval College in a fortnight.'

'You see,' his mother commented, 'neither my husband nor I have tried to influence him, although we have no other son to carry on the practice which, when my husband retires, will pass into the hands of strangers.'

I was conscious of her charm, I admired her. There was something of the patrician about her that impressed me and against which, at the same time, the baker's son in me stiffened.

The Dandurands' house in the Rue des Carmélites must have resembled the apartment we were in now, but I imagine it was even more muted and formal. There was doubtless in the Professor's home the same sense of comfort that you found in his daughter's, an affluence that springs from perfect self-confidence and is not without a touch of hauteur.

'I can understand him dreaming of becoming a desert priest,' said Jean-Paul. 'To my mind, where he went wrong, if he had really set his heart on this, was in not persevering.'

His mother turned towards me.

'Jean-Paul is more practical than his uncle and, upon my word, yes! I believe he is more egotistical too.'

'Egotism is a vital necessity, Mama. Without egotism . . .'

She smiled.

'Let's say that your uncle may not have had as much grit, nor as much singleness of mind as you. After his *bachot*, he entered the Law School.'

'To please grandfather!' the young man remarked.

'Perhaps. Or to avoid conflict. He did not like argument and had an even greater horror of causing pain. One day, while he was at the University, when I expressed my surprise that he never asked any of his friends to the house, he answered awkwardly:

' "You see, most of them aren't wealthy. To bring them here would look as if I . . ."

'I don't remember the word he used. It was at the University that he became conscious of social differences and it worried him for a long time; he was distressed every time my aunt expressed an opinion that smacked of the upper middle classes. He wouldn't argue, but I noticed him grow pale and lose his appetite.

'One of his friends of that time, who was a poet, became the editor of a left-wing paper and indeed I believe he is now a Deputy. My husband could confirm this. I don't know whether he had the same ideas even then and whether he exercised some influence on Robert.

'In any case, it was a relief for him to leave Poitiers for Paris.'

Jean-Paul exclaimed:

'I can understand that.'

'Why?'

'Because it can't be amusing to be the son of the Big Boss. I'm sure many of the students steered clear of him.'

His mother continued, without any sign of disapproval:

'When he came home, on his first vacation, I was no longer a child and he talked to me more freely.'

'He told you about his love affairs?'

'He didn't go that far. He wasn't like you. Besides, women didn't appear to be one of his main preoccupations. I noticed this from the way he behaved towards my friends.'

'At our age you would hardly expect us to appreciate girls of good family!'

Mother and son were extremely outspoken with one another, and they must sometimes have exchanged a few home truths. In spite of their difference in character and temperament, there was a most subtle and indeed delightful affinity between them. At the time of the funeral I had been struck by the way Jean-Paul had lavished little attentions on his mother. Here, too, they could have been taken for lovers.

'What did he tell you on his first vacation?'

'That he had made an attempt to imitate some of his friends who were earning their living at the same time as pursuing their studies.'

'You've never told me about this. He was a clerk in a cinema?'

'No. I imagine he'd have considered that too easy. Just as formerly he had set his heart on the desert army, he now took it into his head to get a job as an unskilled worker with Citroën. They worked there in three shifts, and he managed to get himself signed on for the night one. All he had to do was to join the queue outside the gates with Arabs, Poles, people gathered from every corner of the earth and from the riff-raff of the Paris underworld.'

'How long did he stick it?'

'Three weeks.'

'I consider that pretty good.'

'So do I. I was amazed. However, immediately afterwards, I made fun of him because he had started to have his left arm tattooed. Fortunately he only had one sitting! There had scarcely been time to outline a rose and his initials.'

'In the English Navy all the officers are tattooed.'

'That's a different matter.'

'Why did he do that?'

It was I who replied, seeming to seek his mother's permission with a glance:

'To be like his comrades, like the others.'

Jean-Paul mused about this a while.

'I think I understand.'

He had understood so well that he added:

'After all, in the army too, he would have preferred to be a private soldier rather than an officer.'

We were interrupted. The ladies were sitting in one corner, the men standing in another.

'I too have some questions to ask you,' said Germaine Pétrel as she moved away.

While my wife tackled her anew, it was Pétrel who took me up, as if everything had been arranged beforehand.

'You were speaking of Robert.'

I had no reason to hide it from him.

'He was a strange chap, but with a most engaging personality, and my son admired him tremendously.'

Saucier was with us, refilled our glasses while Jean-Paul, either from discretion, or because he didn't feel that he was quite on a par with the men yet, stayed with the ladies.

'If I were asked my opinion of him, I would say that he was a kind of poet. Moreover, I believe that there was a time when he wrote verses.'

'Didn't *you*?' marvelled Saucier.

'Not that I remember.'

Pétrel's manner of speaking was studied, as if he were proving a point of law before a civil court.

'I wouldn't swear that Robert had no part in Jean-Paul's decision to join the Navy. On the other hand, I cannot fault him for lack of discretion. We saw him hardly twice a year. He seemed to regard himself as the black sheep of the family, and he would forewarn his sister of his visits by telephone as if to avoid shaming us in the event of our having company.'

He went on with phrases that seemed so drawn out that I began to have difficulty in following a conversation which no longer held my interest. Saucier who, especially through his wife is, as it were, half-way between Pétrel and me, put in, in a conciliatory tone:

'He was a bohemian, and that's that! To my mind, it is salutary that some of them still exist in this age of ruthless utilitarianism, if only to give an illusion of levity and to make serious-minded people laugh occasionally. The English, who are the most conformist people on earth, lavish on their eccentrics and originals the same patronizing affections as they bestow on ancient monuments and, in Hyde Park, no one would dream of making fun of a tub-thumper, dressed like a scarecrow perched on a soap box, preaching his newly discovered religion.'

'It's a point of view. It is possible, after all, that my brother-in-law set himself out to amuse others.'

'I don't claim that . . .'

'Yes, indeed! There is something rather disturbing in what you have just said. Several times I tried to speak to him as man to man and he always slipped through my fingers, or replied by a volteface. He can't have liked me very much. In his eyes, I must have been a pompous and icy man of law. All the same, it didn't prevent him from trying to make me laugh, as Saucier has said. It is a pose.'

It was strange to see how fascinated he was by that idea.

'I once had a friend who also thought it his duty to amuse the company. Since he realized that he wasn't funny unless he had had a drink or two, he made a habit of going into a café or bar before turning up at the house he'd been invited to, and he knew the exact amount of alcohol he needed.'

I inquired:

'What became of him?'

'He died of tuberculosis. His wife has had to work as a saleswoman in one of the big stores. I have an idea that Robert was not very robust either. It is often the case with extremely tall men, is it not?'

I was beginning to get worried, for I got the impression that my wife was talking about Lulu and I didn't quite know what she might say about her.

'When all's said and done,' continued Pétrel, 'he led the life he had chosen and he didn't worry unduly. One day, when my wife asked him if he was happy, he answered that he would not exchange his life for any other.

'I only caught a glimpse of his wife the day of the funeral, for I didn't go as far as the cemetery, I had to be at the Palais at midday that day. He never thought it incumbent on him to introduce her to us. Since they were married, however, we had no reason whatsoever not to receive her.

'I think he loved her. In any case, he considered that he had taken on a responsibility towards her.'

'What do you mean by that?' I demanded, irritated by his pedantic tone of voice.

'I am only going by what he said. I was not present when he said the words I'm going to quote to you, but my wife repeated them to me. It was towards Christmas time. He always came to see his sister just before her birthday, and brought her some small gift, a worthless bauble that pleased Germaine. The two of them would sometimes recall the Rue des Carmélites, and I believe they had talked, that day, about the visit Robert had paid his father, also near Christmas, the year he had abandoned his studies so abruptly.

'She must have asked him:

' "You've no regrets?"

'It seems that, after thinking it over for a second, he replied:

' "*At any rate, I've made one person happy and I'll continue to do so.*"

'Then, he laughed, as he always did under such circumstances, mocking himself, and added:

' "*When all's said and done, if each of us undertook the happiness of one single person, the whole world would be happier.*" '

I would rather have heard that phrase repeated to me by Germaine Pétrel's warm voice than by her husband's, but, with all its faults, it moved me just the same.

For the first time, I fancied I had advanced a stage in my knowledge of Dandurand and the immediate result was a wave of tenderness towards Lulu. I was vexed with myself for not going to see her for such a long time, and for having so misjudged her last telephone call.

Saucier also was struck by the phrase, and said to me in an undertone:

'It's what I do with my children. At least, I try . . .'

I gazed at my wife across the room and wondered if I, myself, had really tried.

'Suppose we join the ladies, who look as if they have found something interesting to talk about?'

As I drew near them, my wife was saying:

'You see what I mean? He behaved like a perfect gentleman towards her. Since he had made her his wife, he must have considered it his duty, in so far as I knew him . . .'

I interrupted her with a question to Germaine:

'Did you have a chance to speak to Lulu on the way back from the cemetery?'

'She didn't come back with us. She must have stayed at Thiais with her friend. She appeared to me rather unfriendly but perhaps, after all, she was just nervous.'

My wife opened her mouth, and once again I cut in:

'She is obsessed with the thought that she is responsible for Robert's death. Not only was he everything to her, but she only existed through him. She hardly remembers having lived before she knew him. He carried her like a baby, so to speak. He taught her everything she knows. Her very gestures are modelled on his. He was behind her every word, her every thought. Suddenly, he disappears and she has no one to lean on.'

My wife said:

'Fortunately, she has Mademoiselle Berthe!'

I could have hit her. She sensed this from the look I gave her and turned pale. Her nostrils were pinched as when she knows she has done something wrong but refuses to admit it.

'She has no one,' I retorted, 'only the memory of Bob. That's what she called him, what everyone has called him for the past twenty-three years.'

'So he told us,' murmured his sister. 'It's strange, but when I was five or six years old, I called him Bob one evening at table, because one of my little friends called her brother Bob. My father frowned.

' "Robert!" he corrected.

' "Why not Bob? It's much nicer."

' "Perhaps for a child. But if, one day, he is a well-known barrister, a magistrate or a professor, it would sound ridiculous."

'Father quoted the case of one of his aunts, whom I didn't know, for she ended her days in Indo-China, whose nurse used to call her Chouchou when she was a baby. The name stuck, and my father maintained that when she was twenty-three everyone still called her Chouchou.'

Jean-Paul observed:

'Bob suited him well.'

And my wife:

'I agree with your father. I have never allowed my children nicknames.'

'Perhaps we'd better break up the meeting?' I suggested.

Germaine Pétrel smiled, realizing that my wife and I don't always hold similar views, especially where Bob and Lulu are concerned. I was grateful to her for the way she had spoken about her brother, and I can understand how much pleasure his occasional visits to her must have given him. There was still a question I wanted to ask, and I took advantage of the moment everyone started moving towards the cloak-room.

'Your father was extremely angry with him?'

'He didn't curse him, like they do in popular novels, nor shut the door on him either. I have told you that he respected all points of view. I know quite well that it was a dreadful disappointment to him. He didn't discuss it, merely declared:

' "You go your way and I'll go mine. Each must choose his path." '

'Bob didn't go back and see him?'

'No. He wrote several times. Father didn't reply and my brother concluded from this that he preferred to sever all connections between them. The attitude of both of them remains a mystery to me, and neither one nor the other confided in me about it. I suppose my father was too proud or too unyielding to approve or to seem to. As for Robert, I think a kind of diffidence kept him away. He had no more desire to obtrude himself than he had to impose his wife on us.'

'He didn't see your father again on his death-bed?'

'Father died of a stroke as he and his sister sat reading in the library.'

'Bob didn't go to the funeral?'

'Yes. Without his wife whom he took to Poitiers but whom he left at the hotel.'

Lulu had omitted to tell me about that journey. I thought she had been to Poitiers once only.

'One day when you are in the neighbourhood and have a moment to spare, I should be so pleased if you would call, on the off-chance, to have a chat with me. I am seldom out in the afternoon.'

Jean-Paul overhearing this, seemed to approve.

'Unfortunately, I won't be there. I shall be at the Naval College.'

As we parted, he shook my hand vigorously, as if to thank me for my loyalty to his uncle.

'He was a good sort!' he whispered, 'but you mustn't say it too often to father.'

His mother proved more discreet, but cordial.

'Don't forget my invitation,' she called, as she got into her car.

Hearing this, my wife asked:

'What invitation?'

'To go and see her.'

'For dinner?'

I had my petty revenge.

'No. She has asked me, when I'm in the neighbourhood, to call and have a chat with her.'

'Alone?'

'That's what I understood.'

'Don't you think that's an insult to me?'

'No.'

'At seven in the evening she doesn't even know us. We are introduced, and it's you alone she invites!'

I was satisfied. It was half past eleven. The weather was mild, and the car running almost soundlessly.

I was cruel enough to propose:

'What about going to say hello to Lulu?'

'At this hour!'

'Perhaps you're right, although she rarely goes to bed early.'

I'm sure she was wondering if I had called at the Rue Lamarck as late as this while she was at Fourras. What would she

257

have said if I had told her about my other visits, to the Rue de Clignancourt?

I was tempted to present her with the naked truth, once and for all, to make her face up to the harsh reality, to the true picture of our two selves. But then, by rights we should set about this from the beginning and not allow our wives to fill their heads with foolish notions.

When Bob adopted Lulu, he took upon himself the entire responsibility of his action. He never spoke to her in flowery language. He never even talked to her about love. In short, he took her by the hand like a child, like the little girl she was and, amazed at first that a great boy like him should stoop down to her, she had confidence in him and in life.

I envied them both now. I was beginning to understand the atmosphere of gaiety that pervaded their home. They set no store by inessentials, and that's why people like me acquired new strength in themselves in the studio in the Rue Lamarck.

The curve of Bob's life, from the dream of the desert priest to the Citroën Works to the bistros of Montmartre, was not so very surprising. It's rather as if he had aimed too high, then too low, to settle down at last into a light-hearted mediocrity.

He was a failure, as I have heard people say several times since his death. All right then! but a lucid and conscious failure, who had chosen to be a failure, and he suddenly acquired a kind of grandeur in my eyes.

After wanting to be a saint in the desert, then an ordinary working man, he had finished up quite simply, as he had said to his sister, by concentrating on making one person happy.

'If each one of us . . .'

He was shy about his past, about his background, just as he had been embarrassed by the money inherited from his mother and as he had been a little ashamed, before that, of being the Boss's son.

'Devastating!' he would let fall, with his scarcely ageing smile which held neither bitterness nor malice.

Nevertheless, didn't I sometimes detect in it a touch of nostalgia?

My wife inquired:

'Where are we going?'

I had passed the house and was driving towards Montmartre.

'You're not seriously thinking of knocking at . . .'

'No. I fancy a glass of beer.'

A glass of beer on one of the café terraces in Montmartre, at
the Cyrano, on the corner of that Rue Lepic which Bob had
considered for some time the most humane street in the world
and where I could see the small hotel where he had lived with
Lulu.

'Two halves, waiter.'

'I don't want any beer.'

'What will you have?'

'Nothing. We've had enough to drink this evening.'

We sat there in silence, watching the crowd go by on the
pavement, passing in turn from the shadow to the light and
back again from light to shadow.

In the end, almost remorsefully, hesitantly, I murmured:

'Why do you judge people who are not like you and me so
harshly?'

'You're referring to Lulu?'

'Lulu and Bob.'

'I have never said anything nasty about either of them. Quote
me a single sentence of mine which . . .'

'It isn't worth while.'

'You see! I challenge you to repeat one unkind word. Bob
was a charming fellow, whom I enjoyed meeting now and
again. I am as sorry for Lulu as the next one. But as for wanting
to set either of them up as models . . .'

It was useless to try to make clear to her something she would
never be able to understand as long as she lived. Useless and
cruel. What was the good of upsetting her? Try as she might, at
that moment, to convince herself that she was the one who was
right, she could not but feel some misgivings.

I placed my hand over hers.

'Come on now, you're not such a bad sort!'

'It's a pity I'm not as good as Lulu!'

'What did you say?'

'But that's what you think! Why haven't you the courage to
admit it?'

Yes, why? I left my hand on hers for a second, then withdrew it to drink my beer. A flower-seller stopped in front of us and I bought her a bunch of violets, for no reason, except perhaps because the little barefoot girl was gazing at me with large, grave eyes.

'It's for me?'

'Yes.'

'Ah!'

And after a silence:

'Thank you.'

We went back home. I left my car, as usual, at the edge of the pavement, for the local police know it. I went on tiptoe, to embrace the children who didn't wake. Only the younger one brushed a hand across his forehead as if to chase a fly away and gave a little grunt.

My wife and I sleep in the same bed, like Bob and Lulu. My wife undresses in front of me. She wears an elastic belt which leaves her skin puckered. It is always I who set the alarm, placed on her side, however, for she gets up first and, I don't know why, has always refused to let the servant wake her.

'Good night, Madeleine,' I said, embracing her.

'Good night, Charles.'

If I set the alarm, it's she who streches an arm out to switch off the light. Those are the small habits one acquires in a household without realizing it and which, little by little, develop into rituals one obeys automatically.

I wonder how Bob and Lulu said good night to each other.

I wonder how he said good night to her that night at Tilly, when he had prepared in minute detail what would take place next day at the Vives-Eaux weir.

Because of that thought, foolishly, awkwardly, as at the Cyrano, I had put my hand on my wife's, I embraced her once more, blindly, in the dark.

She didn't react straight away. Perhaps a minute later, with a catch in her voice, she questioned:

'You hate me?'

'No.'

'You're still angry?'

Why the devil, fool that I am! did I long to weep?

Chapter Eight

A virulent type of flu, about which we know hardly anything, and which we are fighting in an entirely hit-and-miss fashion, swept through Paris and kept me extremely busy. My elder son caught it and ran a temperature of 104 degrees.

Almost every evening, I would say to myself:

'I must find time to go and see Lulu, tomorrow.'

Then, the next day, I could hardly manage to see all my patients.

In the end, it was she who telephoned me, just as we were sitting down to dinner. I picked up the receiver from the sideboard.

'Charles?'

I don't know how my wife guessed it was she, perhaps by the expression on my face. Lulu went on, hesitantly, as if she were not sure of herself:

'I'm not disturbing you?'

'Not at all. How are you? I hope you haven't got flu, also?'

'You've got flu?'

'Not I, but most of my patients and one of my sons.'

'I don't think I've got it,' she murmured.

Her voice had a kind of uncertain, irresolute quality. I thought I sensed an embarrassing humility which reminded me of a man begging.

'You're at table?'

I lied:

'We've just finished.'

My wife pulled a face at me.

'I expect you're extremely busy?'

'I have been these last two weeks but I am beginning to see daylight now, and to number more cures than new cases.'

'I've a favour to ask you, Charles.'

By her tone of voice, I wasn't far from thinking that it had to do with money.

'You know I won't let you down.'

I pulled my watch out of my pocket.

'Would you like me to come along at about half-past eight?'

'Thank you, Charles, I'm here all the time. I wouldn't like you to think you were obliged . . .'

I was worried as I resumed my place at the table, and thought aloud:

'I wonder if she's sick or if something's happened that's distressing her.'

'She was crying?'

'No. Her voice is different. You'd have thought it was someone asking for charity.'

'You're going to see her at half-past eight?'

'Yes. I'll take advantage of it by making a couple of calls.'

'I thought you'd finished your round?'

'I'll gain by it tomorrow morning.'

That way, she couldn't suggest coming with me. I went to say good night to my elder son, who has practically recovered and who is making the most of it by reading all day long in a bed littered with picture papers.

'You'll be back late?' my wife asked.

'I don't think so.'

I took the car and set off for the Rue Lamarck. I was surprised to find, not only the door closed, but the shutters lowered and the wooden panel already fixed to the door, so that I had to knock. Footsteps approached, and Lulu's voice inquired:

'Charles?'

'Yes.'

She drew back the bar, then the bolt. Her hair was untidy, she was wrapped in her red dressing-gown, her feet were bare in felt slippers.

'It's kind of you to come.'

I followed her through the unlighted shop into the studio from where, through the open door, I could see the bedroom and, on the unmade bed, the hollow left by a body. Automatically, I looked around me for someone and perhaps I even sniffed.

She watched me and, sitting down, said:

'She's gone.'

'You've fallen out?'

'Not even that. That's not why I asked you to come. I simply told her to go.'

'I thought you were afraid of being alone?'

'I'm still afraid. You saw that I'd closed the shutters and the door. I know it's absurd. I'm sometimes so panic-stricken that my teeth chatter, but I'd much rather put up with that than with what was happening here.'

I hardly dared to look at her, in case she should notice my pitying astonishment. In two or three weeks she had gone so thin that I was alarmed. There was, besides, in her dark-ringed eyes, a staring intensity that I didn't like at all.

'You're not ill?'

'No. Perhaps I've taken my time in not having done with Berthe once and for all, but all the same I realized that I was, in a way, betraying Bob. Perhaps it isn't easy to understand and I'm not very good at explaining myself. Before, I was as I was. It didn't matter much what other people thought; that was how Bob wanted me. The least I could do was to stay the same, wasn't it?'

I nodded.

'With her here, the house was no longer our house. Even our bedroom, our bed, acquired a different smell. Because she's an old maid, she can't understand certain things that a married woman understands instinctively. It's complicated, Charles. She was beginning to dominate me and, at times, I was tempted to think like she does. If it had continued, I would have reached the stage of spoiling our happiest memories.'

'She put up a fight?'

'She assured me that I would regret my decision and that it would be useless to run after her begging her forgiveness. I offered her a small sum of money as compensation. She refused it and, the next day, sent her concierge to me with a note requesting me to put the money in an envelope.'

Suddenly suspicious, I asked:

'You're eating well?'

'As much as my appetite demands.'

'Regular sit-down meals?'

I went and opened the refrigerator, which contained nothing but some cheese, two slices of ham on greasy paper, and half a bottle of milk.

'That's how you look after yourself?'

I surprised myself by using the familiar '*tu*'.

'Sit down, Charles.'

There were not as many hats, bits of cloth and ribbons lying about on the tables as there used to be.

'I take it you've kept on your other employees?'

She looked guilty.

'You haven't kept them on?'

'Only Louise.'

'Why?'

'First, I had to sack Adeline because she was taking things too easy. Mind you, ever since Bob went, they are all doing the same.'

She remembered my association with Adeline.

'I shouldn't have done that? You're annoyed?'

'Not in the least.'

'She met, God knows where, a fellow who is a night-barman in the direction of Ternes. At the beginning, he would come and wait for her on the pavement. Then he got into the habit of coming in and sitting himself down on the corner of the table without even taking his hat off. She wouldn't turn up until ten o'clock in the morning, utterly exhausted. I told her she couldn't do two jobs at a time, for she made no secret of the fact that her friend was introducing her to clients nearly every night. You miss her?'

'Certainly not!'

'The apprentice has found a better situation nearer home, and I haven't replaced her. Don't you see, Charles, I'm in no mood for making hats, for the moment. Only Louise is still coming.'

'She does your shopping?'

'I send her to the baker and the butcher.'

'You don't go out anymore?'

'I haven't had any occasion to. What would I want to do outside? That's not why I asked you to come. Perhaps I was wrong to bother you? Your wife didn't object? I should have been able to take this step myself, and perhaps I'd have found out the truth. You know Doctor Gigoigne?'

His is one of the best-known and respected names in our profession, not only in France, but abroad, and without any doubt no European knows more about cancer than he does.

'He lives in the Boulevard Saint-Germain,' she went on. 'It

appears that he is no ordinary doctor, but a famous specialist who only receives a few patients a day, and then only by appointment.'

'That's right. He devotes most of his time to the hospital and to the clinic at Neuilly where he operates.'

'I have a customer, little Madame Lange. Her husband is an architect, and they lived for a long time in the Rue Caulaincourt. Two years ago they moved to the Boulevard Saint-Germain, but she still comes to order her hats from me. I hadn't seen her since last spring. This afternoon, she came into the shop and, in the course of conversation, asked:

' "Is your husband better?"

'I didn't understand. I said:

' "You didn't know he was dead?"

'She gasped:

' "I never dreamed it would happen so quickly."

' "What do you mean by that?"

'It was her turn not to understand, to be embarrassed. She realized that she'd made a blunder, but she didn't know what it was, nor how to extricate herself.

' "Why did you ask me if he was better?"

' "I thought . . ."

' "You thought he was ill?"

' "I believed so. Yes. When I passed him on the stairs and saw him ringing Doctor Gigoigne's bell . . ."

' "You saw him going into a doctor's house?"

' "At the beginning of the summer. It must have been in June, because we left for the South on the first of July."

' "You are sure it was he?"

' "I am so sure that, as I passed him, I asked for news of you and he replied that you were very well. We live on the floor above the doctor's. It was about three o'clock in the afternoon."

'You can guess what I want to ask you, Charles? If he is such a very busy man, he won't receive me, or else he'll see me for a brief instant and hardly listen to me. Even if he does listen, it isn't certain that he'll tell me all he knows. I immediately thought of you . . .'

I consulted my watch. It was nine o'clock, too late to telephone Gigoigne. He isn't a man to be disturbed for a mere trifle, especially by one of his colleagues. He must be about sixty-five but looks more, or rather ageless. He saw both his father and mother die of cancer. His only daughter succumbed, at sixteen, to an extremely rare form of the disease, and he himself has been operated on twice.

Judging by his measured tread, his cautious movements and soft voice, you might think he was husbanding his strength and, in a way, it's true. He has disciplined himself to a tempo of life which allows him to get through a task that few younger men would be capable of carrying out. In addition to his lectures, he operates up to five or six times a day, either at the hospital, or at Neuilly, and still finds time to examine patients at the clinic and at his own house.

I don't envy him an almost unique responsibility, one he has to meet daily, the responsibility of choice. Because each day has, for him as for other people, only twenty-four hours, he can only accept a limited number of patients, whether paying or free, and his choice often determines a man's life or death.

I was nervous at the idea of asking him for an appointment, but I none the less promised Lulu I'd do so the following day, first thing in the morning. I would have to see him before eight o'clock because, once he has left for the hospital, it is impossible to get him in person on the telephone.

'You will tell me exactly what he says?'

'I promise.'

I don't know why I wasn't altogether satisfied. The idea that Dandurand had committed suicide because he was suffering from an incurable disease had entered my head from the beginning, and I had cast it aside.

'I would like to give you an injection to buck you up,' I said to Lulu.

Without waiting for her permission, I prepared my syringe. Her thigh was flaccid. I was almost certain she had lost ten kilos.

'In spite of everything, try to eat.'

'When I know, it'll be better.'

She was longing to know that Bob's decision had nothing to do with her. For weeks, for months, she had been tormenting herself, wondering why he had left her without a word of explanation.

I made my two calls, and on my return my wife inquired:

'What was the matter?'

'She's discovered that Bob was going to see Gigoigne, the cancer specialist.'

'Poor Bob!'

I didn't discuss it. Next morning, in a bit of a funk, I lifted the receiver and dialled Gigoigne's number. He replied in person. When he heard my name, which he knew, he asked:

'You have a case?'

I explained that I only wanted him to grant me ten minutes' interview, at any time, to ask him some questions about one of his patients.

'What is his name?'

'Dandurand.'

'Didn't he commit suicide?'

He had understood what I wanted of him.

'Come to Neuilly at three o'clock sharp. I can spare you ten minutes between two operations.'

I was before time at the clinic, where I seldom send patients, for it's one of the most expensive in Paris. I was made to wait in a small room on the first floor where a woman of about sixty, seated on an upright chair, her eyes glued to the door, was saying her rosary. There wasn't a sound. The prevailing heat seemed unreal and one felt cut off from the world.

At one minute past three, Gigoigne stood framed in the doorway, in his operating overalls and cap. He glanced at the woman without moving a muscle of his face, without saying a word, probably leaving it to the nurse to tell her the result of the operation.

He signed to me to follow him to the end of the corridor, into an office placed at the disposal of the doctors. He didn't shake hands. I have never seen him shake hands with anyone. His skin is as white and as smooth as china, and he himself is so still, only speaking when it is absolutely necessary, that it is easy to understand why his presence has a chilling effect on those who don't know him.

Going straight to the point, I said:

'I happen to be a friend of Bob Dandurand and his wife. Neither she nor I ever knew that he was ill, except that he

267

suffered periodically from stomach-ache and stuffed himself
with bicarbonate.

'He committed suicide without declaring his intention to
anyone at all, without leaving either a letter or a message and,
ever since, his widow has been torturing herself, wondering if it
was because of her that he wanted to die. Through one of the
tenants in your flats, we learnt that he went to see you at the
beginning of June. I don't suppose he came to you without
an introduction?'

'Bourgeois telephoned to ask if I would see him.'

'The examination was positive?'

He nodded his head in affirmation, adding:

'Cancerous tumour in the duodenum.'

I didn't ask him if he had told his patient the truth, for Gigoigne has the reputation of telling it bluntly to all his cases.

'Operable?'

'Yes.'

'You agreed to undertake the operation?'

Another nod, again affirmative.

'He refused?'

'He asked me if it would cure him. I told him that it was
possible, and that it was equally possible that the disease might
reappear in one year or in ten.'

'What did he decide?'

'Nothing. He said he would think it over. Just as he was
leaving, he inquired:

' "I suppose I would need a great deal of nursing, and it
would be a long time before I'd be able to lead a normal life?"

'I answered with a vague gesture.

'I didn't see him again.'

I had only taken up eight minutes of his time. I thanked him,
and left.

If Bourgeois had sent him, Bourgeois must have been his
doctor and must know more about it. With him, I was on an
equal footing. We had been interns together and, like me, he is
a general practitioner, with this difference that he has a much
more sumptuous set-up in the Malesherbes district. I rang him
up from a little restaurant at the corner of the street.

'When could I see you without bothering you too much?'

'I'm going out in a few minutes. Will you be anywhere near the Madeleine about six?'

'I can be.'

'Then, let's say between six and six-thirty on the terrace of the Weber?'

When I shook hands with him and told him I wanted to talk about Dandurand, he asked rather uneasily:

'You've been to see Gigoigne?'

'This afternoon.'

'He isn't wild with me? The one time I insist on his taking on one of my patients, and he accepts, the idiot decides to commit suicide!'

'You were not friendly with Bob Dandurand?'

'No. Were you?'

'Yes.'

'He must have stuck a pin in my name in the directory, or noticed my plaque on the door in passing.'

'He often came to consult you?'

'Two or three times. He complained of a disordered stomach and, after trying the usual remedies without success, I sent him to a radiologist.'

'It was you who told him he had cancer?'

'I wasn't quite that definite. It wasn't a clear-cut case. I admitted that it could be serious, that I would like a specialist's opinion, and asked if he had the means to meet the costs of a bigwig. He seemed so staggered – like a great boy who hadn't grown up – that I was sorry for him.'

'You didn't think he'd take it into his head to commit suicide?'

'It never occurred to me. It does happen, now and again, but more often than not, as you know, with people who have reached the most painful phase. Now that you mention it, I do remember he asked me a heap of questions. He wanted to know how soon after the operation he would be able to go back to a normal way of living, what kind of life he'd be able to lead, and even if his spirits would be affected by it. Then I asked him if he was married and he said yes.

' "Any children?" I continued.

' "No."

' "Is your profession a tiring one?"'

' "No," he answered, with a smile.'

' "I can't promise anything, but I'm going to try to make an appointment for you with Professor Gigoigne. Only, I must warn you that, since you can pay, it will cost a lot. If you were poor, he would operate free of charge. You're on the phone?"'

' "If you don't mind, I would rather come in person for his answer."'

' "You haven't said anything to your wife about this?"'

' "No. There's no need for her to know."'

'That's all, old man. I wangled his appointment. He kept it, and I had a note from Gigoigne confirming my diagnosis. When I didn't see him again, I assumed that Gigoigne had taken him in hand and, one fine day, I read in the paper that he'd been fished out of the Seine! It's true then? He drowned himself?'

We finished our drinks and parted company after a few generalities more or less relating to our profession and our patients. I wasn't able to go to the Rue Lamarck before half-past nine, and I hadn't even time to go home for dinner, for a message was waiting for me at one of my patients, telling me of two emergencies in the neighbourhood.

Up to a point, I felt a certain sense of deliverance because I didn't need to worry myself about Bob any more. Now, at last, I knew. But, as often happens after any prolonged search for the truth, the result seemed cold and disappointing.

Dandurand's end, however, fitted in with what I knew of his life. There had always been an innate diffidence about him, to be seen again in his nephew Jean-Paul, but here it was offset by tenacity of purpose.

As a young man Bob would sometimes confide in his sister but, she would add:

'... *as if he were talking to himself.*'

Because, after all, she was only a child and wouldn't be able to understand him. He wouldn't have laid bare his heart to a grown-up, but he told her about his dream of the desert, then of his longing to become one of the mass of the ordinary people of Paris.

He had never told Lulu his secrets either and, after they'd been living together for three weeks, he had reminded her that she was under no obligation to him and was free to leave whenever she thought fit. Later on, much later on, he had nevertheless admitted, and then only because she questioned him, that he had realized that he'd loved her ever since that first morning when his father had left the apartment in the Rue Monsieur-le-Prince.

But, to use a household expression, I'm beating about the bush. I know what was puzzling me while I was making my calls. Bob's case was becoming quite simple, too simple. I thought I could hear my wife's exclamation:

'In a word, he preferred not to suffer.'

Others will say so too. Now, I am sure this is not true. I abhor over-simple explanations and people who know everything, reduce everything to categorical statements.

First of all, it is more than likely that he wouldn't have suffered much, and Gigoigne, however sparing of his time and words he may be, would have told him so. An operation is no longer what it was fifty years ago, and no one is afraid of undergoing one.

There would still have been time to decide whether the disease might recur in one year or in ten.

What confirms me in my theory, is that Bob went to great lengths to make out that he had suddenly become passionately fond of pike-fishing, and to arrange a *mise-en-scène* which should logically have put his death down to an accident.

He didn't quit because he was afraid of suffering, but because he didn't want others to have to put up with the sight of his sufferings, and of what, in his eyes, was a fall from grace.

He had done all he could to make Lulu's existence a lighthearted one. People went to see him, to see them rather, to forget their gloomy thoughts, to refresh themselves in an atmosphere of carefree gaiety.

At Tilly, in the small bars in Montmartre, wherever he dragged his great, gangling frame, he was looked upon as a lovable clown.

'*Devastating!*'

His eyes would sparkle, his lips curve into a smile.

What sort of clown would a sick clown be, an anguished clown, a clown on a diet?

My wife won't believe me. I knocked at the door of the Rue Lamarck and Lulu called to me through the panel:

'Who's there?'

'Charles!'

She was as pale and tense as if she were awaiting a verdict from me.

'You've seen him?'

'And also Doctor Bourgeois, who was attending him before he went to Gigoigne.'

'What did they say?'

'Bob was suffering from cancer of the stomach.'

She received the news with a grimace of pain, as if Bob was still alive, as if she were seeing him suffer.

'It was hopeless?'

'No.'

'He might have lived?'

'Gigoigne had agreed to operate.'

'It would have cured him?'

'If not finally, at least for a time.'

'He didn't want this?'

I shook my head and Lulu understood. *She* wasn't deceived about Bob's motives.

'He didn't have enough confidence in me.'

'But he did, Lulu.'

'No, Charles. He didn't realize that I would have been happy to devote the rest of my life to looking after him. He didn't want to force me into the role of sick-nurse. He has always looked upon me as a little girl. Right to the end, he treated me as a little girl. That's why he left me without a word.'

I took her in my arms and I couldn't help noticing she smelled of sweat. After a second, she freed herself:

'Now, at last, we know.'

It was too soon to see whether the truth would do her more harm than good.

'I was forgetting. Your wife phoned.'

'What did she have to say?'

'A woman patient has been waiting in your consulting-room for the last hour. She insists she's been poisoned and is at death's door.'

I knew what it was about, a crank who lives at the bottom of the Rue des Martyrs. Every time she quarrels with her lover, she comes along with the same story.

'Good-bye, Charles. Thank you for all you've done.'

'There's no need to thank me. As for you, try and take care of yourself, or I'll be cross with you.'

She led me back through the shop, lighted only by the reflection coming from the studio, and bolted and barred the door behind me.

To get rid of my patient, I gave her an emetic and, for about ten minutes, her eyes haggard, she clutched hold of my jacket with both hands, moaning that she didn't want to die.

I finally told my wife, shortly before we went to bed:

'Dandurand had cancer.'

'I thought as much.'

She went on with her sewing.

'What has Lulu to say about it?'

'Nothing.'

That was all. I didn't tell her that Lulu only had one employee, nor that she had got frightfully thin. Now that Bob is no longer there, and the atmosphere of the house has altered, I'm pretty sure my wife will fight shy of the place. She is just waiting for me to weary of the whole business and forget the way to the Rue Lamarck.

I found time to go and see Germaine Pétrel, the next day, as if I too were in a hurry to have done with it. Despite her invitation to call at any time, I rang up first. They own a small private hotel next to the Sarah Bernhardt. I only had to cross the ground floor where the offices are and climb a staircase of pale marble.

The apartment into which Germaine Pétrel welcomed me was light-coloured too, modern, flower-filled, and from somewhere beyond several doors came the muffled sounds of a piano.

'It's my daughter,' she said, as she invited me to sit down.

'Will you have tea?'

A housemaid, in embroidered apron and white cap, brought in a tray of tea and petits fours.

'Perhaps you'd rather have whisky?'

'I won't have anything, thank you.'

I hadn't spoken to her about the object of my visit on the telephone. It was she who opened the conversation.

'Do you know that after our meeting at the Sauciers, I was conscience-stricken? In fact, I realized that I hadn't told you the truth.

'I feel that in this way I failed in my duty to Bob. I am not a church-goer, Doctor. I nevertheless believe that we go on living, at the very least in the minds of those who knew us. Now, you spoke to me about Bob with more affection than anyone else did.

'When you asked me how he had got on with his father, I didn't answer you with absolute truth, partly because my son was listening to us.

'Actually, my father never forgave my brother the disappointment he made him suffer. Or should I perhaps call it humiliation? He had made the journey to Paris purposely. The Professors who were to have examined Robert were his friends or his colleagues. That his son should insult them, first, by not presenting himself for his exam, without even letting them know, then by leaving them waiting . . .

'It was beyond his comprehension. When, the next day, father found out that Robert was with a woman, he inevitably cast the entire blame upon her and, for the rest of his life, nothing would make him change his mind.

'I must confess that, for a long time, I, too, thought we were dealing with a schemer who, either from selfishness or stupidity, had prevented him from going to the University that morning.

'My father never actually said to Robert:

' "Choose between me and that girl."

'It was none the less clear that Robert need never show his face again so long as he was living with her.'

It made very little difference, just added the merest touch to the picture I'd finally drawn for myself of Bob.

'I came to tell you why he died.'

'He left a letter?'

'No. I have seen his doctors. Robert had cancer of the stomach.'

'Poor old chap! It's typical of the man who, when he had flu, at Poitiers, would never say a word about it to anyone but hid himself like a sick dog!'

I rose. She held out her hand, her open face lit by a smile.

'His wife must feel relieved?'

'I wonder!'

'It will seem hard-hearted on my part, Doctor, but I am happy about what you've just told me.'

And, looking straight into my eyes, she concluded:

'He made a good end!'

Chapter Nine

With the advance of autumn, Paris became cold and dreary. The *Beau Dimanche* at Tilly had been closed for a long time and I had seen hardly any of its habitués again for, in Paris, we seldom came across each other anywhere except at the Dandurands.

One afternoon, I fell in with John Lenauer on the Boulevard des Italiens, and he insisted on my joining him in a drink because of his 'alarming thirst'.

'You've seen Lulu again?' he asked.

'Yes.'

'How is she? I haven't even had the courage to go to the Rue Lamarck once. I never know how to behave when I'm with anyone sad.'

He talked about Riri and Yvonne Simart who meet even more mysteriously in Paris than they did on the Seine bank.

'You'll be going there next year?'

'Probably.'

The shops were already displaying their Christmas goods, and little stalls were being set up all along the boulevards.

I think it must be the same in all Parisian households as it is in ours. During seventeen years of married life, we must have visited, one after the other, sometimes turn and turn about, at least a dozen different groups. For a month, or six months or ten, you see the same people two or three times a week, invitations to dinner, to a restaurant, a theatre are exchanged then, suddenly, for no apparent reason, you lose touch with one another. Chance may bring you together again several years later and old friendships are renewed.

Sometimes these things have small beginnings. For instance, through my taking Saucier out to lunch while my wife was at Fourras, we had dined at his house with the Pétrels. We promptly asked the Sauciers back, and I thought of Bourgeois also. He has a young and amusing wife, and I was sure that Saucier would be pleased to see them again.

After coffee we played bridge. The Bourgeois invited us back in their turn, then the Sauciers, so that that winter was signalized by what we called our Medicos' Bridge.

October and November passed with a rapidity all the more staggering in that my second son also had flu and my wife was in bed for a week.

We were beginning to think about the children's Christmas presents. Ten times, I vowed I'd go and see Lulu, and, every time, some obstacle had arisen at the last minute. I was ashamed, especially as we found time to go and dine with the Pétrels, who proved to be charming hosts. On this occasion they kept off the subject of Bob.

To be perfectly honest, I even made time, twice, to wander round the Ternes district, with a quick glance into certain bars, in the vague hope of catching a glimpse of Adeline and, not meeting with any success, I paid a visit to her friend.

In the mornings, the lights were kept on until nine or ten o'clock, all day long in my consulting-room because of the frosted glass, and it was dark by three in the afternoon, with constant rain or drizzle.

I'm not trying to find excuses. We went to the theatre twice in all, just my wife and I. And once, at any rate, I did telephone the Rue Lamarck, shortly after November 11.

'Who is it?'

'Charles,' I replied.

It struck me immediately that she'd been drinking. She spoke in a thick voice, stumbling over the words, as if she didn't know what to say.

'How are you?'

'Very well.'

'And your wife?'

'Well also.'

'Your children?'

'Yes.'

It wasn't at all like her. I even wondered if she were quite in her right mind.

'But, what about *you*, Lulu?'

After a silence, during which I could hear her breathing, she said:

'I'm jogging along!'

Now Bob may have been fond of using slang phrases but Lulu, while he was alive, wouldn't have spoken like that.

'You're alone?'

'No.'

There was silence and, embarrassed, I wondered if it wouldn't be better for me to hang up.

'I'm having my fortune told.'

I knew by whom – hideous old Quéven of the pasty face and red-rimmed eyes.

'She foretells good luck for me!'

She laughed, her voice cracked by wine or alcohol. I didn't say anything about it at home.

December was upon us without my realizing it and I sent for the accountant who attends to the making up and despatching of my accounts at the end of the year. Whenever we see him ensconced in the drawing-room, where he wouldn't dream of smoking but sucks cachous all day long, we know that Christmas is near.

I was trying to find some way of persuading my wife to invite Lulu to our Midnight Supper. I knew she wouldn't come if *I* were to ask her, and indeed my wife would have to be extremely tactful and persistent.

'Whom do you intend asking on Christmas Eve?'

'I don't know. And you?'

'I don't know either.'

The year before, as it happened, after we'd eaten some turkey with the children and put them to bed shortly before midnight, we had gone on to the studio in the Rue Lamarck. There were at least thirty others there, and we'd all finished up by improvising fancy-dress with whatever we could find within reach.

'It's going to be sad for Lulu,' I hinted.

'I don't doubt it, but people don't celebrate Christmas while they're in deep mourning.'

I didn't insist, promising myself to bring the subject up again. I didn't get a chance.

On December 15, at a quarter-past eight in the morning, just as I was examining an old man naked to the waist and was listening with my stethoscope to the racket set up by his congested windpipe, the telephone rang. I thought it sounded more shrill and imperious than usual. I had to let it ring for some time before I was able to get to it.

'It's you, Doctor?'

I didn't recognize the voice.

'Doctor Coindreau, yes. Who is speaking?'

'Louise.'

'Louise who?'

'Lulu's assistant. Come quickly, Doctor. Telephone the police. *I'm* afraid to. I daren't even go back into the house. I'm ringing from the butcher's. Lulu's dead.'

*

She had made no fuss either, left no letter, no word of explanation. Beneath her on the bed, near a crumpled photograph of Bob and herself taken fifteen years before, was an empty tube of sleeping pills.

If she had held out for a few weeks longer, she wouldn't have had any need of a drug, for she weighed no more than a child of ten.

'Every day I begged her to eat,' said Louise. 'She would just shake her head, and I'm sure now that she did it on purpose. She let herself waste away.'

I'm sure too, only, it didn't work quickly enough and she had no intention of spending Christmas without Bob.

Perhaps also, now that Bob was no longer there to carry her, she was afraid of falling too low, afraid of becoming utterly unworthy of him.

It was to save herself from this treacherous slope that she had shown Mademoiselle Berthe the door. But hadn't she re-opened it a little later on to a creature like Rosalie Quéven?

She had made up her mind to leave while there was still time.

November

Translated from the French by
Jean Stewart

Chapter One

I don't think I had ever seen anything like it before. It was the second Friday in November, November 9 to be exact. The four of us were sitting round the dinner-table, as on any other evening. Manuela had just taken away the soup-plates and brought in a *fines herbes* omelette, which my mother had gone into the kitchen to prepare.

Since morning, one of the fiercest storms of the whole year had been raging over France and the radio told of roofs being blown off, cars sent flying ten yards along the road, and ships lost in the Channel and in the Atlantic.

The wind was blowing in violent gusts that shook the house as though to uproot it, and the shutters, windows and outer doors seemed about to give way at any moment.

The rain fell with relentless savagery, in heavy drifts, with a noise like waves breaking on a pebbled beach.

We none of us spoke. Our meal-times are usually silent; only essential remarks are made.

'Would you mind passing me the dish, please?'

Each of us goes on eating, isolated from the others by an invisible wall, and that evening each one of us was privately listening to the clamour of the storm.

Then suddenly, without warning, came silence; nature stood utterly still, and the emptiness was almost unbearable.

My father knit his bushy eyebrows. My brother stared at each of us in turn, with a look of surprise.

My mother imperceptibly tensed her long thin neck, as she glanced around mistrustfully. She is always suspicious of everything. She lives amid a hostile universe, forever watchful, forever on the alert, with fixed gaze and straining neck like certain animals, certain birds of prey.

Nobody spoke. We all seemed to be holding our breath as

though this sudden silence presaged some unknown disaster.

Only my father's expression, after that brief frown, remained unchanged. His grey face seldom expresses more than a kind of solemn gravity.

Olivier glanced towards the door, which Manuela had just shut behind her, and I am convinced that he sent her a silent message. I am sure, too, that my mother intercepted that message without even turning her head. She sees and hears everything. She says nothing, but she takes mental note.

My brother soon recovered from the shock of the unexpected stillness of the world. He was sitting in his usual place opposite my father, and I was opposite my mother, who had those telltale red patches on her cheekbones.

It meant that she'd been drinking. She had started on her 'novena', as we call it, but she was not drunk, she's never really drunk.

'Are you feeling tired?'

Why did my father feel compelled to say that? She's no fool; she is far subtler than he is and she knows what words imply. This has been going on for so many years that there's no need for him to underline it.

'I've got my sick headache,' she said curtly.

I don't know which of the two I pity most. It often seems as if my mother deliberately tries to be disagreeable, and even her silences have something aggressive about them. But could my father not be more easy going, show a little tolerance?

After all, he married her, and she cannot have been much better-looking then than she is now. I have seen photographs taken on their wedding-day, in 1938. She has always been ill-favoured; her nose is too long, with a sharp tip that seems to have been added as an afterthought, and her chin is too sharp too.

Was my father ever in love with her? or was he merely proud, being a young lieutenant at the time, of marrying one of the daughters of his Colonel, who was shortly to become a General?

I know nothing about that. It's none of my business. It's not for me to judge them, although I do so involuntarily. We live in a house where each of us watches the rest and leads a life apart.

Only our Spanish maid Manuela, who has been with us two months, sings at her housework and behaves as if everything were quite normal around her.

Pears were served, and my father peeled his more carefully than the most accomplished *maître d'hôtel*. He does everything conscientiously, with a meticulousness that can be exasperating.

Does he feel obliged to restrain himself? Is there something artificial about his calm, dignified manner?

He rose from table first, as usual, just as he invariably sits down first and slowly unfolds his napkin. He has a sense of hierarchy, probably because he is an army man. That may also be the reason, perhaps, why he attaches the same importance to small things as to great ones.

He muttered: 'I'm going to do some work . . .'

That's what he says almost every evening at the same time. He has turned one of the rooms, the other side of the passage, into a study. In the middle there is an enormous nineteenth-century roll-top desk and the glass-fronted bookcases are full of books and journals.

Does he really work there? He brings home a briefcase stuffed with papers from his office. We sometimes hear him tapping away unskilfully on his portable typewriter. More often, there's dead silence. We're supposed not to disturb him. Each of us is careful to knock if we happen to have something to say to him.

He has an old worn leather arm-chair in which I have often seen him sitting with his feet stretched out in front of the fire-place, where he has lighted a small wood fire. He lifts his head from his book and looks at you patiently, offering no encouragement.

'I wanted to ask you if, tomorrow . . .'

Does he even listen? Does it interest him? Does he realize that he's the head of the household and that the three of us depend on him?

Olivier takes little notice of his father and quietly organizes his own life. He often goes out in the evening, less frequently since Manuela has been with us. After dinner he goes up into his bedroom, or into the sort of laboratory which he has fixed

283

up in the attic, and which happens to be just next to the Spanish girl's room.

My mother went into the drawing-room. I followed her. She automatically switched on the television set ... She does so every evening, invariably, whatever the programme, yet this does not prevent her from hearing the slightest noise in the house ...

She sews. She always has some linen to mend, or buttons to sew on. I usually sit down in front of the television set too, but the programme doesn't always interest me and I bury myself in a book.

'It was strange the way the storm ended so suddenly ...'

She looked up for a moment, as though to make sure that my words had no hidden implication. Then she simply murmured: 'Yes ...'

There was a clatter of plates in the kitchen where Manuela was washing up. I knew that as soon as the maid went upstairs my mother would get up, muttering: 'I must make sure she's switched off ...'

But her real purpose would not be to see to the electric light or the gas stove. Some red wine had been left over and she could drink it from the bottle, with an anxious glance towards the door, for she's always afraid of being caught. When she's in this state she will drink anything, whatever comes to hand, and her cheeks gradually begin to flush and her eyes to glitter.

I am sorry for her and at the same time I resent having to pity my mother. Sometimes I feel sorry for my father too. Which of them began it?

We were babies once, my brother and I, myself first, for I am the oldest, I am twenty-one, and then Olivier who is nineteen.

Did our parents behave like most other parents? Did they exchange kisses and loving words as they stood by our cradle?

It seems unthinkable. As far back as I can remember the house has always been just the same, orderly and silent, the days broken only by gloomy meal-times.

I'm not sure that they hate one another. My father is patient, and I realize that it's not always easy. I can understand why he has taken refuge in that study where he spends most of his

284

evenings. But surely Mother might have expected something more than patience from him?

At times I wish they would have a proper scene, a really violent one with shouts and tears and then a temporary reconciliation.

I'm a bad judge. I am not good-looking either. I am rather plain, like my mother, though I have a round thick nose instead of a long pointed one in two sections.

What was the good of thinking about such things? I read my book; I tried to read it and, from time to time, I watched my mother's face. Outside the rain was dripping slowly.

The programme changed to a noisy Western and I got up to turn down the volume. Are there many families like ours living in and around Paris?

At ten o'clock my mother took off her glasses and picked up her sewing, her scissors and reels. She had not been into the kitchen as I'd expected.

'Good night, Laure . . .'

She stood quite still for a moment while I laid a light kiss on both her cheeks. And now she would go through the kitchen on her way upstairs. At last I'd be able to switch off the television and read in peace.

Does my father wait until she is in bed before going up himself? I never see them go up together. There's usually a gap of a quarter of an hour, as if they wanted to avoid any sort of intimacy, even though they sleep in the same bed.

I went on reading. Then the study door opened. My father crossed the passage and stood in the doorway, looking around him with a completely expressionless face.

'Has your mother gone up?'

I glanced at the clock on the mantelpiece. 'Just over ten minutes ago.'

'Did she say anything?'

I looked at him in some surprise.

'No.' What might she have said? About what?

'Has Olivier been down?'

'No.'

'Is he in his room?'

'In his room or in the attic, I'm not sure . . .'

'Good night, Laure . . .'

He moved towards me, and he too duly received a kiss on both cheeks.

'Good night, *papa*.'

It always seems odd to call him *papa*. It doesn't go with his physical appearance, his grave, dignified bearing. He never smiles, or rather, when he tries to smile, it's a mechanical twitch of the lips, with no gaiety in it.

'Aren't you going to bed?'

'Presently . . .'

'Don't forget to turn out the lights . . .'

As if at twenty-one I was incapable of switching off the light behind me!

'Good night . . .'

'Good night . . .'

But that night, the night of November 9–10, was not to be a very good one.

After reading for an hour or so I went to my own room and undressed. I kept thinking about the Professor, and about Gilles, who must surely feel puzzled and resentful.

Professor Shimek is not handsome. He is fifty-two, and has a daughter of fifteen and a merry, dumpy little wife whom he married after he had left Czechoslovakia. He's one of the most intelligent men there are. But from Gilles Ropart's point of view . . .

There are times when I would rather not think, but just let myself go on living. Apparently when I was quite a small girl and my father or mother disturbed me, I used to say with a sigh:

'Can't I be let live?'

I might say as much now. I brushed my teeth, took off the slight make-up I allow myself and, after lifting my heavy breasts with a certain pleasure, I slipped on my pyjamas and got into bed.

I always find it hard to get to sleep. Thoughts and images of every sort flood into my mind, from all periods of my life. I have tried sleeping-pills; I used to drop off more rapidly but would wake up after an hour or two and find it harder to fall asleep again, so that next morning I felt muddle-headed.

I suppose I have inherited my mother's keen sense of hearing.

In any case, our house, although built in the last century, is as resonant as a drum.

I could hear the water dripping from the roof and from time to time a car passing along the road.

Why do I always have the impression that other people are really living and that I am not? Those cars were going somewhere, coming from somewhere. At this time of night there were people at theatres and restaurants, and some of them were laughing. Like Manuela. She's the only one who laughs in our house, regardless of the atmosphere around her. She's my age, she's beautiful, full of health and vitality. Her gaiety seems almost defiant.

I knew what I was expecting and it happened, inevitably. My brother got up in the next room. I could hear his bed creaking. So he must be undressed.

Had he waited long enough? Were father and mother asleep? He opened his door cautiously and crept up the stairs. Although he made as little noise as possible I heard him, and Manuela must have heard him too, for she opened her door before he had time to knock.

This was the tenth time it had happened. It had been going on for about a month; I was conscious of them standing there, above my head, embracing one another. Then I heard Manuela's throaty laugh.

Was my mother listening too? And if so, what was she thinking? My brother is nineteen, and it's natural to be in love at that age.

None the less I suspect her of being bitterly resentful; for it was happening in her own house, in her own realm, and what's more with her maid.

We have never been able to keep a servant longer than six months and Mother treats the Spanish girl more harshly than her predecessors. Manuela seems not to notice. She goes about fearlessly singing and laughing. And for the past month she has readily admitted the son of the house into her bedroom.

They were both in bed now, apparently oblivious of the fact that they were immediately above my head. I could hear everything. But at the same time I was listening, so to speak, to the silence in my parents' room.

If *they* were awake they must be hearing it too.

And then a door opened slowly, their door. Then it closed again, and someone, barefooted, started up the stairs. I could even swear that I heard my father's heavy breathing. I was sure it was him. He took an endless time climbing up to the second floor landing, where he stopped motionless.

Had he only just discovered that Olivier visited the maid in her bedroom? Or, having guessed it, was he looking for proof?

Up in the attic the lovers carried on unsuspectingly.

My father, Captain Le Cloanec, a man of fifty-two, who always seems overburdened by his responsibilities, was standing there barefoot in the darkness, listening to his son and the maid making love.

I had suspected this, but I had refused to believe it; my father was in love, in love with Manuela, which I found inconceivable. He was so much in love as to leave his bed, where my mother might be lying awake, or might wake at any moment, to go and keep watch.

Keep watch for what? He knew now, didn't he? He needed no further proof.

Would he humiliate himself by opening the door and surprising the lovers?

He stood there motionless, torturing himself. I don't know if he really has a bad heart. When anything upsets him he sometimes lays a hand on his chest. Was he doing that now?

I had never imagined him in that situation, nor in such a state of mind. I was distressed by it; I was anxious, too, on account of my mother. He stood there a long time and when at last he came downstairs he went into the bathroom as though to give himself an alibi.

I expected to hear him and my mother speaking, but their room remained silent. He must have groped his way back to bed in the darkness, and if Mother was awake she must have pretended to be asleep.

I had no idea what time it was. My thoughts were becoming confused and I was in a wretched state of mind. I considered getting up to take a sleeping tablet and then, without realizing it, I dropped off to sleep.

In any case, when I opened my eyes, daylight was showing

through the slats of the venetian blinds and when I drew these up, I was surprised to find that the sun was shining. The road was still wet, covered with twigs and even quite sizable branches. There were drops of water hanging to the telephone wires and slipping off one by one. In our front garden a broken branch was lying by the gate.

Downstairs, Manuela was singing. Mother must have been still in her room. She takes nothing in the morning except a cup of coffee which is brought to her in bed, and she seldom comes down until we have all three left the house.

I went to the bathroom. The door was locked.

'That you, Laure?'

My brother's voice.

'I'll be through in a couple of minutes.'

I was a little late. It was past eight o'clock. However, I don't start work at the Broussais hospital until nine and on my motor-scooter the journey only takes me twenty minutes.

My father was probably in the dining-room, drinking his tea and eating toast and jam. We scarcely ever breakfast together, but each of us comes down in his own time.

'Just look at that sunshine! If anyone had told us yesterday . . .'

'Yes . . .'

I heard Olivier getting out of the bath and unhooking his wrap.

'Half a sec . . . I'll let you in . . .'

The door opened. His hair was standing on end and his face was still wet.

He frowned as he looked at me. 'What's the matter with you?'

'I didn't sleep well.'

'Don't tell me you have sick headaches too!'

He has no patience with Mother.

'I've got to talk to you, Olivier.'

'When?'

'Now . . . As soon as Father has left . . .'

For my father goes into Paris by scooter, too, so that Mother can use the car. He only takes it when the weather is bad, as it was yesterday.

'What did you want to talk to me about?'

'Wait . . . I'll come down and have breakfast with you . . .'

I had on my yellow dressing-gown. I combed my hair a little and brushed my teeth while my brother went into his room to dress. He takes no care of his clothes and they always look as if he had slept in them.

We heard Father's scooter starting up and then the gate creaked. He almost always opens it in the morning and shuts it at night.

'Are you coming?'

'In a minute . . . You go down and ask Manuela to do me a couple of fried eggs . . . With sausages, if she's got any . . .'

*

Manuela, serene and smiling, at peace with the world and with herself, called out cheerfully: 'Bonjour, mademoiselle . . .'

On her lips, the words became: 'Z'ou, madezelle . . .'

She has not been in Paris more than a year. She has had two jobs already. She's got a friend whom I once saw waiting for her on the road, a tiny dark creature called Pilar.

'Morning, Manuela. I'd like a big cup of coffee and two pieces of buttered toast. My brother's just coming down, and he'd like eggs and sausages, if you've got them . . .'

She seemed to be laughing. Everything amuses her, even trying to understand what one says to her in a foreign language. She's not much taller than her friend Pilar but plumper, and full of vitality. She moves as gracefully as if she were dancing. She's Andalusian, from a village called Villaviciosa, in the Sierra Morena, somewhere to the north of Cordoba.

She had gone back to the kitchen by the time my brother appeared, with his hair still wet.

'What did you want to say to me?'

'Sit down. We've plenty of time . . .'

It was Saturday. 'Have you got lectures?'

'Only practicals . . .'

Olivier, who is studying chemistry, goes to classes at the Faculty of Science in the former Halle aux Vins. His dream is to have a big noisy motor-cycle, which my father refuses to buy for him.

'Every school-kid has a scooter . . . I look ridiculous on mine, with my long legs . . .'

I am very fond of him. He's a nice lad, but he's moody. He'll flare up over the least thing and abuse me savagely, and then come to say he's sorry.

He must have guessed that I wanted to talk about Manuela and he was curiously and vaguely uneasy. I waited until we had been served. He smiled at the Spanish girl with a tenderness that I had not expected from him. When my parents are not there he can show his real feelings.

I had thought it was only a passing fancy, a purely physical passion, but that single glance of his had shown me something else, while Manuela herself grew a little graver.

'Morning, Manuela . . .'

'Morning, Monsieur Olivier . . .'

She pronounced it 'Olié', and it sounded very sweet and tender. She went off swinging her hips, and closed the door. The dining-room smelt of coffee and fried eggs and sausages but it was also pervaded by the same odour as all the rest of the house, that musty smell of damp wood and hay that you often get in the country.

'Well, what is it?' my brother said impatiently.

I picked my words carefully for fear he should fly into a rage, particularly as one could never be sure that Mother was not behind the door. She lives in slippers, her everlasting red slippers, and she goes about noiselessly.

'You ought to be careful, Olivier.'

He flushed, and retorted with defiance in his voice: 'Careful about what?'

'Last night, something happened while you were up there . . .'

'Mother?' He was on edge already.

'No . . . Father . . .'

'What did Father do?'

'I suppose I'd better tell you . . . You're old enough to . . .'

'What did he do?'

'Some time after you'd gone up, he came out of his room in his bare feet and went upstairs too.'

'What for? To listen at the door? To look through the key-hole, maybe?'

'I don't think so, Olivier. He stood on the landing for a long time and I think he was unhappy.'

'What d'you mean?'

And as I did not answer immediately Olivier thrust his plate aside and stood up suddenly.

'You're not going to tell me that he's ... that he ... that ...'

He could not bear to utter the words.

'Yes.'

'Oh, that would be the end! As if it weren't bad enough to have a crazy mother!'

'Hush ...'

Olivier is pitiless. He treats Mother harshly, especially when she has been drinking, and he makes no allowances for her. He has several times admitted to me that he wanted to leave the house, to drop everything and take a room in Paris, even if he had to work his way through college.

'There are plenty of people at the University who earn their living.'

He was striding up and down the room, trying to contain himself.

'What business is it of his if Manuela and I are in love?'

He turned to glance at a photograph of my father as a young man, a subaltern with a faint moustache.

'What was he doing at my age? ... Unless he's always been as lifeless as he is now, which wouldn't surprise me ... A solemn ... a solemn ...'

He seemed reluctant to speak the word, but it broke out in spite of him:

'A solemn imbecile!'

'Calm down, Olivier.'

'It's obvious you're not the one involved. Does he worry about what you do at Broussais?'

At this I blushed myself, and did not press the point. It's true that it isn't easy to form an opinion of my father's real personality. I myself sometimes dismiss him as a second-rater, trying to maintain a lofty image of himself.

He spent the war years in Algeria, in an office job, and he likes to imply that he was in the secret service. Now, with the rank of Captain but in civilian dress, he works in an office in the Boulevard Brune, somewhere near the Jean-Noël stadium, so that he is only a few hundred metres from Broussais. It's an old building that used to be a private house and now belongs to the War Ministry. The official name of his department is 'Bureau of Statistics'. According to Father, his work is top secret and involves confidential information about counter-espionage.

I learned the truth one day from a young doctor at Broussais.

'I've an uncle in that place too. They're the people who send the money to our agents abroad. They've got round-about ways of sending it so that it can't be traced . . .'

In short, my father is a sort of accountant or cashier.

My brother stopped walking about and stood in front of me.

'What d'you want me to do?'

'I don't know. I only wanted to warn you.'

'Do you admit that he's ridiculous?'

'I pity him.'

'And because he's to be pitied, I've got to be miserable?'

'I didn't say that, Olivier. You might perhaps see her somewhere else.'

'On Wednesdays, then, since that's her only day off?'

I didn't know the answer. It was not my problem. I could not help being uneasy and unhappy about my father.

I'd been quite right to think that Mother might not be far away. She opened the door slowly; she was in her dressing-gown too, with her everlasting red slippers, her hair still dishevelled, her face rather puffy. She looked at each of us in turn.

'Aren't you eating?' she asked Olivier, for he had barely touched his eggs and they were congealing on the plate.

'I'm not hungry.'

He was unnecessarily curt. He added, as though reluctantly:

'Good morning, *maman*.'

'Good morning.'

The greeting did for both of us. She seemed not to notice me.

293

She opened the door and called out. 'Some more coffee, Man-uela.'

She must have been eager for us to go so as to drink some red wine, unless there is a bottle of cognac or whisky in the house. When she is on one of her bouts, anything will do.

She sat down, weary and listless, and Olivier announced:

'It's time I went.'

This was not true, but I could understand his wanting to leave. I finished my breakfast and wondered, yet again, whether there were other families like ours.

'What's going on?' She wanted to make me talk.

'I don't know. Why?'

'I heard voices raised.'

'He often talks like that.'

She knew I was lying. She didn't care. She looked at me with those hard, unhappy little eyes of hers. Manuela, bursting with vitality, brought in her coffee and the contrast between the two women was almost tragic.

'Are you working all day today?'

On Saturdays I sometimes come home at midday. At other times I am on duty all day. When I know that the Professor is going to be there I arrange to stop.

'Did you see your father?'

'No. He'd gone downstairs when I got up and by the time I came down he'd gone off on his scooter.'

Why did she ask me that? Her remarks are never casual. Everything she says has a purpose, sometimes so well hidden that it takes some time to discover it.

'I'm sorry, but I must get ready, I shall be late . . .'

I took a quick shower, for it would have taken too long to clean the bath and run the water. I put on the brown tweed suit I had bought for autumn, although I'm not sure whether it suits my colouring. I can't wear navy blue all the year round.

When I opened the dining-room door again, Mother was no longer there. Nor was she in the kitchen, where Manuela was singing a Spanish folksong. I suppose she had gone down into the cellar.

I left by the back door and went to fetch my scooter from the

294

shed where the car is kept too. The trees were still dripping, after three days' torrential rain. Nature seemed to be slowly convalescing, the sun was still pale. On the road I had to ride through puddles every time I met a car.

Our house is at Givry-les-Etangs, on the edge of a wood. It's a sort of villa of faded bricks with coloured ceramic ornaments and a complicated roof with two pinnacles. It was built towards the end of the last century by an uncle of my father's, another Le Cloanec, who had been a colonial official in Madagascar and then in Gabon.

After a while he had resigned from the service and become a timber merchant. This had enabled him, in a few years, to amass a small fortune and build himself this house at Givry-les-Etangs. There are in fact two ponds not far from here, the Etang-Vieux – the old pond, which has become a kind of marsh, and the Grand-Etang – the big pond, on which we keep an old boat that is always full of stagnant water.

Another villa, further off, has been unoccupied for some years. There's a third, which belongs to the Rorives, a retired dairy owner and his wife.

There was some story about a negress ... For my uncle brought a magnificent negress back from Africa with him, and I'm not sure he did not intend to marry her. I don't know what she looked like, for there are no pictures of her, only a photograph of my uncle, a self-important paunchy figure in a tropical helmet.

She may have met someone in her wanderings around Paris. At all events, she failed to come home one fine evening, and it seems that she was later seen in a brothel where she was employed.

I learned this story through snatches of conversation overheard when one or other of my mother's sisters came to visit her and they gossiped in monotonous voices like a running tap.

My father inherited the house, which is called Les Glaïeuls, and a modest sum of money into the bargain, since his uncle had invested in an annuity.

After Givry-les-Etangs I still have a few kilometres to ride before reaching the Saint-Cloud–Versailles road, where the traffic is denser and I have to take care.

Past that point I feel as if I had severed all links with home and belonged solely to the Broussais hospital.

Professor Shimek is at the head of the immunology department, which includes several laboratories. There are at least twenty girls working there under the direction of Mlle Neef, a spinster of fifty-five who has devoted her life to the Professor.

She cannot endure me, for she knows, even if she has never caught us unawares, that my devotion is not as platonic as her own.

I believe everyone is aware of the situation, even though in public my relations with Stephan are those of a young lab assistant with her chief. I even avoid, during the day, looking him in the eyes, for fear of betraying myself.

Poor Ropart must have been the first to find out, since for over a year I used to go out with him and spend an hour or two in his rooms in the Rue de l'Eperon. He's an intelligent fellow, with a future. The Professor thinks very highly of him and entrusts important research to him. Did I ever think that I might some day marry Gilles Ropart? I'm not sure, but the idea must have crossed my mind, if only when the atmosphere at home became intolerable, which frequently happens.

I always knew I was not in love with him, but with the Professor. I always thought of Gilles rather as a good friend, even though we had a more intimate relationship to which I did not attach great importance. As soon as I began to work at Broussais I fell in love with Shimek, but for a long time I thought him beyond my reach.

Some of the girls make fun of him, because he has retained a strong foreign accent and he is apt to make jokes one can't always understand. And he sometimes talks to himself.

He's very far from the conventional idea of the big chief. He isn't solemn, like my father, and his highly mobile face is rather like that of an elderly schoolboy who loves playing jokes.

None the less he's a member of the Academy of Medicine and he's been mentioned as a possible Nobel prize-winner.

I always arranged to stay on with him in the evenings when he stopped late to dissect one of our animals, a rat, a hamster or more recently a dog. We've got more than thirty dogs in the basement, and the patients in the various hospital wards complain of hearing them howl much of the night.

Shimek carries on his work undeterred by anything, convinced that he is on the right track and that his discoveries will be of capital importance for mankind.

'What's the matter, child?'

He calls all the lab girls 'child'; this makes things easier for him, for he has no memory for names, particularly French names.

'Nothing's the matter, sir. I just wondered if I couldn't help you.'

'Help me, eh?'

He said this ironically, as if he had seen through me.

'You don't seem very keen to hurry home in the evenings.'

'I feel more at home here.'

'Fancy that! And that tall redhead, Ropart, isn't that his name? Have you stopped going out with him?'

I was scarlet with embarrassment and didn't know where to look.

I don't think he was doing it on purpose. Nor do I believe he is cynical. On the contrary; later on, I decided that it was out of a sort of shyness that he spoke like that, as though making fun of himself.

Could he have been jealous of Ropart?

'Have you quarrelled?'

'No. We were chiefly good friends.'

'And not now?'

'I never see him except here.'

'Doesn't he resent that?'

'Surely not. He has understood.'

He went to wash his hands, very carefully, like a surgeon, and muttered a few words in his own language. He seemed vexed. He prowled about tidying up his instruments, then at last he laid his hands on my shoulders.

'In love?'

There was an unfamiliar huskiness about his voice.

'Yes,' I said, looking him straight in the eyes.

'You know I'm married?'

'Yes.'

'That I've a daughter who's nearly your age?'

'She's only fourteen.'

'I see you know all about me.'

I knew, too, that he lived in a big flat in the Place Denfert-Rochereau, opposite the Lion de Belfort.

'What are you hoping for?'

'Nothing.'

'That's about all I can give you. In my position, a liaison is out of the question.'

'I know.'

Did he sense my fervour, my devotion, the quality of my love? I was no infatuated schoolgirl, but a woman. Apart from Ropart I had had a couple of ephemeral affairs.

'You're a funny girl.'

Then he put his arms around me and kissed me with a certain tenderness, first on the cheeks and then on the lips.

We have never been alone in a real room. We have never made love in a bed, except the camp bed which is kept for anyone on night duty.

During the day he treats me exactly as he treats all the others, with an almost fatherly and somewhat absent-minded kindliness.

I have sometimes thought that human beings don't greatly interest him. He sacrifices his time and his health in trying to cure them, to improve their lot, but as individuals they don't exist for him.

I have often wondered what he is like at home, in his family or with close friends, if he has any. He gets on well with the other heads of departments, particularly the cardiologist, but I don't think this could be described as friendship.

As for me, I belong to him. He has grown used to it. He sometimes goes a whole week without taking notice of me, knowing that I am there, that I shall always be there, whatever he may do.

I shall be an old maid. The prospect does not distress me, and perhaps some day, much later, when Mlle Neef retires, I may take her place in the department.

I think I am happy. I should be, if it weren't for our life at home, about which I would rather not think. I hate myself for

298

feeling nothing but a sort of latent pity for my mother. As for my father, I am sorry for him too, though I resent his being the sort of man he is. If he had reacted from the first, instead of bowing his head in meek silence, might not my mother have been different? At the office, he may perhaps take people in. He takes himself in, at all events. He puts on an important solemn air, as Olivier says, but don't the people who work with him make fun of him behind his back?

He is fairly tall and broad-shouldered; he has an erect soldierly bearing, but there's a certain lack of weight and substance about him.

I wonder if other girls of my age criticize their parents? At home, we all spy on one another. Nothing escapes us, not an attitude, nor a word, nor a fugitive gleam in someone's eyes.

'What's the matter with you?'

'Nothing, *maman.*'

Father, on the other hand, does not ask questions; he just frowns, with those bushy eyebrows of his. There are tufts of greyish hair in his ears too.

'You ought to get them cut,' I told him one day when I felt almost intimate with him.

He merely looked at me as if I had said the silliest thing imaginable. How could a man like himself, with his responsibilities, be expected to bother about the hair sprouting from his ears?

And now he was in love with Manuela and had become his own son's rival!

I couldn't bear to think of it. I settled down to work, as usual, in the smallest lab. At that time of day, on Saturdays, the Professor was giving a lecture and his assistant, Dr Bernard, was in charge of the department.

Here, too, I feel myself spied on. Over the past year the news of my relations with the Professor has had time to spread. Do they wonder how I can have managed to attract him, plain as I am? Or do they think I'm a good match for him, with his elderly clown's face? I have heard that comment made several times. It's true that he has a furrowed, extremely mobile face and can grin as broadly as a circus clown.

What other whispers can be going round about us? I get no

privilege, no promotion. On the contrary, it seems a point of honour with Shimek to give me the most unpleasant jobs to do. It's his way of replying to gossip.

'I say, you're not usually so late. It's a quarter past nine.'

'I know. My mother wasn't well this morning and the road was bad.'

'Are you on duty this afternoon?'

'I don't know.'

'One of the dogs has just died, and it was supposed to live several days longer. "He" will certainly want to know what happened.'

And in that case I would stay. I'd eat in the canteen, which I quite enjoy. Olivier would be going out with his friends. Only Father would have no excuse for not returning to Les Glaïeuls, but he makes a point of shutting himself up in his study and pretending to work.

The fact is that we all avoid my mother. Each of us has another life to turn to outside the house, other pleasures, other preoccupations.

She has none. Her only outlet is to take the car to do her shopping at Givry-les-Etangs and once or twice a week at the Versailles supermarket.

She has four sisters and one brother. Her brother, Fabien, manager of the Poulard chocolate factory, lives in Versailles with his wife and two children. One sister, Blandine, lives in Paris, in the Rue d'Alésia, where her husband runs a furniture-removal and road-transport business. As for Iris, who is unmarried, she has a small flat in the Place Saint-Georges and earns her living as a stenographer.

Alberte, whom we call the 'fat one', is the wife of a wealthy Strasburg grocer, and Marion lives in Toulon.

On one of our dining-room walls there hangs a photograph of my mother and her sisters as children, with their father the General in uniform and his wife.

At one time we often had visits from one or other of my aunts, but these have become increasingly rare. I hardly know my cousins; some of them, at Toulon, I have never seen in my life.

I went on working, with my thoughts elsewhere; I was wearing my white lab coat and cap. There are about twenty of us coming and going, bending over test-tubes, looking after small animals to which we have given names.

When the midday bell rang, I felt as if I had only just begun my day's work. I washed my hands, ran a comb through my hair and followed most of my companions to the refectory. The nurses from the other departments were there, but they paid no attention to us, for we are a separate community.

Somebody was saying that Professor Shimek needed horses for a particular serum and wanted to turn one of the garages into a stable. To the nurses, as to their patients, the dogs were bad enough! 'And now we're to have horses in the hospital . . .'

It may or may not be true. There are always rumours going round, particularly about my boss. Nobody questions his great ability, but he's considered an eccentric who would willingly sacrifice three quarters of the hospital to his own researches.

My father and mother must now be sitting *tête-à-tête* in the gloomy dining-room at Les Glaïeuls. Would she say anything to him? Had she been awake when he went upstairs to the second floor and stood waiting for so long, barefoot, on the landing?

I don't expect her to refer to it, except in so subtle a way as to arouse his anxiety without telling him for certain whether she knows.

Olivier must be lunching at the university restaurant, as he does nearly every Saturday. Does he talk to his friends about Manuela? Does he feel the need to confide in them, or does he keep his love a secret?

I went on eating, watching people's faces, thinking, and ended by not being sure what I was thinking about.

Chapter Two

That evening, 10 November, my father surprised me by not retiring to his study after dinner but settling down in the drawing-room, which is divided from the dining-room by a wide opening with no door.

I wondered whether this was in order, later on, to watch Manuela putting away dishes and glasses in the sideboard. As for Mother, she just stared fixedly at him. She was on the second day of her 'novena' and had drunk rather more than the day before. She had begun to walk unsteadily. She would go on drinking more heavily every day until at last, still complaining of her headache, she would retire to bed for two or three days.

I had been mistaken about my father's motives. There was a pre-war film on television, with glossy photography and artful lighting. The men wore short, waisted jackets and sleek hair, the women long dresses and romantic make-up. The whole film was foolishly sentimental, and yet my father watched it with interest, probably with nostalgia. I had the impression that he had seen it long ago, perhaps when he was about twenty or perhaps later, at the time of his marriage. I was surprised to see him staring so attentively at the screen and it seemed to me, at some points, that his eyes were dimmed with tears.

I went up first to bed, for I had not slept much the night before. I don't know if they talked to one another in my absence; I presume not.

During the night I was woken by Olivier's motor-scooter roaring round the house, then by footsteps on the gravel. My brother must have been drunk, I gathered that immediately, for his hand fumbled for quite a while before thrusting the key into the lock. Then he went upstairs with loud, noisy steps, clinging to the banister.

Without pausing on the first floor he went up to knock at Manuela's door, which she opened to him.

My parents, who sleep more lightly than I do, could not have failed to hear; but this time Father did not go upstairs. Over my head, I don't know what they were doing but I could hear the sound of footsteps, furniture being pulled about and my brother's voice raised in anger.

At last I heard him fling himself upon the bed and, after a while, the Spanish girl joined him there.

There was a lull. A quarter of an hour later, somebody went into the bathroom, my brother presumably, and I heard the water being flushed repeatedly.

I did not hear him come downstairs again, for I eventually

302

dropped off to sleep again. Did he spend the night in the maid's attic? Did he go back to his own room? He was being so noisy and clumsy that I must surely have heard him.

Was this not a sort of challenge, a declaration of war? He took no precaution against being heard, quite the reverse.

Next morning, at half-past nine, Manuela left the house before anyone else to go to Mass at Givry. Sunday is not her day off; she takes Wednesdays so as to go out with her friend, who works in the Avenue Paul-Doumer, near the Trocadéro.

Rain was falling gently, a thin steady rain that must have been cold. I watched Manuela walking down the road under her umbrella. She never misses Mass and she always signs herself before meals.

My father finished his breakfast and went into the passage to take down his hat and waterproof. He goes to Mass too. He is a Berton from Pouliguen, near La Baule, where his father used to keep a small bookshop and where his mother still lives in an old people's home.

My brother and I have been baptized. I took my first Communion, but my brother never did, I don't know why.

My mother's family are not Catholics and the General was said to have been a Freemason; I can't say whether this is true or not.

Olivier came down in shirt-sleeves and slippers, his hair all on end and his shirt unbuttoned. His eyes were swollen, his face tired, with red blotches, and, looking at him closely, I noticed the mark of a bite at the back of his neck, below his ear.

'Has he gone?'

'He went to church in the car.'

'Much good may it do him. And Mother?'

'Manuela took up her coffee before going out.'

'Has she gone on foot?'

'You'll find coffee in the kitchen. The pan's all ready for your eggs. Would you like me to cook them?'

'I'm not hungry.'

His expression of disgust was highly revealing. He'd got a hangover, and his head must have been aching.

'Were you with friends?'

'When?'

'Last night, when you were drinking.'

'I chiefly went on drinking by myself after they'd left me.'

'Don't you think you ought to be careful, Olivier?'

He glared at me aggressively.

'So you're on their side too?'

'No, but I feel it's pointless to . . .'

'I've the right to live, haven't I? D'you call it living, the way they exist, the way we all exist in this house? If they're crazy it's not my fault.'

I poured him a second cup of coffee and he sugared it mechanically.

'I'm fed up,' he growled. 'If I only had some money I'd go off with Manuela. She's the only thing that keeps me here. And now my idiotic father has to start running after her with his tongue hanging out. He's making a real fool of himself! If he only knew how he revolts her . . .'

I don't know why I felt a pang. Olivier's brutal words made a keen impression on me and inspired me with pity instead of disgust for my father.

And yet I can understand my brother's bitterness. I, too, sometimes revolt against our life at home, and I keep wondering whether there are many other families like ours.

What's the cause of it all?

What went wrong? Or have things always been like this? Were my father and mother never in love, were they never a proper couple, or did it all happen later, after we were born?

I incline to lay the blame on Mother, who must always have been somewhat unbalanced. Was there ever a suggestion of treatment? did she agree to see a psychiatrist? She has always been somehow out of phase with reality, sometimes so subtly that only members of the family could notice it.

Was my father the right man to take on responsibility for her? Had he done all that he might? I blame him, too. Then I feel sorry for him. I am sorry for all of us, in fact, and if I could not escape to Broussais every morning I think I'd go crazy too.

Olivier asked me: 'Are you going out this afternoon?'

'I certainly am.'

Sundays are deadly at Les Glaïeuls. It's difficult to escape from one another. After lunch, sometimes, we all go up into our own rooms and try to sleep. I don't know about the rest, but that's what I do and I sometimes doze for part of the afternoon. When I go down into the drawing-room, I almost always find my mother watching television and knitting or sewing. Father is in his study, reading newspapers and magazines.

As for Olivier, he makes a point of being out and he seldom comes home for supper on Sundays.

Just now, he was smoking his first cigarette and blowing out the smoke with a defiant air. He had the fierce look of a man in love, ready to challenge the whole world. He glanced at the clock, probably thinking that Mass must be nearly over; Manuela would take a good twenty minutes to walk back from Givry. It was still raining; the sky was hung with low grey clouds, motionless, with darker patches.

'I'm going to take a shower.'

'It'll make you feel better.'

He looked at me irritably.

'So I don't look too good? If you want to know, I got tight on purpose. I was with Marcel Pitet. We had a few drinks and then he wanted to go home. When I was by myself I went into the first bar I came to and drank several brandies at the counter. A woman tried to pick me up and I ended by offering her a drink and telling her all about it. I needed to talk to somebody. I said: "That bastard my father ..." And she offered to console me. At one point I vented my rage on her, perhaps because she made the mistake of saying: "You can always get another girl!" I must have made a scene. The landlord paid himself out of my wallet and then gave it back to me and pushed me into the street.'

'Go and take your shower.'

'That's all you can say, is it? Drink some coffee, some strong black coffee, go and take a shower. And when you come down again try to keep calm and don't make a scene.'

I'd had enough of him. I went into my own room and looked out at the trees, where the yellow leaves that had not yet fallen glistened in the rain.

I sometimes lay the blame for it all on our house, on those everlasting dark woods, on the ponds, the Etang-Vieux and the Grand-Etang, on this godforsaken place where we have no neighbours but that ridiculous couple the Rorives. Not only do they naïvely display their satisfaction at having made good, after thirty years in their dairy in the Rue de Turenne, but they feel obliged, because they're our neighbours, to call on us from time to time. They seem to have noticed nothing. They invariably bring a cake or some chocolates. They smile as if we had welcomed them with open arms and they both go and sit down in the drawing-room.

'Hasn't the heat been trying!' Or the damp. Or the drought. Rorive spends hours fishing in the Grand-Etang, where he sometimes catches a tench. One day when he had caught two fine ones he brought them to us, wrapped up in leaves. 'To take away the taste of mud. You must clean out the insides with a little vinegar.'

My mother is often alone when they come, and if my father is there and catches sight of them in time, he hastily retreats to his study.

And yet it's the Rorives who are normal, surely? I turned to look down the wet road and I saw our car coming nearer. Father was driving and there was someone beside him; I could not make out who but I guessed immediately. When the car came nearer I recognized Manuela's face.

It seemed natural enough. They had both been to church; it was raining. The road was a long one. My father, being alone in his car, had offered the girl a lift home . . .

It might be natural for other people, but not in our family, and I hoped that neither my mother nor Olivier were looking out of the window.

The car skirted the house. I heard the door slam, then the sound of two people's footsteps on the gravel, and Manuela's voice saying something I could not catch.

She's a cheerful creature, the only one in the house; on Sundays as on every other day she goes about looking pertly seductive, with her black uniform stretched tight over breasts and hips.

I often wonder if she does it on purpose, if it's her way of flouting my mother, perhaps my father too. No, her mocking glances are particularly directed at my mother.

Olivier came into my room without knocking while I was still dressing.

'Did you see?'

'What?'

'Father brought her home.'

'It's raining.'

'That's no reason for picking her up in the car and making up to her. I must ask Manuela if he didn't try to put his hand on her knee.'

'Olivier, you're exaggerating . . .'

'You think so? You obviously don't know anything about men, apart from your old Professor . . .'

'Let me finish dressing, will you?'

He was venting his rage on me now, forgetting that he would have known nothing about my private life if I'd not confided in him, one evening when I felt the need to tell someone about my feelings.

'A madhouse, d'you hear?'

He went out, slamming the door behind him. At half-past twelve, when lunch was served – our usual Sunday chicken – we met once more around the table, each in our usual place. Manuela went back and forth from the kitchen, bringing in dishes.

No one spoke. No one felt like speaking. Olivier, very flushed, poured himself three glasses of wine in quick succession, and Father pretended not to notice. Mother, however, was watching his every movement and expression.

One word, one gesture would be enough to make the scene break out and I felt that my brother was finding it hard to restrain his urge to unleash it. This might have relieved him, but it would make life more difficult for all of us subsequently.

Olivier left the table first, after tossing down one more glass of wine. Ten minutes later we were still in the drawing-room drinking our coffee when we heard his scooter and, looking through the window, saw him ride past.

It was my turn next to escape and I went upstairs to put on my boots and fetch my raincoat.

'I expect I'll be back for dinner . . .' I said, half opening the drawing-room door.

The two of them were left together; they could not escape. Their only resource was to stay each in his own little world, my mother in the drawing-room, my father in his study. The bad weather would not even allow them to go for separate walks in the wood or round the ponds. Perhaps the Rorives would call, bringing a tart or a cake, to tell how when they kept the dairy they used to do their shopping in the Halles at three o'clock in the morning. He made the purchases, while she cooked the various vegetables which were subsequently laid out on the white marble table, since many customers in those days bought their vegetables ready cooked to save time.

I made my way to the Champs-Elysées where, in spite of the rain, there were queues in front of the cinemas. Didn't this mean that other people, even couples, even families, felt the need to kill time and escape from their everyday routine?

I had no rendezvous with any friend, nor even with a colleague, for I have no real girl friend. My interests are different from those of the other girls. Many of them have a boy friend with whom they go out on their free days. Others get together in twos and threes and go for picnics in the summer.

There must be some of them, today, waiting for their turn in front of a cinema door.

And I waited too, wondering what the Professor does on Sundays. Perhaps he, too, goes out with his wife and daughter. They have a small country house in the neighbourhood of Dreux, but this was no time of year for staying there.

Do they entertain friends? Are they gay and cheerful? I should have liked to know all about him but there are whole sides of his life which are still hidden from me.

On his desk there is a photograph of his wife and daughter in a silver frame. His wife, in my opinion, is rather ordinary-looking; as for his daughter, who wears her hair long, she has a precociously grave look in her eyes.

What can those two say to one another? What can a father and daughter talk about? I was reduced to imagining their dialogues, for my father and I have never had any real conversations, except of a purely practical nature.

'You're sure you are doing your best?' Father would say to me while I was still at school. 'You're not afraid of failing your *bachot*?'

Then, when I told him I wanted to become a lab assistant:

'That is one of the finest professions for a woman, provided you have the vocation for it. Above all, it needs patience.'

As if he knew! As if he'd tried out everything in his life, whereas he has always worn blinkers and sees only what he wants to see!

I found a seat at the end of a row and, like the rest of the audience, I stared at the screen where people who were in love with each other had to overcome every imaginable obstacle; at the end, needless to say, they were successful.

Was that what the hundreds of people sitting in the darkness of the hall had come to seek?

*

After the pictures I went for a walk in the Champs-Elysées, looking at the shop windows. The rain had stopped. Suddenly a dense crowd had poured onto the pavements.

I went into a self-service restaurant in the Rue de Berry for my dinner. When, plate in one hand and glass in the other, I looked for somewhere to sit, I found myself in front of a very young girl, who couldn't have been over sixteen. Her face was distorted with distress and bewilderment. All the time I sat there she was holding back her tears, and she averted her face in shame whenever I looked at her.

My brother must have come back very late. I did not hear him.

Monday, November 12: the date is marked with a cross in my diary. That means that Stephan asked me to stay on in the evening and that we made love on the camp bed in the little yellow spare room.

It's only in my thoughts that I call him by his christian name. Otherwise, even in our most intimate moments, he's still the Professor and I call him *monsieur*, as we do the heads of departments: an emphatic *monsieur*, with a capital M, so to speak.

He always looks at me with curiosity, as though he didn't quite understand me.

'Are you satisfied with your life?'

He must have noticed my hesitation. 'Don't be afraid to tell me frankly.'

'Here, in your department, I'm very happy.'

'And elsewhere?'

'At home, life is different. I often feel I'm stifled there.'

'Are they strict?'

'It's not that. Everyone's always watching everyone else. I catch myself spying on the others too.'

'Don't you want to have a home of your own, and children?'

Looking him squarely in the face, I replied categorically: 'No.'

'Is your mother unhappy?'

'My father is, too.'

In spite of the many years he has spent in France he still speaks with quite a strong foreign accent. His mobile face is marked with fine deep lines. When he talks to me like that he suddenly appears to me in a different light, like a father persuading his daughter to confide in him. My own father has never sought my confidence. He merely stares at me in astonishment, as though he could not understand my attitude.

There was a separate irony in the Professor's voice as he said to me:

'In short, you want to remain a spinster?'

He does not believe it. He thinks that some day I shall meet someone who attracts me and that then I shall do what they all do. He cannot know that I might have married Gilles Ropart and that it was on his account that I did not.

I suddenly began to think about my aunt Iris and her lonely existence in a flat in the Place Saint-Georges. She works for a big advertising firm in the Avenue des Champs-Elysées.

She was the mistress of her boss, who was young and daring and successful in everything he attempted; he seemed to juggle with life. He had married very young and lived separated from his wife. He was the typical Parisian man of fashion, always in the public eye and able to have any woman he wanted.

Was my aunt jealous or was she satisfied with her share in him, knowing that he would always come back to her?

One afternoon he died suddenly, as though struck by lightning, while he was passing through one of the offices. He was forty-two.

My aunt is all alone now. She must be about forty herself. She's not even a real widow, and she still works for the same firm, although it is now under entirely different management.

She's the most attractive of my aunts, who have all been given pretentious names: Alberte, Iris, Blandine, Marion. The only son, who runs the Poulard chocolate works, is called Fabien. Was this a fancy of the General's, or his wife's?

I should have liked to make contact with her, to visit her sometimes in the Place Saint-Georges, where I have never set foot. I think we might understand one another. She is the youngest of the Picot daughters and she comes once or twice a year, driving her small yellow car, to visit us.

My mother is not fond of her. I don't think she is fond of any of her sisters, which is why I scarcely know my relatives. The others see one another, even Alberte when she comes from Strasburg to Paris, and Marion, the naval officer's wife who lives at Toulon.

Has my aunt Iris known happiness? Is she happy now? I passed her in the street the other day. She did not see me and I did not dare run after her. She has grown much thinner, and this gives her features a certain hardness that reminds me of my mother's.

'You're a funny girl, Laure.'

It seldom happens that he calls me by my first name. His little eyes were, as usual, sparkling with mischief; you never know if he is laughing at you. I believe he was not laughing at me but that he was somewhat touched.

'Well, we shall see what the future has in store for you . . .'

My mother went on drinking, and on Monday evening she smelt not of wine but of brandy or whisky. As there was none in the house I suppose she had driven into Givry or Versailles to buy a few bottles.

On such occasions, she always gets up later. On Tuesday morning I came down early, expecting to be the first. I went into the kitchen and caught my father unawares; I couldn't swear to it, but I am almost sure he was passing a note to Manuela. In any case she quickly slipped a folded piece of paper into her bodice.

'I'd like some marmalade today,' he said to keep himself in countenance.

Poor man! At his age, to be reduced to such childish subterfuges!

I poured out my coffee and announced that I did not want any toast; I was not hungry. However, I sat down in the dining-room opposite my father.

'The wind is from the west,' he said. 'We shall have some more rain.'

I said yes and went on looking at him as he bent over his plate. I think of him as an old man, and it seems ludicrous that he should be in love. And yet he's only about a year older than the Professor. So I'm vexed with myself for being unjust, but I cannot help it.

My brother came down just as I was going out to fetch my scooter. When I returned home for lunch, my mother's eyes were ringed with red and she went about like a sleep-walker. I don't know why I came home for lunch instead of eating in the refectory. My father usually lunches near his office and Olivier goes to the student restaurant.

I seemed to be trying, in vain, to make contact with my family. Just as for a long time I tried to find out where my mother hid her bottles. Father hunted too, I know, with no success. She is more cunning than all of us.

In the evening I went to my English lesson, an advanced class which I attend twice a week.

And on Wednesday, as usual, Manuela stayed in bed late. It's her great delight every Wednesday. She does not necessarily sleep; she lies smoking cigarettes and reading Spanish novels. When she hears no more noise from the ground floor she comes down in her nightdress and dressing-gown and makes herself a great bowl of milky coffee.

I am sure she relishes every moment of her morning, and she only goes out at midday, in her Sunday best, to catch the bus at Givry. As a rule she lunches in a restaurant with her friend Pilar, who works for a wealthy industrialist in the Avenue Paul-Doumer.

Then they go window-shopping together, have dinner some-where or other and end the evening at a dance hall in the Avenue des Ternes, called Chez Hernandez.

She generally comes back on the last bus that drops her at Givry at twenty minutes after midnight.

This Wednesday my father came home rather later than

usual; it was past eight o'clock, and we were waiting for him to sit down to supper.

Mother had not bothered to cook anything. She had opened a tin of soup and bought some cold meat. She even served bottled mayonnaise, which a few years ago she would never have tolerated in her house. She was really unwell. Obviously her drinking bout must be nearing its end, for she could not go on much longer like this.

When we heard the car in the garden, she remarked in a voice she could scarcely control: 'Well, so he's come back after all!'

Olivier and I stared at one another, and I felt that my brother, despite his resentment against Father, was deeply shocked. It was not until we were at table that I noticed my father's face. When he came into the room he had merely greeted us casually. Was I mistaken? I could have sworn that a faint perfume hung about his face or clothes, and his mouth had a bruised look, as though from long and passionate kissing.

And in his eyes there was an almost impish sparkle. I had never seen such an expression on his face. He seemed to have lost his stiffness and much of his solemnity.

So long as Olivier . . .

I watched my brother; he, too, was sniffing the air, with a tense frown.

'So we didn't have any rain after all . . .'

Father's remark met with no response. Nobody echoed it. Mother looked at him with a vicious expression. It was one of the most miserable meals we had ever had. Only Father seemed not to notice. His shining eyes told of his inward exultation. He ate hungrily, resigned to silence since nobody would answer him, but jubilant none the less.

Had he in fact been passing a note to Manuela in the kitchen that morning? Most likely; and it was likely, too, that he had been proposing a rendezvous. I'm sure of nothing, but in our family we are accustomed to interpreting signs.

He had been with her. It must have been the Spanish girl's perfume that still hung about him and that my brother was trying to identify. As for my mother, if she said nothing, she was none the less carrying on an inward conversation with herself and several times she gave a sarcastic smile.

After folding his napkin, my father made for his study and I felt that Olivier was on the point of following him. I stared at him as though to hypnotize him, saying to myself: 'He must not go in there . . .'

He did not go in. He stopped in front of the door. I whispered as I went past him: 'By and by, in my room . . .'

Then I started clearing away, as I do every Wednesday. Mother made a show of helping me, then swayed and clung to a chair for support. I led her to her armchair, murmuring: 'Another of your dizzy fits . . .'

Was she taken in? I switched on the television and escaped into the kitchen, where I began washing the dishes. I don't know whom I was angriest with, Manuela or father.

When I went up to my room I found Olivier stretched out on my bed. He had not bothered to take off his shoes and he had flung his jacket across the room, aiming at a chair but missing it.

'What d'you want?' he asked, aggressively.

'I want to have a chat with you.'

'What about?'

'You know very well. You've got to calm down, Olivier. You can't go on living in such a state of tension.'

'So I look tense, do I?'

Lying there on my bed, indeed, he seemed calm enough, disturbingly calm.

'You mustn't take this business too seriously.'

'Are you referring to that old swine?'

So he had reached the same conclusions as myself. At least, that was what I thought at the time.

'Is that how you speak of Father?'

'I'd like to know how you'd speak of him if you were in my place. I saw them.'

'Whatever do you mean?'

'I'm telling you the plain truth. I'd suspected something. Yesterday I noticed them making signs to each other, like accomplices, and she asked me not to go up and see her.'

'How did you happen to meet them?'

'I didn't meet them. I followed Manuela. I knew where she usually meets her friend, at a restaurant in the Avenue

Wagram. A little before one o'clock Manuela went in. On most other Wednesdays they spend the afternoon visiting shops, or at the cinema.

'They left the restaurant at about two, and went towards the Etoile. There they parted, both in very high spirits, and Manuela went down into the métro.

'I had my scooter and I couldn't follow her. I had a sort of inspiration. I rode as fast as I could to the Porte d'Orléans métro station, the nearest to Father's office. He was there, waiting on the pavement, looking at his watch from time to time.'

'Did he see you?'

'No, I don't think so. In any case, I don't care if he saw me or not. She came up the station and they exchanged a few words before going off towards the Avenue Général-Leclerc.'

He got up, feeling restless.

'D'you understand now? He was as fidgety as a boy and he kept stroking her arm. They stopped in front of a little hotel. Father looked embarrassed. He leaned over her and talked in a low voice.'

'Did they go in?'

'Yes.'

'You went away?'

'You don't suppose I was going to stop there on the pavement while less than thirty yards away they were up to their filthy tricks? Just wait till she comes home. As for him, he can afford to wait.'

'He's your father, Olivier.'

He brought home to me the absurdity of my remark. 'Was that why he went to bed with my girl?'

He was furious: he was fuming with rage. I was terrified that he might go down and create a scene.

'Are you really fond of her?'

'Yes.'

'Even now that you've seen what . . .'

'Even now!'

He was ruthless, threatening.

'You ought to face up to things. You know it can't lead to anything.'

'So love has got to lead up to something, has it? And d'you

315

think your affair with your Professor is going to lead up to anything?'

I was stupefied. 'You know?'

'I've known for a long time. More than six months.'

'Who told you?'

'I happened to be going out, for a short while, with a girl who's a nurse at Broussais. She asked me if I was your brother. She put on an air of mystery that intrigued me and I bombarded her with questions until she told me the truth.'

'What's her name?'

'Valérie Saint. She's in the cardiology department. Her boss and yours are great friends and sometimes work together.'

'I know.'

'You see why I was expecting you to defend him.' He meant Father.

I did not know what to say. I did not even know what to think.

'I assure you, Olivier, it's not the same thing at all.'

'Yes, it is!'

'How can you say that?'

'You're forgetting that you dropped another fellow for his sake – a young intern whose name I've forgotten.'

He even knew about my affair with Gilles Ropart.

'Those old men are all swine and the girls that run after them are tarts.'

'Olivier!'

'Well, so what, Olivier?'

I burst into tears. I couldn't help it. Last time my brother had seen me crying I had still been a little girl. It upset him, and he muttered: 'I'm sorry.'

He was striding about the room, his hands behind his back, and in the study just below Father must have heard the sound of his footsteps, the echo of our excited voices.

Olivier added: 'You're a free agent. You can do what you like with your life.'

'At any rate try to keep Mother out of all this.'

'If you think she doesn't know as much as you do!'

'What makes you believe that?'

'Do you suppose Father can have left his bed and gone up to

the second floor to listen to us through the door without her noticing? And this evening, drunk though she was, she must have seen from his face that he hadn't come straight from the office. The fool didn't even realize about the scent.'

'How is it that she's never said anything?'

'She never says anything. She notices. She's biding her time.'

'Do you think she'll want a divorce?'

'No.'

'What else can she do?'

'She can throw Manuela out, for one thing, and then I'll find the money somehow to follow her, even if I have to steal it.'

I dried my eyes. My head was throbbing and I went to open the window to cool it.

'Anyhow, now you know ... And mind you don't worry about me ... I'm not a kid ...'

He's just nineteen. It's true that I myself am only two years older.

'Good night, Olivier.'

'Good night, Laure. Try to sleep. Take a sleeping-pill.'

'Thanks. You, too.'

I had a feeling that he was reluctant to leave me, that there was suddenly a new bond between us. At last he opened the door and went up into the attic he has turned into a laboratory.

I hadn't the courage to go down and find my mother sitting alone in front of the television set. That evening, I didn't want to see any of them again. I'd done my best. It was not my fault if I had not succeeded.

I took one tablet, then another, to make sure of sleeping. I got ready for bed, lay down and switched off the light.

I must have slept for quite a while, two or three hours or even more, and then I was woken by the sound of merry voices outside the gate; some young men were joking very loudly in Spanish.

Manuela had not returned by the last bus. It was not the first time this had happened. She had found some friends to bring her home and they all seemed in high spirits, probably rather tipsy.

317

They went on shouting jokes at her until she had reached the front door steps and then they drove off noisily.

Had my brother gone down? I turned on the light for a moment to see the time. It was twenty-five minutes past two. I tried to go to sleep again but involuntarily I kept listening. In Manuela's room, I could hear two people's footsteps and soon I recognized Olivier's voice, literally screaming. A chair fell over on to the floor. Someone collapsed heavily on to the iron bed.

My parents could not fail to have heard. Would Father dare go upstairs to intervene? Manuela uttered a single cry. My brother went on abusing her, then suddenly his voice broke. He seemed to be begging her pardon, beseeching her.

Then she spoke to him in a gentle, plaintive tone and, unconsciously, I dropped off to sleep again.

Chapter Three

I expected a catastrophe, of what sort I did not know. It might be the dramatic departure of Olivier, who has no professional training and who, left to himself, would certainly not carry on his studies.

I did not for a moment imagine that my father and Manuela might leave the house together, and I am convinced that this was my mother's opinion too.

In any case, it seemed to me impossible that the situation should grow any tenser without an explosion taking place.

On Thursday morning Olivier came down from the top floor with no attempt at concealment. On the contrary, he stopped to light a cigarette, taking his time, as though he wished to assert the rights he had acquired.

He had shaved, and was fully dressed. He had evidently spent the night in the maid's room and had bathed in her bathroom.

He was looking tired but calm, somewhat over-calm. Father was still at table when Olivier entered the dining-room and the two men exchanged no greeting, but pretended to ignore one another.

318

Was it deliberately that when the Spanish girl brought his coffee and eggs my brother patted her behind with a proprietary air?

My mother was at the end of her tether. The shaking of her hands was painful to watch and she had developed nervous tics, the sudden twitching of certain muscles that distorted her face for a moment and revealed the extent of her deterioration.

She had almost stopped eating, and she was sick every day. It happened to her once on the staircase before she had time to reach the bathroom.

In theory, her 'novena' should be nearing its end, but there was no sign of any decrease in her consumption of alcohol; quite the contrary. We would see her grinning to herself, sometimes with a glance at us, as if to say: 'You're not so clever, the three of you! You imagine I don't know, but I really know more than any of you!'

I cannot say when she first took to drink. I never dared raise the subject with my father, for it's more or less taboo in our house. I have often tried to remember what she was like during my childhood. I can recall her looking melancholy, often depressed and unhappy. I would ask her: 'Are you crying, maman?'

'Don't pay any attention to that. Grownups are unhappy about things that children can't understand.'

I suppose that when she was like that she had already begun one of her drinking-bouts. They were much less frequent in those days. Her brother, her sister and brothers-in-law still used to visit us. Our boy and girl cousins used to come on Sundays and play with us in the garden.

In the afternoon we used to go for a walk round the ponds, the children in front of the grownups. How old was I? At least five, for my brother had already learnt to walk.

This went on for two or three years. Then my mother quarrelled with one of her sisters, the one who married a remover and lives in the Rue d'Alésia.

Then the same thing happened with her brother.

Iris, my only unmarried aunt, still used to come and bring us sweets, and she was on good terms with my father.

From time to time Dr Ledoux was sent for from Givry. He is

still our family doctor, and although his hair is grey I cannot realize that he has grown old.

Two years ago Mother had a particularly bad drinking-bout which ended in a prolonged fainting-fit. Her pulse rate was barely forty-eight per minute and her lips were discoloured. The doctor came immediately and gave her an injection even before carrying her to bed with Father's help.

I followed them. It was the first time I had heard the two men discussing the subject.

'I'll come back and see her tomorrow. She's going to sleep deeply.'

'There's no danger?'

'Not for the present.'

'And later on?'

'If she begins drinking more and more frequently, and more and more heavily . . .'

'Is there nothing to be done?'

'In theory, yes. I could send her to a nursing home for a sedation cure. It lasts about a month. After that she'll go for several weeks or months without drinking. But there are ninety-nine chances out of a hundred that she'll start again.

'What's needed is to find out the precise cause of her behaviour . . .'

I remember my father saying gravely: 'Even when she was a child, her brother and sisters used to tell her that she was ugly and would never find a huband.

'You see she did find one.'

I thought I saw a rather bitter smile on my father's lips.

'She's always been rather withdrawn. Because of her looks, she tended to avoid boys and girls of her own age.'

'Had she begun to drink when you married her?'

'I couldn't swear to it. If she was drinking, it was so moderately that I never noticed. At first she wanted to do without a maid and insisted on doing all the housework herself. I suppose marriage must have been a disappointment to her.'

'But the children . . .'

'She was a very good mother while they were small and depended on her. After that she seemed to acquire a certain indifference. I would not say she lost interest in them, but . . .'

My father made a vague gesture instead of finishing his sentence. It was the first time I had been treated as an adult and allowed to listen to such a conversation, and it was probably at that moment that I felt closest to my father.

'She feels ashamed. After she has spent two or three days in bed, taking nothing but vegetable broth, she wanders timidly about the house like a ghost, with a look of melancholy resignation on her face.

'She sticks to the legend she has created: "Why do I have to endure these dreadful headaches?" '

Mother is wearing herself out, as Dr Ledoux had warned us. She is ageing fast, and like my father she sometimes presses her hand to her chest.

She often irritates me. I bear her a grudge for not having given me a childhood like other people's, and even now for continually jeopardizing the harmony of the family. But what sort of harmony is it, and what sort of a family? We are all at odds with one another. The two men are not on speaking terms, won't even look at each other.

All the same, I'm sorry for my mother. I pity her. I am confusedly aware that she is not responsible and that she suffers more than we do.

Last time Dr Ledoux was sent for, he suggested that she should be examined by a psychiatrist.

'It's worth trying. But when she hears the word she'll probably dig in her heels and declare that she's not crazy. In the broad sense of the word, that's true enough. All the same … I'm not a specialist …'

'What do you advise me to do?'

'I don't know. I'll frankly admit it. The remedy might be worse than the disease. A psychiatrist would want to have her under observation in a hospital …'

'She'd never consent to that.'

'Well, so long as the family can stand it …'

Thursday passed. In the evening I found the remains of a coffee cake in the kitchen. I knew at once that my aunt Blandine must have come to visit Mother, for she invariably brings a coffee cake.

There is no longer any overt disagreement between my

mother and her sisters, even though they seldom see one another. They tend, rather, to blame my father nowadays.

'A proud, surly man, who thinks of nothing but his profession and never says a kind word to his wife.'

Did he ever take her to the theatre or to dine in a restaurant, like other husbands? did they ever travel abroad together?

She was the only one of the sisters who had never left France, who did not know Spain or Italy. We had once spent the holidays on the Riviera, and that was all.

My aunts made no secret of their opinion in front of me. Their brother, Fabien, was even harsher. He would have liked to be considered the protector of the family.

'I cannot understand how you can go on living with a man like that. In any case I never understood why you married him, but at that time Father was still alive and it was no concern of mine . . .'

My mother would sigh. She had gradually got used to playing the part of a victim. I sometimes wonder if she has not acquired a taste for it.

As for Aunt Blandine, she's a big woman with a ringing voice and almost mannish gestures. When she married Buffin, he was a rough, decent fellow who had just bought his third lorry and drove one of the three himself.

Now, he has about twenty of them, some of them travelling daily to Lyons and Marseilles, not to mention four or five removal vans with his name in big black letters against a yellow background.

My aunt has become as vulgar as Arthur, her husband, who is fairly coarse-spoken. One of their sons is already in the family business, while the other, who is said to be brilliant, is studying medicine and planning to go for a course of training next year in the United States.

I had known General Picot, my grandfather, a tall lean man who impressed me with his elegance and breeding. His wife, too, is a person of some refinement; since she became a widow six years ago, she has lived alone in a small flat in Versailles, quite close to her son's home.

For twenty years the General dragged his family about from one town to another, as he was posted to various garrisons. The brother and sisters were now scattered and we ourselves lived in that gloomy house, Les Glaïeuls, because an uncle of my father's had taken it into his head to bequeath it to him.

I sometimes feel that the house is to blame for everything, and that my mother's moods are due to the atmosphere in which she lives all day long.

There's something depressing about the mere smell of damp, the sight of the dripping trees, particularly the two big pine trees.

Friday came, and I was surprised that nothing had happened. On Thursday the Professor kept me back late, but he was pre-occupied, being anxious to know the result of his current experiment. He had inoculated several animals, some mice and a couple of dogs, and was watching them day by day in the smallest of the laboratories, at the far end. The assistants worked in relays, day and night, noting the animals' behaviour hour by hour, their temperature and their blood pressure.

He would trust nobody else with the blood analysis, which he attended to himself. I did not know exactly what he was looking for. He never spoke of it, but one could guess from his nervous tension and the occasional gleam in his eyes that if everything went off satisfactorily he would have made an important discovery.

At midday on Friday Gilles Ropart sat down beside me in the refectory. We had kept on very good terms together. I suppose that like myself he has pleasant memories of our period of intimacy.

'I've a great piece of news to tell you, Laure.'

He had always called me *vous* in front of people and now he had no occasion to say *tu*.

'You're going to get married?'

'Exactly. At least, I've been engaged since yesterday.'

'Someone from Broussais?'

'No, someone who's nothing whatever to do with medicine.'

'Do I know her?'

'No. Her father's an architect and she's a student at the Beaux-Arts.'

'Have you known her long?'

'Six weeks. Love at first sight, in fact!'

He was making fun of himself. He was an odd fellow, very gay, with an enormous sense of humour.

'One of these days I'll introduce her to you.'

'Have you told her about us?'

'I haven't dotted the i's, but she's guessed that I'm no virgin.' He laughed, and looked me straight in the eyes, reflectively. 'And yourself?'

'What about myself?'

'Still the same great love, the same total devotion?'

'Is it ridiculous?'

'No. It's probably very fine. In any case, he's a lucky man. I just wonder what will happen in ten or twenty years' time.'

'I've an aunt who has lived alone for more than ten years and who's not unhappy.'

'You know I nearly asked you to marry me?'

'Why didn't you?'

'Because I was sure you'd say no. Was that true?'

'Quite true.'

'Why?'

'I don't know. Perhaps I'm like those nuns who feel the need to sacrifice themselves.'

'So really, what you needed was a god.'

'If you like.'

It strikes me as odd that life goes on, that thousands and millions of people go on living their lives outside the dramatic atmosphere of Les Glaïeuls.

I have always been impressed, when meeting people in the street, by the thought that each of them is the centre of his own universe and that his preoccupations loom larger than what is happening in the world around.

I am like everyone else, thinking about my mother, my father, and Olivier. I often think about myself, too, about the time when I shall be able to have a flat in town. I can picture myself looking after it in the evening or early in the morning. I don't believe I should mind the loneliness, but, on the contrary, that it would be a relief to me.

When I carry my dream to its conclusion I visualize Stephan coming there sometimes in the evening, to sit down in an arm-chair and chat with me while he smokes. For he smokes cigarettes from morning till night and his fingers are stained brown with nicotine. As his hands are often busy he keps his cigarette stuck to his lips and drops ash everywhere, even on our animals' coats.

The sun was shining, but it was rather cold. I thought about my mother, eating all by herself in the dining-room at home. There were just those two women alone in the house, hating one another. That may not be quite accurate. Undoubtedly my mother feels a real hatred for the Spanish girl who has robbed her of husband and son at once.

But Manuela? She still runs up and down the stairs humming songs from her own country, one in particular, a sort of endless carol of lament of which I have involuntarily learnt snatches.

> *La Virgen s'está lavando*
> *entre cortina y cortina*
> *los cabellos son de oro*
> *los peines de plata fina*
> *pero mira como beben*
> *pero . . .*

Then a gap in my memory. I have a feeling I've got the word-order wrong. It hasn't the least importance since I don't understand it, except perhaps for the last line:

> *porque ha Dios nacido*

I imagine that means: Because a God is born. On Manuela's lips this becomes a love-song. One might expect her, like most other people, to break into a smile only when someone looks at her. But I have often come upon her unawares, when she had not heard me coming, and I always found her wearing the same contented smile.

For her, life is beautiful. Everything is fine. Everything is good. She makes love with my brother every time he visits her in her room. She has made love with my father too, I'm sure of it, simply because he passed her a note asking her to meet him outside a métro station.

She must have other lovers too, at Hernandez' dance hall where she goes every week.

325

I have had several lovers too, but I was not necessarily gay. On the contrary, I was quite clear-headed: I knew that I was not in love but that I wanted to prove to myself that I could attract men. It was during the period when I thought myself plain and gawky.

Gilles Ropart was the last of the series, and I believe he understood, for he always treated me affectionately.

Now I no longer wonder whether I am ugly or not. In any case, I am not really ugly, nor, perhaps, physically unattractive.

True, I haven't a particularly pretty face and I dress badly. I look my best in uniform, especially in summer, when I wear hardly anything underneath the white nylon.

My figure is good, though, my breasts particularly, and most of the men I have slept with have been surprised on seeing me naked.

Did my mother once have a good figure too? There's nothing left of it. She is so thin that you can see all her bones and she's getting bent, she walks with her shoulders hunched up as if she was afraid of being beaten.

I think about my mother too much. I feel that I'm judging her objectively and yet at the same time I am aware of subtle bonds between us. For instance, I tell myself that I might have been like her. If I had got married I don't think I would have been capable of blending with another person's life.

I am fond of children. Sometimes when I tell myself that I shall never have any I feel rather melancholy. But in fact I should not have the necessary patience.

Even a child of Shimek's. I have thought of that. I nearly asked him to give me one. I should have been wrong. I can only dedicate myself to one single person and I have dedicated myself to him once and for all.

I am not even afraid of his deserting me and that is not because I have too high an opinion of myself. I play only a small part in his life, a diversion in the midst of his preoccupations, but he needs that diversion.

Sometimes he strokes my hair with a queer sort of smile.

'My little creature . . .'

And I think I understand what he means. I take up no room.

I'm hardly noticed. I ask for nothing. But I am always there, always ready. He knows it, and he tries to understand my feeling.

There's no question of our being a couple. He is far above me, so far that I don't criticize him, I don't try to understand him.

He *is*. That's enough. And if he took a fancy to make love to other lab assistants I should not resent it, I should be almost glad of it for his sake, provided he came back to me.

Do nuns criticize God and are they jealous of other worshippers?

If I were to talk like this to other people they would probably take me for a fanatic, a hysterical creature, whereas to me it's all quite simple and quite natural. Dear Ropart is the only person who has understood.

I seldom think about myself at such length. It's not narcissism. I am a Le Cloanec, after all, and what has been going on at home for the past week affects me as much as the rest. I have been trying to see where I stand in relation to them, to decide what influences I have undergone.

Then I went back to my work in the lab. The sun was streaming through the wide bay windows and most of the animals were dozing in their cages.

*

The Professor spent much of the afternoon in his room, dictating letters and notes to a secretary. It was past five o'clock when he came into the labs and he went straight into the one that interested him most at the moment, the little one at the far end.

He beckoned me to follow him, as well as one of my colleagues who has a special gift for handling dogs.

'Bring out Joseph.'

This was a reddish-brown mongrel which had been there for over six months, and which owed its nickname to a resemblance to one of the porters.

We held the dog down on one of the tables, and it was so used to this that it never moved, merely looking at us each in turn as though wondering what was going to happen next.

Shimek had adjusted his stethoscope and begun to sound the animal, when the door opened and there stood a stout elderly woman who works at the reception desk.

'There's a policeman who insists on seeing you, monsieur.'

He did not reply, he was not listening, he merely grunted, still bending over Joseph. Framed in the doorway I saw a tall police officer who seemed ill at ease and was very red in the face. He must have been a sergeant, for he had several gleaming stripes.

The Professor did not turn his head, but took his time, and, still preoccupied with the dog, finally growled: 'Another offence?'

'No, Monsieur le Professor. I should like to speak to you for a moment . . .'

'Well, go ahead.'

'I think it would be better . . .'

'Are you worried about these young ladies? Don't mind them. They're used to such things . . .'

'It's about Mme Shimek . . .'

'What has happened to my wife?'

This time he left the dog in our hands and glanced sharply up at the man, seeming surprised to see him in uniform.

'A traffic accident, monsieur . . .'

'How is she?'

'Seriously injured . . . She's been taken to Laënnec . . .'

The Professor seemed more stupefied than anything else. His immediate reaction was disbelief.

'You're sure it's my wife who's involved? There may be other Shimeks in Paris . . .'

'You do live in the Place Denfert-Rochereau?'

Then beads of sweat stood out on his forehead. He had eyes for nobody but the policeman, who scarcely dared speak.

'What happened?'

'She was in a taxi on the Boulevard Saint-Michel. I suppose she was on her way home from the Right Bank . . . Suddenly a heavy lorry coming from the opposite direction drove straight across the boulevard to the left . . . We don't know yet whether the driver, for some reason or another, lost control of his vehicle or whether he was taken ill . . . He's not in a fit state to speak . . .'

'My wife . . .' the Professor urged.

'The driver of the taxi was killed immediately and your wife, gravely injured, was taken to Laënnec hospital. I was told to inform you . . .'

Shimek mopped his brow and reached out for the telephone.

'Get me Laënnec, please, mademoiselle . . . Yes, it's Professor Shimek . . . Hurry . . .'

We no longer existed. Nothing existed for him but the telephone by means of which he was to learn his wife's fate. She had very light blue eyes, a broad Slav face, a kind motherly smile. I thought of the photograph, with his daughter, on his desk.

'Hullo! . . . Is that the houseman on duty? . . . This is Shimek, at Broussais . . . I'm told they brought my wife in a few minutes ago . . .'

He stared mistrustfully at the telephone.

'Tell me about her condition . . .'

The policeman turned his head away.

'What? . . . Before?'

He repeated incredulously: 'Before she got there?'

His face was puckered. I averted my eyes too, because he was unconsciously weeping, his whole face distorted.

'Yes . . . Yes, I understand . . . I'm coming immediately . . .'

He strode through the laboratories without noticing anyone, without trying to hide his tears.

'I didn't dare tell him at once,' muttered the policeman. 'I wanted to prepare him.'

I shed no tears, but my head was reeling and I hurried to the cloakroom to cool my forehead with a towel soaked in cold water. I wanted to . . .

Of course, I wanted to be with him, holding his hand so as to give him courage. Suddenly I was of no use, and perhaps he might even bear me a grudge?

Now that his wife was dead, he might be feeling remorse about our relations. I thought of their daughter Marthe, who was only fourteen and who was still childish and unspoilt, innocent of the powder and lipstick that most girls use.

I had only been to their home once, by chance, when the

Professor had flu and was spending three days in bed. Dr Bertrand, his chief assistant, had given me a report to take to him and I had to wait for an answer.

The block of flats is spacious and well-lighted. On the third floor I pulled a gleaming brass bell-knob and a stout woman in an apron let me in. There were skis in the hallway, for it was winter. I don't know if the Professor goes skiing but his wife and daughter certainly did. I remember that they used to go to Switzerland every winter and that he joined them there for a few days.

The flat seemed cut in two by a broad corridor, broader than those at Broussais, and on either side, right up to the ceiling, there were shelves crammed with books. Not the handsome bound volumes you find in libraries but books of every description, some of them very tattered. In one room, at the far end, a gramophone was playing.

I envied the inhabitants of that bright, airy flat. Most of the doors stood open. There was nothing stiff, far less stifling, about it, as in our house. Life could go on freely there, and nobody had to walk about on tiptoe.

I had to wait for quite a while, listening to the music. Mme Shimek crossed the passage, some distance away from me, and went into the room from which the music was coming, and I heard voices, one shriller than the other but both good-humoured.

Somebody brought me the answer and I went away again. I had had no further occasion to visit the Place Denfert-Rochereau.

'You'd better go home.'

'Why?'

'You're as white as a sheet. Stop in a bar first and have a glass of brandy.'

Anne Blanchet was speaking to me, a tall, likeable girl whom I did not know very well.

'Don't wait to have a fainting-fit. Run off! I'll tell Dr Bertrand you felt unwell.'

It was true. I was overcome with dizziness, and my legs felt limp. I pulled off my lab coat and went downstairs without waiting for the lift.

Just over the way there is a restaurant with a bar. Nobody was there but a waiter laying tables. He called out to me: 'What d'you want?'

'I'd like a brandy.'

He reluctantly interrupted his work, looked at the clock and then at the bottles set out in front of the mirror.

'The barman doesn't come till six and I'm not too sure . . .'

He picked up a bottle and showed me the label.

'Will this do for you?'

I nodded. I was imagining Shimek at Laënnec hospital in the Rue de Sèvres, in front of the probably mangled body of his wife. No doubt he would have stopped weeping. That first reaction must have been due to shock. He had just lost, as though by amputation, a major part of his life, for he was already married when I was born. His wife had also been a refugee in Paris, and was studying there.

When they came to know one another she left the University and, so he had told me, they lived in a single room in Saint-German-des-Prés. He had added, nostalgically, that they had been very poor, and had often lived off a bit of bread and cheese.

'I spoke French very badly. So did my wife, And people laughed at us. Not unkindly. They laughed as if we were very comical . . .'

I supposed that Marthe, their daughter, was at school. I wondered at what time she got out, and who would tell her the news.

Would the body be brought back to the flat and laid out in the main bedroom? I didn't know exactly what the proceeding was and I was very upset. I so badly wanted to be by his side and to share his emotions!

'I'll have another . . .'

The waiter looked at me in some surprise.

'That'll be eight francs. At any rate that's the price written on the barman's list.'

I drank it off at one gulp and I went out. I had no wish to go straight home, where I should be alone with my mother. I preferred to walk about in the gathering darkness. The street lamps were alight and there were lights in the shop windows too. I found myself, eventually, in the Avenue du Général-Leclerc, without knowing what streets I had been through.

'Looking for someone, darling?'

I turned my back on the man who had stopped to address me thus.

I saw the door of a small hotel wedged between two shop-windows. *Hôtel Moderne*. It was a seedy-looking place. An enamel plate announced: 'Rooms to let by the month, week or day.' The door was open, and the passage leading to the office was poorly lit.

The Professor must be holding his daughter in his arms, for he had nobody left but her and she had nobody but him. Wasn't this going to complicate their life?

I suddenly blushed. People might believe that I was hoping . . . No, no! The idea had never occurred to me, whatever might happen . . .

I felt weary. I sat down in a café. When I reached home at last my father's motor-scooter was there, so that I knew I should not have to face Mother alone.

He was in the drawing-room, reading his paper, and I could not resist telling him:

'My chief's wife was in a car crash this afternoon on the Boulevard Saint-Michel. She died while they were taking her to hospital . . .'

He looked at me thoughtfully. He was poles apart from Shimek, whom he had never seen and about whom I seldom spoke, just as I am poles apart from his colleagues, whose names I don't even know.

'Was she young?' he asked at last.

'About fifty, I suppose. Perhaps less. I don't know, I've only seen her from a distance . . .'

He turned to his newspaper again. My mother was upstairs. She must have spent part of the day in bed and I could see at a glance, when she came down, that she had been drinking heavily.

My brother did not come home to dinner. There were just the three of us at table and I tried in vain to make a show of conversation. Nobody listened to me. I stopped talking. In my thoughts, I was at the flat in the Place Denfert-Rochereau.

Were the two of them, father and daughter, sitting down to a meal there? They could not spend all the time watching by the dead woman's bed. Would the undertaker's men come next day and hang the room with black draperies, patterned with silver tears?

I was not accustomed to death. I had known only my grandfather's, and then I was too young to take in details. I remembered chiefly the candles and the branch of box with which people pretended to sprinkle the corpse with holy water.

For my grandfather, even if he really was a Freemason, had had religious obsequies. I vaguely remembered arguments on the subject. My uncle Fabien had insisted on a Mass and an absolution, on the grounds that a secular funeral would damage our reputation; his in particular, I suppose, for Poulard's slogan was: 'The family chocolate'.

My mother went up to bed earlier than usual, for she soon grew drowsy after dinner. As for my father, who went up soon after, I suspected him of retiring early so as to avoid meeting his son.

Olivier came home about eleven o'clock while I was still downstairs, reading an English book but paying little attention to it.

'Are they both upstairs?'

'Yes.'

'I'd sooner see as little of them as possible. If it was in my power, they'd never see me again. How is Manuela?'

'Just as usual.'

'There hasn't been a row?'

'Not since I came back.'

'What's the matter with you? You look as if you'd been crying.'

'My chief's wife is dead.'

'Had she been ill?'

'An accident on the Boulevard Saint-Michel.'

'Young?'

Fifty, for him, was a great age. After a moment's silence he made a cynical comment:

'So now you won't need to hide.'

I was afraid, on the contrary, that my small happiness was seriously threatened. I had held a modest place on the fringe of his home life and on the fringe of his professional life, although I was in some degree a part of that.

But now? There was his daughter, to whom he was bound to devote much more time.

I went up to bed and wept there, while my brother openly and noisily climbed up to the second floor.

On Sunday, when I was on duty at Broussais, the Professor did not come in at all during the day, but merely looked in about ten in the evening to examine his animals.

On Monday I found myself being scrutinized more curiously than usual and this exasperated me. I left the house early and went a roundabout way to work so as to pass through the Place Denfert-Rochereau. The shutters of two third-floor windows, the ones on the left, were closed. This was no doubt the room that had been arranged as a mortuary chapel. Had two prie-Dieu chairs been brought in, as in grandfather's case?

I went straight to the little laboratory where Shimek did his personal research. Good old Joseph was up and about and did not seem to be in pain. He even scratched the wire netting to attract attention.

I looked after the animals as usual. At ten o'clock I heard footsteps in the main laboratory and soon I saw the Professor come in. At first he took no notice of me. His first glance went to the animals.

His face was so drawn, his eyes so weary that he seemed to have grown thinner.

'How is it you're here?'

'It's Monday monsieur.'

He shrugged irritably, and called the two lab assistants.

'Please come, mesdemoiselles.' He did not ask me either to stay or to go and I stood as though rooted to the ground.

'Put Joseph on the table for me.'

I was reminded of the policeman's arrival, when he had been sounding the brown dog as he now proceeded to do.

'You see: there's no rattle in his throat, his breathing is easy his pulse is regular . . .'

He patted the dog's head briefly; his eyes were far away.

'Anything happened?'

'One rat died in the second cage.'

'I expected that. When Dr Bertrand comes, ask him to do the autopsy.'

He looked at me again, opened his mouth and then decided to keep silence.

I did not lunch in the refectory but in a small restaurant nearby. It was a cold grey day. I tried to go for a walk, but I soon felt tired.

How would Shimek spend his time this afternoon? His wife had been alone in Paris when he first knew her. He himself had no relatives in France. He had few acquaintances, and these were almost exclusively colleagues.

He and his daughter must be alone in that flat with the dead woman, apart from the maid, who would stay in the kitchen. He must be feeling hostile towards me, as I had foreseen, because he was angry with himself. It's unlikely that I shall ever regain our former relationship.

And only last Monday . . . I can't believe it.

I ended by going home to dinner. I found my father and mother watching television. A man and woman were embracing on the screen and then the woman burst out laughing.

The stillness of the house was uncanny. I asked Father, stupidly: 'Is Olivier out?'

I had only spoken for the sake of saying something, and he answered curtly: 'I've no idea.'

We had dinner. Only Manuela went on smiling as if, for her, life was good in spite of everything. Afterwards I watched television too, for I hadn't the heart to read. Father retired to his study.

Shortly after ten o'clock my brother came in. I imagined he would go straight up to his own room or to the second floor, but to my surprise he came into the drawing-room.

He was a little tipsy. This seldom used to happen before our recent scenes. He was not a heavy drinker; he seemed to have taken to drink out of defiance.

'Have you got any spirits, Laure? You must know where Mother keeps her brandy.'

She started, but did not even turn to look at him.

'No, I don't know.'

Turning to Mother, he demanded: 'Your brandy, Mother . . .'

'I haven't any.'

'Don't talk nonsense. Tell me where you hide it, so that I can treat myself to a glass or two. Tonight I want to get blind drunk.'

He was drunk already, and he was talking very loud. He seemed to be spoiling for a fight, and he kept looking towards Father's study.

'Well, are you going to fetch me that bottle?'

'Go up to your room.'

'D'you realize that you're talking to me as if I were a kid of ten?'

'Go up to your room,' she repeated in a sort of panic.

He was clearly becoming more and more aggressive.

'If you think I'm going to obey a woman like you . . .'

Then the door opened and my father appeared.

'I wish you'd talk less loud.'

'Perhaps *you* know where Mother hides her brandy?'

'I'd be obliged if you would hold your tongue.'

'And I want to get drunk.'

'Then go and do so elsewhere.'

'I still belong to the family, don't I? This is where I'm supposed to be living.'

'On condition you behave decently.'

'Oh, so we behave decently in this house, do we? Do you behave decently, when you take your son's girl to a filthy, disreputable hotel?'

'I must ask you to . . .'

'And I won't! I've the right to speak, like any other human being, and I intend to do so.'

My father turned to Mother: 'You'd better go upstairs, Nathalie.'

She stayed in her chair, listening, her eyes still fixed on the television screen.

'Manuela!' Olivier called loudly.

'She's gone upstairs,' I said, hoping he would go up to join her.

It was quite true, in fact, that she had gone up and that the light was out in the kitchen. I went in, switched it on, and seized the bottle of red wine, which I brought into the drawing-room with a glass.

'Here you are. This is all I can find.'

Father stared at me, wondering what I was up to. Olivier had reached the point where it seemed best for him to drink as fast as possible and as much as possible, so that he would have to go up to bed.

'Your health, *maman*. You treat yourself to brandy, but your son has to put up with coarse red wine, like a navvy.'

'Olivier, leave your mother alone.'

My father was trying to seem firm, but he failed to impress my brother, who was too far gone.

'You keep quiet! It's the best thing you can do, I promise you. You see, some things are so disgusting that a man who does them loses any right to interfere with other people. As for my poor old boozer of a mother . . .'

'I warn you that . . .'

Father took a step forward, his fists clenched.

'No, really! Don't say you're going to hit me! You forget that I'm stronger than you now.'

'I order you to shut up and above all to leave your mother alone.'

Then another voice spoke; it was my mother's, saying: 'Let him speak, he's quite right. You and I are equally disgusting . . .'

It was all so stupid and pointless. Each of them was trying to find the harshest, most wounding things to say. They were flaying one another alive.

It was scarcely more intelligent of me to threaten them: 'If you don't shut up I shall turn off the lights.'

And for a start, with no particular motive, I switched off the television.

'I shall decide tomorrow what steps to take,' declared my father with bogus dignity, walking towards the door.

'You do that! In the meantime, take care you don't go up to the wrong landing. You might regret it, for up there you're not my father any more.'

He poured himself another glass and gulped it down.

'As for you, *maman*, I think I owe you an apology. Living

with a man like that must be enough to drive one to drink.'

Tears were running down my mother's cheeks and I tried to remember if I had ever seen her crying before. It seemed to me this was the first time.

'Go up now, son.'

She never used to call him that. I was amazed, and so was Olivier.

'Have I hurt you?'

'Don't worry about me.'

He went up to her hesitantly and laid a furtive kiss on her forehead.

'You're a good son, all the same!'

And to me: 'Good night, Laure.'

He made his way laboriously upstairs, reached the first floor landing and then went on up to the attic. Mother cast a brief glance at me, but seemed at a loss what attitude to take.

'It's not his fault,' she finally muttered.

She was obviously referring to Olivier. What did she mean, exactly? That it was not his fault if he had been drinking? That it was not his fault if he had attacked my father and, incidentally, herself? That it was not his fault if he had fallen in love with the maid?

She listened to my father's footsteps as he got undressed. She was waiting for him to be in bed, and perhaps asleep, to go up herself.

'You can go up, Laure.'

I knew she would say nothing more. It was astonishing that she had spoken so much that evening. Indeed, for one moment she had seemed to me almost human.

'Good night, Mother.'

I did not kiss her. I seldom do.

'Good night.'

Perhaps she wanted to be left alone downstairs to have a drink.

Chapter Four

I was surprised, on Tuesday morning, to see the Professor going round the labs, examining some of the animals and giving instructions as he does every day before closeting himself in his office with Dr Bertrand.

Because a person has lost a loved one, we expect him to take no interest in anything but his grief, and yet life goes on, he eats and drinks, talks and works.

I followed him, as usual. There were three of us going round with him, ready to note down his observations, but he seemed not to notice my presence. I was simply there, as if I were part of the background. Two or three times his eyes fell on me, because I was in his field of vision.

Could he really have aged so much in three days? He had lost his prodigious vitality and I had the impression that the man before me was just a man like anyone else, I'm ashamed to say a man like my father. His eyes had lost their brightness, their vivacity, their habitual sparkle.

I felt I had to visit the house of mourning and I dared not go alone; I went from one to another of my colleagues trying to find one who would go there with me at midday. Some of them curtly refused. Others looked at me with an ironical smile. I finally persuaded two, one of whom, Maria, was a stout placid country girl whose parents were farmers.

We ate quickly. Maria had no means of transport but the other girl, Martine Ruchonnet, whose father is a well-known lawyer, had a small car and drove us to the Place Denfert-Rochereau.

The shutters were still closed over two windows on the left-hand side of the third-floor flat. The funeral was to take place next morning and the undertaker's men had begun hanging black draperies over the door.

We went up in the lift. We had no need to ring, for the door stood open. Once again I saw the long, wide passage lined with books. Even the skis still stood in the hallway. A warm smell of cooking mingled with the smell of wax candles.

On the left, the door of the dead-room stood wide open; there were candles burning, a sprig of box, and flowers in profusion, including vases standing on the ground.

She had not yet been laid in her coffin but was lying in state, as it were, on a bed, dressed all in white, with her hands folded over a rosary.

I crossed myself, as I had seen others do. I seized the sprig of box and made the sign of the cross in the air, while I cast a glance at the nun who was praying in one corner.

Had sisters of charity been engaged to watch in turn over the body, day and night, for want of relatives available to do so?

The hands round which the rosary was entwined fascinated me. They were strong hands with square-tipped fingers, the hands of a woman still close to the soil, accustomed to doing her own housework and if need be to undertake heavy tasks.

My mother's hands are long, with slender pointed fingers, and she makes a great fuss when she happens to break a nail.

Were the Professor and his daughter somewhere in the flat, eating a solitary meal together?

Someone came in, a working-class man in heavy shoes, who crossed himself awkwardly and stood cap in hand gazing at the dead woman.

I felt that I was in an unfamiliar world and the impression clung to me all afternoon. I had thought myself close to the Professor. Now I realized that I knew scarcely anything about him and that I had perhaps been an unimportant digression in his life.

When I returned to Les Glaïeuls that evening it was raining again and a strong wind was blowing. I was surprised to find myself the first home. Neither my father nor my brother was there, although it was half past seven. I looked round for my mother and did not find her either in the drawing-room or in the dining-room.

My instinct told me that something was happening and when I went into the kitchen I saw there not Manuela but my mother, wearing her apron.

She looked tired, but less nervous than on previous days. Could her 'novena' be drawing to a close? She was busy putting a dish of ham and macaroni into the oven.

'Hullo, Mother.'

She looked at me as if she were surprised at my speaking to her.

'Hullo.'

'Is Manuela upstairs?'

'No.'

'Where is she?'

'She's gone.'

'Did you send her away?'

'She wanted to go home to her own country.'

This surprised me, but I did not pay much attention to it, for Shimek was still my main preoccupation. I should have liked to comfort him, to be of some use to him. During the afternoon it had been another girl, a tall gawky creature whom I disliked, who had taken the collection for a wreath.

'Are you sure you didn't give her the sack?'

'She left the house of her own accord.'

'You didn't have a quarrel?'

'She must have made up her mind before. She came downstairs in her outdoor clothes, carrying her suitcase, and asked me to pay her what I owed her.'

Father came in presently. He, too, seemed to notice a change in the atmosphere of the house and he called up the staircase: 'Nathalie!'

When he eventually came into the kitchen he dared not ask where Manuela was. Mother provided the information, with a savage irony.

'She's left!'

He seemed not to understand.

'When is she coming back?'

'She's not coming back.'

I broke in, to have done with it: 'She's given in her notice and gone back to Spain.'

He said nothing, but turned away, went to sit in the drawing-room and unfolded a newspaper. He had obviously had a shock. I, meanwhile, laid the table so as to help my mother, but I was thinking only of the Professor and of his wife, who, that night or very early tomorrow, would be laid in her coffin. The folded hands, the rosary, the presence of a man in the dead-room had surprised me, and I wondered if Shimek was a Catholic, if he was really a believer.

In that case, had he been to confess his relations with me, which he must consider a sin? Did he bear me a grudge for having, so to speak, offered myself? For I realized that I had tempted him.

I desperately wanted him to notice me. I wanted to become his mistress. I wanted to be something more to him than an insignificant colleague.

I was sincere then, and I still am. I have dedicated my life to him and I have come to realize, today particularly, that I knew practically nothing about him.

My brother came home at last. He looked tired and preoccupied. He slumped into an arm-chair in the drawing-room, seemingly unaware of my father's presence. He, too, picked up a newspaper, and lit a cigarette.

When he saw me in the dining-room he called out:

'So it's you who lays the table now?'

'As you see.'

'Where's Mother?'

'In the kitchen.'

'And Manuela?'

'She's gone.'

He leapt to his feet, grim-faced.

'What did you say?'

'I said that she'd gone.'

'Did Mother throw her out?'

'She says not.'

'You mean to tell me Manuela went of her own accord?'

'I don't mean to tell you anything at all. I wasn't there. I've only just come in.'

He turned to glare fiercely at Father and then strode into the kitchen.

'What have you done with Manuela?'

And Mother repeated in a dull voice: 'She's gone.'

'What did you say to her?'

'Nothing.'

'You're lying.'

'Have it your own way.'

'Admit that you're lying, that you forced her to leave.'

'No.'

It was beyond him. He rushed upstairs to the second floor, where we heard him moving about, opening and shutting drawers and the doors of the big wardrobe.

When he came down again his look was grimmer than ever, but he said nothing.

'Dinner's ready.'

The soup-tureen was in the centre of the table. We sat down in our usual places, myself opposite Mother and Olivier opposite Father, and helped ourselves in silence.

Dinner was scarcely over when Olivier went off without a word and we soon heard the sound of his motor-scooter. Did he know exactly where Manuela's friend Pilar lived, in the Avenue Paul-Doumer? They must have talked about her; he may even have met her at Hernandez', the Spanish dance-hall in the Avenue des Ternes.

I cleared the table and washed the dishes. I do so whenever we are servantless, which is often the case. Most of our maids stay two or three months, six at most. Some of them leave after a week, unless Mother dismisses them because she considers them lacking in respect for her.

'You're being disrespectful, young woman.' How often had I heard this remark during my childhood and adolescence!

On these occasions I have to get up earlier in the morning and make the coffee, and go to the gate to bring in the bottle of milk, the bread and the newspaper.

Before leaving for Broussais I do my room and my brother's. Finally I knock at Mother's door and put a cup of coffee on her bed-side table.

I don't know if other children are like me. Even as a small girl I avoided, as far as possible, going into my parents' room, because of the smell. Everyone has his particular odour, of course, but when I smelt theirs I felt I was being thrust into an unpleasant intimacy.

This is still the case, whereas Olivier's odour, for instance, does not offend me.

I was sound asleep when my bedroom door was flung open noisily and the ceiling light was turned on. It was my brother, his hair and face wet with rain. The alarm-clock showed nearly midnight.

'What's happened?'

'Don't worry. Nothing that concerns you personally.'

'Did you find Pilar?'

'How did you know . . .'

'It wasn't hard to guess.'

'She hasn't seen Manuela. She's had no telephone call.'

'Perhaps they weren't such close friends after all?'

'Apparently they were. They told one another everything. Pilar knew about my father.'

'What sort of a girl is she?'

'A skinny little dark creature who always seems to be making fun of people.'

'Was she making fun of you?'

' "If Manuela's really gone," she told me, "you'll have to find someone else." '

'Did she add that she'd be willing to take her friend's place?'

'Yes. I went to the airport, for she'd come from Spain by air. They sent me from one *guichet* to another and in the end they told me that they weren't entitled to give any information about passengers.

'At the Gare d'Austerlitz, where I went next, there's such a crowd that the booking-office clerks can't remember to whom they've sold tickets.

'Do *you* believe she's gone home?'

'I don't know. I was as surprised as you were when I got home and didn't see her.'

'I'm convinced she's still in Paris. I expected at least to find a note from her in my room or in her own.'

'D'you think she's capable of writing one in French?'

My objection impressed and comforted him.

'She'll surely find a way to give me news of herself. D'you know what I eventually did? I thought to myself that she didn't know any hotels in Paris and I went into the one to which Father had taken her. They don't remember her there. Her name's not in their visitors' book.

'Who knows? Perhaps Father has set her up somewhere so as to keep her for himself.'

And my brother concluded with a single word: 'Swine!'

I found it hard to get to sleep again. At half-past six the alarm woke me, almost an hour earlier than usual. I went down and lit the gas. The rain had stopped but the sky was still grey and the heavy clouds seemed to be skimming the roof-tops.

I went to fetch the milk, the bread, the paper. I emptied the ash-trays mechanically and tidied up a little, without really cleaning the house. Then I spread the cloth and laid the table.

It seemed pointless to advertise for a maid. The few who answer are invariably the sort of women who can never stop in one place. Presently, no doubt, my mother would ring up the agency, where they know her well.

Even if the house were not gloomy, even if my mother did not have her drinking bouts, it would be difficult to find someone satisfactory because of our remoteness from Paris. Manuela had been a sort of miracle. It was unlikely to repeat itself.

'Do you want sausages with your eggs?'

My brother turned an absent gaze on me and repeated as if the word had no meaning for him: 'Sausages?'

He said it with such a comical air that I could not help laughing.

'Just as you like, I'm not hungry.'

None the less he ate the two eggs and the sausages I brought him and he had not quite finished when Father came down in his turn. The two men deliberately ignored one another and did not even exchange a nod.

As soon as they had left I washed up the pan, the plates and cups, and folded the tablecloth, which I put away in a drawer with the napkins: all familiar actions which I performed whenever we lost a maid. Then I took a steaming cup of coffee to my mother's bedroom. I knocked, but went in without waiting for her to answer. She was lying with her eyes open, staring at the ceiling.

'Have they gone?'

'Didn't you hear Olivier's scooter and Father's car?'

For he had taken the car today, even though it was not raining.

She replied: 'Yes. I'd forgotten.'

It was unreal. She seemed to be living in a sort of dream.

'They hate me, don't they?'

It was easier to say nothing.

'It's not that girl, it's me they're angry with.'

She seldom talks to me as much, and it embarrassed me. Above all, I did not want to hear her secrets.

'I give you my word, Laure, I didn't turn her out. Do you believe me?'

I gave a vague nod.

'Do you hate me too?'

'I don't hate you.'

I was on the point of adding: 'I pity you.'

It was useless. I backed towards the door while she drank her mouthful of coffee between puffs at a cigarette. She seemed better than on the previous days. Her eyes had lost their puffiness, her cheeks their red patches.

'All the same you'd rather have had a different sort of mother.'

'I wish you had better health.'

'I've never had good health. Later, you'll understand. You're too young.'

'It's time I went.'

'Yes. You go.'

I suddenly realized that she would be left alone in the house. It had already happened, between maids, but for no precise reason it frightened me this time. From the landing I looked at her, sitting up in bed, thin and sharp-featured, smoking her cigarette, with her cup of coffee in her hand. She was looking out of the window and it was impossible to guess at her thoughts.

I went first to Broussais, where there was an unfamiliar feeling in the air. Everyone kept glancing at the big electric clock, and Dr Bertrand was in a greater hurry than usual to finish visiting the animals in the three labs. He took some notes and, disregarding the clock, consulted his watch.

Only three girls, the last three to arrive, were left on duty, which was a minimum. Even Mlle Neef went, at half-past nine, to take off her cap and her lab coat and put on a coat with a sable collar and a small black hat I had never seen her wearing.

A quarter of an hour later we all met outside the house in the

Place Denfert-Rochereau, where a number of other people were waiting. Besides the inhabitants of the block of flats, the tradesmen, and a few neighbours, I recognized most of the big chiefs of Broussais, some of them accompanied by their wives.

Those who had not already been up, yesterday or the day before, to pay their first respects to the dead woman went up to the third floor now. I was not among them. I could imagine the Professor standing by the door of the dead-room, clasping people's hands without noticing them, while his daughter and the maid were weeping in some far corner of the apartment.

The hearse arrived, followed by several black cars which lined up beside the pavement, with a police officer directing the proceedings.

The men brought down the coffin, then went back to fetch the flowers and wreaths; these covered the hearse completely and some of them had to be put into one of the cars.

Shimek came down; he seemed to have shrunk, and to be unaware of what was going on around him. He stared at the crowd on the pavement, as though he were going to thank them for being there.

I suddenly saw him as a slight, almost insignificant figure. For one moment, before he got into a car with two of his Broussais colleagues, our eyes met and I wondered if he had recognized me. Perhaps he had, but it was all over in a flash.

I wanted so much to be a help to him, to be needed! I made myself very small. I moved away and mingled with the on-lookers at the back of the crowd, then I went to fetch my motor-scooter and made my way to the Montrouge church.

There, too, I stayed in the background. Most of my colleagues were gathered in groups.

Was it the organ music or the sound of the funeral procession moving up the central aisle that brought tears to my eyes? I did not even know why I was crying. I was not thinking about the woman with the short square hands, lying in her white-satin-lined coffin, nor even, directly, about the Professor, who was standing alone in front, to the right of the catafalque.

I heard the tinkle of the choirboy's bell and the voice of the officiating priest, who wore a great white cross on his black chasuble.

And it all seemed unreal to me, and I had a sense of wasteful chaos. I did not try to clarify my thoughts. Why did I suddenly picture my mother, as I had seen her in bed that morning, with her cigarette and her cup of coffee, staring so strangely through the window at the black trees in the garden?

She was unhappy. She made us unhappy, maybe, but she was the first to suffer from it. And my brother, and my father suffered too. They had become mutually estranged and actually seemed to hate one another.

Was it possible? Would our family ever behave like a real family?

This morning, in front of the house of mourning, Shimek scarcely recognized me, whereas my whole existence depends on him. I have no right, I am well aware of it. Henceforward he would devote himself to his daughter, and become more passionately absorbed than ever in his work.

I blew my nose and wiped my eyes. I was ashamed of weeping from self-pity, for indeed it was for myself that I was weeping.

*

I did not recognize him immediately. I was leaving the hospital and making my way towards the parking place when he emerged from the shadows. He gave me the impression of being inordinately tall, with very long arms and very long legs.

'Did I frighten you?'

It was Olivier, who scarcely ever comes to meet me after my work, unless we have planned to go somewhere in town. My first thought was that he must have some bad news to tell me.

'What's the matter, Olivier?'

'I want to have a talk to you elsewhere than in that damned house. You must know some quiet little café.'

'There's one just opposite.'

This was the restaurant in which I had drunk two glasses of brandy on the afternoon of Mme Shimek's death and it was odd that circumstances should bring me back there on the day of her funeral.

The walls were painted beige and panelled half-way up with dark wood. The room was lighted with small lamps, with imitation parchment shades, standing on the tables. This time the barman was there.

'What'll you have?'

'A coffee. I'm feeling tired.'

'One coffee and one Scotch,' he ordered.

It always surprises me to see him drinking, for it's not so long since he was a child.

'I cut my lectures this afternoon. I wanted to think things out.'

He was looking at me gravely. He was quite sober; he had drunk nothing yet.

'I think I've made up my mind.'

He was frowning as he looked at me. 'Have you got a cold?'

'Are you asking that because of my voice or because my nose is red?'

'You've not got your usual face.'

'I've been crying.'

'Because of what's happening at home?'

'Today was the funeral of my chief's wife.'

He was unmoved by this. He was thinking only of what concerned him personally. But wasn't this the case with me, too?

'You said you'd made up your mind. To do what?'

'To leave home.'

For some time past, I had been expecting this to happen some day, but it came as a shock none the less.

'What about your studies?'

I asked this half-heartedly, for the sake of saying something.

'You know, if I went to the University it was chiefly because Father was keen on it. As for chemistry, I was crazy about it when I was fourteen or fifteen, so as to make some sort of bombs which I used to blow up in the woods. It was just a game. Since I've been studying it properly I don't see where it's going to lead me.'

There is only two years' difference between us, and yet I feel so much older than he is! Is it because he's a boy? Has he remained particularly young for his age?

I felt as if an overgrown child was before me, talking about the vital decisions he had to take.

'I can't stand them any longer, don't you see? Particularly now, after what they've both done to me.'

I understood what he meant. My father had taken Manuela to a shady hotel and Mother had undoubtedly thrown her out. He could forgive neither of them.

'I sometimes wonder whether Mother ought not to be in a mental home. As for the man who claims to be my father, he's nothing but a depraved imbecile.'

He lit another cigarette from the one he was still smoking.

'How will you earn your living? Have you any idea?'

'Not yet. To give myself time to think about that, I'm going to anticipate my army call-up. Or even to enlist, if necessary.'

'Won't you need Father's consent?'

'Do you think he won't give it with the greatest eagerness? He'll be only too pleased to get rid of me. Then he'll be quite free to run after the maids.'

It was painful to find him so bitter and yet so boyish.

'I think you're wrong, Olivier. I'm convinced that he's ashamed of what has occurred. It can happen at his age as well as at your own!'

'Don't defend him, please!'

'I'm giving you my opinion, and I'm asking you not to let your feelings run away with you. Wait a few days. Don't forget that your future depends on it. When you've finished your military service, you'll still not have a job.'

'I shall manage somehow. I'm not afraid of roughing it. At least I shall be my own master.'

He drank a mouthful of whisky and retched.

'Besides, if I stayed at home, I should start drinking. It runs in the family. There! Now you know what's in my mind. Don't you understand?'

'I understand, but I beg you to wait a little, say a week.'

'That's a long time!'

'Not in relation to one's whole life.'

'You know, what sort of life have our parents shown us?'

I felt incapable of persuading him and I could find no arguments, for I too have more than once longed to leave home. I have a job which I enjoy. I could live by myself in a little place which I should always keep spotless, and where I could entertain my friends, both men and women.

Olivier's mind was darting from one subject to another.

'What I cannot understand is how she got to Givry to take the coach.'

'She probably rang for a taxi.'

'She didn't. This morning I saw Léon, the fat taxi-driver, waiting in front of the station. I stopped and asked him if he had called at our house to pick up a girl with a big blue suitcase. He had had no message from the house and he had seen no sign of any girl with a suitcase.

'His mate was waiting behind him and I asked him the same question. He hadn't come to the house either. And there are no other taxis at Givry.'

'It's not much more than a kilometre to walk.'

'With a heavy suitcase!'

'Unless Mother drove her to the station or to the bus stop.'

'Very likely. To make sure of her leaving the district?'

'Do you promise you'll wait a week?'

'Let's say I'll wait a few days unless anything happens in the immediate future.'

'What d'you mean?'

'I don't want any more scenes. It upsets me too much. Afterwards I feel ashamed of myself and of other people.'

'Are you going home now?'

'I shall go in half an hour or an hour's time. I'll be there for dinner, don't worry.'

I called the barman and tried to pay. My brother stopped me.

'Are you crazy? Have you forgotten you're a girl?'

Funny Olivier! I let him have his way. He walked with me as far as the parking place where he had left his scooter. We parted company.

When I reached Les Glaïeuls, I was surprised to find the door open, for it's usually shut. I have become so hyper-sensitive that I was seized with panic, particularly when I found all the ground floor rooms empty. Not only were they empty but they did not smell of cigarette smoke, as on most other days.

The house had not been cleaned. Yesterday's papers were still in the drawing-room and there were breadcrumbs on the dining-room floor.

I went up the stairs and knocked at the door of my parents' room. A voice answered, almost steadily: 'Come in.'

Mother was in bed; her face was far less red than yesterday at the same time. I guessed that she had decided to begin her cure. From one point of view I was glad of it, but from another I was rather frightened.

If we always refer to Mother's 'novena', it is because there always comes a point at which she goes to bed and withdraws, as it were, from the life of the household.

Every day her consumption of alcohol decreased slightly. I once spoke of this to Dr Ledoux, who seemed greatly surprised at my mother's showing so much strength of will.

'In fact, she deliberately tries to de-alcoholize herself. It's horribly painful, at the beginning particularly. She must keep her eyes fixed on the clock, waiting for the moment that she's set herself for a first drink, then for a second. Her entire organism must be upset. I suppose she takes a tranquillizer?'

'I don't know. One scarcely dares go into her room.'

'Does she eat anything?'

'She must go downstairs when there's nobody there, for something's always missing from the refrigerator. She takes no proper meals.'

'It's so painful that I've seen cases of nervous depression and even, though these are rarer, of suicide.'

Her eyes seemed to be sunk deep in their sockets. This was due to the dark shadows on her eyelids. She had not done her hair, probably not washed.

'I haven't done any housework. I've prepared nothing for dinner either, but I rang up Josselin's.'

This was the delicatessen shop at Givry, where they also sold fruit and vegetables.

'I left the door ajar downstairs, so that he could come in and put the cold meat in the fridge. I've ordered eggs, too, and salad.'

I could imagine the effort these simple actions must have cost her. She probably took advantage of being downstairs to remove one or more bottles and hide them somewhere in her room.

'Go off now. It tires me to talk.'

I involuntarily glanced at the empty place beside her in the bed, and thought how, presently, my father would come and lie there. This false intimacy made me feel uncomfortable. As far as I know there has been no affection between them for a long time. They have reached the point where they can scarcely endure one another.

And yet, every evening, they undressed and slept in the same bed.

It was beyond me. It sickened me slightly, especially when I saw my mother in her present state.

She will not admit that she's an alcoholic. Officially, she is ill; she suffers from migraine headaches which make her dizzy.

'I hope you soon feel better,' I said.

She turned on her side and closed her eyes.

I took advantage of being upstairs to go into Manuela's room, where I never set foot while she was working for us. The iron bed was unmade, the sheets and blankets tumbled, which reminded me of the state my brother had been in when he last visited her.

The two of them had lain in the narrow bed, with its single pillow stained with lipstick.

On the floor, I saw a shabby slipper and, bending down, I found its fellow under the bed. She must have forgotten them. The drawers were empty. On the chest of drawers there was nothing but an old Spanish magazine and a novelette with a gaudy cover.

There was nothing in the cupboard except a dirty pair of socks of Olivier's, and in the bathroom I picked up a broken comb.

I went down the stairs and into the kitchen to lay the table. This evening there would only be three places laid. This would go on for about a week, which is the average time it takes my mother to detoxicate herself, after which she returns to normal life.

It distressed me, today, to see her lying in bed, so unkempt and wretched. She must have been tempted, ten times a day, to raise the bottle to her lips and drink as much as on previous days, or even more.

I knew that she despised and loathed herself; Dr Ledoux had

mentioned that too. And yet in a month or two she would begin all over again.

There was some ham, some cold veal, salami and tongue. I laid them out on a plate and I washed and dressed the salad. I could find no tins of soup in the cupboard where they are usually kept. We must have used up the last.

Presently, when my father was in his study, I would go round the rooms with the vacuum cleaner and mop the kitchen floor.

My father was the first back. He, too, was surprised not to see Mother and to find me alone in the kitchen.

'Mother wasn't feeling well, and she's gone to bed.'

'Have you seen her?'

'Yes. She rang up Josselin's to order some food.'

He had understood. He did not go up. He knew he must not. He would just creep into the room as late as possible to go to bed. Then she would at any rate be pretending to sleep.

When Father had gone to read his paper, Olivier came back and remarked with a sneer when he saw me alone:

'Don't tell me Mother's gone off too!'

I resented his harshness a little, just a very little, for I could imagine how painful the situation must be for a boy of his age.

To think that he'd been dreaming of a motor-bike, a real one, one of those hefty machines we see going past on Saturdays and Sundays with a girl behind the rider. Father, for fear of accidents, had always put off buying him one.

If poor Olivier were to leave us and join the army . . .

There; everything was ready. I told them that dinner was served. I apologized for not having had time to make soup and I passed the plate of cold meat to my father.

Olivier and he were still not on speaking terms; they would not even look at one another. I took the plate and passed it to my brother, who helped himself generously.

'Mother said she had eaten,' I remarked casually.

They both knew what course things would take. We are so used to the fiction that we go on playing the game, even when she is not there.

'How is she?' Olivier asked.

354

'Not well. She'll probably be better tomorrow.'

I suddenly began thinking about the Professor, who must be sitting at dinner opposite his daughter. In their flat in the Place Denfert-Rochereau there was also an empty place at table, but there it would remain empty for ever.

Unless Shimek should marry again . . .

I blushed suddenly. And I wondered if I had not just discovered the reason why, for the past four days, he had avoided looking at me.

Did he imagine that the death of his wife had raised my hopes, and that I dreamed that some day he might marry me?

This idea upset me so much that I wanted to get up, walk about, wring my hands. Heaven knows what else. It was horrible. Such a thought had never even crossed my mind.

Would he shun me now, behave ever more distantly towards me, for fear I should claim a place in his life to which I was not entitled? He knew that he was a sort of God to me. He should have known, too, that I claimed nothing from him, except a little notice from time to time, a gesture which would imply just a little fondness. That would be enough. I ask no more from him.

I believe that if in his turn he were to fall in love, I should be frightened. I need to give my devotion freely, without hope of return, and when he happens not to speak to me for a whole day I bear him no grudge. He has other things to think of besides a romantic girl.

Is it really romantic? Is it not, rather, human? Don't we all need to give rather than to receive?

If he had conceived the idea that I was hoping . . .

I was being sincere with myself. I knew that if he offered to install me officially in the big flat in the Place Denfert-Rochereau, with his daughter, I should refuse. I should not feel at home there. I should be awkward and unnatural. I should feel ashamed of my love, which would no longer be freely given.

I looked at the two men at table with me. They both wore the same stubborn look and my father was displaying no more sense than his son.

Was there any hope that, in a few days, life would resume its normal course? We had never had any real family life, except perhaps when we were small. Each of us had, almost always, lived apart from the rest, and laughter was so rare at home that I cannot remember hearing any. The fact remains that we put up with each other, more or less, particularly when Mother was not on one of her drinking bouts.

Now, the feeling one could sense between the two men was almost hatred. My father was ashamed of what he had done and he would never forgive his son for having humiliated him.

And for Olivier it meant the tarnishing of his first experience of sex, of what he must consider as his first love affair.

Each in turn left the table. I cleared away, and filled the sink with hot water to wash the dishes.

Do scenes like this happen at my uncle's home, at my aunt's? It's unthinkable that this should only happen to us, that we should be so exceptional.

Family life is not what we are given to believe and the Professor himself, two days before his wife's fatal accident . . .

But it's not for me to complain of that, nor to blame him for it.

I should so much like life to be clean and beautiful! Clean, above all, without petty hatreds and shabby compromises. People looking one another in the face, gaily, and with confidence in the future.

What sort of future was my brother preparing for himself, for instance. For I was sure, now, that he would not carry on with his studies. He had admitted himself that he had only started them to please my father.

At heart, he was impatient to come to grips with real life, as he said. So long as he was in the house he did not feel free, in spite of his recent outbursts.

And there must be hundreds and thousands like him, with the same vague aspirations, uncertain which path to take.

I felt doubtful whether military service would be good for him. Here too he would have to obey and be dependent on all superior officers, not to mention his seniors in the ranks.

I felt so miserable that I was ready to collapse into a chair and begin weeping again, my head buried in my apron.

Was my brother managing to study, alone in his room? Was it still worth his while?

I was convinced that he was afraid of becoming a failure. He wanted to assert himself, but he did not know in which direction. And I could sympathize with him, and suffer on his account.

I myself had been lucky. I might have failed my exams and been discouraged by some unfriendly teacher. I might have fallen in love with one of the boys with whom I had had intimate relations. They had not really taken me seriously. They had merely been profiting by the opportunity, probably guessing that my main motive was a desire to reassure myself.

I put away the plates and cutlery. I folded the tablecloth. I fetched the vacuum cleaner from the cupboard.

It was one of the few evenings when television voices were silent in the house and it gave one a feeling of emptiness.

Unconsciously, I did the housework more thoroughly than I had intended. I lost count of time. I washed the kitchen floor and polished it.

At one point, when I was on my knees, I saw a pair of legs beside me. It was my father, who was watching me in astonishment.

'D'you know what time it is?'

'No.'

'Half-past eleven.'

'I shall have finished in a quarter of an hour.'

He laid a hesitant hand on my head and I was reminded of the Professor's hand patting my shoulder, at Broussais.

'I'm going up to bed.'

'Yes, I'll soon follow you.'

I had the whole of the ground floor to myself and I took advantage of it to clean my father's study.

As though I felt the need to sacrifice myself, to undergo some self-inflicted punishment.

Chapter Five

My mother did not telephone to the employment agency, and it was just as well. In her present state she would have frightened off any possible candidates.

I myself rang up the butcher's, and then Josselin's, and told them I would call round to do the shopping, so that they should not come and ring at the door.

It was good for me, on the whole, to have something to do when I came home from work.

The Professor had resumed his routine and he spent over ten hours a day in the labs and in his office. His face looked sunken, his eyes were grave, and now, once again, he sometimes turned his penetrating gaze on me.

I dared not smile to him. I averted my head a little, feeling sad and ill at ease. I felt I should never shed that almost physical sadness that clung to me like a sort of fever.

On my way home I stopped at Givry-les-Etangs and bought some calves' liver, then at Josselin's I got a few provisions, bacon and eggs and butter, oranges and grapefruit; I also bought apples and pears, and I did not forget some tins of soup. I had the impression that I was being watched with curiosity and I wondered what the local people thought of us.

On the threshold of the shop I met fat Léon, who used to drive me in his taxi when I was still a child. He was really fat, but surprisingly agile. He joked from morning till night and he was a sort of local celebrity.

'Well, Mlle Laure, has that girl turned up?'

Without thinking, I asked whom he was speaking of.

'Why, that Spanish girl of yours. Seems you've lost her.'

'She's gone back to her own country.'

'Unless she's gone off with a boy friend?'

That evening I did the housework again and I went upstairs to clean out Manuela's attic. I disliked having to touch the sheets in which she had slept with my brother.

At one point I needed a rag. So as not to have to go down two

358

flights of stairs and up again, I went to see if I could find one in the loft, which is full of all sorts of things.

I saw a broken rifle of my brother's and a bicycle that had become far too small for him. My own old bicycle was there too, with flat tyres. One day when I was riding along a path I had bumped into a tree and Dr Ledoux had to put several stitches in my scalp. And there were our old tennis rackets with broken strings.

I went to the far wall, bending down, because the roof slopes steeply, and I was surprised not to find the old green trunk in its usual place.

It had always been there, full of old linen and bits of stuff, and I don't believe it had been used for travelling since I was born. It must have belonged to the time when my father was serving in Algeria and moving about fairly frequently from one garrison to another.

I found nothing that I could use as a duster and I went down to the kitchen to get one.

When I went to bed the two men had already gone upstairs. I fell asleep almost immediately.

Next morning, when I took Mother her coffee, I found her rather poorly, as I had expected. It was the second day of her cure, and one of the most trying. She was staring more fixedly than ever, as if the world around her did not exist, as if her whole attention was concentrated on what was going on inside her.

She was pressing one hand against her chest, which was being shaken with painful spasms.

A few years ago this had horrified me, and I had thought she must be dying. Now I am used, like the others, to seeing her in this state.

'Have you taken your medicine?'

'Yes.'

'It'll pass off in an hour or so.'

Especially when she had drunk a good swig of spirits. Her entire organism was protesting against the enforced deprivation.

'Do you know what happened to the trunk that was in the loft?'

'What trunk?'

'The one that used to stand against the far wall. A green trunk with a yellow band round it.'

She sighed as though in pain and I had the impression that she was trying to gain time. It seemed cruel of me to ask her so futile a question when she was in such distress.

'I don't remember. It must be so long ago ... Wait a minute . . . A second-hand dealer came by one day with his cart; he was travelling from house to house and from farm to farm buying up junk. I took him up to the loft. I know I sold him a table with a broken leg and the two straw-bottomed chairs. He must have taken the trunk too. Nobody used it any more. It was a long time ago.'

No, I had seen that trunk in the loft less than a year ago when I went up to fetch something there one day.

What worries me, actually, was the fact that my mother felt the need to lie. I went to have my bath and then I rode off to Broussais, where everything seems clean and clear and where unlike what happens at home, everyone is not trying to conceal something.

Because of the trunk, or because of the cleaning I had done the previous day, I kept thinking of Manuela again and I tried to imagine her lugging her suitcase of imitation leather as far as the station or the bus stop. There was something phony about that explanation.

In the afternoon I asked Mlle Neef if I might be absent for an hour and I went to the Avenue Paul-Doumer. I found a wealthy-looking block of flats, built of freestone, with very high windows and moulded ceilings. In the lodge there was no mere concierge but a uniformed porter.

Moreover, the word *lodge* is hardly adequate to describe the miniature drawing-room I glimpsed through the glazed door.

'M. and Mme Lherbier, please . . .'

I had got their name from my brother. A smoothly-running lift, with velvet-lined walls, took me to the second floor. I rang and after a fairly long wait, the door was opened by a girl who answered the description I had been given of Pilar; she was small, thin and swarthy, with huge dark eyes and a ready smile.

'Who did you wish to see?' she asked.

Her tiny apron and her cap were made of embroidered muslin.

'I would like to speak to you a moment, Mademoiselle.'

'We're not supposed to have visitors.'

'I might perhaps ask leave of your employer?'

'I don't know whether . . .'

She had the same accent as Manuela but spoke better French. She must have been in France for some time.

A door opened. A woman appeared, dressed in a mink coat, ready to go out.

'Pilar . . .'

The girl went up hurriedly and I saw them whispering together, looking at me. Mme Lherbier finally came towards me.

'What is it you want, mademoiselle?'

'I apologize for intruding in this way. Our maid is a compatriot of Pilar's and a friend of hers. She disappeared a few days ago and I wanted to make sure nothing has happened to her.'

'Pilar! You may answer this young lady's questions if you're able to.'

She made sure, with a rapid glance, that nothing was missing from her crocodile-skin handbag and left the apartment.

'When did you last see Manuela?'

'Wednesday last week.'

'Did you spend the afternoon with her?'

'Yes. It's my free day. In the morning I sleep in, and in the afternoon we look round the shops, Manuela and I, or else we go to the cinema. We went to the cinema. Then she had a date, but we met again afterwards.'

'Did you have dinner in a little restaurant in the Avenue de Wagram, where you often go together?'

'How did you know?

'There was a seat covered with green velvet and we sat down on it,' Pilar said somewhat hesitantly.

'Manuela told us she nearly always dined there with you before going dancing at Hernandez'.'

'That's right.'

'And did you go to Hernandez'?'

'Yes.'

'You've got many friends there?'

'I know nearly everyone. They're all Spaniards there, including the waiters and the band. My boy friend plays in the band. That's why I always stay there till closing time.'

'And Manuela? Had she a boy friend too?'

'She had a lot of friends.'

'Do you mean lovers?'

'She often changed boy friends, don't you see? She liked having fun, Manuela did; she wasn't the sort to stick to one man.'

'How did she get down to Givry?'

'Sometimes by the last bus. Or else one of the gang might have a car. That's what happened last Wednesday. There were five or six of us, including José, the musician. We all piled into a little car and we sang all the way.'

'Was Manuela in good spirits?'

'Just as usual.'

'She never talked of leaving her job?'

'No. She was quite happy. She was always happy.'

'She had no intention of going back to Spain?'

'Surely not. Her mother died ten years ago. Her father has a tiny plot of land and she had to look after her seven brothers and sisters. She'd always dreamed of coming to Paris. When she got her papers she ran away from home, for her father would never have let her leave.'

I was trying to visualize a somewhat different Manuela from the one I knew.

'Did she tell you about my brother?'

'Olivier?'

'You even know his Christian name!'

'He's quite young, isn't he, and rather innocent. She said he'd never made love before and was terribly afraid of making a fool of himself.'

She laughed, a throaty laugh like Manuela's.

'Did he want to marry her?'

'At all events he swore it was serious, and he tried to make

362

her promise not to go dancing at Hernandez' . . . He was jealous . . .'

'And my father?'

'She told me what happened. It was very funny.'

'Why?'

'I'm sorry. You know, Manuela didn't take anything seriously, and we always told each other everything.'

'Did my father suggest her leaving our house?'

'Yes.'

'He wanted to set her up in a little flat, didn't he?'

'I didn't dare mention it. With him, too, you'd have thought it was the first time he'd had a mistress.'

'She didn't accept?'

'Of course not.'

'Why?'

'It's difficult to say. It couldn't lead to anything, you understand?'

'Weren't you surprised at not hearing from her?'

'Yes.'

'What did you think?'

'That she'd got a new boy friend. That perhaps she'd changed her job.'

'You're sure she never spoke of going back to Spain?'

'Never!'

'Did she talk to you about my mother?'

'She's not . . . she's not like other people, is she?'

The word 'crazy' was on the tip of her tongue.

'Nobody at Hernandez' knows any more than you do?'

'I only went back there yesterday. They were surprised to see me alone. I knew already that she'd left Givry.'

'How did you find that out?'

'We used to ring each other up about every other day. I got your mother on the line eventually and she told me Manuela had left for Spain. I said to myself that was an excuse she'd given for leaving her job.'

'Wouldn't she have let you know?'

'I can't understand it.'

'You were really close friends?'

'She used to tell me everything. I was the only girl she knew in Paris. As for boys, she used to laugh and joke and make love with them but she wasn't going to tell them what she was thinking about.'

'Thank you, Pilar.'

'Are you worried, mademoiselle?'

'I don't know. She may have had her own reasons for disappearing. My father's proposal was rather tempting.'

If I had not felt so remote from the Professor I might have talked to him about it and he would have advised me. I dared not. As for the other lab assistants, such problems have never entered their lives.

I became increasingly uneasy, and I was somewhat ashamed of it. I told myself, at times, that I was imagining things, that I tended, like my mother, to dramatize everything.

If Mother was waiting to finish her cure before ringing up the employment agency, I had a full week of cooking and housework ahead of me.

Mother was still not eating proper meals and she was always in bed when any of us came home. Only when she was alone would she come downstairs, unsteadily, and get something to eat out of the fridge. And also, no doubt, take a fresh bottle from her hidden store. It was odd that we had never discovered where she kept it; she was amazingly cunning in this respect.

I went up to see her when I got home, after stopping at Givry again to buy meat and vegetables. She was not reading. Neither was she sleeping, although her eyes were closed.

'Is that you?' she murmured faintly.

'Yes. How are you feeling?'

'Not well.'

'Have you been in much pain?'

She did not answer. Surely it was obvious!

'Has anybody been?'

'I didn't hear the bell.'

'And no phone calls?'

'No.'

'When Pilar rang up . . .'

'Who's that?'

'A friend of Manuela's . . .'

'A Spanish woman rang. She wanted to speak to Manuela. I

replied that she wasn't here any longer. The woman wanted to know where she'd gone and I said she'd gone back to her own country.'

'You're sure Manuela told you that?'

'Yes. I'm not in the habit of lying.'

That was untrue. She lies instinctively. Or else she distorts the truth so much that you can't recognize it.

'Did she call a taxi?'

'I don't know.'

'You didn't hear if she called up Léon or the other taxi-driver?'

'No. I wasn't feeling well. I knew your brother would make a scene.'

'And Father?'

'Your father too. Men are crazy. As soon as a girl comes into the house they're after her like flies.'

'You didn't drive her to the station or to the bus stop?'

'No. That would have been the last straw! She wanted to go, and it was her own business how she did so.'

My mother seemed to have recovered a certain energy.

'I told you I hadn't been feeling well. I went upstairs and lay down. I believe I heard the door bang. I was having a bad attack.'

I could not tell how far she was lying, but there was certainly a false ring about her story.

'Why do you ask me such questions? Isn't it bad enough that I'm laid up in bed, that your father and brother aren't on speaking terms, that we've got no one to do the work and that I'm alone in the house all day?'

She spoke with more bitterness than ever.

'You needn't be afraid; I shall soon be better. In a few days you won't have to bother with anything. I shall do the housework until I can find somebody.'

I was disappointed and slightly sickened. She managed, God knows how, to make me feel guilty. I had just time to prepare dinner and tidy up downstairs a little. My father found me laying the table, and gave me a vague greeting as he made for his study.

'Father.'

'Yes?'

'I want to ask you a question. It's very important. Forgive me for meddling with what doesn't concern me. You offered to keep Manuela in a flat in Paris, didn't you?'

'Who told you that?'

'Her friend Pilar, from whom she had no secrets.'

'And you believe those two girls?'

I looked him in the eyes, my lips trembling, for I felt unsure of myself and this was the first time I had confronted my father thus. It was strange. I was looking at him somewhat as I might look at a stranger and I had a feeling that he was being evasive, that he, too, was prepared to lie.

'I believe them.'

'And what if it were true?'

He was humiliated, unhappy, searching vainly for a dignified attitude.

'You would be within your rights, of course. Your private life is no business of mine.'

He was staring at the floor.

'What I need to know, because it concerns us all, is what has become of her.'

He said nothing. He waited.

'You didn't come back and fetch her to take her to Paris?'

'No.'

'You didn't pick her up somewhere on the way?'

'No, I tell you.'

'And you've not the least idea where she can be?'

'Your brother's the person you should ask. Or your mother, who's quite capable of having thrown her out.'

'Thank you . . .'

Father was not being frank with me, either, and Olivier surprised us in an embarrassing *tête-à-tête*. He looked at each of us in turn, mistrustfully. At home, now, no one trusts anyone else.

'Aren't you going to eat?'

'Are you in a hurry?'

'Yes. I've a date with a friend.'

He never tells us anything about his friends and they never come to Givry. Is it because he is ashamed of Mother? There' a whole side of his life of which we know nothing. He comes and goes, leaves the house at different times, comes home to dinner or not, sometimes goes up to bed without saying good night to us in the drawing-room.

Perhaps it's just a naïve way of proving to himself that he is independent?

'Who've you been out with, Olivier?'

'Some fellows.'

'From the Science Faculty?'

'Maybe. I didn't ask them.'

'Haven't you made any friends there?'

'Most of them are snobs. Or else, like us, they live some way out of Paris.'

'Don't any of them come from Versailles or the neighbour-hood?'

'I couldn't say.'

I did not know whether he went to dance halls, whether indeed he knew how to dance. As for frequenting prostitutes, that was quite out of the question.

'I've seen Pilar.'

'Where?'

'At her work place. I saw the lady she works for too.'

'What for?'

'Her employer happened to be just going out. She allowed me to ask her maid a few questions.'

'What did Pilar tell you?'

'Just what she told you. She doesn't believe that Manuela has gone back to Spain. She might have said so in order not to admit that she was tired of working for us.'

'She'd have told me.'

'You're sure of that?'

'Certain.'

I was less certain than he. A few minutes later, we were sitting together at the round table, in silence.

*

I started doing the housework, as on previous days. But I was still worried about Manuela's disappearance and suddenly, about ten o'clock, I decided to go and see what I could find out at Hernandez'. My brother was out. I knocked at the study door and announced to my father:

'I'm going out for an hour.'

'Don't forget your key.'

It was not raining, but it was cold. When I got to the Avenue des Ternes I had to ask my way. The first few people I spoke to did not know the place. Then a policeman told me:

'About a hundred metres away, on the left, between a shoe-shop and a pastrycook's, you'll see a blind alley. It's down that.'

I left my motor-scooter in the avenue and ventured down, looking rather unfeminine in my anorak. The dance-hall advertised itself in blue and red lights, and in front of the door a few men, in small groups, were smoking cigarettes and apostrophizing the women who passed by. They were all speaking Spanish. Most of them wore brightly coloured shirts.

Some of the women they addressed answered in the same vein. Others blushed and hurried through the door. A big globe hung from the ceiling, made of tiny fragments of looking-glass which reflected the light of the spotlights. This globe revolved slowly over the heads of the dancers, casting luminous patches on their faces and on the white walls. There were two rows of tables around the floor, with paper napkins on them.

Almost all the places were filled and, having taken my bearings, I went up to the bar where only a few men were standing.

'Can I have a fruit-juice?'

'Surely,' replied the barman.

He winked to the others. I was no doubt the only Frenchwoman in the hall, and they exchanged jokes in their own language.

'Do you know a girl called Manuela Gomez?'

'Si, senorita. Yes, mademoiselle.'

'Is she here?'

'Is it Wednesday?'

'No, Thursday.'

'She only comes on a Wednesday, with Senorita Pilar.'

Each of his remarks was greeted with laughter or smiles from the other men.

'Did she come yesterday?'

'What d'you mean?'

'Yesterday was Wednesday. Did they both come?'

'No, Mademoiselle. Only Senorita Pilar.'

I could not tell what was so funny about his answers. It must have been his tone which sent them all into fits of laughter. We seemed to be putting on some sort of comic turn.

'Don't you know where she's gone?'

'Senorita Pilar?'

'No, Manuela.'

I was beginning to lose patience.

'Oh, you mean Manuela. A fine girl, Manuela.'

'Does anyone here know where she's gone? Had she a boy friend?'

'Many boy friends, mademoiselle.'

He pronounced it *mademezelle*, and stressed the word each time. 'Many, many boy friends.'

'I mean: did she go with anyone in particular?'

'Lots of people in particular.'

It was impossible to keep it up. I should learn nothing, and they were laughing at me more than ever.

'Dance, mademoiselle?'

'No, thank you. I must go.'

I paid. They tried to keep me back.

'A glass of Spanish brandy?'

I replied at random and edged my way back to the door. Now I only had to dodge the small groups outside.

I had learnt nothing more than when I arrived, except that Manuela was very popular at Hernandez' and that she was not shy with men. I had already guessed as much. When I reached the corner of the alley I almost collided with someone who was striding forward and just as I opened my lips to apologize I recognized my brother.

'What are you doing here?' he asked, but he had certainly guessed the answer.

'Trying to get news of Manuela.'

'Did you find out anything?'

'No. They made fun of me. She wasn't here yesterday.'

'Are you worried?'

'I don't know. I'd feel more at ease if I knew where she was. I don't like all this mystery about her departure.'

'D'you know what I've been doing?'

'No.'

'For the past two days I've cut my lectures and I've followed Father from morning till night. I think he's bound to look her up at some point and that this is the only way to find out her address.

'So far he's merely gone to his office, lunched by himself in a small restaurant nearby, gone back to work and then come home.'

'Has he noticed you following him?'

'I don't believe so. And even if he should notice I don't care. Things have got to such a point between us now . . .'

'Are you going to Hernandez'?'

'I was going there. I may as well look in there on the off-chance, though I don't expect I'll be any luckier than you.'

'Don't drink too much.'

'I've drunk nothing today but one glass of beer.'

'Good-bye.'

'Good-bye.'

We did not kiss each other. We have never gone in for demonstrations of affection at home. And yet my brother and I are very fond of one another. I worry a great deal about his future and I should so much like him to be happy!

But for that girl . . .

Now I had begun thinking like my mother, and laying the blame for everything on Manuela. Was it the girl's fault if Olivier had made love to her, and should I hold it against her that she had granted him the pleasure he begged for?

My father's case was rather different. She might have . . .

Why? I tried to put myself in her place. I could still hear the barman's voice, the laughter of the men standing round the bar. I had got the impression that practically all of them had been on fairly intimate terms with her.

She was gay. She loved life. She loved love. She wanted everyone to be happy . . .

Why not my father, who had forgotten his dignity and begged for love, too?

No. I hadn't the right to blame him. It was the atmosphere of the house that was responsible.

I was at a loss. I wanted to stop thinking about it. My father had gone upstairs when I came home and I did a little more housework before going to bed.

Next morning I felt weary and listless. As usual, my father came down first to have his breakfast and he cast a surreptitious glance at me.

'Aren't you feeling well?'

'I'm tired.'

'We ought to start looking for a maid. You can't go on doing everything.'

'There's no point in engaging one until Mother has recovered.'

'How is she?'

He had slept beside her but they had not exchanged a word. Last night and this morning she must have kept her eyes closed. So that he had to inquire after her health from me.

'She's feeling bad. The first three days are difficult.'

'Is she eating a little?'

'She goes down to take something out of the refrigerator. She waits until I've left the house.'

'Has she spoken to you about Manuela?'

'I questioned her.'

'What did she say?'

'That she knows nothing. Just what she told us the first day. That Manuela had told her she was going home.'

'Do you believe her?'

'No. I've seen Pilar, her friend. Pilar assured me that Manuela can't possibly have gone back to Spain ... She ran away from home because she had to look after her father and her seven brothers and sisters. She never had a free moment.'

'What can have happened to her?'

Just as my father was asking me this question as if he were putting it to himself, I happened to think of the green trunk. I was on the point of mentioning it.

I didn't, however. I felt I was making up a sinister story and my father would merely shrug his shoulders.

My brother came down next.

'Did you have better luck than me at Hernandez'?'

'I'm still wondering how I managed to get away. I went up to the bar. I spoke about Manuela and they all burst out laughing. I had to restrain myself not to lose my temper, for I couldn't have fought a dozen of them on my own. Anyhow, I'd have had the whole roomful against me. They told me a young lady had been asking the same questions, and they kept nudging one another.'

'The young lady was me.'

'So I gathered.'

'I must make haste if I'm to catch up Father. It would surprise me, actually, if he visited her so early in the morning.'

'I believe you're on the wrong track, Olivier.'

'I'm beginning to think so too. Now that I've begun, I want to carry on to the end. I may as well do that as go to lectures that I don't intend to follow through.'

My colleagues must have noticed that I had been rather gloomy the last few days, but they were mistaken as to the real causes of my depression. In the refectory, however, I tried to join in the conversation of our little group.

It was at about five o'clock that I was suddenly made very happy. I was working in the lab when somebody stopped behind me and I started on hearing the Professor's voice.

'I shall be needing you presently. Don't leave.'

I turned round, trembling with gratitude, but he went off without looking at me. It didn't matter. He had sought contact with me again. He had asked me to stay.

I counted the minutes and I had the utmost difficulty in concentrating on my work. When the six o'clock bell rang most of my colleagues went off to change before leaving. A few of them stayed on to finish some job.

It was not until half-past six that I found myself alone in the small laboratory, where Shimek soon joined me.

'Have you seen to Joseph?'

'Yes.'

'His pulse?'

'Normal.'

'Blood pressure?'

'Still the same.'

'Bring him out, will you? Can you hold him by yourself?'

'He's used to me.'

'It looks as if there's been no rejection . . .'

He dared not yet express satisfaction, for the success of this experiment was something so unhoped-for! Stethoscope in hand, bending over the dog, he went on speaking in the same tone of voice:

'I've missed you a great deal.'

I dared not say anything.

'I did not expect you to turn away from me as you have done.'

'I turn away? Was that what you believed?'

'For over a week you've stopped looking me in the eyes and you never come near me.'

'Because I daren't inflict myself on you.'

'You're speaking the truth?'

'Indeed, I've been so unhappy myself at not being able to come near you, I thought you were vexed with me.'

'About what?'

'I don't know. I might have wearied you.'

'Put the dog back into his cage.'

He followed me with his gaze, and his face was grave.

'I can't quite believe that I was mistaken. You see, it's in moments like those I have been through that one feels the value of true friendship.'

In spite of myself, I burst out fervently:

'I wanted so much to . . .'

'What?'

'I don't know. To comfort you. No, that's too pretentious. To surround you with a little human warmth. I thought of you all the time. I imagined you alone with your daughter.'

He looked at me in surprise, still somewhat incredulous.

'Is it true that . . .'

He held out both hands and took mine, clasping them so strongly that it hurt.

'Thank you. I believe you. It's funny. We were each wrong about the other. It won't happen any more.'

He was tactful enough not to kiss me, but to leave things as they were, looking at me with a sort of gratitude and saying with an assumed fatherliness in his voice:

373

'You must be hungry. Hurry home to dinner.'

'What about you?'

'This evening I've a report to write. I've brought a sandwich and a flask of coffee.'

I did not offer to stay. I knew that when he was writing a report he liked to be alone and even his secretary was not allowed into his room.

'I hope the work goes well,' I said.

My eyes and my whole face were alight with joy. A sense of relief pervaded my entire being and I ran lightly down the stairs instead of taking the lift.

A misunderstanding! There had been nothing more than a misunderstanding between us. Each of us, as he had pointed out, had been mistaken about the other.

I was still thinking about it as I rode out of Paris on my motor-cycle. An idea suddenly occurred to me. If a misunderstanding of this sort had arisen between the Professor and myself, it might also arise between other people, it must certainly arise hundreds of times every day.

Could I be sure that this was not what had happened between us and my mother? I say us, because I knew that my father and brother more or less shared my feelings.

All her attitudes, whether she was on a drinking-bout or not, irritated us. For a long time now we had considered her as mentally sick, even if only to a slight extent, and I had several times thought of consulting a psychiatrist.

Might she not, like the Professor, have been waiting meanwhile for a gesture or a look from us?

I had not dared look him in the eyes. I had been afraid he might think I was glad to see a vacant place beside him. That would have been monstrous of me. I had stayed aloof, waiting for a sign.

And he, meanwhile, had been hoping for some encouragement from me.

He had finally had the courage to speak out and the misunderstanding had vanished.

Had we ever talked frankly to my mother? Had we told her what was worrying us? Hadn't we treated her as if she were outside the family?

It was because of her, more or less, that I had never brought friends home and that Olivier invited nobody to the house. As for Father, he never saw anyone.

We were ashamed. We expected her to be disagreeable or eccentric.

Didn't she know this? Had she not understood it and resented it, long ago? Was this not one of the reasons for her drinking-bouts?

We left her alone all day. We rushed off in the morning, one after the other, on our motor-scooters, and only rarely did one of us go home for lunch. And in the evening we would sit down at table without asking her how she had spent the day.

After which Father would shut himself up in his study, and my brother would go out or up into his room.

Who had begun it? I pondered the question seriously, but it all went back too far into the past for me to find an answer.

If it was all due to a misunderstanding, my thoughts about her were all wrong, and I felt remorseful. I wanted to give her a chance to live with us, as though in a real family, with trustful, affectionate relations between its members.

The Professor had clasped both my hands, looking me full in the face, and his eyes, though still sad, were full of compassionate affection. I was happy, I wanted everyone to be happy.

When I got home my father and brother were at table, eating an omelette. In the kitchen I noticed some soup plates.

'Who prepared the meal?'

'I did,' muttered my brother as though he were confessing a sin. 'I opened a tin of pea soup and broke half-a-dozen eggs into a bowl.'

'Has anyone been up to see Mother?'

They each looked at me in turn as if to say that they had not thought of doing so.

'I'm going up to see if she needs anything.'

I went upstairs, knocked and opened the door. She was sitting up in bed and watched me come in with an impassive face.

'What do you want?' she asked. 'Have you come to spy on me again?'

'No, no. I came to see if you needed anything.'

'I don't need anything.'

'Has nobody come? Has nobody telephoned?'

She said with a sneer: 'I forgot that even when I'm ill I'm supposed to watch this house.'

Her eyes were hard, her voice full of rancour. I felt that it must have taken years of disappointment to bring her to this state.

Had she ever been happy? Even as a child, she was teased by her brother and sisters about her ugliness.

Were those people so very far wrong who said that my father had married her chiefly because she was his Colonel's daughter?

Had she suspected this from the beginning? Or had her eyes been opened in course of time?

I had lived with her ever since I was born, and I had suddenly discovered that I did not know her. When I was able to judge her, or rather when I took it upon myself to judge her, she had already become what she was today and I had no way of discovering the past.

'Aren't you hungry, *maman*?'

'You know quite well that when one's in pain one is not hungry.'

'Is there nothing I can do for you?'

Obviously I was not being very clever. One cannot change one's attitude overnight, or in the course of a day.

'What's come over you?' she asked sarcastically.

'I've been thinking of you a lot today.'

'Really?'

'I've been thinking that we leave you alone too much.'

'Well, now I'm asking you to leave me alone.'

'I want to tell you, too, that I do love you.'

'For heaven's sake!'

I felt I had better go away. I was doing her more harm than good. I was being tactless and ridiculous.

'Good night.'

She did not reply. She lit a cigarette. Over her night gown she was wearing a bed-jacket of a faded blue that intensified the darkness of her hair and eyes.

She would not really be ugly if . . .

I had to stop thinking. My ideas were growing hopelessly

confused and I went down into the kitchen to make myself an omelette.

My brother went upstairs, my father into his study, and mechanically, as my mother usually does, I switched on the television.

Chapter Six

The Professor did not speak to me again nor ask me to stay on after hours, but our eyes met several times during the day. I felt that a sort of complicity had arisen between us, together with a certain peace of heart.

I know that whatever happens to me and whatever happens to him, no man will ever fill his place in my life. I ask nothing from him. That is perhaps what gives me the greatest sense of exaltation. I should like to be the one who gives, while he simply accepts.

My colleagues have known for a long time that there's something between us. They exchange knowing looks when they leave in the evening and see me stay behind, and they involuntarily glance ironically towards the little room where the camp bed stands.

They have understood nothing and I don't hold it against them. Still less do I feel the need to explain to them something which is a very simple truth. As a child I used to watch processions go by, men and women following the Holy Sacrament holding lighted candles, and I remember seeing certain faces lit up with total joy, eyes oblivious of surrounding reality and fixed on some vision beyond the reach of other people.

I felt somewhat like those believers and I calmly braved the mocking smiles of my companions.

Did Shimek realize the place he filled in my life? Could he possibly be aware that my devotion was absolute and that without it I should cease to exist?

I had entered love as others enter the church and that is why, no doubt, I no longer really belonged at home. I prepared breakfast, I cooked dinner, I tidied up and swept. These were only external gestures which formed no part of my inner life.

Today, again, I called at Josselin's to buy something for dinner, and there, rather to my surprise, I saw Mme Rorive, who was gossiping as she did her shopping. She fell silent as soon as she caught sight of me and I suspected that she had been talking about me or my parents.

'I'm so glad to see you. There's nobody ill at home, I hope?'

I haven't the gift of second sight, but I could swear that she was only there because she knew that for the past few days I had been calling in at the same time, on my way back from work.

'My mother isn't very well.'

'Is she in bed?'

'Yes, but it's nothing to worry about. Her usual migraine headaches.'

'Oh, that's so painful! I've a sister who suffers from them too, and when they come on she dare not even cross the road.'

She had finished her purchases. Her shopping-bag lay on the counter beside her but she made no attempt to leave.

She was dressed in mauve, her favourite colour, probably because she thinks it looks distinguished. Her white hair has a mauve tinge too, and her complexion is mauve with a faint trace of rouge on her cheeks.

'Will you give me four jars of *rillettes*, four slices of pâté and two dozen eggs.'

'You know, I was a bit worried. Today, for the third time, I called at your house with M. Rorive and nobody answered the bell.'

Like many tradespeople who have spent much of their lives behind the counter, they referred to one another by their surnames, preceded by Monsieur or Madame.

'Have you lost your maid?'

'She has left.'

'Will that be all, Mlle Le Cloanec?'

'Would you add a little parsley?'

'Yes.'

Mme Rorive left the shop with me.

'Won't you come and have a cup of tea or coffee and a little piece of cake with me?'

There is a pastrycook's opposite, with small white tables round which the ladies of the neighbourhood eat their cakes and gossip. I was feeling uneasy about what she had said of her three visits to our house. She is almost as familiar with our habits as we are ourselves, for she spends much of her time peering through her curtains. She was well aware that my father and brother would not be back for another hour.

I followed her resignedly.

'Tea or *café-au-lait*?'

'Black coffee, please.'

'A slice of fruit-cake?'

'Thank you.'

'I ought not to eat cakes, for I'm fat enough as it is, but I can't resist them. She was Italian, wasn't she?'

'Spanish.'

'With a funny sort of name. Foreigners nearly always have funny christian names.'

'Manuela.'

'Yes, that's it. A girl who was always laughing, a pretty girl who must have had plenty of lovers ... And from what I saw of her she can't have put up much resistance.'

'I don't know what she did on her days out.'

'I remember recently, about a week ago, she came back very late in a car. I wasn't asleep. Sometimes I can't go to sleep and I'd rather sit up. It was at least two o'clock in the morning. There was a whole gang of them piled up in the car with her, singing at the tops of their voices.'

'How do you know it was her?'

'I heard the car stop in front of your house, and then your front door shutting. That's why, when I didn't see her again, I thought your mother had probably got rid of her.'

'She went home to Spain of her own free will.'

'Couldn't she get used to French life?'

'I don't know.'

'Has your mother sent for Dr Ledoux?'

I did not immediately get the drift of her question. 'Why?'

'Because dizziness and cold sweats are often due to catching a chill.'

I still could not understand. What did she mean about catching a chill? I was convinced that for all her apparent naïvety Mme Rorive's remarks were never pointless.

'I did think, that night the dog died, that she was unwise to go out in the rain without even putting on a warm coat.'

I asked involuntarily: 'What dog?'

'Didn't your mother tell you? She probably didn't want to upset you. It was on Tuesday or Wednesday, wait a minute. Tuesday, rather, because I could swear we'd eaten soles for lunch. It's the day the fish comes.

'It doesn't matter. What I'm certain of is that it was raining. Not the heavy storms we'd had the week before but a cold drizzle.

'I was waiting for M. Rorive who had gone into town to do some shopping. I was by the window looking out for him, for I'm worried when he goes off driving by himself.'

I felt distressed for no precise reason. It seemed to me that this chatter concealed a danger as yet unknown, and to keep myself in countenance I drank a mouthful of coffee.

'Aren't you going to eat your cake?'

'Yes. It looks very good.'

'You can't find the like in Paris. Where had I got to? It was some time after dark. A car drove up from the Givry direction, very fast, with its big yellow headlamps lighting up the wet road.

'Suddenly, in the shaft of light, I saw a big dog I'd never seen before. It looked like a stray. It was walking in the middle of the road and the car didn't have time to brake. If I didn't hear the bump, I felt as if I'd heard it.

'I'm much too fond of animals to see an accident like that without being upset. The car went on its way while the dog, which had been practically tossed into the air, fell down more or less on the spot where it had been hit.'

I was increasingly puzzled as to why Mme Rorive felt impelled to tell me this story. She was conscious of my interest, and enjoying it inwardly.

'I was so bowled over that I poured myself a tiny glass of *crème de menthe*. I was drinking it in the lounge when M. Rorive came home. I said to him:

' "We might perhaps go and say hullo to dear Mme Le Cloanec. I made a couple of currant loaves this morning. I might take her one."

'I know your mother adores them. I once took her one and she told me how delighted she was.'

Was all this true or untrue?

'I took my umbrella. M. Rorive wouldn't take his, saying it wasn't raining very hard and that his mackintosh was enough. Just fancy my surprise when I noticed that the dog was no longer on the road. I was sure it was dead. The way it had fallen down, in a broken heap, it couldn't have failed to be dead.'

She went on talking, talking, but without neglecting her cake.

'M. Rorive rang the bell. The ground floor was all dark but there was a light on upstairs in your parents' room. You see I've got to know the house! When you've only one neighbour . . .'

How I wished she would get to the point!

'Well, for the third time, nobody answered.

' "Perhaps she's in the kitchen and doesn't hear?"

'We didn't as yet know that your maid had left. I was a bit worried and M. Rorive said:

' "Let's go and knock at the other door."

'We went round the house and knocked at the back door. There was no light in the kitchen either.

' "Just leave your currant loaf on the doorstep."

' "The rain will soak it."

'Then, I know it was cheeky of me but you must forgive me, I tried the door handle. The door wasn't locked and it opened. I put the loaf down on the table in the passage . . .'

'But the dog? I don't see what the dog has to do with . . .'

'I'm coming to that. Wait a minute. Just as we were going off I heard a noise coming from the direction of the wood. The moon had just broken through and I saw your mother coming through the garden gate. She had no coat or hat on and she was pushing a wheelbarrow . . .'

'Was there anything in the wheelbarrow?'

'No. We didn't wait for her, for fear she might be annoyed to see us there. I suppose she must have seen the dog on the road too. She must have come down to find out if by any chance it was only hurt.

381

'Then, finding it dead, she must have thought of throwing it into the pond with a stone tied to its neck . . .'

Her tone suddenly altered. 'What's the matter with you?'

I replied stupidly: 'With me?'

'You've turned quite pale. You're fond of animals, aren't you? I'm sure you'd never have left the poor thing lying in the middle of the road, just under your windows.'

'I must go back and make dinner,' I said.

'It's nearly dinner-time. Of course you're only having cold things.'

She had noticed what I was buying at Josselin's. She insisted on paying our bill.

'It was my invitation. Did you have some of my currant loaf, by the way?'

'I believe . . . Yes . . .'

Actually, this was not true. For one reason or another, my mother had never mentioned a currant loaf. But then of course she had been in the middle of her 'novena'.

What had she done with it? She had certainly not eaten it herself, because when she is drinking she cannot bear anything sweet. Had she thrown it into the dustbin? Why should she?

What had been her reaction on discovering, when she came back from the ponds pushing a wheelbarrow, that somebody had been into the house?

I went home. Unlike the evening of Mme Rorive's latest visit, the lights were on downstairs. There was nobody in the drawing-room, nor in the dining-room, where the table was laid.

In the kitchen I saw my mother, who had got dressed and was standing very upright, too upright, as though to prevent herself collapsing.

'You've come down?'

She looked at me without answering and heaved a long sigh. I would not have expected her to be capable of coming down today. It was not the first time I'd had evidence of her prodigious strength of will.

She was walking about in a jerky, mechanical fashion.

'I've brought something for dinner. There was a pâté just out of the oven and I took four slices.'

I laid my purchases on the table. The sight of food must have turned her stomach but she gave no sign of it.

'Aren't the men back yet?'

'I'm all alone.'

There are moments when I admire her as much as I pity her. She is alone, indeed, even when the three of us are at table with her. She lives in a world apart, which we do not know, and we have grown used to ascribing her behaviour to eccentricity or to drink.

Perhaps because a few glances from the Professor, that day, had made me happy, I felt a little closer to her, or rather I wanted to be closer to her, to tell her that I understood her, that I knew how wretched her life had been.

Weren't we all a little to blame? I stared at her and felt like crying. I imagined her in the rain, coming back from the wood, from the ponds, going through the narrow gate at the bottom of the garden, whose rusty lock has ceased to function, and pushing the wheelbarrow she had taken from the shed.

Involuntarily I asked her:

'What exactly happened about the dog?'

Her eyes suddenly narrowed and she stared at me with such intensity that I felt ill at ease, and looked away.

'What dog?'

'The one that was run over by a car in front of the house. A big stray dog was walking in the middle of the road.'

I looked up. Her lips had gone white. She must be suffering horribly and I felt ashamed of being unkind, just as I had felt ashamed the night when my father had been humiliated by Olivier. I think humiliation is what hurts a human being most.

'Who told you about a dog?'

'Mme Rorive.'

My mother could see that I was terribly upset. She undoubtedly guessed what I was thinking and I expected her to crack up, to let slip what I might call her mask.

To my great surprise, however, she held firm. I said at random:

'And what about the currant loaf?'

'What currant loaf?'

'Mme Rorive came in by the back door and left a currant loaf on the table in the passage.'

'I never saw any currant loaf in the passage.'

And my mother added a little phrase that astonished me:

'That woman's mad!'

My brother's arrival put an end to our conversation and Mother began putting out the cold meat on a plate.

'Well, so you're up already?'

We are all cruel to her. We ought not to seem surprised at her having got up and tried, by dint of an astonishing effort of will, to resume her place in everyday life.

'Come here a minute, Laure.'

We went into the drawing-room. This, again, is something we ought to avoid, these conversations in corners, lowered voices, whispered remarks. How can she possibly feel at home? How can she not believe that she is different from other people?

'What do you want to tell me?'

'That I've made my inquiries. I can join up in January, with the new draft, and by anticipating my call-up I'm entitled to a choice of arms.'

'You're still thinking of that?'

'More than ever.'

And, with a vague gesture towards the kitchen: 'You've seen her, haven't you? Do you think I'm going on living in this atmosphere?'

'She's being brave.'

'I'd sooner she had stopped in bed. Don't say anything to Father yet. I shall try and get my call-up papers and at the last minute I'll ask him to sign.'

'Suppose he refuses?'

'He won't refuse. After what has happened, my presence here embarrasses him and he'll be relieved not to have me in the house.'

'*What dog?*' she had asked, her face ashen.

And then her final remark: '*That woman's mad!*'

These two little phrases haunted me all through the meal. Father, as stiff as ever, pretended to ignore Olivier's presence. Isn't it possible that with time all this antagonism may lessen and perhaps eventually disappear?

Opposite me, Mother was toying with her food, and I saw her hesitate to pour herself a second glass of red wine, although she was obviously in need of it. So I helped her at the same time as myself, and she looked at me in surprise, but without the least gratitude.

'What dog?'

'That woman's mad!'

I muttered: 'Excuse me.' And I left the table. I hurried up to my own room, reaching it just in time to give vent to the sobs that were choking me.

The dog . . . Mme Rorive . . .

'She told me she was going back to Spain.'

I wanted to be with the Professor, very close to him, and to tell him everything, ask him what I ought to do. I felt hot and cold at once. I lay there with my face buried in the pillow, and I sobbed without even thinking about what was making me so unhappy.

*

I had a terrible nightmare from which I literally wrenched myself, forcing myself to wake up, and I stayed for a long time sitting up in bed, gasping, incapable of distinguishing accurately between my imagination and reality.

In the dream I had not gone to the hospital and my presence had clearly worried my mother. It was raining. It must have been dark outside, for the lamps were alight in the house.

The two men had gone off, Olivier on his motor-scooter, wearing his sheepskin jacket, and Father in the car.

We were both sitting in the kitchen, Mother in her pale blue housecoat, over which she had tied an apron. It was four minutes to nine by my alarm clock. Then three minutes, then two minutes to nine. I don't know why I felt compelled to wait until exactly nine o'clock.

My mother was afraid. She stared at me with enormous eyes and asked: 'What are you going to do?'

I waited to answer till the hand stood in the centre of the clock and I said:

'To make you speak. I've got to know.'

I was calm. I was conscious of fulfilling a task imposed on me by Fate.

'I swear there's nothing to know.'

'The dog?'

'There never was any dog.'

'The dog in the middle of the wet road?'

'Mme Rorive is mad.'

'And the wheelbarrow?'

'I never used the wheelbarrow.'

'What did you do in the wood?'

'I never went into the wood.'

Her face was distorted with anguish and she was wringing her hands.

'And Manuela's imitation leather suitcase?'

'She took it with her.'

'Where?'

'To her own country.'

'She didn't go back to her own country.'

'She said she was going to.'

'You're lying.'

'I am not lying.'

'I insist on your telling me the truth and I won't repeat it to anyone.'

'There's no truth to tell. What are you doing?'

It was a cry of terror, for I was moving implacably towards her.

'Don't hit me.'

'I shall hit you if I have to. I want you to tell me what you've done with Manuela.'

I was holding her by both wrists and they were as fragile as the wrists of a child, with a very soft smooth skin.

'Don't hurt me.'

'Then tell me.'

'I've nothing to say.'

'You killed her.'

She did not answer but gazed at me with wild eyes, her mouth open for a cry that never came.

'Tell me why you killed her.'

'She took everything from me.'

'What did she take from you?'

'My son and my husband. She taunted me, she made fun of me because I'm not a gay person.'

'You were in the kitchen together?'

She did not answer but looked round her as if she had forgotten where she was.

I don't know at what point he had come in, but the Professor was there, in his white lab coat and cap. He had heard everything, even though I had only just caught sight of him. He was shaking his head sadly and looking at me as if he wanted to make me understand something.

Only I could not understand. I knew that I had a job to do, and I was doing it.

'What did you strike her with?'

She struggled a little longer, trying to free her wrists from my firm grip. She muttered at last, turning to glance at the table with its brown and white check oil-cloth:

'The bottle.'

'You struck her with the bottle?'

She nodded.

'Which bottle?'

'The bottle of wine.'

'Was it full?'

'I'd drunk a little.'

'You were drinking out of the bottle when she came in? Was that why she laughed at you?'

'She laughed at me and I hit her.'

'She fell on to the floor?'

'She was staring at me with her big round eyes and walking towards me. The bottle was broken. I took the rolling-pin which was lying on the table and I hit her again.'

'Several times?'

'Yes.'

'Did she fall down?'

'No.'

'Did she stand there a long time?'

'Yes, a long time. And I kept on hitting her. She began to bleed from the nose and mouth.'

'And then she fell down?'

'Yes.'

'Did you know she was dead?'

'Yes.'

'How did you know?'

'I knew.'

'And the dog?'

'There hadn't been any dog yet.'

'What did you do?'

'I went to fetch the trunk out of the loft.'

'So you hadn't sold it to the junk-dealer?'

'No.'

'You lied to me?'

'I always lie. I can't help it.'

'What did you want to do with the body?'

'To throw it into the Old Pond, but I didn't want it to float to the surface. I took the old rags down into the cellar.'

'Are they still there?'

'No. Next morning, after you'd all gone, I put them in the dustbin.'

'Did you take her pulse?'

'No. She was dead.'

She repeated, as though reciting the responses in church:

'She was dead.'

'You put her in the trunk?'

'Yes.'

'You picked up the bits of broken glass and wiped away the stains of wine and blood?'

'There was hardly any blood.'

'You went to fetch the wheelbarrow.'

'Yes. It was raining.'

'Did you put on your coat?'

'No. I wasn't cold.'

'Were you able to carry the trunk by yourself?'

'I dragged it. I'm strong. Nobody believes that I'm strong, but it's the truth.'

'What did you put into the trunk so that it shouldn't rise to the surface?'

'A shoemaker's last that was lying in the shed and your father's old vice.'

I had dropped her wrists and she kept on speaking in a mono-
tone like a schoolchild reciting a lesson.

'Where did you throw her?'

'Into the Old Pond. At the place where there's a hole. I'd
heard say that the mud there is over a yard deep.'

'Were you strong enough?'

'I was strong enough. The hole is close to the worm-eaten
little jetty.'

'And suppose the jetty had given way?'

'It did not give way.'

'And the dog?'

'I came back and I went upstairs to wash my hands.'

'Was there a currant loaf in the passage?'

'No. I saw the dog out of the window.'

'So there was a dog?'

'Yes.'

'Why did you bother about it?'

'I don't know. I didn't like having it in front of the house.'

'Didn't it occur to you that if you'd been seen with the wheelbarrow it would serve as an alibi?'

'I don't know. Why are you so unkind to me?'

'I'm not unkind. I shall have to live with the memory of this
from now on.'

'So shall I.'

'It's not the same thing.'

'Why not?'

'Did you go and fetch the wheelbarrow again and put the dog
in it?'

'Yes.'

'What did you put round its neck?'

'An old piece of an iron grating.'

'Did you throw it into the Old Pond?'

'Yes.'

'At the same spot?'

'No. At the place where the two ponds join. There's a sort of
channel with a little bridge across it.'

I know that my face was relentless and frightening, and she
kept staring at it in terror. The silence made it even more terrible, for I could think of no more questions to ask her.

'You mustn't tell anyone, Laure. Promise me not to tell anyone.'

And as I did not answer, she went on in a little girl's voice:

'I won't do it again. I promise I won't do it again.'

I turned to look for the Professor. He was standing in the doorway. And as I gazed at him with questioning eyes, he nodded to me.

What did he mean? That I must promise? He looked serious and severe. I think he was not pleased with me. He had not spent years in our house and he did not know my mother.

'Don't tell anyone, Laure. I don't want to go to prison. I don't want them to shut me up!'

And then she gave a final cry: 'I tell you I'm harmless.'

I must have cried out too, as I wrenched myself out of sleep, out of my nightmare. I did not immediately think of switching on my bed-side lamp and I sat there in the darkness, listening to the rain beating on the shutters.

I had difficulty in getting my breath back and for one moment I even wondered where I was.

It had been so real! It had seemed so true! Was it possible that . . . I listened, to find out whether my cry might have woken my parents and whether anyone was coming. No. The whole house was asleep. I was bathed in sweat. I reached out to switch on the lamp.

I don't know why I stammered under my breath: 'The dog.'

I could not tell what was true and what I had invented. I got up and went to drink a glass of water in the bathroom. I decided to take a sleeping-pill so as to sleep heavily and dreamlessly.

When I woke next morning at the usual time I was so weary that my first thought was to stay in bed and ring up the hospital presently to say that I was not feeling well.

But my dream immediately recurred to me, with my mother and myself in the kitchen after the men had both left.

I did not want to stop alone in the house with her. I should have been capable of questioning her, of insisting, at all costs, that she should tell me . . .

I took a shower, dressed and went downstairs. I found her making the coffee.

She looked at me and said: 'I don't need anybody.'

'I didn't know whether you were down. We shall have to ring the agency to get a maid.'

I was appalled to find how like she was to the woman in my dream. She had on her pale blue housecoat, which in fact is what she usually wears, and she had tied her apron over it. The illusion was so strong that I turned to the table to look for the rolling-pin.

'What do you want?'

'Nothing.'

I felt I had better leave the room. However, I poured myself a cup of coffee and took it into the drawing-room, where I automatically started tidying up.

I dared not admit to myself that what had disturbed me most was the attitude of the Professor. He had looked at me sadly, as if he were disappointed in me. I'd felt that his eyes were telling me not to go on, not to try to find out.

My forehead was bathed in sweat again, and I was relieved when my brother came down and went to take his usual place at table.

I joined him, as though to put myself under his protection. He was surprised to find Mother serving his breakfast. She said only two words: 'Good morning.'

He looked at me and was surprised to see me in such distress.

'What's the matter with you?'

'I had a horrible nightmare.'

'And is that what's reduced you to this state?'

That remark was enough to show me how hard it was going to be. I wanted to answer, to tell him everything.

But I could not tell anybody anything, I had promised. Had I really promised? It was impossible to be left thus between dream and reality.

'Will you go with me as far as the hospital, Olivier?'

'Why? What are you frightened of?'

'I don't want to feel alone.'

He looked at me curiously as he ate his breakfast.

'I've never seen you like this.'

'If you'd lived through my dream . . .'

'One doesn't live through dreams.'

'While a dream lasts it's as real as reality.'

'Where did you read that?'

Then my father came down and we both fell silent. I was conscious of the passing minute, of our family life, of four human beings together in a suburban house.

My mother was a pale blue figure in the kitchen, drinking her coffee out of a big bowl that we generally use for beating eggs.

My brother had nearly finished eating and was still in his shirt sleeves. My father, fully dressed, was eating his toast and staring straight in front of him.

And I was looking at them all three. I felt I was looking at myself too, seeing myself there amongst them, and my face seemed all puffed up.

The minute passed and there were more minutes, and there will be many more.

'Come on, then!' called out my brother, getting up and putting on his jacket.

He went to fetch his lumber-jacket in the passage. He waited for me to put on mine and my rubber boots, for it was still raining.

We walked across part of the yard, along the gravel path, to fetch our motor-scooters.

'You really won't tell me anything?'

'I've nothing to tell you, Olivier. I assure you it was only a bad dream.'

'I've a feeling you're hiding something from me.'

'I'm a bit blue this morning.'

'And yet Mother's fairly well. I expected her to stay at least two days longer in bed. She's never recovered so quickly from a "novena".'

'You're quite right.'

Why had she made such an effort? Wasn't it because in real life, too, she was afraid?

We rode on side by side and we went through Givry, past Josselin's, past the pastrycook's. Today I would have no need to stop and buy food. I was sure that Mother would order things by telephone, as she always does when she is not on a 'novena'.

I felt a little calmer now that I was out of doors. The rain lashed my face and sometimes took away my breath. My brother adjusted his speed to mine and we reached the road that runs from Versailles to Saint-Cloud. The sky was so grey that it seemed as if daylight had not yet broken and we put on our lights. So did other people making their way to Paris like ourselves, some on scooters, some on bicycles, some under cover in their cars.

From time to time Olivier turned to look at me. He seemed anxious. He was not used to seeing me give way. At the corner of the Boulevard Brune a sullen crowd was emerging from the entrance to the métro station and my brother waved to me before going on his way.

I reached my destination. I was back in the light, whitewashed rooms, among the long tables strewn with test-tubes, spirit lamps, and gleaming instruments.

I went to put on my white things like all the rest and almost automatically I assumed my professional expression.

Chapter Seven

We met two or three times during the first part of the morning, but we did not work together. I tried hard to wear a brave face, realizing how woebegone I must be looking. I felt that he was puzzled, that he was trying to understand, and I hated myself for adding to his worries.

About eleven o'clock he was no longer to be seen in any of the labs and a little later his secretary came to tell me that he was asking for me in his room. The furniture there was of mahogany, with brass fittings, and the walls were almost entirely covered with photographs of leading medical personalities from all over the world.

In this over-solemn setting he appeared smaller, thinner, almost insignificant. It seemed as if he were trying to adapt himself to his surroundings, and he was not the same man as in the lab.

'I didn't want to question you in front of your colleagues. Please sit down.'

He motioned me to the chair in front of his desk, and I felt ill at ease there, as if I were a visitor.

'You're not well, are you.'

'I hardly slept at all last night and the little sleep I got was very disturbed. I apologize for appearing in such a state.'

He looked at me affectionately, trying to understand.

'Have you got family worries?'

'Yes, particularly about my mother.'

I should have liked to tell him everything, to confide in him entirely, but I felt I had not the right to do so. He had just endured his own tragic experience. He had barely recovered from the blow that had fallen on him.

'She has always been rather unbalanced and at times I wonder if she would not be better off in a psychiatric hospital.'

'You're sure it's as serious as that?'

I could not tell him that I was convinced she had killed someone. I had no proof of it. And I was still under the influence of my dream. Wasn't it absurd to attach so much importance to that?

'What do the doctors say?'

'She has always refused to be examined by a specialist. My father dared not send for one against her will. As for our family doctor, he ascribes her eccentricities to alcoholism.'

'Does she drink a great deal?'

'Yes, periodically. For several days she goes on drinking practically all day, in secret. She's fiendishly clever at getting hold of alcohol and hiding the bottles all over the house, so as to have one available at any moment. Then she goes to bed complaining of migraine and only leaves her room when there's nobody else in the house.

'She eats nothing at meal-times. She nibbles secretly at whatever she can find in the refrigerator.'

'How is her health?'

'She complains of those migraine headaches. In fact she only suffers from them when she is drinking. At such times she lives unsteadily in a nebulous universe, and I'm always afraid she may commit suicide. She must be particularly tough, for at forty-seven she has never been ill. Dr Ledoux thinks that her troubles are imaginary.'

It did me good to speak, to see him listening to me and trying to form an opinion.

'She was unhappy as a child. She thought she was ugly and the fact is that she hasn't an attractive face. Now she's so thin that you wonder how she can keep going.'

He wanted to help me. It was the first time he had asked me about my family and I had to restrain myself not to tell him all about Manuela, Olivier and my father. I'd have had to describe the atmosphere of our house.

I was ashamed of taking up his time, of stealing his sympathy.

In any case, how could I confide in anyone, even in him? It was not my secret; it was my mother's. I could keep silent, at least I supposed so, for I am her daughter and I cannot be required to denounce her.

But could somebody else? could he? I did not know the law, I believed however that anyone who knew of a crime was bound to inform the authorities.

I refused to put him into such a delicate situation. I could not accept the idea of making him my accomplice.

I had had a nightmare, because of a few remarks of Mme Rorive's about a dog and a wheelbarrow. That nightmare clung to me and I still found it hard, so many hours later, to feel sure that it had not really happened.

Why should Manuela not have left of her own accord? She had only been with us two months. We knew little about her, and nothing about her real character, except that she went to bed with all and sundry, gaily, because that was her nature.

And because one evening I had come home and found her not there, was it reasonable to condemn my mother?

I was torn between contradictory feelings.

'It's done me good to be allowed to talk to you. I'm grateful. Please forgive me, from now on, if you see me looking downcast or preoccupied. Don't take any notice of me, will you?'

'You don't want to confide in me?'

'For the moment it's impossible. Everything depends on what happens.'

'I won't press you.'

'Will you let me take the afternoon off?'

'Of course. Take a few days' leave if it's any help.'

'It would be worse to spend all day at home.'

I said good-bye awkwardly, as though I scarcely knew him except as the big chief that he is. I went to the door and there turned back for a moment. Why did I get the impression that he was looking at me as though in a dream? His eyes seemed to be trying to send me a message that I could not understand.

I did not want to lunch in the refectory, under the curious gaze of the other lab assistants. Nor did I want to go home to eat, and I went to the little restaurant where I had gone to drink brandy one evening and to which I had subsequently returned with my brother.

I ate at one of the small tables with red tablecloths on them and the barman switched on the gramophone. A soft, subdued music filled the room.

I was not hungry. I felt utterly lost. If I'd been told the police were coming to arrest me I'd have believed it.

However, I eventually ate something and I even took a sweet, which I seldom do.

When I reached home, there was nobody on the ground floor and I was seized with irrational terror. And yet it was quite natural that my mother should have gone to lie down in her room.

I kept on my rubber boots and my sheepskin jacket and, under the drizzling rain, I went out by the back door towards the gate at the bottom of the garden.

The trees were almost completely bare and the ground was thickly carpeted with sodden leaves. Nobody went through these woods in winter. A hundred metres from our house, a track ran from the road to the Big Pond, but we always used to take a short cut along a scarcely visible path.

I am ashamed to admit that I was looking for the marks of the wheelbarrow. There were none, needless to say, among the dead leaves. I followed the bank of the Big Pond as far as the wooden bridge that crosses a sort of narrow channel joining the two ponds.

Here there were no leaves and on the muddy soil the traces of a single wheel were still clearly visible. Some rushes had been

attened and even broken as if a heavy, bulky object had been
ushed over them.

No landscape had ever seemed to me so sinister and I have
ever felt such a sense of loneliness. The rain made little rings
n the surface of the pond and the trees stood out blackly
gainst the low sky. I felt cold in spite of my lumber-jacket. I
vanted to talk to someone.

And I suddenly realized that I should never be allowed to
alk.

I went back, hesitantly, towards the house, thinking about my
ather and Olivier and what attitude they would take if they
knew the truth. Did my father not suspect it? If he did, as I
elieved, he must be unwilling to learn it, preferring to remain
n uncertainty.

As for my brother, I believed him to be incapable of keeping
a secret like this one. He would go into the army as he had
decided. And it was probably better for him.

I felt really cold. I had to make an effort to stop my teeth
rom chattering. My mother had heard me come in. Was she
vatching me from a window?

I stopped in the shed where the wheelbarrow was kept and I
made out some fresh scratches on the side of it.

A pile of old iron had always stood in one corner and I could
save sworn that this pile had dwindled, I could see neither the
rusty vice my father had used in the days when he used to tinker
about the house, nor the cobbler's last.

I felt lost and utterly alone in the midst of the hostile universe
and I was afraid to go back into the house.

I had not the heart to condemn my mother. I felt that we
were all guilty, we who had let her gradually sink into an abyss
of solitude and despair.

I thought I saw the curtain stir over the kitchen window. I
could not remain outside indefinitely. Nor could I go back to
town and wait to come home until my father and brother were
back.

I pushed open the door with a reluctant hand, pulled off my
boots, hung up my jacket on the coat-rack.

Mother was there, standing in the kitchen, three yards away
from me, looking at me with a fixed stare.

Chapter Eight

I went forward, and I was no longer cold or frightened. M
mother was not a threatening figure and her gaze expressed onl
her own terror.

I had the impression that in her eyes I figured as a judge an
that her life depended on me. She did not speak. She ha
nothing to say. She waited.

And I said, in as natural a voice as I could manage:

'I didn't feel well and I left the lab early.'

That did not explain my visit to the wood or to the shed. I
explained nothing but my evident distress. In spite of myself
gazed at her intently as if I wanted to understand everything
She was so pitiable with her flat chest, her clothes hangin
loosely about her, her long thin neck and pointed nose.

It was as if I fascinated her. She stood as motionless as a
animal on the alert, with only an occasional quiver of the nos
trils.

What was the good of telling her that I knew? She was con
scious of that, and she was waiting for my verdict. So I sai
casually,

'I wonder if I haven't caught a chill.'

What would they do with her? Would they send her to prison
for the rest of her days? Or else, on the grounds of diminishe
responsibility, would they shut her up in a mental hospital?

She seemed shrunken with fear. I had never before live
through or even imagined minutes like those I then endured. I
seemed to me that the world had stopped turning, that it ha
ceased to exist, that there was nothing but the two of us face to
face.

If they tried to shut her up anywhere my mother would kil
herself, I'm convinced of that. Was this a solution? Was it th
only one?

I rejected it. And I knew that by holding my tongue I wa
assuming a heavy burden, that I was making myself responsibl
for my mother.

I had dreamed of a tiny flat in Paris where I should be alone my own home. I had imagined that some day, much later, ̶himek would come to visit me there and that he'd have his ̶wn arm-chair beside the fire.

I realized now that I should have to stay here, to look after ̶er, to avoid fresh dramas.

I would be the only one to know, alone with the bare, hor-̶ible truth.

What was the good of putting questions to her, of asking if ̶hings had happened as I had dreamed?

She was surprised to hear me say:

'I feel like drinking something to warm me up. A hot toddy ̶or instance. Is there any rum in the house?'

She spoke at last, under her breath, as though talking to her-̶elf.

'I believe there's a bottle in the cellar. I'll go and see.'

I put some water on to boil. There are some familiar gestures ̶hat one performs unawares at the most painful or dramatic ̶noments. You put on water to boil, you set out two glasses, two ̶poons, some sugar, a lemon.

It was untrue that I needed to warm myself up. It wasn't ̶ossible to stay any longer face to face in silence.

The rum represented a sort of absolution, a promise that ̶here would never again be any mention of Manuela, who had ̶oved life so much. Had not her gaiety, her greed been a kind of ̶nsult to my mother?

And then my brother, shamelessly, had visited her room; my ̶ather, barefoot, had crept up to the second floor to listen ̶ehind the door, and then had taken her to a shady hotel.

Manuela took everything!

Had she really surprised my mother in the kitchen that day, ̶lrinking red wine out of the bottle, and had she laughed at ̶ler?

I should never know.

What was there left for the woman who now came upstairs ̶vith a bottle of rum and poured some into the two glasses? She ̶vas ashamed, she had been ashamed all her life, ashamed of ̶eing ugly, ashamed of her drinking-bouts and of the tremors ̶hat seized her when she stopped drinking.

I would never speak to her of what had happened between

her and Manuela, even if it meant that I should never know the real truth myself.

She had guessed that I knew. It was not the same as uttering the words.

I poured boiling water into the glasses. Neither of us wanted to sit down. I should have felt as if I were paying a call.

But henceforward I would always be here. From time to time the Professor would keep me back after work at the lab. None the less I would become an old maid, like my aunt Iris, except that I should not have a place of my own, a little flat that would reflect my personality, as Iris had her flat in the Place Saint Georges.

'Inspector, I have come to tell you that my mother . . .'

It was unthinkable. It would be monstrous. And yet she was still shaking. She could not believe that her nightmare was over.

I pictured men dragging the pond and bringing up the green trunk.

'Drink up,' I said, seeing her hesitate.

Heavens, how fragile she seemed, how insubstantial! I found it hard to realize that she was my mother.

And though I felt bitter against her for making me take this decision, I had not the heart to condemn her.

The rum sent a warm glow through my chest. My mother must have felt her legs giving way, for she sat down on the edge of the kitchen chair, as if she dared not take a more comfortable seat.

'Did you ring up the agency?'

'Yes.'

'Have they got anyone?'

'They'll ring back tomorrow morning.'

Under my eyes, year by year, my mother had gradually become an old woman.

And I, slowly but surely, was going to become an old maid.

She was looking at me, still watchful but already with a gleam of gratitude.

She was no longer utterly alone.

*Epalinges
19 June 1969*